Shadow Scorcher

Sentinel Flame Book 4

By Adam Freestone
Alaskan Writer of Imaginative Creativity

8370 Eleusis Drive, Anchorage, Alaska 99502-4630
books@publicationconsultants.com—www.publicationconsultants.com

ISBN Number: 978-1-59433-766-6
eBook ISBN Number: 978-1-59433-792-5

Library of Congress Number: 2025909150

—First Edition—

Manufactured in the United States of America

Hyroc's mind is contacted by a mysterious voice filled with malice that wants them dead. The group beats a hasty retreat, willing to take their chances with The Ministry, only to find they are trapped in the forest by a powerful enchantment. They cannot leave. Their only course of action is to find whatever is projecting the enchantment and destroy it. The Devouring Thicket it is known as because once someone went in, they were never heard from again. And this is where our story continues.

Alaska's Master of Imagination
In loving memory of My Uncle, David Cory Taylor.
1965 – 2024
Though you lived in a faraway desert, you were always close to our hearts. Thank you for all the fun times.
Adam Freestone –

Sentinel Flame: The Story So Far (Recap)

THE SENTINEL FLAME SERIES TAKES place in a medieval-style fantasy world about a boy named Hyroc. Hyroc is different because his face and head resemble that of a wolverine. He has claws and a covering of black fur, with dark brown stripes running from his sapphire eyes down his back. He knows nothing of his parents or his past, and no one knows what he is. Everyone besides him is human. He was adopted by a man named Marcus. Marcus holds a high standing in his town and with The Ministry of the Silver Scythe he once served. The group aims to seek out anyone who utilizes dark magic and destroy them and any of their creations. Hyroc falls under their consideration as something to eliminate. Due to Marcus's past work with The Ministry and his favorable reputation with them, Hyroc is protected, though he is still viewed as something evil and is often met with disdain from others.

At the age of nine, Hyroc's life takes a bad turn when Marcus falls ill and passes away. Marcus' sister, June, stepped in to care for Hyroc. She has inherited some clout from The Ministry and can prevent Hyroc from being killed.

When Hyroc is fifteen, he accidentally injures someone. The accident removes his protection from The Ministry, and he flees for his life. He escapes alone across the Plains of Forna in search of safety. A group of Witch Hunters ambushes him. A white bear appears and kills the hunters before mysteriously disappearing.

Hyroc arrives at the village of Elswood, which lies at the edge of a vast forested wilderness where The Ministry holds little sway. Hyroc discovers an abandoned cabin outside the village and makes a new life. He is unsure how the villagers will react to seeing him, so he stays hidden until he can determine what they will do. While doing so, two giant spiders attack him. He slays the creatures, sustains a venomous bite in the process, and loses consciousness. When he wakes, he again encounters the white bear. The bear (named Ursa) saved him from the spider venom. Ursa is tasked with protecting him. She then disappears until she is needed again.

Hyroc stumbled upon a girl named Elsa. A wolf is hunting Elsa, and he kills it to protect her, revealing his presence. Fearing for his life, Hyroc returns to his cabin, ready to run, and watches for signs of pursuers. No one comes. Thinking he's in the clear, he resumes his routine. Days later, he reencounters Elsa. He is surprised to learn Elsa wants to thank him. Through no fault of Elsa, her oldest brother Donovan and father Svald capture Hyroc. Hyroc is brought to the village elders. Thanks to Hyroc saving Elsa, the elders take no punitive action against him. The villagers are perplexed by his animal-like appearance and are incredibly cautious of his intentions; he is allowed to trade with them. Slowly, Hyroc befriends Elsa's family.

Hyroc settles into his new life at Elswood. His sixteenth birthday comes and goes, and winter arrives. While hunting with Elsa and Donovan, they come across a lone wolf. Before they can slay it, a wolf pack surrounds them. The animals behave strangely and have purple eyes. Then they attack. Hyroc is separated from his friends and encounters a doglike shadow demon called a Shade Hunter. Hyroc destroys the creature, realizing he has more than just The Ministry hunting him.

Book two, Tree of Memories, starts a few weeks after the end of book one, Hyroc. Donovan and Elsa are unsettled by their encounter with the shadow demon, but they keep it to themselves. But their patience for him to explain runs out, and they force the issue. Hyroc answers as best he can, but this only heightens Elsa's and Donovan's growing mistrust. Donovan is suspicious enough to bring his concerns to a man named

Harold in the village. Harold, an ex-witch Hunter, ambushes Hyroc and is determined to get the answers he seeks. Ursa steps in and disarms Harold without harming him. She explains the situation to him. At first, Harold assumes she is a witch, but she persuades him neither she nor Hyroc threatens the village. Harold departs peacefully and agrees only to tell Elsa and Donovan enough to exonerate Hyroc.

Hyroc has not seen Ursa since the attack, and he demands answers, the most pressing of which is who his second enemy is. Ursa is just as ignorant about his second enemy as he is, except that they sent the demon from somewhere to the west beyond the borders of Arnaira, the kingdom he lives in. He repairs his relationship with Elsa and Donovan.

Ursa comes to Hyroc one night, leading him to a strange stone. When Hyroc touches the stone, his consciousness travels to an enormous tree inhabited by blue crystalline versions of forest animals. Hyroc is supposed to choose an animal. He chooses a brown bear. He returns from the tree, and then, to his utter astonishment, he transforms into a bear. Ursa informs him that he chose what animal he could transform into when he touched the stone. His transformation isn't permanent, and he can go in and out of his animal form at will. Ursa tells him there are advantages to using his animal form, but there are also dangerous tendencies it exerts upon its host. Ursa offers to train him to control these tendencies; otherwise, he will succumb to them and become much more animal-like. He may even become a danger to his friends. He agrees for Ursa to train him. This means leaving Elswood and coming with her into the untamed wilderness.

When Ursa brings him to a suitable location, she tells him of his origins. He hails from a place called Wulfren. Invaders once threatened the kingdom, and they had gained favor with a powerful Guardian named Wearla. She bestowed upon the inhabitants of Wulfren the gift of this transformation to fight off the invaders. The invaders were defeated, and there was peace in the land for a time, but the inhabitants of Wulfren used the transformation gift to attack a weaker kingdom, which was expressly forbidden. Because of their misuse of the gift, Wearla curses them. Thus, they became the Wol'dger.

Hyroc is shocked and depressed to learn he is some cursed creature. To him, he is the monster everyone has said he always was. Despite this spirit-crushing information, he moves forward with his training.

When he transforms at the beginning of his training, he is locked into his animal form and cannot transform out of it for the duration of his training. He is deprived of all human comforts and must live like a bear in the wild. Through a series of brutal, grueling, and thoroughly unpleasant tasks that test his resolve to its limits, he masters those dangerous tendencies.

Returning to Elswood after completing his training, he settles back into his life. He keeps his bear form a secret from Elsa and Donovan because he doesn't know how to break it to his friends without them thinking he is a witch and turning on him purely out of fear. He is guilt-ridden, keeping his new ability from his friends, feeling he is being deceitful, and desperately wants to tell them.

When he works up enough courage to tell them, disaster strikes. Giant spiders, corrupted by the residual essence of the Shade Hunter demon, attack and drag his friends away to their nest. With no time to seek assistance, Hyroc rushes off to save them. He tracks the spiders to their lair in an abandoned mine. Hyroc fights his way into the dark subterranean depths of the mine. During one spider encounter, his torch is extinguished, plunging him into complete darkness. When all hope seems lost, a blue flame materializes in his hand. Its illumination saves him and allows him to reignite his torch. Then, the flame mysteriously vanishes. Hyroc reaches his cocooned friends and their family. His elation turns to sorrow when he cannot save his friends' parents and grandfather. But Elsa, Donovan, and Curtis are alive. He drags them out of the mine and finds Ursa outside.

When he asks Ursa about the blue flame, he learns he is a type of Wol'dger called an Anamagi. He is descended from people who had remained loyal to the instructions of Wearla. Because of their loyalty, she offered to spare them the Wol'dger curse. They refused because they did not wish to be separated from their brethren. Because of their willing sacrifice, Wearla gave them a portion of the power of the Guardians and their bloodline.

This dispels Hyroc's somber feelings about being cursed and gives him a sense of worth. He helps his friends bury their parents. Ursa offers to teach Hyroc how to use the powers of the blue flame, known as the Flame Claw. Hyroc knows of his origins but has learned nothing of his parents. Those questions still linger, and the motives of his unknown adversary remain a mystery.

Book three, Outcasts, takes place two years after the events of book two, Tree of Memories. Things are not going well for Hyroc and his friends Elsa, Donovan, and Curtis. Shortly after the deaths of their parents by the corrupted spiders. Rumors, fueled by distrust of Hyroc, began to spread that the four of them had conspired to murder their parents. As a result, during the two intervening years, the villagers have withheld any assistance to the group. They are essentially outcasts. The lives of the four have become difficult, and they are living very near to starvation.

Hyroc has finished his Flame Claw training and has access to potent magic. He uses it to assist their situation whenever possible, but it is still insufficient. And with the completion of Hyroc's training, Ursa has since departed. The villagers are becoming more hostile toward him, and he is wary of an attack. He brings his pet mountain lion, named Kit, with him to the village to deter this. With the added advantage of his Flame Claw, Hyroc can handle anything the villagers throw at him. The only challenge is magic is taboo in the region, and no one knows about his ability beyond his friends. Though Hyroc is allowed into the village if his secret is revealed, his life in Elswood is over, and this will severely complicate things for his friends.

But with the worsening villager hostility, it is only a matter of time before he is forced out. As a result, he has been preparing for a journey to the Wol'dger kingdom, the land of his birth. But he is reluctant to depart with his friends in such a desperate condition and feels he must remain because it would be a dishonorable repayment for their kindness. He only entertains the notion of leaving when their situation is stable or the villagers force him out.

The four continue to stave off starvation, but one day, Hyroc and Donovan encounter something unsettling. They find a mutilated deer.

This is clear evidence of a witch in the area. After Hyroc's experience with the Shade Hunter demon, he knows this is the work of his unknown adversary. Hyroc and his friends notify Harold, the Witch Hunter. The five of them proactively search for the whereabouts of their latest adversary. The clues they find are scant and unhelpful. But there is another development. Ministry soldiers arrive at Elswood. They are led by an Inquisitor named Keller. He is almost fanatical in his devotion to The Ministry. Keller had pursued Hyroc when he fled Forna nearly four years prior. He maintained his search even after losing Hyroc's trail. During the four years, Keller has steadily worked through the towns and villages bordering the wilderness at the edge of Arnaira. These are the most reasonable locations because these sentiments often have little to no Ministry presence and are where witches are the most likely to go unnoticed. Now, he has finally reached Elswood.

The Ministry doesn't know Hyroc is here, and the soldiers are just commencing another search. The villagers are even more distrustful of The Ministry than Hyroc. They refrain from notifying the soldiers about Hyroc. Because they have knowingly consorted with him – what The Ministry considers a dark creature – if they say anything, an Inquisition will be undertaken, with the entire village under investigation for witchcraft. An Inquisition is incredibly unpleasant for its subject and, oftentimes, deadly for several citizens. Remaining quiet, even if it means losing out on a chance to rid themselves of Hyroc, was preferable to the problems posed by an Inquisition. But despite the threat of The Ministry to Hyroc, this may be a fortuitous turn of events. The Ministry may eliminate the new adversary of Hyroc and his friends. Since the witch they pursue is a recent arrival that sticks to the isolation of the surrounding forest, the village would be insulated from the requirements of an Inquisition. Maybe Hyroc and his friends won't have to lift a finger.

But then, one morning, their hope is shattered when the home of Hyroc's friends is attacked. Harold is injured, and the witch kidnaps Elsa. Hyroc and Donovan rush to rescue her, fearing their enemy has dire plans for her. They find the witch and slay them, narrowly surviving the encounter, but Elsa is nowhere to be seen. Hyroc recognizes the elements of a ritual the witch was performing and realizes they had an accomplice, and that's who had Elsa. The witch had bound a blood werewolf to them, and this creature was commanded to destroy Hyroc and everyone in Elswood. A full moon is approaching, so they must rush back to the village to have any hope of saving Elsa and everyone else. Ministry soldiers discover Elsa – to them, she is just another citizen – and free her, but the full moon has already arrived. The creature is temporarily distracted while annihilating The Ministry soldiers, allowing Elsa time to flee. As soon as it finishes with the soldiers, it tears after Elsa. The creature quickly overtakes her, but Hyroc, Donovan, Curtis, and Harold arrive just in time. Hyroc is in his bear form, and with the assistance of his Flame Claw, he takes the creature head-on. While Hyroc draws its attention, the others engage the creature at range. At first, Hyroc stands toe to toe with their enemy, but the injuries he sustains quickly take their toll. Weakend he can no longer distract the werewolf. One by one, the creature incapacitates his friends until only Hyroc and Elsa remain in the fight. Despite everything they had thrown at it, their defeat and the destruction of their village seemed inevitable. Then, something amazing happened.

The trauma of the fight on Curtis triggers latent magical abilities in him. He strikes the werewolf with an incredibly powerful bolt of lightning. This attack severely injures the creature, enabling Elsa and Hyroc to strike the final blow. But all the commotion of the battle attracts the attention of another group of Ministry soldiers. With Hyroc's animal transformation secret out and Curtis' brilliant display of magic in the middle of the village for all to see, accusations of witchcraft are unavoidable. Hyroc and his friends attempt to flee the village. They are surrounded, but through a heroic sacrifice, Harold secures their escape. Hyroc and his friends get away, but The Ministry pursues them. They gather supplies and gear and plan how to move forward. Escaping west to the neighboring kingdom of Mastgar seems the best course of action. But it is also a massive gamble because tales about the kingdom described it as a barbarous, lawless land full of witchcraft and murderers. Similarly unsavory descriptions were also laid upon Hyroc by the Ministry, but all were false, and he argued Mastgar is probably also none of those things. The kingdom may not share the same intolerance toward magic as the Ministry. Though he is not certain, it's their best option.

Their main obstacle was a considerably long journey as Mastgar lay far to the west. All the while being pursued by Ministry forces. It would be impossible for them to go unnoticed over such a vast stretch of Ministry lands. But a broad swath of forested wilderness intruded upon the northern reaches of Arnaira. This is unfamiliar land to The Ministry soldiers, and encumbered by their battle gear and sheer numbers, they would be bogged down in this terrain. Elsa and Donovan know much about this area and can guide the group more quickly than their adversary. They would lose their pursuers and stay ahead of any messengers that would spread the word of them to the Western region of Arnaira. By then, they were confident they would safely be in Mastgar beyond The Ministries' reach. That was, assuming it wasn't an evil place.

Another problem they faced was a shortage of food. Since they could not properly provision themselves for such a journey with any supplies from Elswood, they could only rely on what they had. This would only carry them part way through their long journey. They would be in the middle of an uninhabited wilderness with no food. Starvation was a serious possibility. But Hyroc assured them he could help stretch out their meager supplies with his Flame Claw magic. But even with his assistance, it was a considerable risk. With this grim possibility on their minds, the group set out.

Hyroc is still injured from his fight with the werewolf when they leave Elswood, and it is a painfully arduous effort on his part. He's slowing the group down with The Ministry closing in. But through some quick, ingenious use of the abilities of his animal form and his Flame Claw, they evade the Ministry forces that follow them out of Elswood. They quickly put enough distance between them and The Ministry that their trail goes cold. They were in the clear. Or so it seemed.

Days since any Ministry sightings, one night, Hyroc and his friends are set upon by hooded figures wearing strange plague masks. Throughout the fighting, it is revealed the figures are humans infused with shadow demon essence. After the defeat of these twisted creatures, the group is baffled to find Ministry markings upon them. These entities are called the Hand of Death. They are named so because one touch from their empowered hand is lethal. They hearken back to the time when the dark sorcerer Feygrotha ruled Arnaira. The Ministry's use of such creatures contradicted their doctrine and was a form of absolute hypocrisy. It is clear someone within the Ministry had gone rogue and become so desperate to eliminate Hyroc that they wholly disregarded the tenets of their ideology to turn to witchcraft. Keller is the apparent culprit.

But beyond Keller's apostation from the beliefs he devoted himself to, the Hand of Death has another more pervasive danger. They can track the Quintessence of magic users. The unique properties of Hyroc's Flame Claw protect him from this vulnerability, but Curtis is fully exposed. They are unable to shake their pursuers and are attacked multiple times. The group fears it is only a matter of time before they are overwhelmed by these Ministry demons. Unable to run, they devise a cunning ambush to turn their enemy's ability to their advantage. They were hopelessly outnumbered by The Ministry forces overtaking them, but there were very few Hands of Death among them. If they could kill all the creatures, nothing was left to track Curtis. They can then disengage and safely resume their journey. It was a perilous gambit, but it was their only chance of saving Curtis.

They executed the plan, unsure if everyone would come through unscathed or if any of them would live through it. Through a mixture of stealth, confusion, and sheer terror from a showy display of Hyroc's Flame Claw, they sprang their trap. They used the chaos to pick off as many demons as possible before leading the creatures away from The Ministry forces. Once separated, they battled with the creatures up close. Hyroc and Curtis slay them, but no sign of Elsa and Donovan exists.

While Hyroc and Curtis anxiously wait to see if the rest of the group has come through alive, Hyroc hears a familiar voice. It's June. But he left his beloved aunt behind many years ago in Forna; why was she here? Then, to his horror, his aunt reveals herself as one of the demons. Keller had twisted her with shadow essence. Enough of June's mind and love of Hyroc, which remains intact, and she can fight Keller's control, but she can only do so for so long. Knowing she is the last one capable of tracking Curtis, she asks Hyroc to end her torment. With a heavy heart, he does as she requests. Now, he has nothing left tying him to Arnaira. Then, Elsa and Donovan arrive.

The group exits the other side of the wilderness. Free of The Ministry, for the time being, they head to the nearest town to resupply for the final stretch of their journey. Wanted posters of Hyroc have long since populated the region, so Hyroc must wait outside while his friends get their provisions. Restocked, they head to the border of Mastgar. Before they reach safety, a force of mounted Ministry soldiers overtakes them. The group is forced into a swath of forest, where the horses would get slowed down in the rougher terrain. But strangely, there is no sign of pursuit amongst the trees. The forest is quiet.

The group seems to have escaped their pursuers. They stop to catch their breath at a stream near unnaturally beautiful rose bushes. But the insidious purpose of these roses is quickly revealed. The roses are merely the lure of a monstrous plant creature that bursts out of the ground with the sole intention of devouring them. They destroy their adversary, but

Chapter 1

Inescapable Trap

THE FOREST WAS AWAKE. THE forest was searching like reaching vines blindly stretching forth. Malevolently, it sought the trespassers whose steps had stirred it from its slumber. Striding on two legs, they brought pestilence. Others had come before, and their remains nurtured the trees. But not these. These had survived! They had overcome the thorns that none other had lived through. But one wielded the power of a thunderstorm. It was raw and dangerous, reminiscent of the dark ones. Terrible deeds the dark ones had committed against the verdant forest. Pain they had wrought. Remorselessly they destroyed, caring not for their deeds. But vengeance belonged to the boughs of the woods. The trees purged the darkness until no shadows remained. The final sleep was their reward. The green thicket despised the footsteps of all those who trod upon its ground.

But another among them was familiar. He wielded the azure flame of those charged with safekeeping the wooded places. The failure of the safe keepers echoed through the trees – the pain and abominations they could not prevent. The forest hated them for their negligence. This one was no different. He was destined for justice. He would draw no more breath. With misery, the trees would close his eyes to the binding connections that knit all roots together. Keep him from seeing the branches stretched toward him as the unseen snare drew around him. None of them could escape the shade of the leaves. They would feed the forest with their corpses.

Hyroc watchfully drew his fur-covered head from side to side. His body resembled something similar to a wolverine that walked on two legs. Beneath his red rust-colored jerkin, dark green cloak on his back, black pants, and supple brown leather boots, his lean frame was covered in black fur. His dark coloration was only broken by two dark brown stripes that went from his eyes over his head and ended in a spade shape on his back. His Sapphire blue eyes carefully scanned the shaded forest surrounding him. His hairy hand, with small white claws on his fingers, hovered near the hilt of his falchion protruding from the scabbard on his belt, ready to draw it at the slightest sign of danger. He also carried a strung bow looped over his shoulder and a quiver full of arrows. The cool forest air flowing through his snout was heavy with the smell of leaves and pine resin. He was accustomed to breathing the smoky scent from years of hunting game in Elswood, but here in these woods, something about it wasn't right. That familiar sharp, clean smell put him on edge. It seemed to confer a sense of danger, as if the forest watched their every move, waiting for an opening to strike. It was devoid of birds twittering and the buzzing of insects. Apart from the fullness of the timber, the forest seemed utterly empty of life. Or, at least, the typical kinds of life. There were living things here, but they were unlike anything Hyroc had ever seen, and he was in no hurry to meet them again.

When he saw nothing, he raised his black fur-covered arm and waved forward, indicating to Elsa, Donovan, and Curtis that it was safe to proceed. His three companions were humans with a light olive-skinned complexion and siblings to each other. They were his best and only friends. Though Hyroc wasn't of their blood, for all intents and purposes, they had adopted him into their family nearly four years ago when he arrived in their village of Elswood.

Donovan was a young man the same age as Hyroc, with a strong fit build beneath his dark brown jerkin, cloak, and white tunic. He had short brown hair and light brown eyes. He carried a steel-headed spear with one hand, resting the wooden shaft on his shoulder to ease the strain on his arms while he walked. A quiver full of arrows was strapped to his back as he was also a decent shot with his bow he had stowed away in its buckskin tube. He was quick-witted and tended to exemplify any strangeness they faced or deflect the seriousness of their situation with levity and sarcasm. But he was dependable and could be counted upon to have everyone's back in a fight

Donovan's sister, Elsa, was the oldest by only a few years, with a fetching feminine figure under her jerkin, cloak, and blue tunic. She had gray eyes, and her long blonde hair poked out of the edges of the hood she had drawn up over her head. She held a bow with an arrow at the ready and was the best shot among the group, having brought down more game than Donovan and Hyroc combined. She was lethal from a distance but only had a hunting knife for anything that got close, so it was up to Hyroc and Donovan to keep enemies away from her

Curtis was the youngest with the lanky appearance of a pubescent child. He had amber eyes and dark brown hair and wore a gray tunic and green cloak. Apart from a small knife, he carried no weapons, but, despite his unarmed, youthful appearance, he was arguably the most powerful member of their party. Recently he gained the ability to use lightning magic. His power was potent and volatile – something a rampaging werewolf experienced firsthand – but with the assistance of Hyroc, the boy was rapidly taming it. When he first gained this power, he was sending out single bolts of lightning so powerful he depleted his body's Quintessence – energy which enables the use of magic – reserves and knocked himself unconscious. They were incredibly deadly attacks, but only to a single target, and then he was at the mercy of his enemies. Now, he made his lightning much less energetic and could take down several opponents.

Hyroc was a few paces ahead of the group, acting as a pathfinder. His companions trailed behind him, leading their supply-laden donkey while watching their surroundings. None of them knew what dangers lurked behind every trunk.

This was a cursed place where some sinister force stalked them. This entity sought their distraction, and it seemed to control the forest. It employed a subterranean menace disguised as beautiful red rosebushes. If something disturbed the flowers or one of the thick green vines spreading out from the plant, a floral monster with thorns for teeth would erupt from the ground. The roses were enchanted to draw in unsuspecting victims who gazed at them. They were like the colorful lure used by a skilled fisherman to attract fish. This dark entity had also cast a powerful enchantment over the entire forest. If they came to the forest's edge and tried to leave, the enchantment would send them walking back into the trees. That left them a single option. Find whatever was responsible for the enchantment and kill it before it snuffed them out.

But not even Hyroc, the most knowledgeable of the group in such matters, knew what monsters awaited them in this place. Hyroc snapped his head to the side at the sound of rustling leaves, the muscles in his arm tensing in preparation for swinging his sword.

Kit's four-legged feline shape and reddish-brown coat slinked through a bush enveloped in the shadow of the trees. His ears attentively swished as if they had a mind of their own, listening for danger. His heightened hearing served as their best defense against an ambush. A roar or a guttural growl from Hyroc's pet cougar would signal an approaching threat.

Hyroc moved forward, and the big cat followed him from a distance. Ahead of him, he noticed a place where the trees thinned. Reduction in the forest canopy potentially indicated a river or where a road had once been. Even if it were overgrown, it should be easier to navigate than the rugged, root-riddled terrain they had thus far encountered. A river would be less helpful, but at least their surroundings were more visible, making it easier to spot anything harmful while moving along its shore. Hyroc indicated the thinner spot with a repetitive waving motion.

He jolted to a stop, whipping a halting hand into the air. Everyone stopped, ready to fight. Not daring to speak and potentially give their location away to anything within earshot, he indicated two patches of vibrant roses between them and the thinner area. Though Hyroc suspected the hypnotizing effect only worked at close range, he was taking no chances. After the near disaster of the group's first encounter with the floral horrors, they were wary about their danger.

The group had fled into the forest to escape mounted soldiers of The Ministry of the Silver Scythe. Flat plains surrounded where they had originally entered the forest. They would have been trampled if they had tried to fight. Fortunately, Hyroc and his friends were close enough to enter the forest ahead of the soldiers. The soldiers were robbed of their speed advantage past the tree line as their mounts would have difficulty moving in the tangled terrain. The group's strategy had been incredibly successful, but in doing so, their situation had deteriorated more than they ever could have imagined. Now, the four of them pined for The Ministry soldiers. It appeared The Ministry soldiers knew of the deadliness of the thicket, and were wise enough to avoid entering.

Wordlessly, Hyroc indicated an alternate course around the rosebushes with a curving motion of his arm. Elsa pointed to confirm the direction and then nodded. When Kit deviated from the new direction, Hyroc made a clicking noise out the side of his long Wol'dger mouth to get the big cat's attention. Kit looked at him attentively. Hyroc jerked his head sideways, instructing his companion to follow before moving away to meet with the rest of his party.

Hyroc kept a watchful eye on the green leaves below the roses, ensuring the party didn't accidentally wander too close. Everyone came to a startled stop when they heard a branch break. Elsa fitted an arrow to the string of her bow and joined everyone in scanning their surroundings. After a tense moment, nothing appeared.

The Ministry hunted the group because of witchcraft – or rather because the organization ignorantly perceived all types of magic as witchcraft and dark arts. In Arnaira, the use of witchcraft or any association with it was strictly forbidden and punishable by death. The trauma of a fight with a werewolf threatening to wipe out their village had triggered Curtis's latent lightning magic. The boy, with the assistance of his brother, sister, and Hyroc, had dispatched the werewolf with a blazing lightning bolt. This occurred in full view of the village and The Ministry. Charges of witchcraft were certain for the group, so they fled. The nearby kingdom of Mastgar was their destination, as the kingdom was reported to be accepting of the use of magic. The group had journeyed across Arnaira, but right when their destination seemed inescapably close, they were ambushed and forced into this horrific forest.

When Hyroc and his companions reached the thinner patch, the area was overgrown, with shorter, younger trees than the surrounding forest. A line of unnaturally flat plant-covered terrain hinted it was the remains of an abandoned road.

When last Hyroc looked at the map of this area, he noted a road linking Arnaira to Mastgar. Perhaps they had found it. However, based on the dense plant growth, his map was severely outdated. Following the road seemed the best decision for now.

Elsa stopped when she spotted a small black shape scurrying down the trunk of a tree at the edge of the decaying road. Instinctively reacting to it like they were in imminent peril, she shot it with an arrow. The shape tumbled down the trunk to the ground. Cautiously, she and Hyroc moved closer to investigate. Hyroc grabbed the arrow shaft, tentatively lifting the thing it had impaled. It was an unfamiliar species of squirrel. Its mouth had pointed tusks and two horned protrusions on its head. It had black fur with some brown around its belly. Elsa looked abashed about her reaction. She was so on edge anything unknown moving within her sight triggered her to attack.

"Is that a squirrel?" Elsa asked quietly as she came to Hyroc.

"I think so," Hyroc whispered.

"Nasty looking critter. Normally, I would use it for supper tonight, but in this place, I don't know if anything we eat will poison us. Best to be rid of it."

Hyroc nodded. He removed the arrow and chucked the squirrel carcass as far into the trees as he could.

"What was it?" Donovan softly asked as he held the reins of their donkey.

"Some kind of weird squirrel," Hyroc answered.

"It had fangs and horns," Elsa added.

"Oh, fangs and horns," Donovan said mischievously. "So you're saying I shouldn't tease a seasoned hunter for getting spooked by a squirrel and taking a needless shot." Unamused, Elsa gave his arm an annoyed shove. Still smiling, Donovan continued. "We probably shouldn't expect anything in this place to be normal."

"I know," Elsa agreed.

"At least now we know *there are* animals here," Hyroc added.

"Yeah, but after those man-eating plants, it makes me wonder what else is waiting for us?"

"Don't bother wondering too much," Hyroc said gloomily. "I'm sure we'll find out soon enough."

"Yes, thank you for showering me with your delightful rays of sunshine," Donovan said.

The group followed the remnants of the road until the lengthening of the shadows. It was still light out, but they knew not to be fooled by it because night always came fast among the trees. There was no telling what new dangers awaited them after sunset. They opted to camp at a bend in the road at the top of a shallow incline.Usually, being out in the open and exposed was risky while being hunted, but they wanted the maximum visibility to see anything approaching them. But they didn't know the capabilities of the *thing* that wished to kill them. For all they knew, its gaze was unavoidable no matter how careful they were.

Donovan turned to head off and collect firewood.

"Donovan," Elsa called to him. "You shouldn't go alone. *None of us should.* There needs always to be at least two of us together. That way, this *thing* doesn't have a chance to separate us and attack someone alone."

"I'll go with him," Hyroc volunteered. He flipped his bow off his shoulder and into his hands. Around the road, the trees were thin enough for him to effectively shoot an arrow with some certainty of hitting its intended target.

Elsa and Donovan nodded.

Donovan approached a suitable tree and used a wood hatchet to cut branches for firewood. Hyroc fitted an arrow to his bowstring and vigilantly stood guard in the fading bronze sunlight. He became aware of whispering in the back of his mind. After he and his friends had avoided being consumed by an army of plant creatures, the entity after them had spoken to him in his thoughts. Little of what it said was remotely coherent except it wanted them dead, and it appeared furious. He had learned to block out its voice, but if he concentrated, he could hear it whispering. Even then, its voice was too faint for him to understand. Now, it was getting louder suddenly.

Hyroc tightened his grip on the arrow's feather fletching as he scanned his surroundings. Besides the wind rustling leaves, Donovan's chopping was the only sound echoing through the trees. Hyroc turned his eyes to his friend. Donovan severed another branch. The whispering was now loud enough for him to understand plainly.

"Bark is eaten!" the entity growled. "The limb decays. It grows no more. Metal teeth gnaw and ravage it. Death. It brings death. The shadows return! Pain they bring. The greedy fire watches. He knows not their oath. The rain washes away the stain of their life water. The trail of the hunters is on them. Tooth and claw will be their fates…."

The last part caught Hyroc's attention. "Tooth and claw will be their fates" was ominous. But that *thing* had been quiet for a while. What had suddenly riled it up? Donovan hacked through another branch. The voice got even louder.

"Their trail emerges in the twilight!" it said. "They cannot hide from their sins. The flies will swarm to rot. They will be washed by the benevolent sun no more!"

A surge of inspiration and alarm shot through Hyroc. *It was reacting to the chopping*! Hyroc lunged forward, seizing Donovan's arm mid-swing.

"DONOVAN, STOP!" Hyroc yelled. "*It knows we're here.* We need to move *now*."

Donovan cursed as the two of them dashed back to Elsa and Curtis. Elsa and Curtis had already started offloading their things from the donkey to make camp.

"Stop, stop," Hyroc called. "We've got to get out of here!" With a small frying pan in one hand, she shot him a stunned look. "The chopping gave us away. That *thing* knows where we are."

Without question, she stuffed the frying pan back into a saddlebag. Donovan helped her resecure the saddlebag onto the donkey before everyone rushed toward the incline.

"KIT!" Hyroc shouted to the tree's upper branches where the big cat rested. "DANGER, FOLLOW." His companion scrambled down the tree. Kit's ears rapidly flicked in all directions. Hyroc caught glimpses of shadowed shapes darting between the trees. "On your guard!" he called out. "There is *a lot* of *something* out there. Get ready to fight."

"I see them," Elsa said.

"I can't tell what *they are*," Donovan stated.

Hyroc used his Flame Claw to form a bright blue sphere in one hand. He tossed it above his head, binding it to hover above the donkey. It bathed the twilit group in pale blue light. He saw Curtis falling behind and dropped back to protect him. Kit snapped his head toward the side of the road, issuing a sharp, snarling growl. Hyroc turned to see what looked to be a wolf covered in orange and red scales with a brownish-graysnout and limbs of a matching color. He turned his bow horizontally to quickly get it into position to send an arrow at the creature as it charged toward him. Before he could fire, it leaped. It smashed into him, sending him stumbling backward and pinning him against a tree. The creature opened its mouth, revealing black fangs like sharpened sticks. Behind these, it had no tongue, and its whole maw was full of thorns. What Hyroc had initially taken as scales turned out to be leaves. This was no animal; it was another plant monster!

As the leaf wolf brought its head forward to tear into his flesh, Hyroc lifted his bow to block it. Wood and thorns snapped and crackled as the creature sank its floral teeth into it. The beast fiercely pushed toward him, jerking its head from side to side as it tried to yank the bow from his grip. The wolf wasn't nearly as heavy as Hyroc had expected, which allowed him to hold it at bay with only moderate difficulty. Then, to his astonishment, its front legs merged with the bark when they touched the tree his back was against. This prevented Hyroc from slipping underneath the creature. With the sound of groaning wood, the creature exerted much more pressure, and the tree seemed to be drawing it closer. Hyroc could use one hand on the bow to hold the beast, but there wasn't enough room for him to draw his sword. He grabbed his hunting knife instead and repeatedly jammed the blade into its side. The leaf-wolf didn't react with the slightest sign of pain. As he continued to stab, preparing to channel fire through the knife before the pull of the tree on the wolf overwhelmed his strength, he felt the blade glance off something hard. Hoping it was something vital, he aimed at it with his next strike. It felt as if the blade had struck a hollow chunk of wood. There was a loud crack. The creature instantly dissolved into a pile of leaves and sticks, covering Hyroc in a shower of lifeless debris. Hyroc stared down at the material all over him in bewilderment.

He turned his attention to Curtis and Kit to see three more creatures moving onto the road. Curtis fried one with a blazing bolt of lightning, but the remaining two were too close for him to hit before they were on him. Kit swiped his claws across the side of one, drawing its attention, but the other knocked Curtis off his feet. Hyroc sheathed his knife and threw his broken bow aside as he rushed to aid the boy. He rammed his shoulder into the leaf wolf on top of Curtis. The creature landed on its side and scrambled to its feet, sounding like numerous animals moving through thickly clustered bushes. He drew his sword before it could fully stand, delivering a downward strike to its neck. The creature's head separated from its shoulders as it collapsed into a pile of leaves and other plant refuse. Hyroc pulled Curtis to his feet.

A surge of dread shot through him when Kit let out a fierce, pain-filled roar. Hyroc spun around to see the third creature mauling the mountain lion's shoulder. Hyroc darted over to his companion, wrapped his arm around the leaf wolf's neck, yanked it backward, and drove his blade through the side of its neck. As it disintegrated, he saw three more creatures attacking Elsa and Donovan. Multiple arrows protruded from the leafy body of one. It was having trouble moving from an arrow sticking in what functioned as a joint. Donovan dispatched it with a spear thrust through its chest. Hyroc threw a fireball, and Curtis shot a lightning bolt at another heading for Elsa. Their combined attacks turned it into a smoldering pile of ash. The third creature moved toward their donkey. The animal brayed out in alarm, rearing back.

It smashed its front legs into the creature's head. With a loud wooden crack, its skull caved in, and it collapsed. The leaf-wolf maintained its shape but stopped moving. It appeared disabled. But taking no chances, Donovan stomped on its back, shattering that hard, vital thing within its body, and it fell apart.

A pained groan pulled his attention back to Kit. His companion had a bleeding wound on one of his back legs and another on his shoulder, and he was limping badly. He arduously walked toward Hyroc before collapsing onto his side. Hyroc felt a thrill of fear as he sheathed his sword and rushed to Kit's side.

"You're okay, you're okay," Hyroc said comfortingly, trying to keep the fear from his voice. Kit's fur was sticky with blood. Hyroc stroked the top of his four-legged friend's head. As the stress of the fight diminished, he again became aware of the entity talking.

"...blue fire and thunder burn leaves," it said in a storm of rage. "The Guardian silences wolves it was sworn to protect. But the pack remains. They come. Now they come. The trap ensnares the destroyers. The oath breakers. No escape exists!"

"More of those things are coming," Hyroc yelled out. "We have to go!" He frantically assessed Kit's injuries. They were severe but still within his ability to heal with his Flame Claw. But with who knew how many more of those leaf wolves on the way, there was no time for that.

"I'm sorry, buddy, this is going to hurt," he told Kit. "But we've got to get out of here, or we'll die. Okay, don't kill me when I do this." He shoved his arms under Kit and lifted with all his might. Kit tensed and roared in pain but offered no resistance to being moved. Hyroc draped him over his shoulder and used his arms to support his companion's back end. Then he rushed over to the rest of the group before everyone moved down the road as fast as they could.

Donovan retrieved an unlit torch from the donkey and turned with it held out toward Hyroc, indicating for him to light it with his Flame Claw. Hyroc had just enough movement in one hand to aim it at the blue orb following the donkey. He then moved his hand down toward the torch. The orb dropped onto the torch and flowed over it. A blue flame crackled to life before turning the natural orange color.

This eliminated the drain on his Quintessence from the light. He also figured removing the light was good because its illumination was much brighter than the torch. Hyroc heard things moving through the foliage back where they had been fighting.

"We need to get off the road!" Elsa called back. "Those things will see us out in the open like this."

"I agree," Donovan said. He glanced over his shoulder at Hyroc. "Can you make it in the trees with him?"

Hyroc nodded though his arms started to tire from bearing Kit's weight. He would hold on as long as possible. "Go up ahead with that torch," Hyroc said. "I can see just fine without it." Donovan nodded, quickening his pace. There was hardly any remaining light from the sunset, but his Wol'dger eyes allowed him to see better in the dark than his friends.

The group turned off the road and headed into the trees. Encumbered carrying Kit, Hyroc lagged behind in the rougher terrain. He glanced toward the top of the incline they had just come from to see four-legged shapes emerging onto the road. Then he heard sounds directly behind him. He darted behind a cottonwood tree's thick, rough trunk, pressing his back against it. Elsa and Curtis led the donkey behind a knoll where a clump of birch trees grew in a line. Donovan spotted Hyroc and dropped back to assist with Kit. Hyroc stopped him by shaking his head emphatically and waving him away. The things behind them were too close for Donovan to arrive without them seeing him. Donovan jumped behind the nearest tree, peeking around the side of it, ready to act if the creatures noticed Hyroc.

A deep rumbling growl from Kit filled Hyroc's ears. Hyroc shushed his companion by reassuringly rubbing the back of the mountain lion's head. He heard footfall behind him on the other side of the tree. Turning his head, out of the corner of his eye, he saw two leaf wolves walking into sight. An instant later, their footsteps were all that betrayed their presence. Hyroc realized how fast and loud he was breathing. With a mental effort, he tried slowing his breaths. Sound near the right side of the tree drew his attention. He saw one wolf investigating a bush at the edge of the road. It made no sniffing noises, presumably because it didn't have a functional nose or need to breathe. It turned suddenly at hearing an animal. Both wolves trotted away to investigate.

"...the Guardian makes no sound as the stillness of death," the entity said. "We cannot see." Its voice quieted. "We will wait for its *flame.* It depends on it. It is addicted to the withering of all that it crushes underfoot. But the trap yet remains..." Its words faded to imperceptible whispering in the back of Hyroc's mind.

He breathed a sigh of relief. "All right, I think we're safe," Hyroc said. "They're gone." That's when he realized Kit was breathing shallowly. "No, no," Hyroc said. "Come on, Kit." He rushed over to the knoll where Elsa and Curtis were. "Don't do this to me," he pleaded. He carefully lay Kit on the ground. The big cat had an exhausted look in his eyes. Kit issued a weak groan. He had lost much blood.

"Donovan, we need to get a fire going," Elsa said. "Curtis, go with him. And no chopping!"

"Yeah, only collect dead wood that's already fallen," Hyroc added. "Otherwise, our enemie will find us all over again."

Elsa knelt next to Kit and placed his head on her lap. She stroked his head while talking calmly. Hyroc assessed Kit's wounds to figure out the best way to heal him while fighting a surge of fear. Was he about to lose another friend? He had already lost so many. When he looked closely at the two injuries, he noticed blood-covered thorns from the mouth of the leaf wolves embedded in both wounds. It appeared the thorns were made to snap off and get stuck in anything the wolves bit to cause further bleeding and prevent the wound from closing, inevitably leading to infection. They had to come out. Even with magic, the lacerations wouldn't heal if the thorns remained.

Hyroc drew his knife. "Hang in there, buddy," he said.

Elsa grabbed his arm, stopping him as he moved it toward Kit. "You used that to stab one of those wolf things," she said, holding up her knife. "Use mine; it's sharper and cleaner."

Hyroc accepted it, carefully dislodging the thorns with the blade tip. With his experience skinning and dressing animals, he was adept at the wound's debridement. He only hoped the thorns weren't poisoned. His Flame Claw might not be able to counteract that.

Kit growled weakly, garnering a comforting shush from Elsa. Hyroc set the bloodied knife on the ground and placed his hands on Kit's shoulder wound. He concentrated hard on bending his body's Quintessence to mend the injury. A soft blue glow emanated from his hands, and he felt a steady stream of energy flowing through them. Imperceptibly, at first, the skin slowly began stitching together. Hyroc was heartened to see the mending but hoped his diminishing strength wouldn't hold him back from completing the process. Healing was far more taxing on his Quintessence than throwing a fireball or forming a barrier to shield himself, and he wasn't well practiced at it. Just like the more someone did something and got better at it, so too did his utilization of Quintessence.

As he started on Kit's leg gash, he felt the drain on his strength. The fatigue incessantly urged him to stop, but he knew he could not. Kit would not survive if he relented. He fought through it; he was almost finished. He started having trouble holding himself up and became lightheaded. His strength was nearly exhausted. He would lose consciousness if he fully depleted His Quintessence reserve, which was his body's way of keeping him from killing himself. The wound was now closed. All that remained was for the skin to regenerate. Encroaching blackness formed on the edges of his vision. Then, he had completed the process!

He fell forward with a gasp, barely catching himself before he went face-first into the pine needle-covered dirt. Elsa grabbed him by the shoulders and gently eased him against a rock jutting out of the knoll.

"Easy," she said. "You finished. He's okay now."

Hyroc sat there breathing heavily, resisting a powerful urge to sleep. Though there was no immediate danger, he couldn't rest until he was confident his feline companion was mending. He stared at Kit's still form, momentarily unable to concentrate on anything around him. His memory flashed back to his first meeting with the mountain lion as a cub on the river shore in Elswood. Then, the tiny cat had taken down a troublesome weasel that stole Hyroc's fishing bait. He was his very first friend after fleeing Forna, even before meeting the

Shackletons. Then he remembered roughhousing with the big cat and how much the two of them had enjoyed it. Was their time together about to end? His companion was no longer in danger of bleeding to death, but he had lost much blood in the process. Hyroc didn't know how to heal anything beyond the outside flesh and muscle. The rest was up to Kit.

Awareness lethargically filtered back into his mind. He noticed Donovan and Curtis were getting a fire going. How long ago had they returned, he wondered sluggishly. They had brought back a bundle of sticks. It was sufficient for the night. And for the first time since he noticed Kit was injured, he realized his hands were covered in blood. He felt nauseous from knowing whom it had come from. He hastily retrieved his waterskin from his belt and used its contents to wash away the crimson liquid. After he wrung out his hands, he grabbed Kit by the shoulders and gently slid the big cat's head into his lap. Kit's eyes opened a slit, but he was partially unconscious. Hyroc stroked his companion's head soothingly. The mountain lion resonated with a soft, rumbling purr. That seemed like a good sign but Hyroc feared the sound merely distracted him from thinking of the painful sting of loss he might soon feel.

Elsa settled into the crutch of a tree in front of them. "Now that he's taken care of, what about you?" she asked. "How are you?"

"Tired," he said, looking up from Kit to meet her gaze. "Healing him took everything I had, but I think I'm okay."

She nodded, then reached into a small pouch tied to her hip. She retrieved a mashed-up wad of white and green yarrow and held it out to him. He gave her a puzzled look. She indicated his shoulder with her other hand.

"You've got a little spot on your shoulder," she said. "I think Kit may have accidentally gotten you with his claws when you were carrying him."

Hyroc reached under his jerkin to the indicated area and found a spot wet with blood that stung at his touch. It was a minor injury, but he was amazed he hadn't noticed it until now. He accepted the yarrow and applied it to his wound.

Donovan and Curtis came over to them. Donovan held a hunk of bread and divvied portions for everyone's supper. Only after Hyroc took a bite of his piece did he realize how hungry he was.

"How is he?" Curtis said before taking a bite.

Hyroc sighed. "I healed him as much as I could," he said. "The rest is up to him. We'll have to see what happens tonight."

"He's tough. I'm sure he'll be all right."

Despite his younger friend's words of comfort, Hyroc wasn't nearly as optimistic. For all he knew, the bite of those creatures was poisonous. There was nothing he could do about that. He forced his thoughts away from pursuing that route of thinking; it was too painful even to consider.

"I'm concerned about what happens next," Donovan said. "Who knows what monsters come out at night in this place?"

"I think we all agree with you there," Elsa noted. "We need to keep a lookout. I can take the first watch. Then Donovan, and –" she trailed off, looking between Hyroc and Curtis. "Hyroc, you definitely need to rest."

He offered no objection. He wasn't sure how much longer he could remain awake. The urge to sleep was overcoming his will.

"Curtis, you think you can take over for Hyroc?" Elsa continued.

"Yeah, I can do that," Curtis said. Hyroc nodded his thanks.

"Everyone stay close to the fire; it should keep any dangerous animals away."

"*Should*," Donovan emphasized with a sniff.

Elsa and Hyroc gave him a flat look.

"Well, there's not much we can do if it doesn't," she said. "Other than, you know, for us to kill anything brave."

"That reminds me of something I needed to ask. Hyroc, what were we breaking inside those plant wolves that made them fall apart?"

Hyroc pondered his answer a moment. "I'm pretty sure it was a Quintessence vessel like this," he answered. He indicated a ruby spike that hung from a necklace around his neck. "This gemstone can hold a small amount of extra Quintessence. I'm able to tap into it in an emergency. And if I wanted to, I could also use it to power minor spells and enchantments without energy directly from me to make them work. And I'm assuming those wolves had something similar inside of them. Just a lot more fragile. And once we broke it, we released the Quintessence contained within. Without it, there was no energy to maintain the spell that held those creatures together, so they disintegrated."

"So they really were made out of nothing but sticks and leaves," Elsa said.

Hyroc nodded. "I'm guessing they were constructs composed of forest debris."

"But why would someone want to make those things from such brittle materials?" Donovan questioned. "Why not something stronger like rock or metal?"

"Maybe that's all the thing after us has to work with in here," Hyroc suggested. "Or its torch isn't all the way lit, if you catch my meaning. It sounded rabid every time I heard it talk."

"Well, thankfully, they are easy enough to kill," Elsa said.

"The only problem is I'm positive there are many more of them than us," Hyroc cautioned. "So, despite their fragility, if enough of them come after us at once, they'll overwhelm us."

"I don't relish the thought of those things eating us alive," Donovan said darkly.

"We'll just have to keep the *thing* in here from noticing us," Elsa said.

"Until we can kill it, that is," Hyroc said. "And escape this nightmare."

"All right, that's enough talk for the night; everyone needs to get some sleep while they can. We don't know how restful it'll be tonight. Especially with the scent of blood on us."

Hyroc looked down at Kit, unsure what morning might bring.

Chapter 2
Wolf Den

HYROC JOLTED AWAKE, THE STRANGE call of an animal disturbing his sleep. It was still night. The orange light of their campfire danced across the trees. Curtis kept watch while fiddling with a stick out of boredom. Donovan and Elsa slept nearby. Hyroc saw something brightly glowing on Curtis' shoulder. Groggily, he focused on it, realizing it was some bird of prey made of lightning sitting on Curtis' shoulder. It was a magical creation Hyroc had taught his younger friend how to make. Hyroc turned his attention to Kit, who lay partially in his lap. A jolt of dread shot through him when he thought his four-legged companion wasn't breathing. Hyroc's mind raced as he ran through anything he might do. He was sure he could use his healing to restore Kit's breathing if only he knew how. Hyroc felt a stab of cold anxiety in his chest. He saw Kit's chest rise and fall. He slumped back against the rock behind him, breathing a sigh of relief. His reaction immediately felt absurd. He was letting his nerves get the best of him.

"How is he?" Curtis asked. He made a half-waving motion – the lightning bird faded out of existence – before crouching beside Hyroc. He scratched between Kit's ears, which garnered him a faint purr from the mountain lion.

"Better," Hyroc said, blowing out an uncertain sigh. "That wolf really hurt him, and I patched him up with my Quintessence as best I could, but there's nothing else I can do. We'll have to see how he's doing in the morning."

A shrill shriek drew Hyroc's attention to the trunk-filled darkness beyond the light of the fire. He saw points of light that were animals' eyes gazing in his direction. Most of the eyes were at the top of the trees; he figured they were the eyes of squirrels and owls. Lower, on the forest floor, he saw strange eyes he had never seen. They didn't glow like the eyes of a wolf or cat. The light of the fire glinted off them as if they were black onyx. Then, the eyes melted into the darkness. He heard a soft hiss and the clicking of mandibles. His first assumption was it was a giant spider, like the ones he had killed in Elswood, but the noises didn't match. It was hard for him to gauge the creature's size, but whatever it was, it was big.

"I think there's some kind of weasel out there," Curtis said. "Right before you woke, I saw the eyes of something coming closer. Judging from how its eyes were moving and how I thought it was shaped at the edge of the light, I think it was a huge weasel thing."

"No, whatever I just saw was no weasel," Hyroc said, scanning the forest. He was quiet for a long moment as he unsuccessfully searched for the strange creatures. "Have you had any sign of those leaf wolves?" he asked.

Curtis shook his head. "Nah. None."

Hyroc nodded. "Good." He closed his eyes and folded his arm. "I'm going to try to go back to sleep. Wake me if you need anything."

Curtis acknowledged him by saluting him with the stick.

Hyroc thoughtfully studied Kit in the subdued morning light filtering through the tree canopy as he chewed a piece of cheese. He winced from a flare of pain in his shoulders and arms as he gingerly lifted his hand to his mouth to take another bite. His arms ached, but that's what he got for carrying Kit, an adult mountain lion that weighed almost as much as he did, and running several yards to safety. It amazed him how he had even been able to do that. He was stronger than he thought. But he faced a dilemma: barring another surprising burst of strength, how would he move his companion if need be? He had healed all of the cougar's external injuries, but Kit was still too weak to walk. His walking would eventually return; Hyroc just wasn't sure how long it would take. It could be hours or days. In this place, staying put and losing time to his friend's mend seemed risky. Every second they stayed here was another second for something to attack them.

After Hyroc finished eating, he brushed his hands off and grabbed his waterskin. He unstopped it and offered the end to Kit's mouth. Kit opened, allowing Hyroc to give him a drink. The big cat's eyes were open, and he curiously watched and listened to his surroundings. That seemed a good sign he was recovering.

Elsa came into sight from the direction of the road with her hood drawn over her head, running in a crouch. "There's a bunch of those leaf wolves back where we killed that group," she said, and pointed in the direction. "They're still looking for us. We can't stay here with them so close." Hyroc let out a displeased growl. "How's Kit? Can he walk?"

"No, he's very weak," Hyroc said. "I think it will be at least a few days before he can properly move on his own."

She quietly cursed. "It wouldn't be much of a problem if we could build a litter to carry him on, but we can't cut the branches without alerting, our enemy, to our location. And unless we want to dump supplies – which seems a terrible idea – there's no room for him on the donkey's back." She studied the big cat thoughtfully. "Two of us might be able to carry him, but I don't know."

"I've got a way."

"You changing to a bear?"

Hyroc nodded. "I'll carry him on my back. His weight won't be a challenge for me in that form. Someone will have to carry my sword and knife."

"Sounds good. Let me help my brothers break camp, and we'll help you get Kit situated."

Hyroc rubbed one of Kit's ears with his thumb. His companion happily flexed the toes of one paw and rumbled a deep purr.

"You're not going to like this," Hyroc said sympathetically. "But we can't stay here."

He carefully slipped out from under Kit and stood. He unbelted his sword and knife, followed by his jacket, setting them against the rock. Next, he retrieved a length of rope from the donkey and tied it loosely around his bare fur-covered stomach. After finding an even patch of ground, he dropped down on all fours. He closed his eyes and focused on seeing a full moon's silvery disc. When it was the only thing in his mind's eye, it triggered the transformation. He felt his bones and limbs thickening and his muscles gaining strength. His whole body became heavier as he settled into a bear's strange but familiar shape. The rope pulled snugly against his middle.

His friends stepped over to him while Curtis finished rolling up the sleeping beds. Hyroc sidled up to Kit. Elsa undid the knot in the rope on Hyroc's back but kept it from slipping to the ground. Donovan settled into a crouch next to the mountain lion.

"Kit, Donovan is going to pick you up and put you on my back," Hyroc said reassuringly. "Don't fight him. Okay?" The big cat stared at him, irritably thumping his tail on the ground. Hyroc nodded to Donovan. "That means he's okay with it but doesn't like it."

"I hope so," Donovan said indignantly. "I'll be angry with you if he shreds me with those knives on his paws. If there's anything left of me, that is."

When Donovan scooped him into his arms, Kit gave a curt meow. Donovan arduously hoisted the mountain lion onto Hyroc's back. He laid Kit butterfly spread on Hyroc's broad black back like an animal rug on someone's floor, with the big cat's arms dangling around his neck. Hyroc waited nervously for his companion to settle into a somewhat comfortable position, hoping Kit would not slip and dig his claws in. When the large feline stopped wiggling, Elsa retied the rope to hold him securely onto Hyroc. Kit meowed with displeasure.

"It's just for a little bit," Hyroc said over his shoulder. "Until we get to safety. Then we can rest. But you've got to be quiet." Hyroc spoke under his breath. "And this won't be any fun for me either."

Elsa gave Kit a comforting scratch behind the ears. She collected Hyroc's sword, knife, and quiver. Then she searched around the rock as if something was missing.

"Something wrong?" Hyroc asked.

"I can't find your bow," she said

He sighed. "It's not there. One of those wolves got a hold of it with their mouth, and it wasn't usable anymore. I threw it away. I didn't think wasting Quintessence on a spell to repair it was a good idea while I'm still recovering from what it took out of me to heal Kit." His bow was his most valued reminder of Marcus, the only man who had been a father to him. Now, he had lost it just as he had lost his necklace, which was his sole link to his mother. Little by little, his past was slipping away. Soon, he feared there would be nothing left.

"Sorry to hear that," Elsa said sympathetically.

Hyroc nodded his thanks.

She handed the extra quiver off to Curtis, and the four of them headed out.

Hyroc moved carefully to keep Kit in position on his back. The big cat held firmly onto Hyroc's neck to help keep himself from sliding around. The proximity of Kit's sharp claws to his throat made him nervous. If he slipped and dug them in, the consequences would be *unpleasant*. This was a precarious arrangement, and Hyroc felt vulnerable. He would have difficulty fighting if they encountered more of those wolves or, Hallowed forbid, something else. He would depend almost entirely on his friends to defend him. This was new to him. He was used to being the one defending others and not the one in need of protection. It made him uneasy. His friends may miss a threat and let some unknown thing single him out like a predator picking out the easiest target amongst a herd. Was this how animals felt when he hunted them? He shook off the thought. Elsa and Donovan were just as good of hunters as he was. They wouldn't miss anything.

They moved parallel to the road but from a distance in the thicker foliage. The black feathery shape of a raven fluttered to the ground in front of the group, and a patch of silver markings decorated the side of its neck. It was Shimmer, the Guardian servant Hyroc and his companions had befriended. He spent most of his time in the air monitoring their progress, and it was not uncommon for him to disappear for entire days. He had gotten into the routine of landing and conveying adjustments they needed to make in their course. He also kept an eye on the overgrown road for leaf wolves. From his agitated squawking whenever he landed, he indicated the wolves were still there. Once he stopped seeing them, they could return to the path‘s gentler terrain. That would significantly improve Hyroc's ability to balance Kit on his back. He expected one misstep to send Kit tumbling to the ground, ending in much pain for both of them. He had to concentrate on every step. It concerned him how slowly he had to move, especially with those creatures so close by and potentially coming toward them from behind.

Elsa and Donovan spotted a sizable patch of the deadly rose plants stretching toward the road. Because of the wolves, this forced the group to move farther into the trees. They planned to go around the plants, but an elongated hill obstructed their path. Though the slope had a gentle incline, it was steep enough to cause Hyroc problems keeping Kit on his back. So they attempted to go around it. They followed the base of the hill, but it seemed never ending. Eventually, it was apparent they had to climb it, or they risked losing the road and their bearings.

Hyroc reluctantly agreed. It wouldn't be easy, but he would manage. Before starting the ascent, Donovan tightened the rope around Kit. He and Elsa flanked Hyroc on both sides. They stayed close to assist if needed. As Hyroc stepped onto the incline, Kit tightened his grip and pressed his legs against Hyroc's lower back. This caused Hyroc no pain, but hefelt the sides of Kit's claws against his skin. He would bleed if he made any mistake.

He warily picked his way up the hill. The thick foliage between the trees made for slow going. They had to alter their course when they came to an impassable line of thorny devil's club. Moving sideways on the hill was far more challenging for Hyroc. Kit drooped to the edge of Hyroc's back, half of his companion's body dangling in space. The big cat meowed in alarm as Hyroc felt him starting to slip. Knowing claws capable of shredding a deer were about to pierce his flesh, Hyroc resumed his original position. He began walking sideways once Kit had reoriented himself. This slowed the group's pace to a crawl. Pushing through the foliage this way was also more taxing on Hyroc's strength.

He quickly felt his limit fast approaching. He would have to take a break soon.

They had cleared the line of devil's club, but a small boulder against a clump of trees was the final obstacle. Hyroc could drop down the hill a little and come around the trees. But that would require him to step sideways down the hill or walk backward. There was a high chance of him losing his footing because he couldn't see where his feet were going. The other option was for him to climb over the boulder.The latter seemed the least accident-prone plan.

Hyroc sidled up to it and started climbing over the boulder. Carefully, he slid his belly across its cool surface. Then, one foot slipped. His backend dragged him down the rock from the pull of the incline. He scrabbled his paws against the unrelenting surface, getting a tenuous grip on the edge. But it wouldn't hold! The weight of his body was too much. Kit yowled in surprise, bracing one of his back legs against a tree trunk to keep himself from sliding off Hyroc's back. Hyroc knew he was seconds from receiving several gashes from the mountain lion falling. Dread engulfed Hyroc at how much it would hurt when he landed.

Donovan and Elsa pressed their shoulders and hands against Hyroc's rear, arresting his slipping. They gave him a moment to reorder his grip.

"Move – your – rump!" Donovan said in a strained voice. "You're a lot – heavier – than I thought."

"Hurry," Elsa said with a grunt. "We can't – hold you – for long."

Hyroc anchored his paws on the boulder's edge and heaved himself up. He got his chest over the lip, pressing a back leg against a tree. Elsa and Donovan gasped in relief when he took his weight off them. Hyroc scrambled off the rock. Breathing heavily, he leaned against a tree to rest a moment.

"I guess now we can say you've become a *belly-dragger*," Donovan called to him jokingly.

Hyroc rolled his eyes. "Oh, haha," he said humorlessly. "Make fun of the bear."

Donovan laughed as he helped Curtis lead the donkey down and around the trees.

"All right, quiet, you two," Elsa insisted.

Hyroc waited for the donkey to arrive before continuing. Thankfully, no more significant obstacles blocked their path. Hyroc was grateful when they made it to the top. The hill flattened out into a small meadow. Grasses covered the ground, punctuated by patches of harmless wildflowers.

Kit suddenly became excited and meowed urgently. He squirmed against the rope, insisting to be free of it.

"All right, we can take a break for a little bit," Hyroc agreed. "But you'll have to wait until the others catch up. They can –" Hyroc interrupted himself with a surprised yell when Kit grabbed one of his ears in his jaws. The big cat gently tugged on it, pulling Hyroc's head back.

"Okay, okay," Hyroc said defeatedly. "We don't have to wait for the others." One of his paws glowed blue as he swiped with it. The knot in the rope undid and fell away. Pleased, Kit let go of Hyroc's ear and, on wobbly legs, slinked to the ground. He gave a couple of flowers an investigative sniff before lying down in the shade. By now, the rest of the company had arrived.

"Let's take a break for a bit before we head down the other side," Elsa insisted. She offered Hyroc a drink from her waterskin. Curtis did the same for Kit. When Elsa finished, she sat against a tree in front of Hyroc. "What's the plan here? How do we find this *evil thing*?"

"I don't know," Hyroc admitted. "I haven't had time to think about it."

"It would probably help if our lives weren't constantly in danger," Donovan noted. Elsa, Curtis, and Hyroc nodded their agreement.

"Finding our adversary depends on what it, or they are," Hyroc said. "If it's a witch, I assume they would probably have some ritual area. They would have to in order to create something as complicated as those leaf wolves, killer rosebushes and that enchantment at the forest edges."

"That sounds like a lot of work," Elsa said. "Would they have enough Quintessence for something like that? I mean, is that something you could do?"

"I doubt it even if I knew how. But there are ways around that. If this witch is skilled enough, as seems to be the case, it could be harvesting Quintessence from the trees. Plants possess a small amount of Quintessence."

"But if the Witch drains all of it, doesn't that kill plants?"

Hyroc nodded. "Yes, but they wouldn't completely drain the plants. They must be siphoning off a tiny amount. Such a small quantity from a single plant is useless, but that's a huge amount if they do this to the entire forest. That's the only way I see the witch being able to maintain the enchantment that keeps us from escaping. I think this because when we were attacked last night, they only found us when we chopped wood. This suggests the witch is somehow linked to the trees, and something is blocking me from communing with the trees. Our chopping must have altered the flow of Quintessence from that tree, and the witch noticed it. That's what gave us away."

"But how does knowing that help us?" Donovan asked.

"Because for the witch to obtain the maximum amount of Quintessence, they would want to be in the exact middle of the forest."

"So, you're saying we need to find the heart of the forest?" Elsa said. Hyroc nodded. She stood and swept her eyes across the forest below. "Okay, what are we looking for?"

Donovan joined her effort.

"An opening in the trees," Hyroc said. "Like a clearing. Or anything that sticks out."

Elsa pointed. "There!" she said excitedly. "I see a gap right there."

Hyroc stood on his back legs to get a better look. He confirmed what seemed to be a clearing not very far away. "That's –" he looked at it thinking a moment "– that's North."

Donovan consulted their map. "But if I'm reading this correctly," Donovan said. "The road goes off to the northeast. We might lose it if we move away from it."

"Does anyone see a better option?" Hyroc asked. Elsa and Donovan shook their heads. "That's our best bet. Just give me a few more minutes to rest, and then we can head out." He turned to look at his friends and noticed Donovan deep in thought. "Donovan, did you see something?"

"No," Donovan said. "But there's something that's bothering me about our predicament. You think what has us trapped in this forest is a witch?"

"Yeah, that's my best guess."

"Then why were you able to hear them? Elsa, Curtis, and I didn't hear anything. The last time you heard voices like this, we ran into a Shade Hunter. Could this *thing* be a shadow demon?"

Hyroc shrugged. "I don't know. But why is it using those rose plants if it's a shadow demon? I've never heard of one using plants to kill people."

"I hope our luck isn't so bad we run into something you haven't heard of."

CHAPTER 3
Dark Water

HYROC PUSHED THROUGH A CLUMP of bushes, their cool, wet leaves brushing across his broad bear body. Earlier in the morning, a short rainstorm had deposited water on everything. Getting to the gap they had spotted in the trees took longer than expected. It was now the afternoon of day two of their journey there. They hoped, if everything went well, to arrive by dusk. But when they reached it, they faced a powerful witch. Hyroc had been in this position not long ago when he and his companions still called Elswood home. He had killed a witch once and could undoubtedly do it again. Then, when he had slain his enemy, the four of them could finally escape the enchantment in this wretched forest.

Elsa quickly lifted her hand, signaling for everyone to stop. Everyone halted. Hyroc stopped mid-step, holding a paw in the air. He listened carefully to his surroundings. Something was moving through the trees, but he couldn't discern a direction. Everyone scanned the forest alertly. Elsa drew their attention as she raised her bow to aim at something. When Hyroc followed her gaze, he spotted a dark shape approaching her.

Hyroc gently lowered his paw and trotted over to her as quietly as the foliage would allow. The shape resolved into a dark brown stag with black antlers and red eyes. It was bigger than the deer he had hunted at

Elswood. What concerned him the most was it had serrated spikes of horn pointing forward and could cause serious harm if it charged them. He or Curtis could efficiently dispatch it with an attack spell, but Hyroc didn't want to waste the Quintessence if it could be avoided. Maybe they could get it to move on without having to fight it.

The buck stopped, regarding them with crimson eyes. It had an intimidating glare, and Hyroc wondered about preemptively charging the animal. But he was hesitant, encumbered by Kit on his back, and with sharp horns to contend with, it was a recipe for disaster. He could try posturing. Hyroc let out a loud, groaning call. The stag stiffened alertly, focusing on him. He met its gaze unblinkingly. The animal pivoted and trotted back the way it had come. Hyroc kept his eyes fixed on it until it slipped out of sight.

"You see the look of that buck?" Donovan said quietly in a mixture of awe and anxiety.

"Now there's also Red-eyed deer in here," Elsa noted.

"We need to be careful of those," Hyroc said. "That had some nasty-looking antlers. I don't want to get in close to fight one."

"I don't blame you," Donovan agreed. "We should go in case it decides to come back."

Hours later, Hyroc felt something was wrong but couldn't figure out what. He glanced around. There were only trees and greenery as far as he could see. He took a deep whiff of air through his ursine nose, but a flood of unfamiliar scents prevented him from discovering anything. He pushed the disconcerting feeling aside. The sense of wrongness seemed to grow the farther he went. He looked through his surroundings again; there was…wait. It was unusually dark, and when he glanced up, he saw the canopy was much thicker, the leaves blocking out a substantial amount of sunlight and sky. When he lowered his gaze, the trees appeared broader, with pale gray bark and extensive roots split the ground. He didn't see a single pine tree or spruce. The forest was more crowded here. The change had been so gradual he almost hadn't noticed. Maybe this was an indication they were nearing their target. He needed to be wary. A fight could come at any moment.

The trees thinned out when they reached a shallow rise to form an open area beyond.

"I think we're here," Hyroc said quietly. "Get Kit off my back."

Elsa and Donovan untied the rope holding Kit in place. The big cat climbed off Hyroc and sluggishly walked over to a tree, where he lay down.

"How do you want to play this?" Donovan asked.

"First, I'll transfer out of bear form." Hyroc closed his eyes to initiate the process. He continued when he was back in his natural form. "You and Curtis will come with me," Hyroc suggested as he belted on his sword. "Elsa, you should remain here with Kit."

Elsa shot him a questioning look. "Stay here with Kit?" she asked, slightly indignant. "If you're going after this sorcerer, and he is as powerful as you think he is, you'll need as much help as you can get."

"It's just because Donovan and I have the most experience fighting a witch. I also have my Flame Claw; he has a spear, and Curtis can use Quintessence. You only have your bow and a knife, and the last witch we went after could turn arrows to ash before they hit with almost no effort. I don't think you'll be able to do any good out there. Someone needs to stay back to watch our supplies and Kit. We shouldn't leave anything unattended in this place." Elsa opened her mouth to speak, but he cut in first. "*But* that doesn't mean you can't still cover us with your bow from the tree line. Maybe you can catch the witch by surprise, or at the very least, give him one more thing to worry about. All right?"

"Okay, that sounds reasonable. If things are going sideways, I'm jumping in to help." She grabbed her bow and positioned it against a tree in front of Kit. Donovan tied the donkey to the skinniest tree. Curtis, Donovan, and Hyroc headed into the opening.

As they entered the area, a golden sheen settled on the ground. Hyroc realized he was looking at water. What he and his friends had assumed was an area cleared for performing dark rituals, was merely a lake. A mass of tangled roots covered most of the shore, and the ends of some dropped into the lake. Opposite them, the lake drained into a stream. Perhaps the lake was fed by a spring submerged in its depths. The water was brownish-black, and he couldn't see beneath its surface. He scanned the area but couldn't see anyone or anything that stood out. Beyond the ominous color of the lake, there wasn't anything here.

"There's nothing here," Hyroc said in a mixture of relief and disappointment. "I guess it's safe for Elsa and Kit to join us."

Donovan lifted his fingers to his lips, whistled, and waved Elsa over. Elsa led the donkey to them, and Kit slowly trailed behind her. As they waited for her to join them, Curtis grabbed a rock. Hyroc grabbed the boy's shoulder when he pulled his arm back into a throwing position.

"Don't," he said sternly. "There isn't anything here we can see, but we don't want to stir anything that might be hiding in the lake."

Curtis nodded apologetically and dropped the rock.

"So, this place is empty," Elsa stated. "Well, this did seem like the best lead."

"Yes, but I made us lose the road," Hyroc said, feeling stupid.

"Hey," Donovan said, putting his hand on Hyroc's shoulder. "You shouldn't feel bad about this." He indicated the forest around them with a waving motion. "This place doesn't exactly follow the *normal* rules. I'm certain we'll find the road again."

Elsa put a hand above her eyes, looking skyward. "I can't quite tell the sun's position through all of this," she said. "But I think it's pretty late in the day, so we should camp here before we lose what little light we have."

They found a suitable place on a small patch of ground without any roots, but it was uncomfortably close to the lake's edge.

Elsa drank from her waterskin, looking displeased. "We have another problem," she said. She upended the waterskin to display the last two drops falling out of it. "I think we're about out of water." Everyone checked their waterskins, confirming her words. "That means we need to get some from *that*." She pointed at the lake.

"We don't know if something is waiting in there for someone to do just that," Donovan said before Hyroc could.

"But we need water. We're not going to get very far without more." Donovan signed in resignation.

"I'm pretty sure we can handle anything that comes at us," Hyroc said reassuringly. "I'll be right next to her, ready to hit anything trying to grab her."

Elsa moved to the mouth of the river. Hyroc positioned himself next to her, sword at the ready. The water seemed to become more threatening.

"Ready?" Elsa asked.

"Yeah, go," Hyroc said.

Cautiously, she dipped her waterskin in the river. Nothing near them moved. Elsa set her filled waterskin aside and grabbed another. She gave her surroundings a quick look before doing the next skin. This attempt made Hyroc even more nervous. They could have just gotten lucky on the first attempt and had caught anything off guard. But now, anything in there was aware of them. Nothing happened. Hyroc tensed, giving everyone a start when a water bug floated in front of Elsa. Everyone smiled at their preposterous reactions. Elsa filled the remaining water skins without incident.

She sniffed the opening in the skin and looked unenthused. "It doesn't smell good at all," she said. She handed it to Hyroc, and he responded similarly when he smelled it.

"Are you sure it's safe to drink?" Donovan questioned.

"There's only one way to find out," Hyroc said.

"All right, I'll try it."

"No, I should be the one to try it," Elsa admitted. "And before either you say anything, it's because one of you can carry me if something happens, but I can't carry either of you if something happens to you. I'm not trying to demean myself by saying I'm the least useful out of you three, but I'm the one that makes the most sense to do this." Hyroc and Donovan nodded in agreement. Elsa lifted her waterskin to her mouth and took a drink. She frowned but didn't seem entirely disgusted by the flavor. "Well, it doesn't taste as bad as I thought, but it's still pretty bad."

"Feel any differently?" Hyroc asked tentatively.

She shook her head. "No. I feel fine. I think it's safe."

Hyroc breathed a sigh of relief. Then he saw Kit come over and take a drink, followed by their donkey, which they had temporarily relieved of its packs to let it rest.

"Good," Donovan said. "But just because that water's drinkable doesn't mean this lake is safe. We should probably build up a barrier on our side closest to the lake, just in case."

Elsa and Curtis split off to find fallen firewood while Hyroc and Donovan got to work on the barrier. Hyroc used his Flame Claw to form a small mound of dirt, and then he and Donovan piled rocks on top of it. Next, they added the dead branches of a thorny bush. Lastly, they sprinkled dry leaves across their makeshift fortification and around their camp so they would hear anything trying to sneak up on them during the night.

Hyroc and Donovan stepped over to the lake's edge to wash the dirt from their hands. As they did so, Hyroc noticed tracks on the ground beside him. But they didn't belong to any animal he had seen. A partial drag mark at its center was as wide as a person, and several indents beside it went in the same direction.

"Are those spider tracks?" Donovan asked, dropping into a crouch to take a closer look.

"No, this is something else," Hyroc answered. "But I don't think we want to run into whatever it is."

"We'll need to keep an especially close eye out at night."

"The forest seems to have changed here, so there's a good chance what we'll find from now on will be even more dangerous."

"Splitting up might not be a good idea anymore."

"Agreed."

Elsa and Curtis returned with firewood. Hyroc used his Flame Claw to get a fire going.

"You know, there's something I've always wondered," Donovan said, pointing at the fire as it turned from blue to orange. "You're supposed to be all in tune with nature and whatnot. I mean, you can even talk to trees."

"I don't talk to trees," Hyroc corrected, annoyed.

"Right, you see what they're feeling."

Hyroc shook his head disapprovingly. That was better, but still not entirely correct.

"And might I say? The most interesting feeling I imagine them having is delight from an animal depositing excrement in their vicinity. That sounds like the most boring company ever."

Hyroc waggled his head in agreement.

"Anyway. So, with nature in mind, why does your ability only seem to come in the form of fire? Fire seems bad. I mean, forest fires burn down many trees, kill animals in the most agonizing way possible, and destroy pretty much everything in their path. Why would you want to use something so dangerous to the forest?"

Hyroc gazed at him thoughtfully. "This is how Ursa explained it to me," he said. "Yes, fire can be devastating, but it also brings life. When a forest fire rages through the forest, it destroys that area. But by doing so, it allows new life to flourish. It burns up all the dead trees and whatever else has accumulated. Clearing all that out makes room for new seedlings to take root. If you go to a burned-up area right after a fire, there's green cropping up all over the ashes. Yes, it kills trees, but they are quickly replaced with seedlings."

"So it's sort of the forest's way of cleaning," Elsa said. "But instead of sweeping things away, like with a broom, it burns it up."

"I guess you could look at it that way. So my Flame Claw combines an incredibly destructive force with the powers of renewal. I can defend myself with it, as with fireballs, or use it to heal." He indicated the fire. "Or use it as a tool to save us some work by lighting a campfire."

Donovan nodded. "That makes a lot of sense," he said. "Thank you."

"You're welcome."

Hyroc lay back, gazing at the dimming sky above the lake. He just couldn't use his Flame Claw to get everyone out of this terrible place.

Chapter 4
The Village

Hyroc felt something tickling his ear and face. Groggily, he rolled onto his side. Then, something pulled the side of his cloak away, exposing him to the cool morning air. He opened his eyes to see what interrupted his fleeting sleep. Kit playfully held the corner of Hyroc's cloak in his mouth. Hyroc snatched the fabric away and lay back down. His eyes closed partway before shooting open as he sat bolt upright. Kit was moving around unhindered! He appeared to have fully recovered from almost being exsanguinated to death. This was excellent news.

"Kit, you're better!" Hyroc yelled excitedly. Kit jumped on the makeshift wall and crouched into a playful pouncing position. Hyroc hunched his back and invitingly spread his arms. "Come on, come on. Get me!" His companion leaped on him, knocking him onto his back. The cougar grabbed his head and shoulders in a massive hug, lightly pinning him in place. Hyroc wrapped his arms around the big cat's powerful shoulders and wrenched them sideways to yank Kit onto his side. Kit lightly resisted the move, pawing at Hyroc's face without claws. The exuberant mountain lion purred happily as they wrestled back and forth. Kit firmly pinned Hyroc and started licking his face.

"No, stop, stop it," Hyroc said, trying to wriggle away from the wet saliva assault of his companion's sandpapery tongue. "Stop that. Ahh, that doesn't feel good. You're going to remove my fur with that!" Hyroc got a hand free and pushed away the head of his feline companion. "Yes, I'm glad you're feeling better. I don't want to be bald." Kit affectionately rubbed the side of his head against Hyroc's hand.

"Looks like *Somebody's* in a good mood," Elsa said happily.

"I was worried how weak he was after that wolf mauled him," Donovan said. "Those things have some nasty teeth, thorns, or whatever you want to call them. But I'm happy our friend was determined to prove me wrong."

Curtis stepped closer and made a clicking noise with his mouth to call Kit over to him. The big cat pulled away from Hyroc to accept the boy's attention eagerly. After a few scratches, Curtis magically created a tiny glowing ball he sent zipping across the ground for Kit to chase. Kit frantically slapped at the ball with his wide paws in a rapid thumping motion. Everyone chuckled joyfully. It was a welcome diversion from their horrid situation. For a moment, the forest seemed brighter.

Hyroc brushed off his clothes and unwrinkled them. "I'm glad I won't have to walk on all fours anymore," he said. "I don't feel comfortable in this place going without my sword. From what that creature did to Kit, I don't relish the thought of getting bitten. I am a much bigger target in bear form, so there's more of me to get bitten in a fight."

As Hyroc belted on his weapons, a strange noise came from the other side of the barrier. It was a crisp sound like many leafy plants were constantly getting stepped on. Looking toward it, everyone saw what appeared to be vines creeping out of the lake. Everyone warily backed away. The vines grasped the barrier and started pulling it apart.

"Those don't seem to like our little wall," Elsa said.

"Hey, those are freaking me out. Let's leave!" Donovan exclaimed, grabbing the reins of the donkey and leading it away.

Wordlessly, they acknowledged his instructions. Hyroc's foot caught on the crook of a root, and he stumbled. He fell, catching himself with an outstretched hand on a taller root. A searing pain drilled into his head, and his consciousness washed through the tree. Their enemy's voice said, "Clever prey, they flee where eyes cannot see. But not even boroughs can hide their evil." Hyroc pushed himself up and pulled his hand away, severing the connection. Then, he was struck by an epiphany.

"It's a tree!" Hyroc said, staring at his hand, awestruck. "That voice I keep hearing is from a tree."

"Hyroc, what's that you're saying?" Elsa asked as she helped him to his feet.

Hyroc looked at her. "Our *enemy* is a tree."

She cocked an eyebrow. "A tree?"

"Yes."

"Okay? I guess as weird as everything is in this forest, something that bizarre shouldn't come as a surprise to me. Explain as we go." She ushered him forward.

"It's a tree. That explains the flesh-eating plant creatures, the leaf wolves, the voices, and why I can't commune with the trees to learn anything about this area. It's a Warding Tree."

"A Warding Tree? Is that anything like a Watcher Tree?"

Hyroc shot her a curious look.

"It's something our parents used to tell us. 'Hunt quietly and shoot straight, but remember the eyes of the Watcher tree. It knows every leaf and sees every kill. Treat animals justly. Do not waste, or needless destroy, for the ire of the Watcher tree is dire.'"

"That sounds like the same thing. Guardians are powerful protectors of the natural order, but they can't be everywhere all at once. So they created the Warding Trees or Watcher Trees to tend the wild places in their stead. These trees know everything happening in the forest they are charged to look after. Or at least anything impactful that happens. This is what my communion ability is derived from. The Warding Trees are unable to sense subtle events in the forest. A pack of wolves hunting a deer will go unnoticed because their activity really doesn't involve the trees, but if something like a bear tears into a tree with its claws or a moose starts vigorously scraping its antlers on a tree, then it will notice. That's why it found us when we started chopping wood the other day. We were effecting the trees.

"They have magical abilities enabling them to manipulate trees and the foliage within their influence. They control, guide, and maintain the natural balance of their forest."

"Do you know what their disposition towards people is?" Donovan said. "How do they react if someone starts chopping down a tree? Do they usually kill them?"

"They're generally peaceful," Hyroc answered. "They're not supposed to do anything if someone fells a tree, so long as that person's actions don't disrupt the balance or they are overly destructive. If someone cuts down trees to build a house, the Warding Trees don't mind. But if someone cuts down trees and doesn't do anything with them, they leave them to rot; the Warding Tree won't like that. Or if someone purposely starts a forest fire or abuses the animals of the forest. Something like killing animals simply for the fun of it rather than for food or to, in some way, make use of the carcass. But even if someone does any of that, they have to do quite a lot to make a Warding Tree angry."

"What happens when the tree gets angry?"

Hyroc's expression turned more serious. "It gives the person a warning. It tells the person about their transgressions, trying to scare them into knocking it off. But if they don't get the hint, well, it kills them."

"Do you know how it kills?"

"Not really. Ursa never shared that with me. She must have thought I wouldn't get into a situation where I would have to worry about that. My guess is with the trees. They probably use roots or something to smother, stab, or beat someone to death."

"Lovely," Elsa noted sarcastically. "But what did we do to piss off this Warding Tree? We haven't done anything remotely bad here. We only fled into the forest. We're not even chopping firewood. If anything, we've treated this forest more kindly than Elswood."

"Why is this one using all these strange creatures to attack us?" Donovan asked.

Hyroc threw a hand up and shrugged. "I have no idea," he said. "Nor do I understand why it would want to trap us here. But whenever I have heard it talk, what it says is barely coherent. I don't think that's how they are supposed to sound. I think there's something wrong with this forest."

"Could it be sick?"

Hyroc shook his head. "I wouldn't expect so," he said dismissively. "If it were sick, it should get weaker and be less of a threat, like when a human, Wol'dger, or animal is unwell. I don't think it would be strong enough to create those wolf golems made out of forest refuse, let alone the enchantment preventing us from leaving."

"Beyond piquing our interests, knowing that doesn't improve our situation," Donovan noted.

Hyroc sighed in dejected agreement. "But what gets me," he said, rubbing his head. "Is how it's able to block my communion ability? I don't think it's supposed to be able to do that."

"Well, it's doing all kinds of odd things," Elsa said. "Why not also that?"

Hyroc studied the trunks of the trees they passed. Why did his communion ability hurt? Was the warding tree attacking him? But if it knew precisely how to target his mind and prevent infiltration, wouldn't that also reveal his location? His frustration grew with each tree they passed. The answers were all around him, but he couldn't glean anything from the trees. What he needed to know was there; he was sure of it.

He stopped, looking a tree up and down. If he got past the pain, could he learn something valuable? He knew how to cope with tremendous pain; he was a bear. He placed his hand on the tree, concentrating hard. Pain drilled into his head. He willed himself through the discomfort and forced his mind into the tree. The tree resisted fiercely. It would not yield its secrets willingly. But it could not withstand the will of an Anamagi. The pain intensified. Gritting his sharp teeth, he maintained his effort. There had to be something here! Then, he noticed a familiar feeling. Hyroc groaned, breathing heavily from the pain. He couldn't endure this much longer. What was that feeling? The pain clouded his thoughts, making it hard for him to think. He focused on the feeling. There had to be something to this. If he pushed just a little harder. He suddenly smelled acrid smoke. His eyes and nostrils burned from choking fumes. In his mind's eye, he saw a tree engulfed in blazing flames. Was it a memory from the tree? No, it was not a memory of the tree; it was bigger than that. It was a collective memory from the forest. He felt his consciousness being stretched like a sheet across the area. He was everywhere, yet still within his body. Then he saw young men and women being knocked to the ground, wearing horrified expressions. An instant later, leaf wolves fell upon them, tearing into their bodies. Hyroc now recognized the feeling. It was anger. A colossal amount of anger! Rage like he had never imagined could exist in the world.

He felt himself drawing out of the tree. Something with a will was pulling him away. His consciousness shrank back into his body. He opened his eyes to see Elsa pull his hand away from the tree. Then, he noticed the severe pain erupting in his head. His legs buckled, and he fell against the tree, holding the side of his head while screaming in agony. Elsa dropped to her knees before him and grabbed his shoulder as if trying to wake him from a nightmare. She spoke, but he couldn't understand her through the roar in his ears. After a moment of torment, the pain subsided.

"Hyroc, Hyroc," Elsa yelled. "What happened? What did you do?"

"Wooked – in – tree!" Hyroc moaned through clenched teeth. His shoulders rose and fell with rapid, deep heaving breaths.

"What in the *sunless plains* were you thinking? We already know this Warding Tree wants us dead without you needing to torture yourself like an idiot, you bullheaded moose."

"I ound – sometin. I'll – explan wen I stop – anting – tubi unconscious!"

"What's with all the yelling?" Donovan said, coming around the tree with his spear ready. Kit came in behind him, frantic and startled. The hackles on the big cat's neck were raised. "Where's the –" Donovan stopped talking abruptly and jolted his head back in surprise. "Whoa. Shadow! What happened to your eyes? They're all red and bloodshot. Did something knock you on the head?"

"No, it was something *stupid*," Elsa said. She held the back of Hyroc's head, treating him with the only kind of comfort she could offer.

Hyroc pulled away from her hand, demonstrating his self-inflicted discomfort had subsided. "I needed to learn something," he said.

"You look downright demonic right now."

"Wonderful. I look even more frightening. That's what I've always wanted," Hyroc said sarcastically.

"I hope whatever terrible thing you just put yourself through was worth it," Elsa said.

Hyroc nodded. "It was, I think. The Warding Tree isn't what's blocking my communion ability; it's the trees themselves. It's like nothing I've ever felt. They're angry. Really angry. Their animosity radiates from them almost like poison meant to repel pests. But it's nothing we did. Something happened before we ever arrived, something terrible. And whatever *it* was, it infuriated this entire forest. This whole place is drowning in anger."

"Ah, so, basically wrong time, wrong place," Donovan said unhappily.

"Seems so. That terrible thing involved people, so this Warding Tree considers all people enemies and it wants to punish anyone coming into its forest. The enchantment that traps us here is to ensure no trespassers, human, Wol'dger and apparently Anamagi alike, don't escape its wrath"

"Well, that's unfortunate, but regardless of what this terrible thing was, that tree still wants to kill us. We have no choice but to find it and destroy it before it kills us. No matter how terrible what happened here was. It's us or *that tree.* Did you learn anything new about how to find it?"

Hyroc blew out a breath. "No."

"Well, finding the road is a good place to start," Elsa suggested. "It could lead somewhere useful, but at the very least, it should make traveling easier while we figure something out."

Hyroc nodded. "If we keep heading east, we should come across it eventually, I hope. But here's something odd." He spoke with an ironic smile. "Or, I guess, something else that's odd, considering what we've seen. This tree thinks I'm a Guardian. I assume it sensed or recognized the power of my Flame Claw derived from Guardian magic. But if it thinks I'm a Guardian and the rest of you are my allies, why is it trying to kill us? Guardians are protectors of nature, and the Warding trees are supposed to aid them."

"Yeah, that does sound counterintuitive," Donovan said. "But have you considered this tree could just be crazy?"

"The thought had crossed my mind. The things it says don't sound sane."

"See. We have to focus all of our attention on destroying it if we want to make it out of here alive."

The group headed in an easterly direction. As they moved forward, the air gained a fetid smell. It reminded Hyroc of the moldering smell of fallen leaves in autumn, wet from the thawed morning frost just before the winter snows. Then he spotted giant, waist-high mushrooms with dark brown tops growing from the ground beside the trees. Hyroc and his companions wound their way through the forest, trying not to touch any giant fungi from an abundance of caution. No birds were singing here, only the haunting screech of some feathered creature. Hyroc heard things moving all around them beyond his sight. The noises were soft, suggesting the creatures were small. Then he saw whitish filaments stretched between the branches of trees. He couldn't tell if they were strips of moss or the gossamer webbing from giant spiders. Those frightening creatures tended to avoid sunlight, and these were perfect conditions for them to thrive.

The terrain rose to a mild hill. The canopy overhead thinned as they climbed, letting through light and weakening the gloom. It didn't fully open to the sky but was a welcome reprieve. Through a gap in the leaves, Hyroc saw the dark silhouette of an eagle against the bright blue sky. What did the forest look like from above, Hyroc wondered. Did it look more inviting or less? The hill gradually sank back into the darkened trees. As it leveled out, the space between the trees increased. An unusually straight, long patch of unobstructed forest materialized. Everyone breathed a sigh of relief; they had found the road. Going south led to where they had been a few days prior when they had headed for the black water of the lake. The other way stretched off in a northeasterly direction. With the change in the forest, heading east seemed to lead them closer to their target. At least, everyone hoped that was what it indicated. They followed the road as it went to the northeast.

Save for the occasional bend around a troublesome feature, the road maintained its course without substantial deviations. Close to the time when it would have been ideal to set up camp for the night, the road turned fully toward the north. When the travelers turned the corner, large black shapes came into view. The shapes startled the group, as everyone feared they were new forest monsters. But upon further scrutiny, the shapes resolved into boulders. They had an unusually squarish shape, and Hyroc realized they were the remains of buildings. Many more similar structures came into view. Was this a village?

The structures were dilapidated and in a far-progressed state of decay. The corners of several buildings had collapsed, spilling their rotted wood innards into the flat areas that vaguely resembled the paths between them. Some even had gaping holes in their roofs where trees had taken root and grown through the opening. Moss and thorny vines clung to the outsides of the most intact buildings. Thick patches of forest flora crowded each building, filling every gap and crevice they could take root in. No one had lived here for a very long time.

"How is there a village here?" Elsa asked, taken aback.

"I have no idea," Hyroc said, taking in their surroundings.

"This place gives me the creeps," Donovan said. "Maybe we should think about making camp elsewhere."

"No, it's almost dark," Elsa noted. "I don't relish getting caught after sundown before we've made camp and have a fire going. Better to shelter for the night in a suitable place."

"We should look at that one," Hyroc said, pointing to a structure. "It still seems mostly intact from here and shouldn't have any widow-makers hanging from what's left of the rafters."

They moved to the building, but a glimmer caught Hyroc's attention. He cautiously broke away from his friends to investigate. Something crunched under his boot. When he looked down, he saw a grayish bone poking out of the ground. It looked human. Scanning his surroundings, he noticed more remains. Upon closer inspection of the one he had stepped on, he realized it looked like the vertebrae around the neck had been crushed by powerful jaws. The nearest next skeleton had a large patch of dark discoloration spread across it as if it had been exposed to the licking flames of a fire. Most of the other skeletons had a similar appearance. When he returned his eyes to the glimmer, he noticed it emanating from a large wolf's skeleton, nearly twice the size of any he had ever seen. The animal's remains had numerous broken bones, chips, whitish lines of cuts, and fractures, indicating it had been killed in a vicious fight.

Then he realized it wasn't a mere wolf. He saw circles of silver around each of the animal's ankles. And the glimmer was from a square-cut emerald on a bronze chain hanging around its neck. But he knew the gem wasn't for decoration. It was a power gem capable of storing Quintessence. He was looking at a dead Guardian. If these people's

activities attracted the ire of a Guardian they were certainly into something vile.

"All right, the building looks sound," Elsa said as she approached Hyroc. "It also still has a partial roof, so it won't be a problem if it rains tonight. What's caught your interest with these bones? It looks like you've got a wolf there. A huge one."

"It's not a wolf," Hyroc corrected. "It's a Guardian."

She was stunned. "A Guardian? Guardian, as in protector of nature? Guardian, as in Ursa? That kind of Guardian?"

"Yes."

Elsa was quiet. "So they *can* be killed."

Hyroc nodded. "They're damn tough and mighty, but, yes, they can be killed. This one didn't go down without a fight." He indicated the human remains around them with a sweeping motion "This wolf took many of its enemies down with it."

"What were these people doing to get on the bad side of this Guardian?"

"It was something dark they would have been better off leaving alone."

"Yeah. Come on, it's not a good idea for you to be out here alone this close to dark."

"I just need to do something real quick."

Hyroc reached for the emerald but pulled his hand back reluctantly. He wasn't keen on taking from the dead.

"I'm sorry," he reverently said to the bones. "I'm not desecrating your remains. But you've got something that could help me and my friends get out of here." Finally working up enough courage, he snatched the necklace from the skeleton. Hyroc whispered prayerfully, "May you rest peacefully, honored Sentinel, your watch is ended. He stood and followed Elsa to the structure. There was a gaping hole in the ceiling, but enough of a corner of the wall remained to form a sheltered recess. Donovan and Curtis cleared away rotted wood in what was left of the floor to build a fire without risking catching the moldering building on fire. Across from where they stood, Hyroc saw a room with a foot locker. Curious, he walked over to it. The hiss of a muskrat startled him and made him instinctually reach for his sword. The minuscule animal scampered out of an unseen recess and disappeared through a hole in the wall. The foot locker had a lock, but the metal was severely rusted. Hyroc drew his wood hatchet and smacked the back of its head on the lock. With a metallic clank, the lock fell away. When he tried opening it, the top of the chest snapped off. After tossing the lid away, he pushed aside pieces of rotting cloth and parchment to find a book's mostly intact leather wrapping. Maybe it was a journal from one of the townsfolk? That might help him discover what had befallen this village and where the Warding tree was. He carefully carried the fragile book to his friends.

"Did you find something?" Elsa asked as she divvied out food among her brothers.

"Yeah, it's a book," he said without looking at her while concentrating on each step to ensure he didn't stumble and destroy what he carried.

He lowered himself to the deteriorated, moss-covered floor and opened the book. Curtis and Donovan sat down on either side of him, looking at the book expectantly. Elsa stepped behind him and peered over his shoulder.

"Maybe it's a journal from one of the villagers," Hyroc said. "If it is, it might be able to tell us what happened here, and maybe there's something in it that will help us find the tree."

"What's it say?" Curtis asked as Hyroc turned another page.

Hyroc leaned forward, suddenly becoming more interested. "Hmm, it's written in Runeisk." His friend shot him a quizzical look, not understanding what this meant or even what that was. Hyroc shook his head in self-deprecation, feeling a little embarrassed when he realized he was the only one who knew what he was talking about.

"Oh, sorry, Runeisk is the language witches use. Considering all the skeletons around that dead Guardian, it shouldn't have come as a surprise. They would be the kind of people to vex a Guardian. It's been a while since I read it. I haven't since before Marcus, my adopting father, passed. And these rot smears on the parchment aren't helping. This may take me a while to translate. What I've been able to decipher so far mentions what herbs are best for treating minor ailments. This book must have belonged to an herbalist."

Elsa and Donovan nodded with less interest and resumed , getting the donkey settled and removing its saddlebags to let the animal rest.

"Let us know if you find anything," Donovan said.

Elsa gave Hyroc a hunk of bread, and he continued reading as he ate. He read until everyone settled down to sleep.

"Have you found anything yet?" Donovan inquired sleepily while stretching his arms.

Hyroc shook his head. "Not yet," he answered. Hyroc laughed half-humoredly. "Now I'm into the best herbs to use with injured livestock or the best ones to be baked into bread. But it's hard to tell with this in the way." Hyroc indicated a page with a patch of rot over a large portion.

"Fascinating," Donovan said sarcastically.

Hyroc carefully closed the book before lying down to sleep.

Chapter 5
Weapons

The next morning, Hyroc carefully turned the rot-pocked page of the herbalist's old book. Halfway through, the page split off from the spine of the book. Hyroc flipped the disconnected page over, laying it on the book to read what was on the other side. Now, he either read how to treat toe fungus by submerging someone's foot in water infused with herbs or the best seasoning to use on a cooked toe. Not only was he unpracticed reading Runeisk, but keywords were unreadable due to the decay of the parchment. This forced him to piece things together, and sometimes, he had to outright guess about the things he read. It was a slow, tedious process. Then, to compound his frustration, it might be a complete waste of time for him to comb through it for anything useful about the Warding tree.

"Anything yet?" Donovan asked as he absentmindedly entertained himself by trying to toss a piece of wood into the opening of the broken chest.

Hyroc shook his head. "No, still nothing since last you asked," he said, his tone bored.

Curtis tossed a piece of wood at the chest. He got it in! He thrust his arms into the air in a soundless celebration.

"I'm not sure if I'm going to find anything," Hyroc continued. "Everything so far has been pretty –" he trailed off abruptly. "Hold on, what's this?" He put a finger on what he read to help his focus. "I think this says something about *black vein*." He again noticed his friends looking at him quizzically, clearly not knowing what he spoke about. "Sorry," Hyroc said, squeezing his eyes shut in slight embarrassment. "It's what happens when a shadow demon, like a Shade Hunter, bites somebody. The veins around the wound turn black. If not cured, the veins slowly spread across the body, and if they reach the chest, the person dies.

"Marcus once explained this to me and showed me drawings of it. He learned that during his work with The Ministry, a witch summoned a Shadow Hound to terrorize a village. They killed the creature and the witch, but not before several people were bitten. Most of them died, but it was a monumental challenge for the ones he managed to save."

"Okay, noted, don't get bitten by a shadow demon," Donovan said. "Did Marcus ever talk to you about anything that wasn't disturbing?"

"Well, when you're a child, and everyone thinks you're an unnatural creature of destruction, you must be extra sure you don't do anything wrong. He drilled this information into me to keep me safe. However, I think he unintentionally overlooked the nightmares caused by telling me said information. So, in hindsight, it might not have been his best idea to reveal that to a child, but those things sure seem to have come in handy as of late."

Donovan waggled his head in agreement.

"Anyway," Hyroc continued, "the black vein indicates someone got attacked by a shadow demon, and the villagers were dabbling in summoning. This more thoroughly explains how they drew the wrath of a Guardian. They do not take kindly to shadow demon incursions."

"As I've heard," Elsa said. "All right. Donovan and I have been thinking since we're going after a Warding tree, it might be a good idea to look around the village for any weapons we could salvage. The three of us can handle anything potentially dangerous, so you stay here and keep going through the journal."

"Seems reasonable," Hyroc said. "But if I haven't found anything by the time you return, I doubt there's anything in it. Oh, and be careful of any leftover runes drawn on the ground or any of the buildings, especially if they're glowing; they may be enchanted to do something harmful."

"We'll keep an eye out."

"Oh, I almost forgot. There's one more thing before you go." He placed the journal on the uneven, rotting wooden floor of the building, rose, and stepped over to Curtis. He pulled the emerald necklace from his pocket and handed it to his younger friend. "That emerald is a power gem, just like the one I've got." Hyroc pushed the pointed ruby that hung around his neck forward for emphasis.

"That's great," Curtis said excitedly. "Where'd you find it?"

Hyroc's smile faded, and he nervously scratched the back of his head. "It came from, uh, actually, you don't want to know."

Elsa stifled a laugh.

Curtis was suddenly less enthused.

"But I made sure it was clean. I would never give you anything that I wouldn't want to wear. I just wouldn't put it in your mouth, is all. But the important thing is it can store a small amount of Quintessence. Having some extra Quintessence on hand could be useful in an emergency. This is how you fill it." Hyroc put his hand over his ruby, and Curtis mirrored him. "Concentrate on the gem. Think about energy flowing down your arm into your hand. Now, think about that energy moving out of your hand and into the gem." Curtis concentrated on the emerald, which glowed a soft green, signaling Quintessence flowed into it. "Okay. You've got it." The light faded from the emerald. "Just remember sending Quintessence into the gem is the same as using a spell, which will sap your strength, so make sure you only do a little at a time. I usually siphon some into it before I sleep at night because sleep and rest help regenerate Quintessence. By the time morning arrives, I'm as good as new. Whenever you know you won't need to cast spells, it is a good time to fill it. And you do that until it's filled."

"Thank you, Hyroc," Curtis said eagerly.

"You're very welcome," Hyroc said. "Okay, the three of you, be careful. I'll be here."

"We hope with something useful," Donovan said encouragingly.

"I don't have much hope of that, but yes, I hope I'll have something useful to share," Hyroc said, waving as the three of them headed out.

Hyroc pushed his arms into the air to stretch and yawned after hours of reading. He rubbed the soreness out of a spot on the back of his neck. Kit sauntered over and started chewing on a discarded page that had fallen out of the journal. Hyroc snatched it away from his feline companion.

"Don't eat that!" he said indignantly. "Who knows what kind of weird mold is growing on it." Hyroc used his Flame Claw to incinerate the page, thus eliminating the temptation. The cougar lay down, flicking his tail in irritation.

Hyroc resumed reading. Now, the journal dealt with protocols for treating animal bites. It was knowledge he might benefit from if only the names of the herbs and how to administer them were readable. He grimaced as it went into a graphic description of a particularly gruesome wound. The sound of footsteps outside the building drew him from the gory details.

"Elsa, Donovan, or Curtis, is that you?" Hyroc called out, putting his hand on his sword. It might have been a mere instant before something attacked him if it wasn't them.

"Yes, it's us," Elsa's voice answered

Hyroc continued reading as he spoke. "Did you find anything?" he said.

Elsa ducked into the structure. "Oh, there's lots of stuff here, but most is too rusty or decayed to use." Multiple wood hatchets – their metallic heads scarred with dark orange rust – hung from her belt, and she carried tools and pieces of scrap metal in her arms. She stuck her salvage into one of the donkey saddlebags lying on the floor. "I found a bunch of tools, and though they're pretty rusty, they're still in good enough condition for us to get some use out of them and maybe save the sharpness of our blades. But take a look at this." She stepped over to him and held her open palm in front of him. The silver heads of five Shadow Killer arrows glinted in her hand. Without an arrow shaft attached to them, they were useless against a shadow demon, but their silver was worth a considerable amount if they ever got out of this forest.

"That's a nice find," Hyroc said.

"You've got to look at what I found," Donovan said excitedly.

"Oh, yeah, we also came across this," Elsa said.

Donovan came inside the structure carrying a rusted Boar Spear. The shaft was shorter than the spear he had brought from Elswood, with a heavier leaf-shaped head that made it better for thrusting and more capable of slicing.

"That's an impressive find," Hyroc said. "I'm surprised you found that in functional condition."

"I know; I was amazed," Donovan said. "I don't think this rust scale goes too deep into the blade, so I can get it off with a whetstone."

Hyroc smirked. "Or you could just let me do this." He lifted his hand toward the blade. A flowing blue shimmer engulfed the blade. The rust on it shrank and disappeared. "There."

Donovan looked at the blade happily. "You didn't need to do that, but thank you."

Hyroc nodded his appreciation.

"That spear also frees up Donovan's old one for me to use," Elsa said. "Arrows barely slow down those leaf wolves, and now, I have more than just my knife to rely on. What about you? Have you had any luck?"

Hyroc shook his head. "I've read many ways to treat injuries, but I don't even know if I translated most of them correctly."

"Keep trying until we've gotten everything ready for travel."

Hyroc returned his attention to the book. The book shifted from injury treatment to praising someone. Much of the writing was unreadable, making it difficult for him to figure out who they were or what they had done deserving of praise. He turned the page, and his eyes widened with astonishment.

"Oh, what!" Hyroc said. He looked from Donovan to Elsa, who had noticed his reaction and pointed at the book. Unable to form words into an explanation, he just read it aloud. "… A rainy summer day, one of the most powerful among us (unreadable)… The king spat on our offer and unjustly murdered (unreadable)… We will not, ideally, take these insults. The strongest among us have been called to bring retribution (unreadable)…Lord Feygrotha will call us out of the shadows to join him when all his enemies lay dead."

"Did you just say Feygrotha?" Donovan questioned. Hyroc nodded. "As in the terrible sorcerer Feygrotha who ruled over Arnaira almost one hundred years ago and was so evil my ancestors were forced into rebellion against him and his followers?"

"I'm afraid so. The shadow demons, the dead Guardian – it all makes sense now. After the king of Arnaira killed Feygrotha's family for their use of forbidden powers and cast him out, he must have fled to this place to plan his vengeance."

"But then why is everyone in this town dead?" Elsa asked. "If he was that powerful, what could have wiped out this place?"

"I know. It's strange." A thought came to Hyroc. "While you were out, did the three of you happen to see any bodies?"

"Yeah, there's a lot of them."

"Did any of their necks look damaged, like something had bit them there?"

"Actually, yes. I took a close look at some of the remains, and, yes, the neckbones were damaged."

"That's because leaf wolves killed them. The other day, you know, when I made my eyes go bloodshot?"

"And you were wailing in agony," Elsa interjected. "Yeah, we remember."

Hyroc felt mortified imagining how he must have looked during that ordeal. "Yes," he said subdued. "Well, I saw someone get killed by one of those wolves, and the creature went for the person's neck. I also saw a burning tree, and I don't think it was from a forest fire. Knowing what witches tend to do in areas they reside in, they must have started draining Quintessence from this Warding tree after killing the Guardian, who tried to stop them. Ursa told me draining Quintessence from a living thing is incredibly painful. Who knows how long this tree had to endure that? They probably left it with just enough Quintessence to keep it alive after a session, then they let its energy reserves regenerate before doing it all over again. This tree must have also witnessed those witches doing unspeakable things to the forest. All of that combined must have been unbearable. That's why I can barely understand it when it speaks. They drove it into madness!"

"It sounds like those witches got what was coming to them," Donovan said.

"Feygrotha probably spurned on the actions of those witchs' in preparation for his campaign of vengeance," Elsa suggested.

"Probably," Hyroc agreed. "Summoning many shadow demons to use against the king of Arnaira would have required a ton of Quintessence, and they had a whole forest of living things from which to draw energy. And they would not have humanely extracted it from the animals or the Warding Tree."

"But if the tree couldn't do anything to stop them, how did it kill everyone in this village?"

"That's a good question."

Hyroc turned to the last page of the journal and read it aloud. "The forest hunts us. It is dragging people off to the northeast by (unreadable)…. The plants surround us (unreadable)…. The Warding tree will not let us leave! The edges of the forest are unreachable. We are holed up in the village and will hold out until Feygrotha returns."

Hyroc closed the journal. "That's the last thing written."

"We know the rest," Elsa said darkly. "But if they were doing all those horrible things to the tree, and it couldn't do anything, how was it suddenly able to kill everyone?"

"I think I know. Feygrotha took the strongest of the villagers with him to kill the king of Arnaira. That would have left less able fighters behind in the village. The weaker fighters might not have been able to control the tree. And no longer restrained by them, it made those wolf golems to attack the villagers. The tree then steadily closes in on them until everybody's dead."

"That's not much different from what it's trying to do to us."

"Let's leave this place and leave the dead to their rest," Elsa said. "So, to the northeast?"

Hyroc nodded, tossing the journal to the floor. "Yeah, I believe that's where the Warding tree is."

"All right, let's end this nightmare," Donovan said sternly.

Chapter 6

The Warding Tree

HYROC AND HIS COMPANY PUSHED through a cluster of dark brown bell-shaped mushrooms, engulfed by the ominous shadow of the thick forest canopy. Hyroc looked up to see small, scattered red eyes watching them from shaded branches. He hoped he and his friends could soon escape the gloom of these nightmarish woods and return to one without greenery intent on killing them. The snapping of a branch drew his attention back to ground level. He glimpsed a shape between the trunks of two trees before it slipped out of sight.

"Yeah, I've been seeing it, too," Elsa said, stepping beside him. "I haven't gotten a good look at it either, but something *is out there*. And it's big."

"It's probably an animal of some sort," Hyroc said. "But who knows how the Warding tree might have altered it? I don't think it's noticed us, so if we're careful, we can probably avoid attracting its attention."

Elsa snickered half-humoredly. "Right. And when has our rotten luck been that good?"

Hyroc shrugged. "That's why I said, 'probably.' That way, I'm covered in the ever-diminishing likelihood we're okay or if something awful happens."

"Good thinking," she scoffed."But if something awful does happen, I don't think either of us will care who called it."

"Probably not."

Past the leathery bells of the mushrooms, there was a gap in the trees. A scraping noise emanated from the edges of the clearing. Hyroc and Donovan broke from the group, approaching the sound with weapons ready. A brown weasel, the size of a fox, raised its head above the foliage and yipped in alarm. It regarded them with frightened, beady eyes before dashing away. It left behind the remains of an animal it had been gnawing on. Hyroc and Donovan lowered their weapons.

"False alarm," Donovan said as he and Hyroc returned to the group. "It was just a big weasel-looking animal scavenging what was left of an old kill. We scared it off, but we should get past the carcass quickly in case something else smells it."

They hastily moved past the kill and stopped to take a break when they were a safe distance away.

Donovan leaned against a tree and stretched his arms. "Where is that stupid tree?" he asked, mildly annoyed. "We're going on two days now of searching."

"The journal only indicated it was to the northeast," Hyroc said. "I read nothing about distance, or, at least not from what was legible."

"I hope whoever wrote it didn't use another reference point."

"Let's hope not. I don't want us to spend a second longer than we have to in this forsaken place."

"All right, let's head out," Elsa announced.

A branch snapped behind them just as Elsa took hold of the reins of their donkey. Hyroc, Kit, and Donovan cautiously fell back to guard the group against a would-be attacker. They warily watched their surroundings but couldn't see anything. Another branch snapped from a different direction, followed by the rustling of leaves.

"I think it's that big animal from earlier," Elsa said. "The one we couldn't identify."

"And there's more than one!" Donovan yelled.

Everyone pulled close to the donkey, with their backs against each other. Hyroc heard a clicking noise that made his neck hair stand up. "I just heard something click." The giant spiders that had claimed the lives of his friend's parents, Svald, Helen, and Walter, had made the same noise. It was a sound they all had tried hard to forget.

"Click, you mean as in *spiders*?" Donovan asked.

"I believe so," Hyroc answered as he continued to scan the forest with his eyes. "But it sounded louder."

"Oh. So maybe it's a bigger spider. Great."

"I just saw something pretty close," Elsa said, startled. "It kind of looked like a big snake."

"A snake?" Donovan and Hyroc questioned simultaneously.

"Sure, why not a huge snake!" Donovan said sarcastically.

They heard clicking from multiple directions.

"Are snakes known for making clicking noises?" Donovan said.

"I don't think –" Hyroc's answer was cut short when a black shape burst through the trees. It was no snake – it was an enormous black centipede! Its segmented black carapace glistened in what little light made it through the canopy. Innumerable thin, blood-red spindly legs supported the creature's long body, and its movements were serpentine. Sharp mandibles protruded from its mouth, and two venomous claws flanked either side of its head. It had large white eyes, and bright orange antennae protruded from its head and rear.

Elsa rushed toward it menacingly, jabbing her spear at its head. The front third of the creature lifted off the ground like a snake preparing to strike. Antenna flailing, the centipede bobbed its head and jutted forward, trying to find a way past her weapon. Curtis hit it in the head with a lightning bolt shattering a sizable chunk of its black shell. The enormous insect recoiled, issuing a sharp, squeaky clack of pain.

Another centipede rushed toward Elsa from the other side of the donkey. Hyroc dashed forward to intercept it. He swung his sword at its head, but the centipede jinked its body sideways out of the way of his strike. It jutted its head toward him to attack, and he darted under it. He stabbed upward at the carapace on its underside. The creature pulled out of the way of his blade and repositioned for another attack.

Kit issued a loud shrieking roar as he pounced on its head. The centipede hissed angrily, its head dropping from Kit's sudden weight, and it swiped its head wildly from side to side as it tried to throw the cat off. Barely maintaining his hold with his paws and feet, Kit bit at the creature's exoskeleton but couldn't get any purchase on it with his teeth. The centipede finally shed him with a sharp twisting motion of its head. When Kit landed, the creature rammed its head at him. Kit jumped sideways out of the way of its attack.

"Get away from him, you overgrown insect!" Hyroc yelled, flashing his sword through the air to regain the creature's attention. "Yes, that's right, bring your face to my steel." The centipede charged, and he blocked its strike with a barrier from his Flame Claw. The force of the collision curled the creature's long black body like a gigantic pill bug. Hyroc dismissed the barrier and started hacking away at his opponent's head. The creature clicked furiously; then, there was a chitinous crunch and a burst of greenish-yellow blood when Hyroc severed one of the claws on the sides of its head. The creature jolted back, and Hyroc formed a blue flame in his hand. He stepped toward the ebon beast, yelling menacingly while jabbing the flame forward in his outstretched hand. Clicking rapidly, the creature retreated into the shadows.

Sparing a glance at Kit to confirm his feline companion was uninjured, Hyroc turned to Elsa, Donovan, and Curtis to see the first centipede lying dead, but they were engaged with a third creature. The centipede swung its head at Elsa and knocked her off her feet. Before it could strike, Donovan stabbed it in the side. Its carapace cracked as the heavy spear punched through its armor. The creature thrashed violently as it pulled away from him.

Hyroc spotted a fourth centipede weaving through the trees toward the donkey from behind. Hyroc bolted toward the donkey. The pack animal was vitally important to their survival here! It carried all their food; they would be in a nasty predicament if it got injured. Sensing the approaching danger, the donkey brayed in alarm as it ran away. The centipede rapidly closed the distance. Hyroc felt a knot of dread in his stomach when he realized he wouldn't get there in time and his adversary was too far away for him to hit with a fireball.

The centipede dropped its head down and rammed the donkey's rear at an upward angle. The strike lifted the donkey's feet off the ground and sent the animal flying. It landed with a half tumble and lay in a heap. The centipede surged forward like a hunting python to finish off its prey. Now within range, Hyroc hurled a fireball at the creature. The front of the beast erupted into blue flames. It made a screeching clack so loud it hurt Hyroc's ears. In a panic, the creature smashed its head into multiple trees and erratically snapped every branch unfortunate enough to get in its path as it desperately tried to douse the flames. It bashed the back of its head into a thick, unyielding limb and fell to the ground. Hyroc slashed the centipede's head while it was bringing its head back up, knocking it back down. He grabbed the hilt of his sword with both hands and jammed it through one of the creature's eyes as hard as he could. The creature went limp as greenish-black blood spurted out of the wound. He pulled his blade free and rushed over to check on the donkey. The animal was conscious, but blood seeped out of a wound on one of its back legs, and one of its front legs was sticking out in the wrong direction. The injuries were bad, but neither were immediately fatal.

When he returned his attention to his friends, they still fought the third centipede, but it had sustained many more injuries. Hyroc found Elsa's bow, which she had stowed away on the donkey. When he found an arrow, he cast a piercing enchantment on it and let it fly. The arrow shot clean through both sides of the centipede's head before flying out of sight. The creature collapsed to the ground, unmoving. Just for good measure, Donovan and Elsa drove their spears through it. They turned to Hyroc, looking relieved, until they noticed their donkey.

Hyroc set Elsa's bow aside and returned to the donkey for a more thorough examination. The laceration on its back leg issued a concerning amount of blood. Luckily, the injury was only to the muscle and viscera. He could heal that with his Flame Claw. It was an entirely different matter if it had gone to the bone. He placed his hand over the wound and performed a quick healing spell. The bleeding stopped as the tissue knit back together. The joint above the foot on the donkey's front leg was out of its socket. Hyroc wasn't sure if he could use his Flame Claw to fix that. The donkey wouldn't be able to stand in this condition. By now, the rest of the group had arrived.

"I think its ankle joint is dislocated," Hyroc said.

"It is," Elsa confirmed with dismay.

"I don't know if I can heal that."

Elsa gently ran a hand over a lump in the animal's skin. "Okay, good," she said, sounding mildly relieved. "Nothing feels broken. We need to put the joint back into the socket. Donovan, Curtis, hold the back legs; he won't like this."

"You've dealt with this before?" Hyroc asked.

"No, but my father once showed me when our neighbor's plow horse stepped in a ground squirrel's hole and dislocated its ankle. To get the joint back in, I will have to pull down on the foot to reopen the socket. At the same time I do that, I need you to push up on the joint – that bulge in the skin right there. Do it carefully but firmly. Push up until you slide it back into its proper place. Ready?" Hyroc nodded. "On three. One, two, three."

The donkey loudly brayed in pain and fought against them as Elsa yanked on its foot below the dislocation. Hyroc pushed up on the joint and slid it back into its normal position with a pop.

"Okay, done," Elsa announced happily, slapping Hyroc on the shoulder. "You did well, and we did it all without magic."

Hyroc nodded his appreciation at the compliment.

"But the bad news is, he won't be able to put weight on that leg for hours."

"All the while, we'll be sitting here right next to those dead *things*," Donovan said, indicating the dead centipedes with his spear. "And apparently, *there is* something worse than giant spiders." Everyone let out a quiet and mildly cynical laugh.

"Hopefully, these carcasses won't attract scavengers until after we leave," Hyroc said.

"I shudder to think what kind of carrion eaters would feed on them in this forest."

It was nearing dusk by the time the soreness on the donkey's leg had subsided enough for it to walk. The donkey moved its limbs gingerly, but with some gentle coaxing, they led it onward. To ease the animal's pain, Hyroc went into bear form, acting as a pack animal for their supplies with saddlebags tied to his back. They weren't going far, so he didn't have to endure the indignity long. Even so, he was grateful to be moving again because he heard something poking around the area and had no interest in meeting it. They made camp for the night on a raised parcel of ground surrounded by large ghostly white mushrooms with broad tops bigger than dinner plates giving off a silvery glow.

"So what's our plan?" Donovan asked the following day. "Keep going northeast?"

"Yes, I think we should for now," Hyroc answered. "But if we don't find anything soon, we can try something else. Does that sound good to everyone?"

Everyone agreed.

"I'm getting concerned about the situation with our supplies," Elsa said. "There's nothing to worry about for the time being, but if we can't eat anything here because it's probably poisonous, running out of food will be a serious problem."

"I know," Hyroc agreed. "I can't get that fact out of my mind either. Let's hope we find that tree before we run out of provisions."

The group moved past the mushrooms back into the darkened forest. They heard things moving all around them, but nothing appeared. Everyone was especially vigilant to make sure nothing followed them.

Hyroc began hearing extremely faint whispering. "Can anyone else hear that?" he asked.

Everyone stopped to listen.

"You're going to need to be a little more specific," Donovan said. "I hear all kinds of noises around us that I don't like."

"That whispering? Do you hear that?"

"No, there's no whispering as far as I can tell," Elsa said.

Hyroc nodded eagerly. "Good, I think that means we're going in the right direction," he said. "The voice of the Warding tree I hear in my mind is getting louder. Stay alert; I don't know what we'll find close to that tree."

As they continued forward, the volume of the whispering didn't increase, and it was still too faint for him to make out what was being said.

The noises around them suddenly ceased. Kit's ears snapped sideways as he let out a warning roar.

"WATCH OUT!" Elsa yelled.

A leaf wolf exploded out of the foliage, running straight for her. She swept her spear sideways at it. The creature sprang backward out of the way. Hyroc darted forward and decapitated it with his sword. A strong breeze dispersed its leafy form through the air.

"*It* seeks the heart," the Warding tree snarled in Hyroc's head, its voice crisp and clear. "But the Guardian oath breaker and his puppets will not claim it!"

Five more wolves weaved through the trees as they tore toward the group. Donovan sidestepped a lunge from one wolf and drove his spear through another, darting at him. Hyroc tossed a hastily formed blue fireball at the wolf Donovan had dodged. The creature dissolved into a flaming pile of ash. Elsa slashed through a wolf in midair as it hurtled at Donovan from the side. There were sounds of movement behind them.

Hyroc knew their enemy was trying to keep them pinned down to buy time while it gathered an overwhelming number of the wolf constructs to send against them. All remnants of secrecy were now lost. They had to be near the tree. Every construct in the forest had to be on its way. Their only chance now was to locate the tree and destroy it before all the wolves arrived and tore them to pieces.

"We need to move!" Hyroc urged. "We must find that tree before there are too many wolves to handle."

"Which way?" Elsa asked.

"Keep going the way we were."

Everyone surged forward as fast as they could. A wolf shot toward Hyroc from the side, and he dispatched it with a quick slash from his sword without stopping. The trees thinned out ahead, and there appeared to be the broad trunk of a massive tree. The tops of its branches were covered in green lichen, with streamers of brown moss hanging from them. That had to be it! It was long past time they ended this.

"There!" Hyroc called out, pointing to the tree with his sword. "That's the Warding tree."

"What should we expect?" Elsa said as they ran.

"I'm not –" his words were cut short when he saw a spear thrust at him out of the corner of his eye. He dodged it with a sideways jump and jogged backward, making a half circle to face back toward whatever had attacked him.

His attacker walked on two legs. It had two arms and a head and appeared to be a person. After an instant of confusion, Hyroc realized it was another plant construct. It had rough, bark-like brownish-grayish skin with some green. The creature's legs looked like long miniature tree trunks supported by short, flexible roots that reached across the ground to keep it stable while it walked. One arm had no hand, with the arm ending in a rectangular wooden shield. The other arm had a hand grasping the shaft of a spear with a sharp wooden tip. The creature's head had no mouth, and two glowing green eyes, and its shape reminded him of a skinless human skull.

Hyroc used his sword to deflect a stab from the creature's spear. It then bashed him with its shield, which sent him stumbling backward. It snapped its attention to the side and jolted back as Donovan swung his spear at it. The creature blocked a sword strike from Hyroc as he rushed forward and pushed Donovan back with a kick. When it turned to attack Donovan, it left one of its legs exposed, and Hyroc gave it a hard slice. It collapsed onto one knee. Donovan knocked its spear aside and stabbed it through the chest. There was a loud crack, and the creature collapsed into a wood pile.

"That couldn't have been a person?" Donovan said as more of a statement than a question.

"No, it was a golem, the same as those wolves," Hyroc said. "It was just a little more complicated." He grabbed Donovan by the shoulder to usher him forward. "We need to keep moving! If it surrounds us and pins us down, we're dead."

They rejoined Elsa and Curtis, who were anxiously waiting for them. Curtis eliminated a leaf wolf with a quick lightning bolt, and everyone started moving again.

"Okay, what's the plan for dealing with this tree?" Elsa said.

Hyroc cursed. He hadn't given that any thought. Avoiding getting killed by the Warding tree had been his only concern since getting trapped here. Up until this moment, in his mind, destroying it had been a straightforward process: make it die. That's how he dealt with practically every threat he had encountered for the last several years. Stabbing his enemy or inflicting some lethal injury was basically how he had killed all of them. But he faced a vast tree. Stabbing it was laughably useless, and none of the weapons he or his friends possessed could hurt it in any meaningful way. And even if they had axes, they would be overrun by constructs well before they could chop away enough of the trunk to do anything.

So what did that leave him with? Using Quintessence or magic was obvious, but how to utilize it was the question. Trees are wood, and wood burns, so fire? Except, using fire had a similar problem to using axes; the constructs would kill them long before the flames consumed the tree. There was another option he hadn't considered. He could try talking to it. He could speak directly to the Warding tree if he touched it. This direct link would bypass the extreme pain he experienced when using his communion ability. The pain was caused by the anger of the trees, not by the Warding tree itself. Or so he hoped. By talking to it, even as deranged as its mind was, he may convince it he and his friends were not its enemy and not a threat. Then, it should let them leave.

"All right, I have an idea," Hyroc said. "If I can get close to the Warding tree, I think I can use my communion ability to convince it we are not a threat."

"Hyroc, I thought that hurt when you did that," Elsa questioned. "Remember, the whole screaming in agony and your eyes getting bloodshot?"

"The trees of the forest caused *that pain*. If I talk to the Warding tree directly, that shouldn't hurt."

"And what if you're wrong?" Donovan asked. "What if the pain is too much for you? What do we do then?"

Hyroc shook his head. "I – I don't know," he said. "But it's the best thing I can think of."

"That's one hell of a gamble."

"I know it is, but we're going to run out of food eventually, so it'll still slowly get us one way or another if we don't try something. You've all trusted me so far. I'm asking you to trust me now."

"I trust you," Donovan, Elsa, and Curtis said one after the other.

"Let's end this," Hyroc said sternly.

They rushed toward the looming Warding tree. They weren't moving as fast as Hyroc knew they could. Running while leading the laden donkey forward was slowing them down. It was either lay everything out on the table, hold nothing back for a complete win, or death for all of them. Supplies wouldn't matter if they failed. They had to cut the animal loose! They could retrieve it later *if there was a later*. Without them controlling the animal, the Warding tree was less likely to go after it. It would be safe – unless there were more giant centipedes nearby.

"We've got to cut the donkey loose!" Hyroc urged.

Elsa, who lead the donkey, looked at him, stupefied. "Cut it loose?" she yelled. "Are you insane? It's carrying all our food. We can't eat anything in this place, remember?"

"I know. But if this doesn't work, we won't need it."

"Okay," she acknowledged gravely, understanding the weight of his meaning. She let go of the reins.

Hyroc darted over to the animal and grabbed it firmly around the neck. The donkey brayed in surprise as it skidded to a stop. "When it's safe, come find us," Hyroc said into the animal's ear. He gave it a hard slap on the rear. The donkey bolted forward, fleeing away from the Warding tree. Hyroc turned his attention to Kit. "Kit, you, too. Get going!" Kit regarded him with a supremely puzzled look but remained where he was. "You've done all you can. Get out of here." Kit chuffed at him defiantly. "Don't argue with me! If this doesn't work, we're done with or without you. When it's safe, find me. And if it doesn't get safe, you've been a great friend, and I love you, buddy." Reluctantly, Kit bolted off into the trees. Hyroc hastily waved everyone forward.

They were almost to the tree! Hyroc caught movement out of the corner of his eye. He jumped sideways out of the reach of a spear thrust and stumbled to a stop. Donovan charged the construct, swinging his spear at it wildly. The construct blocked an attack from him. His spear hit the construct's shield with a loud *thunk*! Hyroc came at the creature from the side with a strike from his sword. It dodged his attack by jolting backward. It landed on one foot, and before it could stabilize its stance, Donovan shoved his shoulder into it, knocking it off its leg. Hyroc finished it off by driving his blade into its chest.

Turning back toward Elsa and Curtis, they saw Elsa thrusting her spear through a leaf wolf. A second wolf came at her from the back, knocking her to the ground. It lunged forward to bite her, but she blocked its mouth with the shaft of her spear. Curtis threw himself on the back of the creature and stabbed it repeatedly with his hunting knife. There was a loud cracking sound, and the wolf turned into a pile of leaves covering most of Elsa's body. She shed the leaves when Donovan helped her to her feet.

They were now beneath the canopy of the Warding tree. Its thick, leafy, moss-covered limbs and towering trunk rose above the forest's trees. Its size gave the illusion they were slowing down as it seemed things took longer to change. The leaves on its branches blocked nearly all light from the sun, but a faint blue glow from the trunk prevented the area from getting dark. It wasn't as big as the Tree of Memories, but if it were turned into lumber, its wood could have been used to construct an entire city. Enormous mushrooms grew sparsely beneath its shadow, and large roots protruded.

The immediate area around them was clear, but across from them, Hyroc saw numerous leaf wolves and two-legged constructs rapidly heading their way. He wondered how many more were coming toward them, out of sight behind the trunk. The outcome would be grave if they didn't get to the Warding tree before those creatures arrived.

The creatures swarmed around the sides of the Warding tree, trying to intercept them. The shapes merged into an encircling army. Everyone exchanged a severe look. There was only one certain consequence for failure. If this didn't work, they wouldn't regret it for long. Hyroc ran with an outstretched hand and pushed it against the warding tree.

"STOP!" Hyroc commanded as powerfully as his mind could project. "WE ARE NOT YOUR ENEMY. We will not hurt you."

He pulled his mind from the connection, opening his eyes to confirm a spear wasn't about to be plunged into his chest. Elsa and Donovan stood beside him with the tips of their spears pointed outward. Curtis stood between them, lightning crackling in one hand in preparation to cast an attack spell. The horde of constructs had halted. Hyroc returned to the tree.

"The kin of oath breakers parlays?" the Warding tree said seeming almost confused.

Its mind felt powerful and ancient, filled with the weight of countless years of memories. Hyroc detected enormous, chaotic activity just beyond his reach.

"Yes, to parlay, and we – my friends and I, bring peace," Hyroc answered. "We bring no darkness."

"There is no peace amid the gnashing of teeth."

In Hyroc's mind's eye, he saw images of him and his friends destroying leaf wolves. "We were defending ourselves from attack as the mother bear protects her cubs. If there is no danger to us, we are at peace."

"And what darkness do you bring with you?"

"None. We abhor the darkness. I am Anamagi. The azure flame welcomes no darkness."

"The blue flame does not," the Warding tree agreed.

"We are friends; we only wish to –" the tree cut him off.

"But the flame is feeble! Their weakness spread darkness and pain."

Hyroc saw the wolf Guardian, who had been killed. More figures stood farther away, performing incantations or throwing a fireball or ice spikes at the wolf. The magic attacks smashed harmlessly into a blue shimmering barrier protecting the Guardian. The wolf opened its mouth and breathed out a cone of blue fire, incinerating, some of the figures. One of the humans drove a spear into the Guardian through its unprotected flank. The wolf knocked the person off its feet and buried its teeth into the human's neck. Then, a large ice spike stabbed through the Guardian, killing it. Hyroc saw the ghastly treatment of forest animals and the performance of a series of depraved rituals. The images ended with blood splashing on a tree and the bark being stripped from it before its life-sustaining Quintessence was drained away.

"Their failure is not mine," Hyroc said. "The darkness they brought does not reside with us. Our ancestors are blameless."

"Can there be trust from the words of the son of oath breakers?"

"You can have trust in mine." Hyroc projected the memory of his fight with the Shade Hunter, ending with the demon's decapitation. "The darkness has also caused me pain, and I will not tolerate it."

"PAIN!" The tree screamed so forcefully into Hyroc's mind it felt like he had been punched. "YOU KNOW NOTHING OF THEIR TORTURE, GUARDIAN WHELP! The darkness of cold winter with no summer breeds suffering. Their malice and our suffering are carved into the land. The green of the forest was made to wither. Your ignorance is displayed for all to see."

"I'm sorry, I'm sorry," Hyroc quickly apologized. "You're right. I don't know what you went through. But I do know some of what *he* did." Hyroc projected memories of him as a child learning about the atrocities Feygrotha had committed in Arnaira. "His evil legacy has haunted me my entire life, and I only wish to be free of the echo of his actions The Ministry continues."

"The cub understands," the tree said.

"Yes, I understand," Hyroc said. "We all understand."

"You wish for the migration of your flock as the beating of wings escapes winter."

"Yes, we wish to migrate through your woods and leave your forest peacefully."

"Peace?" The tone in which the tree spoke made Hyroc uneasy. It sounded as if the word meant something terrible. "Can it be trusted? The fox will strike cunningly, surprising the rabbit." There was a rising amount of anger in its voice. "*He,* too, proclaimed friendship before *he* brought suffering."

"No, I promise only peace," Hyroc pleaded. "We promise only peace. There will be *no suffering.*"

"Are its promises unbreakable? Is its word bounded to justice, or is it as the snare of a hunter?"

"My promises are genuine, as unmovable as a mountain. I swear on my mother's grave, we wish only to depart in peace. We will do you no harm."

"It swears on its mother's grave, but we do not know her. We do not know what was done in her name. Without a name, there is no certainty to guard against a lie. We do not know its mind."

"No, you can be certain of my mind. I am Anamagi. I carry the blue flame of the Guardians. Guardians do not lie. They are trustworthy, as I am. I do not deceive you. Let us depart in peace."

"No, they lied! They said they were protectors. They said they would keep the darkness away. They deceived us and let terrible evil take root. *They did nothing*!"

"No, please, we will not hurt you," Hyroc pleaded. "I cannot atone for their failure, but we are innocent. Please. I'm begging you, please let us pass. We will leave peacefully."

"They turned an eye without sight toward us," the tree continued, seemingly unaware of his words. "Our suffering was of no consequence. Giving passage to one imparted with their knowledge invites suffering and the obscuring mist. Evil cannot …"

Hyroc pulled his mind from the Warding tree, interrupting it as it steadily descended into an infuriated stream of incoherent ravings. He opened his eyes to give his friends a regretful look of despair. It would be mere moments before the Warding tree was riled up enough to return its attention to them and kill them.

He threw up one hand in defeat. "I'm sorry," he said sorrowfully. "It just wouldn't listen. I –" he cut himself off, narrowing his eyes in determination. *This was not how he was going to let it end.* He still had his original simplistic plan to fall back on: destroy the tree. It wouldn't be without a fight. If they were going down, their opponent *would not* escape this unscathed.

The words, "Forest fires can be destructive, but they are also a powerful force for rejuvenating a wild forest," popped into his head.

"No, we're not done yet!" Hyroc said commandingly. "If we go, we're taking a piece of this damn tree with us." He stepped away from the tree. "Everybody get away from the trunk." His friends followed him to an open space in the mass of constructs. The creatures stood still, their skull-shaped faces staring forward emotionlessly. Hyroc knew these things would resume trying to kill them at any instant. "All right, Curtis, you need to hit that tree with the biggest lightning bolt you can make. Don't hold anything back." He pulled off his ruby necklace and tossed it to his younger friend. "Use the Quintessence I stored in that ruby necklace and anything you have in your emerald to make it even more powerful."

"What if I make it too big and knock myself out?" Curtis asked tentatively. "You need everyone to fight, right?"

"No, that's exactly what I want you to do. You need to strike with every bit of energy you have. It's okay if you knock yourself unconscious from using too much Quintessence. If that happens, we'll carry you; I promise we'll keep you safe. You know you can trust us."

"I trust you."

"Okay, so I'm going …"

Hyroc cut his words short when, with a reverberating creaking sound, every construct snapped their faces toward him and his friends. Hundreds of eyes focused on them. Donovan and Elsa stabbed the two closest constructs through the chest. A tsunami of teeth and spears surged toward them from all sides. Hyroc made a wide sweeping motion with his arms, surrounding everyone in a circle of blue fire. Several constructs did not heed the fire, stepped into it, and were incinerated. The remaining horde stopped where they were.

Hyroc opened his mouth to tell Curtis to attack the Warding tree but realized the constructs blocked his shot. "Hold up, Curtis," he said. "You need a clear shot; otherwise, your bolt will be bled off on all these constructs. I'm going to clear you a path. As soon as you have a clear shot, hit that tree with everything you've got, and I mean *everything*."

Curtis nodded.

Hyroc pulled his arms in, took a deep breath, and then threw his arms out. A wave of fire shot off in the direction of Hyroc's arms. A loud whoosh of air and a strong gust of wind pulled at Hyroc as the constructs erupted into two massive fires. With the creatures being a combination of wood and other flammable forest material, the flames spread like a plague, and everything erupted into an inferno. Hyroc used his Flame Claw to form two long shimmering blue barriers toward the Warding tree. With a straining effort, he made a grasping motion with his fingers before pulling his arms sideways as if ripping something apart. The two barriers swept the burning constructs out of the way, creating a clear line toward the trees.

"CURTIS!" Hyroc yelled. "HIT IT!"

A bright white light emanated from Curtis's hands as he formed a lightning bolt. The light grew in intensity, and soon Curtis's entire body was enveloped. Hyroc shielded his eyes with his hand. Rising energy rippled through his body, and all his hair stood on end. Then, a burning heat shot across him, and he barely managed to stay standing from the concussive release of a massive lightning bolt. The bolt slammed into the Warding tree, shooting up one side, and with a deafening crack, the tree was blown in half. One half remained standing while the other careened to the ground. That half landed so hard it tossed Hyroc and his three friends off their feet. After landing, everyone scrambled to their feet except Curtis. Curtis was unconscious but okay.

Everything was burning. Thick smoke filled the air, and glowing orange embers rained down on everything. Hyroc slapped into submission a spot of fire on his arm that ignited his hair. Everyone hacked and coughed from the choking smoke.

"We need to move!" Donovan said. He handed Hyroc his spear and picked up Curtis.

Hyroc cast a spell to form a bubble around them to repell the smoke. "This way," he said, waving everyone forward.

They weaved through burning piles of dead constructs turned back into their base materials. They had now cleared the diminished shadow of the Warding tree, but the fire had already spread to the surrounding forest. Animals stampeded between the trees, desperately trying to escape the flames. They got a start when two giant centipedes darted past them. Hyroc yanked Donovan back out of the way of a deer with serrated horns as it thundered past. Above all the commotion around them, he thought he heard a donkey's braying and a mountain lion's yawl. Kit and their supply-laden donkey emerged from the smoke. Elsa seized the reins of the animal. Kit brushed his head on Hyroc's hand.

"Good. Everyone's here," Donovan said.

"Now, we just need to avoid burning to death," Hyroc said.

"It's all your fault if we do."

Hyroc laughed half-humoredly.

Chapter 7

Uncaged

HYROC SNEEZED IN BRIGHT SUNLIGHT, holding his hand up to shield his watering eyes. This was the first time he had been in unobscured sunlight in weeks, and the warmth felt amazing on his face. Was he finally going to escape the nightmarish forest trapping him and his friends for what felt like years?

"You have some soot behind your ear," Elsa said, reaching over and removing a piece of ash.

Hyroc rubbed the spot.. "I don't want any souvenirs to remember this place," he said.

"Except maybe *for this*," Donovan said proudly, holding his boar spear.

"I don't think what we went through was worth even *that*," Hyroc noted.

"Only because you lost your bow to a leaf monster."

Hyroc rolled his eyes. "Yeah, I'm sure that's the *only* reason."

"At least now that Warding tree is not going to hurt anyone ever again," Elsa said.

Everyone nodded in agreement. Hyroc stood in a break in the tree line where, a short distance away, the forest continued. In front of him was a line of red flowers stretching out in both directions. The flowers represented the edge of the destroyed Warding tree's reach and the enchantment preventing them from leaving. The Warding tree was destroyed, so he assumed the enchantment was no longer active. If he was wrong, something else powered the spell, and they would have to find that thing in this vast woodland. He approached, carefully stepping over the flowers. Looking over his shoulder, he was relieved to see his friends still behind him and not in front of him, which should have happened from the enchantment turning him around.

He waved. "The enchantment's gone!" he called out happily. "We can leave."

Hyroc sat on top of a hill with his back against a rocky outcropping, holding the unrolled map of Mastgar. The group had lost their bearings while staying alive in the Warding tree's domain. They had to figure out the four cardinal directions to find Mastgar. He gazed at the sun, ensuring he didn't stare directly at it. A bright green afterglow hung in his vision when he returned to the map. He rubbed his eye to help clear his sight, then lowered the map to speak to his friends.

"Okay, so this is our situation," Hyroc said. He indicated toward the sun with his hand. "It's past noon, which means that way is west. The only problem is I don't know how far north we may have wandered. And if we've gone beyond what's shown on the map, there's no way of knowing what's around us. So going south to try to find the road, again, is our best bet. According to the map, this should be connected to the one we followed before confronting the Warding tree."

"If it's overgrown like the road was in the forest, it will be hard to spot from a distance," Donovan noted.

"Exactly," Hyroc agreed, unenthused. "But that brings up another thing. Once we find that road, we're in Mastgar and have to think about all the bad stuff The Ministry said about the people here. I'm pretty sure all of that is untrue, and The Ministry believes this is an evil place simply because the people use magic."

"But you can't be completely certain about that," Elsa interjected.

Hyroc nodded. "Yep. There's a chance they were telling the actual truth, and Mastgar is as bad as they suggested. This means we need to be wary of people until we know for sure they aren't going to attack us. And if they do, I will feel like an idiot."

"We all will," Donovan said.

"We also don't know how people will react to seeing me. We're no longer in Arnaira and beyond Ministry lands, but the people here could be just as hostile to me as anyone there. And if that's the case, this may be where I have to say goodbye." Hyroc blew out a morose breath. "It's better for the three of you to find a good place to live than for none of us. I can make that sacrifice if it comes to it."

"We'll figure it out, okay," Elsa reassured, rubbng his shoulder. "But I'm sure that's not the case if The Ministry dislikes the people here so much."

"I'm sure that's not the case," Hyroc repeated, hoping saying it aloud would conjure it into existence.

"There's one last issue," Elsa said. "We're almost out of food. Our unplanned delay in the Warding tree's realm depleted our supplies, and we need to restock."

"Well, if my judgment of our location is correct," Hyroc said. "According to the map, there's a town named Forestgold farther west on the road where we should be able to restock."

"Assuming the townsfolk aren't murderous barbarians," Donovan added.

"Yes, assuming that."

"You could try climbing a tree to help us get our bearings." Donovan pointed at two tall spruce trees growing close together. The two trees almost touched. On the side where the trees were nearest, there were few branches. Typically, a spruce tree's spindly needle-covered branches were so tightly bunched it was practically impossible for him to scale one. This was a rare opportunity to look at their surroundings, and he needed to take advantage of it.

"Yeah, that's a good idea," Hyroc agreed. "I was so wrapped up in looking at the map I hadn't even noticed them."

"What would you do without me?" Donovan said smugly.

"Replace you with a better friend?" Hyroc joked.

"Don't go getting too big of a head," Elsa said, jabbing Donovan in the shoulder with a knuckle.

"Hey, that's not nice, Hyroc," Donovan said, feigning hurt.

Hyroc kicked off his boots. He anchored the claws of his hands and feet into the bark. A startled squirrel chattered at him from a branch at the midpoint of the other tree. When he reached the top, he was surrounded by a sea of verdant green. For the first time, he noticed bits of ash drifting through the air. In the distance, huge black clouds of smoke billowed from the forest as the fire Hyroc and Curtis had ignited continued to rage. The flames would cleanse the festering wound Feygrotha and his followers had inflicted on this forest, and new, untainted life would flourish. Hyroc couldn't help wondering how long that blaze would last and how far it would spread. However, he suspected the more it destroyed the tainted forest, the better.

"Can you see anything?" Elsa called up.

Hyroc scanned his surroundings while his claws kept him secured to the side of the tree. The sky was overcast with holes revealing the occasional spot of blue sky. He didn't see any indications of a road, but to the southwest, a hazy area suggested cooking fires. Cooking fires meant people and possibly a town or village. When he focused more on the area, he made out faint white curls of smoke as if they came out of chimneys, but he was unsure. With their supplies dwindling, a mistake could be costly.

Hyroc pointed toward the smoggy area. "I think I see some smoke haze that way," he said. "And maybe some trails of chimney smoke, but I'm not sure of either."

"Any sign of the road?" Elsa called up.

"None that I can see, no. And I don't recognize any landmarks from the map."

"All right. Go ahead and come down."

Hyroc carefully descended, speaking when he returned to the ground. "That's also to the Southwest, where we were going to go, so we wouldn't be wasting any time."

"Shimmer!" Elsa called out. Their raven companion spiraled down from a branch overhead. The black bird alighted onto her shoulder, and she stroked his feathery head. Elsa indicated the southwest. "There might be a town in that direction. Can you check for us?" Shimmer bobbed his head happily. As much as they could tell, that meant yes. Elsa gave him an encouraging stroke on the head. "Good bird. We'll also be walking that way so you can find us again when you return." He bobbed his head again before sidling onto Elsa's forearm. She obligingly flung her arm skyward to assist his takeoff.

Shimmer returned a few hours later.

"You're back," Elsa said in greeting. "What'd you see?"

Once on the ground, Shimmer pointed with one wing toward the smoke. He cawed excitedly twice, then shuffled forward, but it wasn't his regular walk. His movements seemed exaggerated, as if he were trying to tell them something. He stopped and looked up at everyone. When no one showed signs of understanding, he continued walking in the same manner before stopping to look at them again.

"I think he's trying to tell us there are people where we sent him," Elsa said.

Shimmer cawed energetically at her words and hopped up and down.

"Seems so," Hyroc agreed.

The raven then pointed northward, away from where he had indicated the smoke trails.

"And now I think he's trying to tell us that's where the road is," Elsa interjected.

Donovan pointed at Hyroc and laughed. "Ha, see, I thought we were going the wrong way," he said.

Hyroc shrugged. "Well, it's hard to tell when all these trees surround you."

"Excuses, excuses, excuses."

"Okay, judging from how long he was gone," Elsa said. "We're probably a day away from the road, and from there, it will probably be another day before we get to where the people and smoke were. So that's probably around two to three days. Our supplies will last that long, but there won't be much left afterward."

"Which means things will get *complicated* if the people of Mastgar really are monsters," Hyroc noted. "And we can't get our supplies replenished."

“If that’s the case, we’ll have no choice but to resort to thievery,” Donovan said unenthusiastically. “But if they turn out to be bloodthirsty lunatics, none of us will feel bad about stealing from them.” Everyone gave him a flat look. “What?”

“One thing at a time,” Hyroc said. “Let’s just focus on getting to those people for now. But we need to be wary about being seen. At least, until we know they’re not exactly how The Ministry described them. And if any part of that description holds, it’s a good bet they can use magic, or some of them will be able to, like Curtis and I. Which will make them especially dangerous, so don’t let your guard down.

“I hope we didn’t go through all we did to get here,” Elsa said, “just to get into another life-or-death situation.”

Chapter 8

Mastgar

HYROC CROUCHED BEHIND A TREE, shrouded by the darkness of night, gazing toward a campfire ahead of him. He and his friends were off the side of the dilapidated road where Shimmer had directed them. Four figures gathered around the fire, unaware of his presence. Their attire was similar to that of his and his friends, though maybe nicer, suggesting they were hunters. He wasn't close enough to make out what they said as they chatted, but they sounded friendly. But he and his friends were now in Mastgar. The Ministry had depicted their neighboring kingdom as a harsh, lawless land full of witchcraft and darkness where danger lurked around every corner. This kingdom could be just as wretched as The Ministry said. Coming here could be a lethal mistake.

Even if Hyroc had made the correct assumption, how would the citizens react to seeing him, a Wol'dger? Pretty much the first reaction of anyone he encountered in Arnaira was to try and kill him because they thought he was a demon or some harbinger of destruction. The parents of his friends had taken him in, but even as compassionate as their father and mother were, Svald had seriously considered ending Hyroc's life. Hyroc's noble action protecting Elsa from being ambushed by a wolf was the deciding factor proving to the villagers of Elswood he wasn't a threat. But he had no such proof with these hunters. All he had was his word and the words of his friends, and he wasn't optimistic about that being enough to overcome the effects of any fear caused by his appearance.

If they reacted to him fearfully but accepted his friends, their harrowing journey here was worth it to him. He would gladly part ways with his friends if that meant they were safe. They deserved as much after everything they had done for him. Then, he would resume the lonely journey he had started when he fled from Forna so many years ago.

But he was getting uselessly far ahead of himself. The four of them needed to figure out the best way to introduce themselves. They needed to do that calmly and as least surprisingly as possible.

"How do you want to handle this?" Hyroc whispered to his friends. "I can't go first because –" he gestured to his face, gritted his teeth in a savage snarl, and growled to help demonstrate the point. "Grrr, you know."

"I figured," Elsa said. "So I'll go."

Hyroc and Donovan shot her a skeptical look.

"You?" Donovan asked. "Are you sure that's the best idea? What if they are just as dangerous as The Ministry said and try to hurt you? No, I feel much more comfortable if you let me go first."

"Yes, I thought about the danger. But I think they will react better to seeing a pretty girl coming out of the woods than to you."

"Who said you were pretty?"

Elsa shot him a venomous glare and punched his shoulder. Hyroc swatted the top of Donovan's head with his hand.

With a gleeful smile, Donovan returned to the topic. "So you plan to go over to that group of strangers and, what, use your feminine wiles to disarm them?"

"Something along those lines, yes."

"That's a stupid plan."

"I'll be fine," Elsa said. "Besides, the three of you will be here covering me with your bows and magic in case anything goes wrong."

Donovan blew out a breath. "All right. But be careful. This is an unfamiliar land. We have no idea what kind of people we're dealing with here. At the first sign, anything is amiss; get out of there."

She nodded and walked toward the firelight. Hyroc and Donovan exchanged an uncertain look, then each nocked an arrow and held their bows ready.

The hunters were startled when she made her presence known. The hunters didn't reach for the hunting spears and bows lying on the ground near where they sat, which seemed a good sign. She and the hunters talked, and then she gestured toward the neglected road as if answering a question about where she had come from. The hunters suddenly became agitated at her explanation. She raised her hands placatingly to try to dissuade the hunters from whatever they were reacting to. This seemed to have no effect.

Donovan cursed. "Get ready; I think this is getting out of hand," he said.

A sinking feeling formed in Hyroc's stomach. This couldn't be happening. The Ministry was correct! How could they have been accurate? They were wrong on so many things. Why did everything have to turn out so rotten? On their way here, he and his friends had battled soldiers and shadow demons and survived creations of a mad Warding tree. And this was what waited for them? Where were they going to go now? The Northlands. No, they couldn't live there. That was suicide.

Elsa reached down to her belt and drew her knife. Instead of holding it out to defend herself against the four hunters as Hyroc had expected, she held it up, purposely showing it to the hunters.

Donovan raised his bow and aimed.

"Wait, wait," Hyroc said, pushing his friend's bow back down. "I don't think she's in danger. She's showing them something."

Donovan gazed at him uncertainly but complied.

Elsa used the knife to cut her thumb.

Hyroc Donovan, and Curtis exchanged a confounded look. Now, none of them had any idea what she was doing.

She held the knife up and her bleeding hand for the hunters to see. One hunter tentatively grabbed her hand and examined it. The hunter nodded to their companions, letting go of Elsa's hand. The group relaxed, and she slipped her knife back into its scabbard. The hunter withdrew a handkerchief from a pocket to bind Elsa's cut. After exchanging words with the group, she turned and beckoned toward Hyroc, Donovan, and Curtis.

"She wants us to come over there," Hyroc said.

"I guess it's safe," Donovan said. "Finally, some good luck for a change."

"I'll hold off until you know how they'll react to seeing me."

Donovan nodded his understanding as he and Curtis headed over. The hunters greeted each of them in turn and chatted excitedly with them. The donkey beside Hyroc brayed loudly at being left with him and Kit. Hyroc cringed and reached to clamp the donkey's mouth, but the damage was already done. The hunter pointed in Hyroc's direction, aware of his presence. Knowing the futility of denying his whereabouts, Elsa waved him over. She wore a guarded expression, unsure how this was going to go. Hyroc grabbed the reins of the donkey and led it toward the fire. Hyroc's features came into the light.

"A Wol'dger?" one hunter said in surprise. They knew what he was called? That seemed a good sign. They knew what he was and didn't seem overly concerned about his appearance. If things continued this way, Mastgar would be a much better place than Arnaira. And if the citizens here knew what a Wol'dger was, maybe there were more like him in this place.

"... and traveling with humans," the hunter continued, but his tone indicated this was unusual. Hyroc was too excited by the idea of other Wol'dgers being in this place to think about why his traveling with humans would be strange. Meeting others of his kind had been at the forefront of his thoughts since he had learned from Ursa he wasn't alone. Nothing had worked out enough for him to explore that desire. Now, the opportunity presented itself again.

"Yes, these are my friends," Hyroc said.

The hunter nodded his understanding. They cursed, noticing Kit trailing the donkey, and the four of them made a move to seize their weapons.

"NO, HOLD!" Hyroc yelled, jumping in front of Kit. His companions joined his effort to reassure the hunters. "Hold, just hold. He's with me – I mean, he's my pet mountain lion."

"You have a pet cougar?" one hunter asked in astonishment as a question about his sanity.

"Yes. I raised him from a cub."

"Don't worry, he's friendly; he's safe," Elsa assured them.

"Yes, we've been traveling with him for a while now without any issues," Donovan said.

"If you say so?" the hunter questioned. "Just keep your *pet* back away from us, all right?"

"I can definitely do that," Hyroc agreed, grabbing Kit by the collar. "I didn't mean to give all of you a start." He spoke quietly to Kit. "You need to stay back; you're scaring them. They're not used to seeing mountain lions this close." The big cat growled irritably but stayed where he was.

"It's all right," the hunter said.

The hunters settled back down, warily watching Kit. "So strange to find you traveling on the *old road*," another hunter said. "You four are the only travelers to come by this way for as long as anyone can remember. They say the woods down that way are cursed, and none who enter are ever heard from again." He indicated Elsa. "We thought your friend here was an apparition."

"She scared us half to death!" another hunter commented.

"Sorry again for that," Elsa said, somewhat embarrassed. The hunters gave her a friendly, dismissive wave. She held up her bandaged hand. "I didn't know how else to prove I wasn't a spirit, so I thought cutting myself might convince you. I had heard ghosts don't bleed because they have no blood."

"I thought you had lost your mind there for a moment," Donovan said.

"So, is there really a curse?" the youngest of the hunters said.

"Not anymore," Hyroc said proudly. "We made sure of that."

The hunters cocked their heads in surprise.

"You must tell us of what you speak," the first hunter said. "Come, share our fire."

Hyroc smiled. He wondered if this was what it was like to be treated the same as everyone else.

Chapter 9

The Pack

Hyroc woke in the steely gray morning light. A depleted campfire smoldered weakly nearby. The rest of his company stirred, but there was no sign of the hunters who had mistaken Elsa for a ghost. They were probably adhering to a strict hunting schedule and didn't have the luxury of waiting to give them a proper sendoff.

Hyroc realized with surprise last night was the first time in weeks he had talked with someone or something which wasn't intent on killing him or his companions. They had finally reached Mastgar. Considering what they had faced, it seemed impossible they had reached their destination alive. They had fought a small Ministry army, monsters, and demons and even faced down a deranged Warding tree attacking them with bizarre plant creatures. It almost felt as if he were dreaming. But, no, it was all real. And best of all, there were Wol'dgers here! He had waited his entire life to meet another of his kind. This was the beginning of his finally learning the answers he had sought for so long.

He didn't need to hide how he looked for fear of being attacked. There was no Ministry here; he no longer had to cower beneath their seemingly endless reach. He was free of them! But now he was in Mastgar, what was the next step for him and his friends? Firstly, they needed fresh supplies before considering anything else. Thankfully, things were easier here as he didn't have to worry about going unnoticed. He could actually participate in the process of acquiring provisions. This was the first time he could remember not having to carefully observe a shopkeeper's or their customers' movements for any prelude to an attack.

Despite his new prospects for the future, he still had to make it to the town and out of the wilderness. He needed to contain his enthusiasm a bit longer.

After eating breakfast, they moved out. The uneven surface of the neglected road and the encroaching forest underbrush gave way to a better-maintained path. It felt like years since he had walked on anything this smooth. Until now, well-traveled paths such as this were dangerous obstacles conferring a higher chance of him being spotted by someone who wanted to harm him. But that wasn't going to be a problem anymore. In Mastgar, he and his friends were just another group of travelers.

Traveling on the well-kept road, they covered a significant amount of ground. The road wound through a forest of mainly spruce and deciduous trees giving way to the mottled shade of a birch thicket. Then, the trees thinned out, revealing a plain of rolling lush green grasses. A gentle stream flowed to one side of the road. The path followed the meandering course of the creek for most of the day, but the stream widened as it fed into a large lake. It was bigger than their lake at the foot of Wolf Paw Mountain, and they could barely see the opposite shore. Hyroc pushed aside a feeling of longing for Elswood. Even after the terrible encounter with a witch and a vicious fight with a blood werewolf-forcing him and his friends to flee their home, a part of him still missed it. It was too late in the day for them to reach the opposite bank before dark. They would go as far as they could before dusk. Compared to the deep forest, they could precisely determine how long until they lost the light, guaranteeing night wouldn't catch them unaware.

As sunset neared, other smaller paths connected with the road. They started encountering other travelers. Hyroc eagerly looked at each of their faces as he passed them, hoping they were a Wol'dger. Though some of the passersby returned a look of uncertainty, likely from rarely laying eyes on his kind, they were all human. The road arrived at a ferry crossing, splitting into two paths in either direction along the lakeshore. Travelers hurried past him and his friends to catch the last ferry trip for the day. Getting on the ferry was tempting, but they read a required toll posted on a piece of parchment outside the closed door of a small guard shack. With little of their initial supply of Flecks, they could only buy essentials, such as food, so they opted to travel by foot. Away from the ferry crossing, they made camp on the lakeshore beside the road. With the last of the light, Hyroc fished but caught nothing.

A light rain woke them the next day. Just before noon, they reached the other side of the lake. They arrived at the endpoint of the ferry crossing, where another guard shack was situated, but there was also an inn. The establishment's owner had likely chosen this location to capitalize on the constant flow of travelers coming on and off the ferry.

The road split off in several directions, and signposts pointed in each direction. Hyroc read through them, and one name stood out: Forestgold. He double-checked the map of the area, confirming it was the town's name. Everyone agreed with his decision to go there.

The rain let up as they moved toward Forestgold – small patches of blue sky formed in the dark gray rain clouds. Trees again came into view on the grassland. They appeared sparsely at first, but their prevalence steadily increased. In the distance, the terrain returned to forest, but the trees here weren't as thick as the previous area. The road curved onto a small rise; beyond was the town. Most structures sat at the forest's edge, with some going into the tree line. Stone walls surrounded the town, with a handful of guard towers sprinkled across it. Guards milled around the main gate, and two alertly watched the flow of travelers, ensuring everything stayed orderly. When the two spotted Hyroc, they only paid slightly more attention to him than to the other travelers. This indicated to Hyroc seeing a Wol'dger was not uncommon. That was a good sign. Maybe here he would finally encounter another of his kin. They looked startled, shying back a little when they saw Kit sauntering closer. The guards tightened their grip on their weapons but made no move to prevent entry by the big cat.

Past the gate, townsfolk busily attended to their errands. Forestgold gave the impression of an essential hub for travelers and traders. Stores and stands displayed various goods, from furs and food to tools and weapons. It was a promising hint he and his companions could make a living here. But before they did anything, they needed to replenish their supplies. The four of them watchfully moved through the streets until they spotted a shop to buy grain.

Hyroc felt a thrill of excitement when, down the street, he saw the snout and pointy-eared figure of an adult Wol'dger male. He wore a short-sleeved shirt that exposed the dark brown fur on his arms and had a sack of grain slung over his shoulder. Hyroc's friends gave him an encouraging smile. Elsa motivated him to talk to the stranger with an emboldening gesture. Hyroc stepped in front of the Wol'dger with the friendliest expression he could muster.

"Hello, my name's –" he managed to get out before the Wol'dger cut him off.

"Out of my way, whelp!" the stranger demanded fiercely. He rudely bumped Hyroc with his shoulder as he pushed past.

Hyroc cocked an eyebrow, unsure of what had just happened or how he should feel about it. His friends mirrored his confused expression. Donovan shrugged. Hyroc returned his attention to the stranger and followed him from a distance. Maybe if he watched the Wol'dger for a bit, he could figure out why the stranger had reacted so rudely. Hyroc and his friends had only arrived in the kingdom days ago. Maybe there was some custom he was unaware of and had unknowingly violated it.

He followed the man into the open space of the town center. A gray stepstone fountain topped by sculptures of the heads of cranes sat in the middle of the space. One sculpture had an open mouth from which a steady stream of clear water flowed into a square basin. A group of dogs and a couple of Wol'dgers sat on the steps. Then, he realized those weren't dogs. They were wolves. Unsure what to make of this strange scene of wild animals in the middle of a bustling town, he noticed each wolf had the glowing paw print of a wolf on their shoulders. These weren't animals; they were Wol'dgers in animal form. But each of their animal marks was red instead of blue. He also became aware there were many guards in this area. These guards acted more cautiously and vigilantly than the ones at the gate. They were here to protect the town from these Wol'dgers. If the guards thought this group might do something terrible, he should be wary of them, too. His thoughts turned back to his unknown adversary, who he had learned at Elswood was supposedly to the west, and Mastgar was a fair distance to the west from there. Had he and his friends ventured into the domain of his adversary? Were these Wol'dger's a part of that danger? It was probably best if he just steered clear of them entirely.

He heard the click-clack sound of the donkey's steps coming up behind him. As he turned to warn his friends about the potential danger, he saw one Wol'dger male with dark brown head fur wearing a dark green jerkin and black pants at the fountain rise to his feet and walk toward Elsa. Hyroc felt a sinking feeling. He wasn't close enough to block the Wol'dger's approach. Kit rattled out a displeased growl. This wasn't going to end well.

"You there, human, hold up," the Wol'dger called to Elsa. Donovan was in front, leading the donkey by the reins, with Curtis behind him and Elsa at the back. Distracted handling the animal, Donovan was slow to notice the stranger.

Elsa saw the Wol'dger and glanced around uncertainly to ensure he wasn't talking to someone else. "Me?" she said, pointing to herself.

The Wol'dger nodded. "Yes, you," he answered. "Hello there." He gave her a sharp-toothed Wol'dger smile. "You are very pretty. Has anyone ever told you that? I thought there were only ugly humans."

"Thank you," Elsa said, feigning politeness as she tried to move past him, but he blocked her.

"Hey, hey, I just want to talk." He brushed aside a strand of hair hanging over her face. Elsa pulled away, irritating him. When he reached for her again, Donovan caught his arm.

"She's not interested," Donovan growled.

"I wasn't talking to you, *Flat Face*!" the Wol'dger bristled, freeing his hand. He looked Donovan up and down scornfully before returning to Elsa to resume his unwanted advances.

Donovan leaned in, grasping his spear, the shaft pointed toward the Wol'dger. "I said she's *not interested*," he said, threateningly emphasizing the last two words.

The Wol'dger looked at him with defiant arrogance. "And what if I'm *not interested* in what you have to say?"

Hyroc had seen that expression mirrored many times on the faces of his bullies at the boarding school in Forna. It was a look of supremacy from assuming they were unbeatable and their coming out on top was assured. Hyroc stole a glance at the fountain. The Wol'dgers were focused on Donovan. It was a good bet they wouldn't take kindly to what his friend was about to do. Hyroc was a few steps behind Donovan and could easily protect his friends by forming a wall of fire between them and the fountain.

Donovan stepped back and smashed the Wol'dger in the face with the shaft of his spear. The Wol'dger's head snapped back. Donovan jabbed him in the abdomen with the butt of his spear, and when his opponent doubled over, he struck him in the back of the head, which sent him to the ground.

Every Wol'dger around the fountain bolted to their feet, stampeding toward Donovan. Hyroc swiped one arm sideways, forming a wall of fire in front of the approaching group. The group skidded to a halt and did something unexpected. Every Wol'dger there turned their attention to Hyroc and fixed him with a savage glare.

"ANAMAGI!" the group snarled. They were so enraged they didn't seem frightened he summoned blue fire out of nothing. The group wheeled around and shot toward Hyroc. Feeling a thrill of fear, Hyroc dismissed the fire to conserve Quintessence and grasped the hilt of his sword. Kit let out a threatening roar, baring teeth but with no effect.

Yelling erupted from behind Hyroc, and the metallic scraping of chainmail filled the air. The Wol'dgers stopped. Over a dozen guards with shields and swords drawn rushed forward, inserting themselves between Hyroc and the group.

"STOP!" sternly ordered one guard in front of Hyroc. "Fighting in town is expressly forbidden. Disperse! Take this business of yours outside the walls, or face the consequences."

The Wol'dger leader, a large solid black wolf, indicated they should follow before he walked away. The group obeyed. Hyroc breathed a silent sigh of relief and slipped his sword – which he had pulled halfway out of its sheath – back into its scabbard.

A guard clad in chain mail, greaves, and a wide kettle helmet. approached Elsa. "Are you all right, Miss?" he asked. "They're gone now."

Elsa nodded. "Yes, I'm fine," she said. "Thank you."

The guard indicated Hyroc. "And what of this one?"

Hyroc pointed at himself, taken aback.

"He's with us. We're all traveling together."

"Then, tell both your companions *we* aren't here to risk our lives protecting a Wol'dgerling and his friend who have more hutzpah than is good for them, and they have a death wish. Especially when, of all things, they chose to pick a fight with *The Pack*. And if it weren't for us, the townsfolk would be cleaning what was left of them off the streets for a week." He spoke pointedly to Hyroc. "And since I assume *he's* new here, I'll let him go with this warning about magic. Only those on royal business are allowed to use magic in any cities or towns under Mastgarion rule. Otherwise, magic is strictly forbidden, and I'll clap you in irons if you do it again. Understood?"

"Yes, sir," Hyroc answered resolutely.

The guard nodded. "Good. And you had better not cause any more trouble." The guard walked away. Two others joined him as he headed off. Hyroc noticed one of the guards paying more attention to him. The guard's expression looked impressed. Then Hyroc noticed the guard wasn't wearing chain mail. He wore dark blue leather armor. Unfamiliar runes inlaid in silver adorned it, and those markings were absent from the armor of the other guards. A mage, perhaps? Magic was dangerous, so it made sense the guards in this kingdom had magic casters among them to counter the threat. The guard regarded him with intrigue and nodded before walking off. Donovan leaned in and spoke quietly. "What in the world is hutzpah?"

Hyroc shrugged. That was also the first time he had ever heard hutzpah. "Nothing good, I think, from how he used it."

"Let's leave the town center in case those Wol'dgers decide to return," Elsa suggested.

"That's probably a good idea," Donovan agreed.

"I just want to say one thing first," Hyroc said. "Nice work with the shaft of your spear." Donovan beamed at the compliment. "That was an excellent hit to his face."

"You think *that* might have been a tad of an overreaction?" Elsa asked sharply.

Donovan laughed uncomfortably, holding the back of his head in embarrassment. "Yeah, in hindsight, that may have been a little more than was necessary. But, Wol'dger or not, I wasn't about to sit there and let him disrespect you like that. He treated you the same as someone buying a horse or livestock. And that *was seriously not okay*."

"I appreciate your concern for my well-being, brother, but I can take care of myself! That almost ended badly for all of us. We didn't come all the way here to get torn to pieces by wolves. If those guards hadn't been there …"

"It's what brothers are supposed to do!" Curtis snapped. Elsa and Donovan wheeled around, looking stupefied at their younger brother's uncharacteristic chastising outbursts. "We're supposed to look out for each other, no matter what."

Elsa blew out a breath. "Okay, I'm just saying, in the future, don't do it if we're going to get killed in the process."

"I make no guarantees," Donovan said jokingly, giving Elsa an affectionate smile indicating he understood completely.

"I think we may want to wait on getting our supplies and leaving town, considering what just happened," Hyroc said. "What did the guards call that group, The Pack? Most of them were wolves, so, yeah, that has to be it. Since we pissed them off, and they don't seem like the type to let go of a grudge, they may be waiting for us outside the town to even the score. Finding a tavern and staying out of sight there until morning is the best thing for us to do."

"We're almost completely out of Flecks," Elsa said. "But I think we have just enough to pay for a room for one night without cutting into buying provisions."

"I agree," Donovan said. "But did you see how idiotically angry they got when you made that fire wall? They went berserk, practically ignoring me, and went straight for you."

"Yeah," Hyroc said. "That was strange. I figured it would frighten them and make them back off, not infuriate them into murdering us. They shouted 'Anamagi,' so they knew what I was, and I assume they also knew what I could do with my Flame Claw. They didn't seem to care."

"And I saw it," Donovan noted. "The crazed look in their eyes. They seriously wanted to *end you*. It was like nothing I've ever seen."

"And their animal marks," Elsa questioned. "The ones on their shoulders showing what animal they can turn into; why were they red? Aren't those supposed to be blue?"

"I don't know," Hyroc answered. "I thought all animal marks were supposed to be blue like mine. I'm not sure why their marks are different."

"Maybe they're a different tribe or clan than you," Donovan suggested. "I assume Wol'dgers have something similar. Maybe it's so you can tell each other apart, so you don't make a mistake while dealing with each other."

"I guess," Hyroc said.

"Well, don't give yourself too much of a headache over it," Elsa suggested. "We just got here, and those were the first Wol'dgers you –we've met, so I wouldn't expect you to learn everything about them immediately. Let it go for now and ponder it more after you've had a good night's rest. Seriously, when was the last time you slept in an actual bed?"

"I thought dirt was a bed," Hyroc joked. Elsa gave him a flat, half-humored look. "I really can't remember."

"I'm sure something will pop into your head in the morning."

They wandered through the streets until they found a tavern with a stable for them to house their donkey. The light was turning the dull orange of dusk when they arrived, and the streets were steadily emptying. The establishment was named The Wheezing Cottonwood. It was a moderate-sized beer hall with a small staircase to the left of the front counter leading to the upper floor. It was sparsely filled with patrons. Elsa and Donovan volunteered to acquire a room for the night while Hyroc and Curtis went to find a table to order something for them to eat. Everyone in the tavern was human except for a single Wol'dger male with dark gray fur wearing a brown tunic and pants but nothing on his feet, leaving his white foot claws exposed. He sat alone in a corner, studying the contents of a wooden mug. The Wol'dger wore an incredibly grumpy expression, suggesting a high probability they would harm anyone who bothered them.

Hyroc found a table against a wall. Kit attracted many circumspect stares as they took their seats. The cougar surveyed the room uncertainly, finding his proximity to many strangers disagreeable.

"Kit, here," Hyroc said, invitingly patting the floor beside his chair. "Lay right here." Reluctantly, Kit lay down. He began cleaning his paws, pausing to glower at anyone who walked past.

Nearby, a bearded man sat on a stool with his back against the same wall, smoking a pipe. The puffs of smoke the man issued steadily grew smaller. A second man sat at a table across from Hyroc with an inkwell and piece of parchment, and he scratched away on it with a feather. Hyroc did a double-take when he realized the man wasn't holding the feather. His writing implement moved on its own. The man waved one of his index fingers as he manipulated the feather with Quintessence. He was a mage. Hyroc pulled his attention away from the man and looked for a waiter. The man with the pipe pulled it out of his mouth to look at it with displeasure as the fire within fizzled out. Hyroc glanced around to make sure no guards were within view before he summoned a tiny blue flame between two of his fingers. He approached the man and motioned at the pipe with his empty hand. The man held it out to Hyroc with a curious look. Hyroc deposited the flame into the pipe. A stream of white smoke slowly flowed out of it. The man gazed at his pipe in awe. He waved the pipe toward Hyroc in supreme appreciation. Hyroc happily nodded his thanks and sat back down. Then, he became aware the mage was now staring at him with intrigue. The feather stiffened before collapsing to the table. The man collected his things and walked over to Hyroc's table. He got a start when Kit growled at him, just now seeming to notice the giant cat.

"Knock it off," Hyroc said disapprovingly.

The man motioned toward an empty chair in front of Hyroc. "May I?" He asked.

Hyroc gave the man an appraising look. Why did this person want to talk to him? Beyond his friends or a villain planning something dreadful for him, no one ever wanted to talk to him. The people of Mastgar seemed relatively indifferent toward him, but he practically knew nothing about the goings-on here. If he wasn't careful, his ignorance could easily get his friends and him embroiled in something illicit. The near-disastrous incident at the fountain he and his company had blundered into was still fresh in his mind. If he was careless, he could very well repeat his mistake or make an even bigger one. He had also used magic a moment ago to light that other man's pipe. Magic wasn't allowed in town, and the man was similarly attired as the guard mage he had seen earlier. The man likely wanted to question him about his blatant disregard for their laws. Hyroc chided himself for his careless act of charity. Now, he had attracted even more unwanted attention. How could he be so foolish? Unless the damage was already done, it was probably best he demonstrated he wasn't interested in talking. Hopefully, that would make this man move on.

"No," Hyroc said. "I think you had best be moving on. My mountain lion doesn't like strangers."

The man frowned, taken aback by the refusal. He glanced down at Kit, who was glowering at him, then studied Hyroc's face for a long moment. The man indicated Hyroc's hand, which he had used to light the pipe. "Don't worry; I'm not here to get anyone in trouble over such a trivial infraction. I'm fascinated by that blue flame you created just now. I've never seen that. And I can make it worth your while." The man reached into a coin sack on his belt and laid several Flecks on the table.

The coins immediately drew the desirous gazes of Hyroc and Curtis. With the group nearing destitution, it was an enticing offer. All Hyroc had to do was talk to this stranger. Hyroc glanced at the man, weighing any difficulties incurred by divulging his information. He came up with nothing and decided the reward was worth the risk.

"I accept," Hyroc said. "Take a seat. Kit, calm, he's friendly."

The man's expression brightened. He took a seat and laid on the table his inkwell and a fresh piece of parchment. He made a waving motion toward the inkwell. His writing quill dipped itself in the ink and hovered above the container. "What kind of magic did you use to make the fire?"

Hyroc cautiously scanned the room to ensure no unsavory-looking characters overheard him before answering, "Flame Claw," he said.

The man looked puzzled. "My apologies, not what you call it. I meant, what type of magic did you use? There's ice magic, fire magic, and so on. You were using fire magic, but what did you use to make your fire blue?"

Hyroc gave him a comprehending nod. "Oh – oh, it's Guardian magic. It's what Guardians use." Then it occurred to him this man may not even know about Guardians.

The man looked at him in amazement. "Guardians? You mean to tell me you're using Guardian magic?"

Hyroc nodded.

"Incredible." The man's writing quill rapidly scratched words onto the parchment, dictating his thoughts.

"You know what a Guardian is?" Hyroc asked.

The man nodded. "Very much so. They are powerful beings in the form of animals that usually don't interfere in the kingdom's affairs, preferring to keep to themselves, but yes, I know what a Guardian is." The man shook himself, suddenly realizing something. "Where are my manners?" He pushed his hand out to Hyroc. "My name is Darius Ashfin."

"I'm Hyroc Foxclaw," Hyroc said. After an awkwardly long delay, he shook the man's hand. It felt like an alien motion. He thumbed toward Curtis. "And this is my friend Curtis."

The man's expression changed as if he wanted to ask a question, but he refrained as he shook Curtis' hand.

"It's nice to meet you, Hyroc and Curtis." He withdrew his hand. "Hyroc, how did you come to acquire this, Flame Claw, I believe you called it? Was it from a Guardian?"

"I'm an Anamagi."

"Anamagi? I'm not familiar with that term. Is that what you Wol'dgers, your people, call a mage?"

"No, I don't think so."

"Ah, it's something new. Interesting. Go on." He pointed his hand at a pack he had set at the foot of the table and swept it toward the parchment he wrote on. Three sheets of parchment flew out of the pack, garnering a look of excitement from Kit as they neatly settled onto the table. Kit stood, inquisitively poking his head over the edge of the table. Hyroc pushed his head back down. Darius waited for his writing quill to finish filling the current piece of parchment before using his hand to replace it with a fresh one. Hyroc pushed Kit's head down for a second time.

"There's a lot to tell, and I don't think I have the time to tell you everything right now," Hyroc admitted.

"That's more than all right. Even from the little you said, you have already given me plenty to consider. I'm sure I can get the full story another time." He paused, realizing something. "You're that Wol'dger that caused the commotion at the fountain."

"I wasn't trying to start anything," Hyroc stated quickly. "I was just backing up my friend. I'm sorry if –"

"No, no, I didn't mean to make you think you did something wrong," Darius interjected. "That reminded me of something, is all. You see, I was sent here by the mage Council of Mastgar to study the Wol'dger situation."

Hyroc narrowed his eyes. "Wol'dger situation?"

Darius looked at him strangely. "Why are the two camps of your people fighting? We want to understand what's going on."

Something clicked in place inside Hyroc's head. Is that why that group of Wol'dgers earlier wanted to rip him limb from limb? Had he stumbled into some Wol'dger conflict? Wol'dgers were still basically human, so it made sense they still fought each other. But over what? What was going on here?

"Didn't you know?" Darius asked.

Hyroc shook his head. "No, my friends and I had only arrived here this afternoon."

"Really. Where from? Are there other Wol'dger communities?"

"From Arnaira."

Darius' mouth fell open. "Arnaira!" he said dumbfounded. "How in the world did you avoid getting killed by The Ministry? They are completely intolerant of the use of magic. They label any magic as witchcraft."

"I know, *believe me*. And to make another long story short, I was smart and lucky."

"Indeed. So you mean to tell me you know nothing about the situation here?"

"I'm afraid I don't. I didn't even know there were Wol'dgers here until I arrived today."

"Then, why did you come here?"

"We needed supplies so we could continue to the capital of Mastgar. We assumed this kingdom was safe for mages and magic users. You see ..." he indicated Curtis. "We recently learned my friend Curtis here can use magic. The Ministry found out and has been after us ever since."

Darius became more interested. "He's a mage, you say. What type are his abilities?"

"Curtis, show him."

Curtis laid his hand on the table, summoned a ball of lightning in his palm, and formed it into a cat. The tiny cat with a body of crackling lightning hopped onto the table.

Darius's eyes lit. "*A lightning mage*," he said in amazement. "It's exceedingly rare to find one who can manipulate the energy of Quintessence into lightning. And of all things in a child; you are very special, boy."

"Can you help us?"

"I definitely can."

Elsa and Donovan walked over to the table. Donovan held two mugs of ale in his arms, and Elsa carried one, along with a smaller mug, presumably filled with tea or milk for Curtis. They set their cargo on the table and distributed them to everyone.

"All right, I got us a room for the night," Elsa said. "But after we purchase our provisions, we're not going to have anything left, so we need to figure out where we're going and how to make a living." She looked toward Darius inquisitively. "Hello. Hyroc, who is your new friend here?" She noticed Darius' writing quill moving independently and was momentarily distracted.

"This is Darius," Hyroc said. Darius stood and shook Elsa's hand before moving on to Donovan. "Darius, Elsa, and that's Donovan."

"It's nice to make your acquaintances," Darius said. He politely waited for Elsa to sit before sitting.

"Darius here is a mage," Hyroc continued. "He's here to learn about Wol'dgers, but I think he can help us."

"Yes." Darius indicated Curtis. "Your friend –"

"Brother," Donovan corrected.

Darius gave him a comprehending nod. "Ah, your brother can use lightning magic. That is a scarce talent among mages. His abilities would greatly interest me and my associates within the Council. We have a school for mages where we educate and teach magic users to hone their abilities. I believe it would be advantageous to enroll him. They have the best teachers, trai –"

"Yes!" Elsa interrupted excitedly. "Yes, of course, we will enroll him. That's exactly what we hoped to find when we came to Mastgar. And he'll be safe there?"

Darius nodded. "Of course, I would even wager the school is the safest place in the kingdom."

"Good, good. Do we need to do anything? All you have to do is ask, and we'll do it."

"Beyond traveling to Vettenfelth, the capital of this kingdom, you don't have to do a thing. I'll take care of everything. However, there is one minor obstacle to enrolling him. As your friend said, I'm here to learn about Wol'dgers, which complicates things. I am honor bound to put my work first. This will delay me in helping you, but I promise I will assist you as soon as possible."

"How long of a delay are we talking about?" Donovan asked.

"No more than a few weeks."

"So should we stay here until you can help?" Elsa said. "Near this town, I mean."

“That would be advisable, yes. I only need to remain in contact with you. So long as you fulfill that requirement, you can still travel somewhat through the vicinity.”

“That also means we’re going to have to find some sort of work here,” Donovan said. “Because we’re not going to be able to sustain ourselves until then on our practically nonexistent Flecks.”

“Unfortunately, I was only provided with enough coin to buy food to keep me fed while I worked,” Darius admitted. “So I can’t be of much help in that regard. But I can spare this.” He added a few more Flecks to the coins on the table. “That will at least cover your meals for the night and pay for your room. First thing in the morning, I’ll send a messenger pigeon out to my colleagues in the Council. I hope that will speed things up. But it will still take me some time to get word back, and with any luck, I will get permission to postpone my work until everything is settled.”

“We’ll figure something out,” Elsa said.

“I promise to keep you apprised. I think I’ve taken up enough of your time for one night. So I wish you all a good night, and I’ll take my leave.” Everyone wished him well for the night. He stood, making multiple hand motions to his writing supplies and bag. The writing quill dropped into its inkwell, and the sheets of parchment organized themselves before floating into the bag. Darius slung his sack over his shoulder and collected the inkwell and feather.

“By the way,” Hyroc questioned as Darius turned to walk off. “What type of mage are you?”

Darius turned back toward him with an amused smile. He held his hand over Hyroc’s mug. Ice formed in his hand, and he deposited a ball of ice into Hyroc’s drink. Darius playfully raised and lowered his eyebrows before walking off. Hyroc quizzically tipped his mug toward himself to gaze at its contents.

“I believe that’s worthy of a toast,” Donovan said happily. He held his mug up and waited for everyone to join him. “To a new beginning.”

“To a new beginning,” Hyroc, Elsa, and Curtis echoed before everyone clapped their cups together.

Chapter 10
Otter Trap

HYROC WALKED DOWN THE STAIRS of The Wheezing Cottonwood tavern, which led from the top floor to the bottom level. Kit thumped down the steps behind him. Hyroc lifted a fist to his mouth and let out a wide, wolfish yawn. He couldn't remember the last time he had slept so well. His friends waited for him at a table as they ate breakfast. It was morning, and the dining hall was practically empty.

"Well, you look well-rested," Elsa said as Hyroc sat.

Hyroc nodded happily as he tapped the floor beside him, telling Kit where to lie. The mountain lion sprawled out on his side at the indicated spot and impatiently drummed his tail on the floor.

"Yes, that was the most comfortable *floor* I have ever slept on," Donovan said sarcastically.

"Hey, there was only one bed, and it wasn't big enough for all of us."

"So, naturally, it had to go to the oldest."

Elsa gave him a wicked grin. "Yes, naturally."

"So, does anyone have any suggestions on what we should do?" Hyroc asked before he bit into a piece of sausage. He offered a morsel of the meat to Kit, who eagerly snapped it up. "We'll be here a while. We need to find a way to earn a living until we hear back from Darius."

"Well," Elsa said. "The original plan was to use the last of our Flecks to restock our provisions before we continued on our way. But spending our coin on that is much less important now, so we have some leeway with spending what we have, but not much."

"We are hunters," Donovan said. "We should hunt. We could use that *leeway* to replace our dwindling supply of arrows, which we lost most of when they found residence inside shadow demons and flesh-eating plant *things.*"

"Okay, what should we hunt?"

"We can hunt deer, which will keep us fed and give us hides we can then tan and sell for leather."

"That seems doable, but remember, we have no tannin or any of the tools we had in Elswood. We'll either have to buy or make anything we need. And considering our situation, the former is beyond what we can afford."

"I could probably use my Flame Claw to make that scrap metal we salvaged into any tools we need," Hyroc added.

"That's a good point, but let's hold off on that for now, at least until we find a place to go. We can do pelts, hides, and leather. Even if we only brain tan, whatever we get should still go for a decent price. We could also see if there are any special beasties around here, things everyone here is too scared to go after because they'll, you know, die. And with magic on our side, I'm sure Hyroc and Curtis can take down whatever we encounter."

"Unless it's a Dragon," Hyroc interjected. "Because even with magic, I doubt we would be a match for one of those."

"Dragons exist?" Curtis questioned.

Hyroc stared at him, thinking. Now that he thought about it, he wasn't entirely sure dragons were real.

"Well, we didn't think werewolves were real, and one almost killed us and everyone in Elswood," Donovan said. "So, with our luck, they probably do exist."

"Okay, then, if we hear anything about a giant fire-breathing lizard," Elsa said. "We should avoid it, but beyond the possibility of something horrible like that existing, and it happens to be here, what do you think we should do about deciding what to hunt?"

"I think the best way for us to figure that out is to go to any hunters and trappers in town and see what they're going after," Hyroc suggested.

"We could also talk to the merchants here and see what types of animal pelts they're trying to get. It might be worthwhile to go check the market or the shops in town."

"Good idea," Donovan said. "But watch out for those crazy Wol'dgers – what were they called, again?" He snapped his fingers. "The Pack. We need to watch out for them." He indicated Hyroc. "Specifically you. They detest *you*."

"I know," Hyroc scoffed. "I'm used to my mere existence pissing people off. But I'll say this: bashing one of them in the face might have also had something to do with it."

"No, no, you seem to have forgotten that I bashed him *three times*," Donovan joked. "Three times. Once in the face, once in the stomach and once in the back. Get it right." Elsa, Hyroc, and Curtis shook their heads, trying not to smile. "Okay, to the merchants."

They made their way through town to the market, doubly sure to avoid the fountain. The market was in an open square near numerous shops at the western edge of town. Most merchants displayed wares from within the protective walls but more extended outside through an open gate.

"Okay, Curtis and I will look through what's here," Elsa said. "Donovan, why don't you and Hyroc see if there's anything outside that gate?"

"And what if you run into one of those crazy Wol'dgers while we're gone?" Donovan asked. "Especially that rude one whose schnoz had a meeting with the blunt end of ma spear?"

Hyroc pointed out the guards around the square. "Donovan, there are a lot of guards here," he said. "I'm sure she'll be fine even if she meets one of those Wol'dgers. And we'll only be split up for a bit."

"I'm sure I'll be safe here," Elsa assured.

"If you're sure, that's good enough for me."

"But I should probably be the one worrying about you, considering what happened yesterday. Try not to get into a brawl while you're out there."

"I just might," Donovan joked. "Meet again back here?"

Elsa nodded, and Donovan and Hyroc headed out. They swept their eyes through the merchandise beyond the gate. Overall, the items out here were lower in value than those within the walls, but more inexpensive. Most notably, unrefined leathers had yet to be turned into anything and retained the shape of the animal they had come from.

"Do you see anything you like?" the merchant prodded politely, a man in his thirties who wore a black jerkin and a woolen hat. He regarded Kit cautiously when the big cat came over to give his wares an investigative sniff.

Donovan indicated a hide. "What did you get that off?" Donovan asked.

"Ah," the man said, noticing the bow and quiver poking over his shoulder. "A fellow hunter, I see. I got most of that there from deer my brother hunted, some moose, elk, and a boar."

"What did he take it down with?"

The man rubbed his chin thoughtfully. "He used a longbow with a heavy draw and two steel-tipped razor arrows."

"I've heard those longbows are pretty good."

"Yes, my brother says they are fantastic. But their draw will definitely make your arms sore in the morning."

"Do you know where he got that deer?" Donovan asked, indicating himself and Hyroc. "My friend and I, we're new here and don't know the area, so we're trying to get a feel for some good hunting grounds."

The man regarded them inquisitively, deciding if telling them anything might bring unwanted competition to where he hunted. "Well, the deer aren't from anywhere special; the kind I have here are fairly common, and you can find their trails almost anywhere in this area. But the other animals are harder to find." The man gazed at them thoughtfully. "But there is a way we might be able to help each other. Scyth Horn hides are quite valuable, and I'll pay you well if you can bring me one."

"Scyth Horn? What is that?"

The man was taken aback. "It's a big deer, with black horns and crimson eyes. Once you've seen one, you'll never forget."

"Ah, one of those. Yes, I believe my friend and I have seen one."

"If you manage to kill one and bring me its hide, I'll make it worth your while. Just be careful; they have a real angry side. They're as aggressive as a moose cow with young, but they'll try to impale you with their horns. And those horns of theirs are sharp, so be wary."

"Thanks for the warning."

"You're welcome, newcomer."

Hyroc and Donovan left the merchant. The man appeared especially glad when Kit departed.

"So we should try to get a Scyth Horn," Donovan said.

"Yeah," Hyroc agreed. "That was one deer we ran into while trapped in the forest. We need to be careful of those horns because they look nasty. Let's go tell your sister and brother."

"Yes, but before we do, I see someone selling arrows over there. Let's go look at them first."

After purchasing arrows from the fletcher, they returned to Elsa and Curtis. The two were examining fox pelts when they found them.

"Did you find something?" Elsa asked.

Donovan nodded. "I think so," he said. "There's a deer called a Scyth Horn; apparently, its hide is worth a lot. What about the two of you?"

She pointed a thumb over her shoulder, indicating the merchants behind her. "Well, all the furriers have lots of fox, mink, beaver, and river otter. I also saw clothing made from wolf, bear, and mountain goat, with some cheaper clothing from deer, rabbits, and squirrels."

"So there don't seem to be many differences between what people hunt and trap here and Elswood," Donovan acknowledged.

"No, not a whole lot, except for maybe that Scyth Horn, which, am I right in assuming it's dangerous?" Donovan nodded. She seemed unsurprised. "But, so far, I've heard nothing about anyone wanting the hides of any nightmarish creatures."

"What do you think we should try for?" Hyroc asked. "Should we see if there are any nearby rivers where we might find some beavers or otters?"

"We could start with that," Elsa said. "But if we don't find anything after a while, we should head into the forest for something else."

"All right."

"But before we head out, since we don't know how long we'll be doing this here, we should get a tent, so we don't have to be exposed to the rain when it eventually decides to rain again. And I saw one right over there."

They purchased the tent, essentially a cloth tarp oiled to allow it to shed rainwater. Then, they bought a sack of cold-flour before heading out. The incredibly unpleasant, tasteless gruel it made would keep them from starving if they were unsuccessful hunting game.

They moved off the main road leading out of town, heading for a small stream shown on Hyroc's map of Mastgar. They knew animals tended to congregate around water sources, and it was the best spot for them to start their search for fur-bearing creatures.

It was a forested area consisting mainly of white birch, and the trees weren't as thick as they were at Elswood. No hunting trails had been cut here, which made for slow-going, but they had purposely chosen this place. No trails meant few, if any, people used this area for hunting or trapping, so they didn't have to worry about competing for any captured animals. Of course, there was also the chance no one came to the spot because there weren't any animals. The ground rose as they climbed the flanks of a hill. The top flattened out, ending in a small ridge. Below them, they saw the winding gap in the trees where the stream flowed. It wasn't far from the bottom of the hill.

Carefully, they picked their way down. This side of the hill was steeper, causing their donkey difficulty navigating it. They had to move in a zigzag pattern down the slope. Their donkey prevented them from going straight, and they had to search for the safest descent to bring their supply-laden pack animal on, lest they risked it breaking a leg. Thankfully, there weren't many trees in their way to further complicate the situation. It took longer than expected, but they reached the bottom without any issues. They were at the stream after moving through a thin band of trees.

Foliage filled the space between the trees and the shore. The plants grew right to the water's edge. The ground abruptly dropped off though it was a mere step or two to reach the stream. Grass and roots drooped down along the edge, making it hard to see where the ground was precisely, and it would be easy for someone to misstep and twist their ankle.

Hyroc thought, right now was an awful time for any injury. They continued along the shore. The drop-off turned into a sandy bank at a bend in the stream. It was now dusk. The sandy bank was lower than the shore with the drop-off, so they set up their tent on the higher ground in case the river flooded at night. This way, they had more warning to escape the rising water.

Their tent consisted of oiled animal skins knitted together into a tarp. They went with a five-point anchor system, meaning they used wooden stakes to hold the four corners of the tent in place, with a center post pushing the middle up to give them headroom. The only downside to their tent was it had no walls and provided no protection against the wind. Also, if they got blowing rain, they were likely to get wet. But if they built up walls of branches and forest debris, they would be sheltered from the wind. They could only utilize this technique once they had found a permanent location to make camp.

After the tent was set up, with the last remaining light, Hyroc attempted catching fish in the stream using a hand line. Elsa moved downstream to avoid accidentally getting hooked and established a dropline to try snagging fish to eat for breakfast. In the fading orange light of sunset, it was hard for Hyroc to see the dark shapes of fish gliding through the stream. Though his Wol'dger eyes gave him superior night vision, the changing conditions of sunset and sunrise disrupted his ability. At these times, he saw no better than his human companions. He spotted a shadow and used his Flame Claw to form a shimmering blue barrier to pin the fish to the bottom of the stream.

"Cheater," he heard Donovan yell from the tent as his friend started a fire.

Before Hyroc could move, Kit splashed into the water, pushing his head underneath the barrier and grabbing the fish with his teeth. Kit pulled his sodden head out of the water, the fish wildly waving its tail. Hyroc dismissed the barrier. The mountain lion stopped at the shore, staring at Hyroc with clearly mischievous thoughts entering his mind.

"Don't do it!" Hyroc sternly called out, knowing his feline friend was considering stealing his fish. "That one isn't for you. But you can have the next one."

Kit studied him for a long moment, then walked over to him, and after delivering a killing bite to the fish's head, dropped it at his feet. Hyroc nodded obligingly before making another cast into the stream. Not long afterward, he caught a fish. He pulled it in and dispatched it with his knife. When it stopped moving, he tossed it to Kit, who snatched it out of the air. The big cat happily sauntered over to the tent. Donovan had just gotten a fire going, and that's where Kit went. He stared at Donovan expectantly. Rolling his eyes, Donovan held his hand out. Kit dropped the fish into his proffered hand. Donovan stuck it on a skewer, cooked it, and returned it to the big cat. Kit bedded down next to the fire to enjoy his supper.

Hyroc hadn't caught any more fish when night arrived. He collected his single fish and moved into the firelight to gut it, saving the innards to use as bait. Divided among the four of them, there wasn't much fish to go around, but it was a welcome addition to go with bread. After dinner, everyone lay their sleeping mats underneath the tent as close to the fire as possible. Kit lay down next to Hyroc with his head resting on Hyroc's arm. Shimmer fluttered underneath the tent, lowered himself into a sitting position next to Elsa upon landing, and went to sleep. Everyone else quickly followed suit.

The sky was overcast, with a cool breeze the following day, but rain seemed unlikely. Hyroc was the first to wake. He added wood to the smoldering remains of their fire and used his Flame Claw to reignite it.

"Cheater," Donovan said groggily but playfully.

"I'm just putting my Flame Claw to good use," Hyroc said, reaching for the pack with their food. He retrieved some bread, tore off a hunk, and handed it to Donovan. Donovan nodded his thanks before eating. Similarly, he gave bread to Elsa and Curtis when they woke.

"Hyroc and Donovan," Elsa said after breakfast. "I think you two should head out and see if you can hunt us our dinner while Curtis and I get to work finding places for traps."

"Sounds good," Donovan agreed. "Hyroc, I'll just go with my spear, and why don't you use my bow since you don't have yours anymore? Does that work for you?"

"Wait," Hyroc said, an idea coming to him. He indicated Elsa. "If you're going with your spear, why don't I switch with Elsa? She's a better shot with a bow than either of us, which will maximize our chances of downing something when we find it."

Donovan looked at him, agreeing with a nod.

"Because," Elsa said. "It will be easier for the two of you to carry whatever you kill – especially if the carcass isn't nearby – than it will be for me and Donovan."

"Oh, I see," Donovan said accusingly. "You just want the two *men* here to take on the difficult task while you save the easiest for yourself."

"Why else do you think I keep you two around?" Elsa joked.

Hyroc hung his head with a sigh, feigning dejection. He spun on his heel without moving his head and went to the tent to retrieve Donovan's bow and quiver before heading out. Kit excitedly followed behind him.

Hyroc and Donovan moved to the stream and crossed it to follow an animal trail cutting through the foliage. The trail ran from the stream, maintaining a relatively straight course. It stayed straight for a time before turning into a wild path that followed no discernible pattern. It moved over a hillock, heading down the other side into a swath of short, scraggly spruce trees. They passed an eagle watching them imperiously from its perch on the barren gray top of a tree. Hyroc dismissed the idea of shooting the regal bird because they weren't desperate for meat and could be picky about what they hit.

A flash of white fur and a darting shape appeared at the base of one tree. But before Hyroc could aim, it was out of sight. Kit flew after the shape, disappearing in the green needle-covered skirts of the trees. The rustling of foliage and the breaking of dry leaves and sticks quickly faded as he ran out of earshot.

Hyroc and Donovan headed after Kit. Not long afterward, they heard the mountain lion's footfall again. Kit rejoined them, carrying a lifeless rabbit in his jaws.

"Good job," Hyroc said, giving his companion a congratulatory pat on the head. Kit rumbled happily. Hyroc retrieved the rabbit and tied it to his belt.

The spruce trees gave way to the green leafy canopy of white birch and cottonwood. A squirrel chattered at them from some unseen place. They quickly found it perched on a branch by following the direction of Kit's ears. Before Hyroc could lose an arrow, an eagle snatched it off the branch. Hyroc and Donovan exchanged a look and laughed. Kit tipped his head in confusion.

"I was not expecting that," Hyroc said.

"Me, neither," Donovan agreed. "But that's not the first time I've seen that."

"How much further do you think we should go? We're getting kind of far away, and the farther we go, the farther we'll have to carry it back."

"Don't worry, I know. Let's check up here before we turn around."

Hyroc nodded.

Kit stiffened, abruptly stopping. Hyroc and Donovan did the same, knowing the cougar had heard something. Kit's ears slowly rotated as he tried to discern the precise location of the sound. He dropped into a low crouch and stalked forward silently. Hyroc and Donovan followed, carefully placing each footstep. Ahead of them, Hyroc spotted the long-necked shape of a lone doe grazing in a gap in the trees. He quietly lined up a shot. Donovan misstepped, crunching a twig. The doe bolted. Kit tore after her. Hyroc and Donovan rushed after their four-legged companion, but that was merely to make sure they didn't lose track of him. Their two-legged forms were no match for the two animals' speed. Whether or not the deer got away was entirely up to Kit.

Their attention was focused on listening for sounds to follow. Kit was now beyond their hearing. Something rustled through the bushes behind them. Hyroc and Donovan wheeled around.

"What was that?" Donovan asked, not bothering to keep his voice down because Kit's deer was too far away for it to make a difference.

"Kit and that deer were in front of us," Hyroc noted. "There's no way that was him or that deer."

"A black bear, maybe?"

They listened intently but didn't hear anything else.

"We might have scared it off," Donovan suggested.

They alertly scanned their surroundings. At the edge of Hyroc's vision, he caught a glimpse of two eyes in his peripheral vision staring back at him. Startled, he snapped his attention back to that spot. There was nothing there.

"I just saw something looking at us!" Hyroc said. "And it didn't have bear eyes."

"Where?"

"Over there."

"Okay, you move toward that spot. I'll hang back to ensure it doesn't come behind you."

Hyroc nodded, warily walking forward.

"Yeah, maybe we scared –" he trailed off as a rustling sound and the impact noise of something hitting the ground came from behind him.

Hyroc spun around to find Donovan lying on the ground on his back and a huge black feline with a white chest flare, bigger than Kit, standing on top of him. The cat held the claws of one paw to Donovan's throat.

"Lower your bow!" the cat snarled in a man's voice.

A blue paw on the cat's shoulder identified him as a Wol'dger. *Great, another one of those crazy Wol'dgers from town,* Hyroc thought to himself.

"Do it, now!" the Wol'dger shouted. "Or I'll slit his throat. Toss your bow one way and your arrow and quiver another. *Slowly.*"

Hyroc tossed his arrow aside, then his bow in the opposite direction. He unslung the quiver from his shoulder and kicked it behind him.

"Now, your sword and knife the same way."

"Don't," Donovan cautioned.

"Be quiet," the Wol'dger growled.

"It's okay, Donovan," Hyroc said reassuringly. "I know what I'm doing." Hyroc discarded his sword and knife.

"The next time either of you speak, it will only be to answer my questions."

Trying to take advantage of the Wol'dger distracting himself by talking, Hyroc covertly lowered himself to get on all fours and transform into bear form.

"Stop right there!" the Wol'dger yelled, pressing the tips of his claws against Donovan's neck. "*I'll slash his throat* and be gone before you have a chance to move. And I give you my word, that's what I'll do if I see you trying to change. Stand up, all the way." Without taking his eyes off the Wol'dger, Hyroc stood up. "Eagle should know better by now than to have two of his lackeys sneak up on me."

Eagle sounded like the name of a person and not the bird of prey. Hyroc hadn't met anyone named that. Perhaps it was the name of one of those Wol'dgers at the fountain the other day. Did this Wol'dger think he and Donovan were chasing him? Could this be a misunderstanding? Or was this Wol'dger mixing him up with someone else? But one thing was clear: this Wol'dger was extremely dangerous and should not be trifled with. Hyroc didn't relish fighting him, even with the advantage of his Flame Claw, but he had to save his friend.

"We weren't following you," Hyroc said. "We were following a –"

The Wol'dger laughed mockingly. "Yes, that's exactly what I expected a Feral assassin to say. That's what all the others said right before they tried sticking me with a dagger. It's been a while since I ran into one of you, and I started to think Eagle was losing his touch, or, I should say, losing it more."

"Hyroc, just tell him everything," Donovan said. "He's not going to believe us otherwise."

"Hyroc?" the Wol'dger said, sounding surprised. The Wol'dger focused on Hyroc and was instantly more interested. When he spoke, there was a change in his voice; it was softer and less harsh. "Your Hyroc? Your name is Hyroc?"

"Yes, my name is Hyroc," Hyroc said.

The Wol'dger blinked as if to clear particulates from his vision. He shook his head. "No, you can't be," he said as if he had just seen a ghost. "You're dead. Hyroc died long ago. *They all did.*"

"Why do you speak as if you know me?" Hyroc asked guardedly. "Who are you?"

A guttural growl interrupted the Wol'dger's response. Kit materialized out of the foliage next to the Wol'dger, his teeth bared and hackles raised. The Wol'dger disengaged from Donovan, leaping away into a more defensible position.

"Kit, hold!" Hyroc called out.

The Wol'dger returned his attention to Hyroc. "I'm your uncle!"

Chapter 11

Fenrald

HYROC STARED AT THE WOL'DGER. He felt as if he had been punched in the gut. This was impossible. Hyroc was almost unable to comprehend what this person had just said. This was his uncle? No, this was preposterous, not to mention convenient. This had to be a trick. This Wol'dger was trying to make him lower his guard to gain an advantage. The witch in Elswood had attempted the same strategy. He needed to remain cautious and not get distracted.

Donovan scrambled to his feet and retrieved his spear. A spot of blood from the Wol'dger's claws showed on his neck. Hyroc kept his eyes glued to the Wol'dger, not daring to retrieve his sword. The power of his Flame Claw alone could neutralize the stranger.

"Nobody move!" the Wol'dger commanded. "Everyone stop. Just stop. I mean you no harm."

"That's rich," Donovan scoffed. "For you to say right after attacking us. How stupid do you think we are?"

"You threatened to rip my friend's throat out," Hyroc spat. "Forgive me if I think you're untrustworthy and likely to stab us in the back the moment you get a chance."

"I know what I said, all right," the Wol'dger said. "I made a mistake – that's all it was. A mistake. I thought the two of you were someone else. I apologize for attacking you. I genuinely don't mean any harm to either of you. Please forgive me."

"It will go a long way towards proving that if you transform into your natural form. Get rid of those claws."

"All right. I'll transform." He spread his legs so each had equal weight and closed his eyes. His body began changing from a four-legged creature into something walking on two legs. Skin, muscles, bones, and organs steadily altered shape to suit a more humanoid form.

Where there had been bare fur was now covered in clothing. The Wol'dger wore a dark brown jerkin and black pants. His fur was black, with a gray chinstrap of hair under his jaw, and he had hazel eyes.

"Okay, now stand," Hyroc said. "Slowly." The Wol'dger slowly rose up on two legs. He and Hyroc were the same height, but the stranger was broader in the chest and had thick muscular arms. "Keep your hands where we can see them."

"I assure you I am unarmed," the Wol'dger said. "Blades and other metallic weapons prevent me from transforming."

"We know how that process works," Hyroc said sharply.

"I wasn't trying to imply you didn't. Okay, I did as you asked. Now, kindly ask your friend to lower his weapons?"

Hyroc studied him pensively, mulling over the request. Just because this Wol'dger wasn't armed and without flesh-shredding claws didn't mean he still wasn't dangerous. His fists were still more than enough to make him a threat. But Hyroc knew he could call upon his Flame Claw if this Wol'dger tried anything. Kit was also ready to strike, and his companion would probably react faster than he if anything happened. Neither he nor Donovan needed a weapon to defend themselves.

"All right, Donovan, you can do as he says. Lower your weapon."

"Are you sure?" Donovan questioned.

"Yes. I'm sure. Do as he says."

Donovan lowered his spear.

The Wol'dger then indicated Kit, who had a murderous gaze fixed on him. "Him as well."

"Kit, calm."

Kit regarded Hyroc with uncertainty as if to say, "He attacked us, and should not be excused." He chuffed in protest before settling onto his haunches in a prone position with his paws beneath him. His posture was relaxed, but he glared at the Wol'dger, ready to strike at any instant.

The Wol'dger nodded appreciatively.

"Now, give us your name," Hyroc demanded.

"Fenrald," the Wol'dger said.

"Okay, Fenrald," Hyroc said. "You said you're my uncle. Is that true?"

"Yes, I promise I'm your uncle."

"Can you prove that?"

"No, I don't have anything on me to prove it. Only my word. But I can get you the proof you're asking for."

"Okay, where is it?"

"I live in a village a day's walk to the east. That's where I keep what you seek," Fenrald said.

Cautiously, Hyroc retrieved his map of Mastgar from his knapsack. "This map doesn't show any village to the east," he said.

"We only built it a few years ago. You'd be lucky to find it on any map of this region."

"We? What do you mean by *we*?"

"Other Wol'dgers, from Wulfren."

Hyroc pushed down an upwelling of excitement. A village of Wol'dgers! He had searched his whole life to find such a community. But that was only if Fenrald wasn't fabricating the entire thing. Though he seemed honorable enough, he might still be trying to trick them.

"I'd be careful of what he says," Donovan cautioned. "It's probably an entire village of those crazy Wol'dgers with the red markings. It might be a trap."

Fenrald looked at them, puzzled. "Red marks?" he said. "You mean the Ferals? No, I can guarantee there are no Ferals there. Our proper name is Guidance Wol'dgers, but we've taken to calling ourselves Glacials for short because our blue animal marks look similar to ice. The Ferals are trying their damnedest to wipe us off the face of the earth.

Where have you been hiding all these years for you to know nothing about them? They slaughtered everyone I ever cared about in Wulfren, including your parents!" As he spoke the last part, Hyroc caught a tinge of pain in Fenrald's voice.

Hyroc felt a cold sensation run up his back and a flare of rage. The unknown enemy who had killed his mother had haunted him his entire life. His adversary was responsible for ripping him and his three friends from their home in Elswood. If this Fenrald were making any of this up for personal gain, Hyroc would take it out of his hide.

"What did you say?" Hyroc said coolly. "I hope you're not trying to deceive me with *that.*"

"I would never do any such thing!" Fenrald said with an indignant glare.

"I think the only way we're going to resolve this is to go to the village," Donovan suggested. "It doesn't sound far."

"No, it's not far," Fenrald confirmed. "It's less than a day's walk."

"And what if it's full of those savage Wol'dgers with the red marks?" Hyroc questioned.

"I guess we'll have to figure that out when we get there," Donovan said. "But first things first; we must return to get my sister and younger brother."

"And while we're at it," Hyroc suggested, "we can send Shimmer out to confirm the village exists."

Donovan nodded his agreement. "You're going in front of me," he said, pointing his spear forward. "Forgive me if I'm not ready to turn my back on you yet." He lightly rubbed around the delicate, freshly formed scab on his neck for emphasis.

Fenrald nodded before falling into step.

No one talked during the walk back to the tent.

"Hey, you two," Elsa called out when they arrived. "I found some –" she trailed off when she noticed Fenrald. "Oh, now, who is this?"

"This is Fenrald," Hyroc said. "He says he's my uncle."

"He – he what?" she said, dumbfounded.

"Yeah, he says he's my uncle. And he says he can prove it if we come with him to a Wol'dger village to the east."

Elsa leaned in and lowered her voice. "Do you know if we can trust him? Could this be a trap?"

"I don't know, but we can send Shimmer to do a flyover of it to make sure."

Elsa lifted her fingers to her lips and whistled. A distant caw answered. The black shape of Shimmer spiraled down out of the sky, landing in front of her. He squawked a greeting. Taking notice of Fenrald, he inquisitively tipped his head sideways.

"Shimmer, we need you to fly east," she said, pointing the direction. "We need you to see if there is a village close by – not the town where we came from. It's a smaller settlement." The raven cawed his acknowledgment before taking flight. "It won't take him long to return."

Fenrald gazed at her quizzically. "How do you command a Guardian servant?" he asked. "You are human."

"We don't command him," Hyroc noted. "We ask for his help. He can choose whether to obey."

"I see."

"I'm Elsa, and that's my younger brother, Curtis, over there."

"Nice to make your acquaintances." Fenrald turned his full attention on Hyroc. Hyroc saw the Wol'dger studying him.

"What?" Hyroc said.

"You have your mother's eyes."

It made Hyroc uncomfortable to have his features scrutinized by the stranger. It reminded him too much of what he had gone through in Forna and his initial experience with the villagers at Elswood. He put his back to Fenrald, acting as if he hadn't heard the remark. An awkward silence settled on the group until Shimmer returned. Upon landing, he pointed his body east and excitedly jumped into the air, fluttering.

"I think that's a yes about the village," Elsa said. "But that's probably about all we can learn from a bird's-eye view without visiting it."

"Which means we have to break down the camp we spent all last night setting up," Donovan said unenthusiastically.

"Yes, but it's not much work."

"It'll go much faster if I help," Fenrald volunteered.

"I don't see why not," Elsa agreed.

"We should keep an eye on him," Hyroc whispered into her ear as he moved past to assist with the task. The breaking of camp went quickly.

"Fenrald, lead the way," Elsa said, putting him at the head of the group.

They moved north away from the river to find more easily traversable terrain, then turned east. The forest turned to a mixture of white birch and tall spruce trees punctuated with patches of cottonwood.

"Where do you hail from, Hyroc?" Fenrald asked as they walked.

Hyroc studied him warily, wondering if he should divulge that for his safety. But there didn't seem to be a way for the stranger to use the information against him.

"Arnaira," Hyroc said.

Fenrald stared at him incredulously. "Ministry lands?" he said. "I've heard they don't take kindly to –" he indicated himself, "– our kind. How did you survive?"

"I was smart and lucky."

"Indeed. How long did you live there?"

"All my life. Probably around nineteen years."

"Nineteen? Has it really been that long?" He shook his head in disbelief. "You're at the right age. It is you." He paused. "Do you possess the transformation gift?" Hyroc nodded. "And you are Anamagi?" Hyroc didn't answer, unsure if he should answer truthfully, considering how violently the Wol'dgers in town had reacted to seeing blue flames. "You still think I'm being deceptive. But just from your silence, I know the answer is yes. You would have inherited that from *her*."

"Who is *her*?" Hyroc said though he suspected the answer.

"Your mother." Fenrald sighed dejectedly, appearing distant as if a memory had momentarily taken hold of him. "What animal did you choose? What is your animal form?"

"A bear."

"Strength? Interesting. Why a bear?"

"It's personal," Hyroc said, sharper than he had intended.

Fenrald threw his hands up apologetically. "I wasn't trying to pry," he apologized.

"Just – just focus on showing us where to go."

Fenrald nodded.

Hyroc drifted to the back of the group.

"You okay?" Elsa asked.

"I'm fine," Hyroc answered. "Fenrald was asking things that were a little too personal."

She nodded.

The forest didn't change much for the rest of the day. They stopped for the night to camp at a rocky outcropping at the base of a bluff.

It was a clear night, so they didn't see the need to bother with the tent. Hyroc pulled a hunk of bread out of a pack and divided it among Elsa, Donovan, and Curtis. He was about to stow away what was left when Elsa tapped him on the shoulder.

She cleared her throat. "Hyroc, aren't you forgetting something?" she said.

Hyroc stared at her, perplexed. Then it dawned on him. He had been so used to worrying only about his friends for years he hadn't even considered giving food to Fenrald. The Wol'dger hadn't eaten all day and had to be starving.

"Fenrald, here," Hyroc said, holding the remainder of the bread out to the stranger, followed by his water skin.

Fenrald accepted the proffered sustenance. "Thank you," he said, holding the bread up appreciatively.

After everyone had eaten, they settled into sleep. With nothing else to offer, they gave Fenrald the knitted skin of their tent for him to use as a makeshift sleeping mat and blanket.

"I know this probably goes without saying, Fenrald," Hyroc said. "But they'll be keeping an eye on you." He indicated the branch of a cottonwood where Kit was lying. The big cat glared at the Wol'dger threateningly, seeming to say, "I dare you to try anything." Then Hyroc indicated another tree. Shimmer was perched on it with one wing held out as he preened it with his beak. The raven stopped to regard Fenrald before resuming. "And don't try deceiving them either. They'll alert us if you do anything suspicious. And Kit, the cougar, isn't known for his restraint." Fenrald nodded his understanding before leaning back against a tree trunk and closing his eyes. "Good night."

The following day, the sky was draped by ephemeral cirrus clouds, and a mild breeze kept it a pleasant temperature.

"How much farther is the village?" Donovan asked as they finished preparing their donkey for travel.

"Not much further," Fenrald said. "We should be there by midday."

Donovan nodded.

After departing, they encountered a road Fenrald said led to the village. It wasn't as neat and uniform as the one going in and out of Forestgold. It was clearer than a hunting trial but roughly hewn through the forest. Plants sparsely populated the road, indicating enough traffic tread on it to trample anything trying to take root. As they followed it, a four-legged shape came into view, moving toward them. They realized it was a bear.

"Bear!" Elsa called out. She reached for an arrow, but Fenrald stopped her.

"Hold," he said. "That's not what you think. Look closer. See that on its back?"

Everyone focused on the bear. Brownish lumps protruded from its sides. They were leather packs filled with goods. It was a Wol'dger in bear form, using their form as an improvised pack animal. They also relaxed when they saw the animal mark on its shoulder was blue. It was a Glacial. The bear regarded them with a passing glance. Then, it suddenly seemed surprised when it realized humans were in the group. It stopped, watching them curiously.

Everyone soon smelled burning firewood, and the village appeared. The village was a sparse grouping of structures with a haphazard layout similar to Elswood. The chief difference was the roofs reminded Hyroc of drawings of North Lander dwellings he had seen at the boarding school in Forna. Their roofs had a distinct triangular shape intended to help keep winter snow from accumulating in dangerous amounts and potentially collapsing the building. Unfamiliar decorations and runes in a language he couldn't read adorned the outside of each structure.

Three Wol'dgers congregated in front of the nearest buildings, talking to one another. Their conversation ceased when they noticed Elsa, Donovan, and Curtis. They stared in puzzlement at the three humans.

Fenrald led the group away from the buildings, going down a path ending at a small log cabin in a tiny clearing.

"This is your home?" Hyroc asked as he looked around, taking in his surroundings.

"Yes," Fenrald answered. "It's not much, but I am happy to call it home. Make yourself comfortable while I retrieve what will prove I am who I say."

He stepped onto the porch outside the front door and reached into a hand-sized recess in the boards. He pulled out a rudimentary key, unlocked the door, entered, and returned with a necklace with a silver disc.

"I believe this should do it," Fenrald said, handing the necklace to Hyroc.

On one side was the name Fenrald, and animal symbols were on the other, below the name Foxclaw. That was Hyroc's last name. Fenrald was his uncle!

A flood of emotions billowed through Hyroc. He had lost all hope he would meet other family members one day. Now, here he was, in the presence of his uncle. Questions exploded into his mind. There were so many things he had spent his whole life searching to answer. He could finally solve the enigma of his past.

"Unc – uncle," Hyroc stammered, thunderstruck by the enormity of the situation. He had to force the words out of his throat. They felt foreign, as if they came from a forgotten language. "Uncle. You're my uncle!"

Fenrald nodded happily. "Yes," he said. "I'm your uncle, nephew."

Almost without realizing it, Hyroc rushed forward and embraced Fenrald in an excited hug.

Fenrald laughed. "I never thought I would see you again as long as I lived! You were just a babe last I saw you. Now look at you. You've gotten so big. You're already a man."

"I had given up all hope of meeting anyone from my family," Hyroc said. "And – and, here you are."

"Yes, here I am."

Hyroc stepped back from Fenrald, wiping his eyes on the back of his hand. "I have so many questions. I – I – I don't even know where to start."

"Yes, I imagine you must. You all must accept my sincerest apologies for what happened when you first saw me," he said to Donovan. "Especially you. I truly thought the two of you were Feral trackers. I hope there aren't any hard feelings."

"Nobody got hurt," Donovan admitted. "Or at least, it was nothing permanent. Consider it forgotten."

"I appreciate that. Do all of you hail from Arnaira?"

Everyone nodded.

"We came from Elswood," Elsa said. "It's a village far to the east, at the foot of Wolf Paw Mountain."

"What brings you to – as I've heard The Ministry describe Mastgar – these dark and savage lands?" Fenrald said ironically.

The happiness drained from everyone's face.

Fenrald nodded his understanding. "Ah, I see it's nothing pleasant," he said. "You don't have to share it if you prefer not to."

The four of them nodded their appreciation.

"But may I ask if it's the same reason your parents aren't with you?"

"Sort of, yeah," Elsa said.

"I'm sorry to hear that," Fenrald said somberly. "You have my deepest condolences. I have endured my share of loss and know all too well the hole left behind. You're welcome to stay here as long as you like. I don't know if there's enough room for all of you inside."

They nodded thankfully.

"Thank you for considering my friends," Hyroc said. "I appreciate it."

"You're welcome, but thanking me is unnecessary."

"Fenrald, when you accidentally ambushed us, where were you coming from?"

"Oh, I was returning from business regarding the king's court. But that's a conversation to be had later."

"And what's a Feral? You've said that name a couple of times."

"Ferals, that's what the Wol'dgers with the red marks are called."

"Oh, the crazy ones," Donovan said.

Fenrald nodded. "Some are, yes. But it's more complicated."

"Why are their marks red and ours are blue?" Hyroc asked.

"I promise I'll answer all your questions, but there's something I need to take care of first. I need to get my daughter."

"Daughter? I have a cousin?"

"Yes. Well, sort of."

CHAPTER 12

The Honor of Foxclaw

FENRAL LED HYROC AND HIS friends through the Wol'dger village proper. They passed a building where a Wol'dger in the form of a big cat with grayish fur lay on the roof sound asleep, their head resting on their paws. Kit let out an alarmed yowl when he came around the side of a building to face a large wolf carrying a basket full of herbs in its jaws.

"Pardon me," the wolf apologized to the group in a woman's voice.

"No problem," Donovan responded as he politely stepped out of her way.

He and the wolf did a double take, looking back at each other in mirrored surprise. Most Wol'dgers they passed looked at the group with curious stares. The onlookers paid no mind to Hyroc or Fenral; their human companions drew attention. It felt bizarre to Hyroc for him not to be the center of attention. It was nice, for once, to avoid gawking eyes and to blend into the background because everyone looked like him. But he felt something new: empathy. He empathized with his friends, who were watched by so many eyes. From years of experience, he knew having people scrutinize every action and movement wasn't pleasant. However, no one here appeared to think because they looked different, they were dangerous or some hideous demon. Was this what his life could have been like if not for the fear The Ministry had installed in the citizens of Arnaira?

They exited the other side of the village, returning to forested surroundings. A farm came into view in a large swath of cleared area. Brown lines of tilled soil surrounded the structure. A Wol'dger in a white tunic stood near a dirty white stag with patches of black across its body and dangerous-looking pointed horns protruding from its head. The animal wore a harness across the chest attached to a square sled. Stones weighed down the sled, with rows of spikes on the bottom furrowing the ground. The stag arduously pulled the plow through the stubborn earth while the Wol'dger assistant and ensured the animal continued walking straight.

"Silka, Unresh," Fenrald called out as they came to the front of the building.

A Wol'dger woman stepped out the front door. She had brown eyes with black fur on her head and strips of white running down it. She wore a long blue tunic, a bronze necklace ending with a disk of silver hung from her neck. and she had sandals on her feet with her claws sticking out.

"Ah, there you are, Fenrald," she said.

"Silka," Fenrald said in greeting.

"I hope everything went well on your journey."

"It went as well as expected."

She nodded.

"Is Elizabeth ready?"

"Elizabeth!" she yelled. She pointed to Hyroc and his friends. "Who are your friends? I don't recognize them."

Fenrald shook his head in joyful disbelief. "You're not going to believe this," he said happily. He put his hand on Hyroc's shoulder. "This is my nephew, Hyroc."

Her mouth fell open in astonishment. "No, you're kidding me," she said as she came over to take a closer look at Hyroc.

"No, I assure you, this is no jest."

"Another Foxclaw? After all these years? You survived."

"Survived?" Hyroc asked, puzzled. "What did I survive?"

Her expression became baffled. She turned to Fenrald. "You mean he doesn't know?"

Fenrald shook his head somberly.

"Ah, you've got a lot to tell him."

"Tell me what?" Hyroc asked, steadily growing more concerned. "What do you *have to tell me*?"

Fenrald patted him on the shoulder. "Later," he said. "I promise I'll tell you later. This isn't the proper place to have *that* conversation, and you'll want to be sitting down."

Hyroc wondered anxiously if he genuinely wanted to know despite having waited his whole life for this moment. Now that those answers were right in front of him, knowing them seemed substantially less enticing.

"Who are your companions?" the woman asked Hyroc. Hyroc pulled himself from his thoughts and introduced Elsa, Donovan, and Curtis. "It's nice to meet all of you." She dropped into a crouch when she noticed Kit sauntering forward and, seemingly unafraid, held her hand out, letting him sniff it.

"And that's Kit," Hyroc said. "Don't worry, he won't go after your deer."

She laughed softly. "Oh, I don't think we have to worry about *that*."

Hyroc regarded her in confusion, puzzled by her confidence.

A lean male Wol'dger appeared in the doorway. He had gray eyes and dirty white fur with some dark brown under his chin. He wore a white tunic and dark gray pants and was barefoot. The Wol'dger walked with a bad limp and leaned heavily on a walking stick.

"Unresh," Fenrald said in greeting to the Wol'dger

"Fenrald," he said in kind as he ambled forward.

The woman stepped over to Unresh and whispered something into his ear. He mirrored her earlier look of bewilderment before turning to Hyroc.

Then, a herd of half a dozen Wol'dger children clamorously stormed around the side of the building. They were all boys ranging in a color mixture of brown to black, to white, and all wearing gray tunics. Then, a young Wol'dger girl with amber eyes and black fur, wearing a light blue dress and a pink scarf wrapped around her head, peered around the building. A human girl with dark brown eyes and a matching dress about the same age followed her.

"There you are, Elizabeth," Fenrald said. He walked over to the two girls, holding a hand out. The human girl took his hand and shyly stayed behind him as he led her toward Hyroc. "Love, there's someone special I want you to meet."

Hyroc stared at her perplexed, realizing she was Fenrald's daughter. But how was that possible? She was human!

Donovan leaned in close to Hyroc. "You didn't, by chance, start out looking like a human?" he asked, sounding similarly mystified.

"No," Hyroc answered. "I did not."

"Didn't think so," Donovan said.

Fenrald smiled, knowing what the two of them were thinking. "I see you noticed a problem about her being my daughter," he said humorously. Hyroc and Donovan nodded, flabbergasted. "She's adopted."

Hyroc and Donovan drolly smiled in comprehension.

"I was going to say," Donovan said amusedly.

"Elizabeth, say hello to your cousin, Hyroc," Fenrald said encouragingly.

The girl tried even harder to conceal herself behind Fenrald before reluctantly waving. Hyroc returned the gesture.

"She's a little shy around strangers, but she'll warm up to you once she gets to know you."

"Hello," a young man's voice said to Elsa.

"Hello," Elsa said, turning toward the voice and back to looking at Elizabeth. She did an astonished double take, realizing the greeting had come from the deer pulling the plow. It wasn't a work animal but a Wol'dger in the form of a deer. "My name is Iskall."

The deer extended a hooved foot toward her. Elsa stared at it, then slowly grabbed it by the ankle to avoid a patch of accumulated mud and shook it.

"I'm Elsa," she said.

The deer nodded happily, lowering its foot and heading to Donovan, Curtis, and Hyroc to do the same. Kit tipped his head, perturbed and stumped about whether to treat the deer Wol'dger as prey or something he would get in trouble for attacking.

Elsa looked coyly at Hyroc. Hyroc shrugged, smiling back his understanding of the peculiar situation.

The other young adult male Wol'dger came over to introduce himself. He had dark brown eyes and brown and white fur. He wore a white tunic, gray pants, and reddish colored leather boots. "I'm Shawnren, Iskall's older brother," the Wol'dger said, indicating the deer before wiping his dirty hands on a rag. He shook everyone's hands before returning to the field.

The group of boys rushed Elsa. They appeared to be between seven and twelve years old. They gazed at her with exuberant interest.

"Are you really a *human*?" one boy blurted out.

Elsa lowered herself into a crouch so she was at their level. "Yes, I'm a human," she politely confirmed.

"Wow," they all said in unison.

Hyroc realized this was probably the first time they had seen or been able to talk to a human. This was beyond his comprehension. He had known humans all his life and had never pondered what it would be like not knowing their kind. He figured it would be close to how people reacted to seeing him for the first time.

"Do you really have five toes on your feet?" the youngest boy asked.

"Boys!" Silka called out disapprovingly. "Manners. You don't need to ask our guests those kinds of questions."

"It's okay," Elsa said, smiling. She pulled a foot out of her boot and displayed her toes for an instant before putting the boot back on.

One of the boys nudged another boy with his elbow. "See, I told you it wasn't four like *we have*," he said triumphantly.

"Shut up," the other boy said.

The group noticed Curtis and moved over to him.

"Hyroc, do you only have four toes?" Elsa asked, turning to him.

Hyroc nodded. "Yep," he said. "I can only count to eighteen on my fingers and toes."

"Huh, I didn't know that."

"Wait, you can count?" Donovan chimed in comically.

Elsa and Hyroc regarded him with a flat look. Kit yawned as if offering his criticism of the joke's failed frivolity.

Fenrald helped the limping Wol'dger over to Hyroc.

"Hyroc, I want you to meet my good friend, Unresh," Fenrald said.

Unresh ground his walking stick into the dirt to steady it and held his hand out. "Hyroc, it's nice to meet you," he said as they shook hands. Hyroc nodded. "I can't believe, after all these years, you're standing before me."

"If I had known you were here, I would have come sooner," Hyroc said.

"Well, all that matters is you're here. I was in Forestgold a few days back and heard you got into it with those Ferals from The Pack."

"I was just backing up my friend, Donovan, and I wasn't expecting *all of them* to come after us! Things would have gotten ugly if the guards hadn't stepped in."

"Is it true you summoned a wall of azure fire?"

Hyroc nodded. "Yes, but I wasn't trying to rile up those Ferals."

"So it is true; you are an Anamagi."

"I am."

"I never thought I would again meet another of your blessed kind. Yes, Anamagi are the only things they hate more than us."

"Why do they hate you?"

Unresh stared at him in astonishment.

Fenrald leaned in. "I've got a lot to fill him in on," he said.

"Indeed," Unresh agreed. "Well, no matter. I'm glad to have met you, Hyroc. I hope I'll have more opportunities to do so from now on."

Hyroc nodded his thanks. Unresh turned to return home, but his young sons surged toward Hyroc, obstructing his path.

"Boys, *careful*," he cautioned.

Kit let out a startled chuff at the throng of boys rushing toward him. The boys jolted back with a gasp.

"Kit, be nice," Hyroc said, comforting the big cat with a pat on the head. "We're surrounded by friends." He relaxed. The boys studied the cougar uncertainly for a long moment before tentatively drawing closer to Hyroc but at a slower pace.

"You can make blue fire!" two boys said simultaneously.

"That boy traveling with you said so," a different boy said, pointing to Curtis.

Curtis regarded Hyroc apologetically.

"I can," Hyroc admitted.

"Whoa," all the boys gasped in amazement.

"Show us!" one boy demanded.

"Don't make a nuisance of yourselves," Unresh said disapprovingly.

Hyroc raised a placating hand as he spoke. "It's not a bother."

He created a small blue flame in his palm. The boys exclaimed, staring mesmerized at the flame. Hyroc formed the flame into a sphere and tossed it into the air. It exploded, the conflagration flaring in the shape of a howling wolf's head. Every child in the vicinity laughed, clapping excitedly.

"Do it again!" a boy shouted.

"All right, all right, that's enough, boys," Unresh said. "Go ask your older brother for a ride or something."

The boys sighed disappointedly and walked off.

"Well then, we should get going," Fenrald said. "As always, thank you for your hospitality, my friend."

"You and your nephew are always welcome," Unresh said. "As are any friends of yours."

"Come, my love," Fenrald said affectionately to Elizabeth. "It's time to go."

Elizabeth waved goodbye to the Wol'dger girl, who returned the gesture. The group waved farewell to the Wol'dger family before heading off.

When they arrived back at Fenrald's house, it was nearing dusk. Kit eagerly investigated the area around Fenrald's home. Everyone got to work setting up the tent and readying a place for the group to sleep. After sniffing the perimeter of the structure, Kit suddenly became intrigued by Elizabeth, as if noticing her for the first time, and moved toward her. He halted when Fenrald blocked his path. The Wol'dger gazed at Kit guardedly.

"No, it's all right," Hyroc said reassuringly, moving over to them. "I promise he's not going to hurt her. He knows to be careful around children."

Fenrald's gaze darted between Hyroc and the mountain lion before cautiously stepping aside. Kit studied Fenrald warily before continuing to Elizabeth. He playfully lowered his head and went to rub against the girl but accidentally came too fast, knocking her over with his whiskery face.

This gave Hyroc and Fenrald a start. Mortified, Hyroc rushed forward to pull Kit away from the girl. Fenrald stopped him with an outstretched hand when Elizabeth laughed. Hyroc shot Fenrald a dumbfounded look. Fenrald's eyes were wide with wonder.

"That's the first time I've heard her laugh," Fenrald said, stunned.

"What?" Hyroc said. "Really?"

Fenrald nodded, his eyes fixed on the laughing little girl as Kit gently rubbed his face on her as he joyfully purred.

"How long have you known her?"

"About three years now."

"How did the two of you meet?"

"Supper first," Fenrald urged, a hint of sorrow in his voice. "You and your friends are probably hungry. It's not an enjoyable tale."

Hyroc nodded his understanding, then made a clicking noise with his mouth to call Kit off the girl. Kit sauntered to his side, and Fenrald helped the girl to her feet and caringly dusted her off. The joy faded from the girl's face, returning to an indifferent expression. Hyroc recognized that look. She had gone through something traumatic, something her young mind could not cope with. Up until recently, Curtis had worn a similar expression every day after spiders killed his parents. Fenrald led Elizabeth by the hand into his home.

Fenrald put together a stew pot with pieces of smoked venison and fresh, crisp leeks. He cooked everything on a cooking rack in a small stone hearth. Then he doled out a bowlful for everyone. He didn't have a table big enough to seat everyone, so everyone found a seat inside wherever they could. After tossing a chunk of meat to Kit, Hyroc joined them.

"Is that a rack from a scythe horn?" Donovan pointed to some serrated antlers mounted on one wall.

Fenrald nodded. "Indeed, it is," he said. "I see you've come across one."

Donovan nodded. "What did you use to kill it?"

Fenrald gave him a wiry smirk and raised his hands as he spoke. "My bare hands, or, rather, I should say, my bare paws."

Donovan nodded, impressed.

"I ambushed that buck while I was hunting in animal form. It put up more of a fight than I expected. I would have had its head mounted, but that particular region of its body wasn't in ideal condition if you catch my meaning." Everyone gave him an understanding chuckle. Fenrald spent the rest of the meal regaling Hyroc and his friends with stories of his hunting escapades in the area.

"Thank you for the meal," Elsa said gratefully after everyone had finished eating. "It was excellent."

Fenrald nodded his thanks for the compliment as he collected her bowl. "Okay, Elizabeth, time for bed," he said after he had put everything away. She looked at him unenthusiastically from the open doorway of the house, where she was petting Kit's head.

"Buft Ketty," she said, pointing to Kit.

"Elizabeth," Fenrald said more sternly. "Bed. You can play with Kitty in the morning."

She regarded him with adorable pleading eyes.

Fenrald pointed to her bed in an adjoining room. "Bed. Now. I'm going to –"

"Fenrald," Elsa interjected. "If she wants to stay up, I don't mind watching her."

"You sure?" he said. "I don't want to bother you."

"It's no trouble. I expect there's a lot for you and Hyroc to talk about."

He studied her thoughtfully before answering. "All right. Just keep a close eye on her."

"I promise we will."

"You can come and get me if she starts making a fuss."

Elsa nodded her understanding. "Elizabeth, let's go play with Kitty out here," she said, ushering the little girl away from the door.

Elizabeth's face lit up, and she excitedly complied. Elsa pulled the door partway shut behind her.

"I'm sure you have many questions," Fenrald told Hyroc.

Hyroc nodded.

"And I hope I can answer all of them." He opened a cabinet in one corner of the room, uncorked something, and poured a dark caramel-colored liquid into two waiting cups. "Where should we start? How about I answer your questions first, and then you can answer whatever I have?" He walked over to Hyroc with a cup in each hand, giving him one. "Does that sound fair?"

Hyroc nodded, absentmindedly taking a sip. As soon as the liquid reached the back of his mouth, a hot, burning sensation erupted in his throat and nostrils. Hyroc's eyes flew wide open as he blew out a pain-laden breath and coughed uncontrollably.

Fenrald looked alarmed and embarrassed. "I'm sorry," he said apologetically, snatching the cup from Hyroc's hand. He laughed nervously. "I'm not used to entertaining guests unaccustomed to this drink."

"What in the Shadow was that?" Hyroc choked out, his eyes watering.

"The finest Wulfren scotch. It's got a bite if you're not used to it."

"That's an understatement!"

Fenrald handed him a waterskin, which Hyroc took a swig from and gargled with water. With his mouth full, he looked for something to spit in, but finding nothing and unwilling to soil the floor of his uncle's house with his saliva, he swallowed.

"What were you saying again, uncle, before you tried killing me?" Hyroc joked sarcastically.

Fenrald chuckled. "What do you want me to start with?" he said.

Regaining his composure, Hyroc stared at Fenrald, thinking. "What was my mother like?" he asked. "I want to know about my parents. Can you tell me about them?"

Fenrald nodded. "Your father, Jasok, was my brother," he said. "He was tall; you got your height from him. Also, you got your black and brown coloration from him. He was strong but not quite as thick in the chest as me. He was very caring and gentle, but he was not someone you wanted to get into a dust-up with when he got riled up. He probably pulled me out of half a dozen messes I accidentally got involved in, as any good big brother would.

"Your mother, Shrana, was mostly gray, with strips of brown. She was slender and gorgeous by any standard among us Wol'dgers. She had the same dark blue, sapphire eyes as you, which, I should add, is somewhat rare with our people. She had the same gentle demeanor as your father. It has been a lifetime since I referred to him as someone's father. She was cunningly intelligent and fiercely protective, and even without the Flame Claw, she was someone most men would avoid trifling with. And when you were born, you were the most important thing in her life."

"What animals could they transform into?" Hyroc asked.

"Shrana could turn into an eagle, I think. Or she could have been a hawk. I had trouble telling the difference between the two species. But I will say her ability to fly was immensely convenient. If we ever ran out of anything, she could return from most markets outside the city in less than an hour. However, her having to remain in animal form for several hours afterward was an inconvenience. So, often, a meal was shared outside with her.

"Your father was not blessed with the transformation gift."

"My Guardian mentor mentioned not all of us gain the ability to transform," Hyroc noted.

"It was unfortunate your father did not. I can imagine how much fun we could have had if he had chosen a big cat. But he never let his lack of inheriting the gift get him down. Many others had difficulty dealing with the fact they had been passed over. To him, my ability was just another part of what made me, *me*, and I never held over him his lack thereof."

"Why did you choose a cat?"

Fenrald rubbed his chin. "I respect their strength and power, the clean, fluid way they move, but most of all, I admire their ability to go unnoticed. Cats can sneak up on prey unawares and pounce before the animal knows it is there. Granted, if everything went smoothly, you didn't make a mistake; nothing unfortunate happened, such as a sudden change in the wind or any other bad luck. I also enjoyed hunting, and many aspects of that form complemented the task. While we're on the subject, why did you choose a bear?"

"Well, where I grew up in Arnaira – a town called Forna – I attended a boarding school."

"A boarding school?" Fenrald asked, surprised. "A boarding school in Arnaira, with human children, in Ministry lands?"

Hyroc nodded.

"You have to be toying with me."

"I promise you I am not."

"How was this possibly allowed?"

"A good man named Marcus took me in. He was a retired Light Bringer –someone in The Ministry who researches witchcraft to find ways of countering it. He was one of their best, and even though he was retired, he had a relatively high standing and influence with them. This enabled him to negotiate an exception to keep me alive; otherwise, they would have killed me. He convinced them he could turn me from darkness – because they thought I was a shadow demon – and make me into something to help others."

"So you were an experiment?"

Hyroc waggled his head uncomfortably. "Yes, I guess you could say that, but that was only outwardly how it had appeared to The Ministry. Marcus believed no such thing about me. He treated me well."

"All right, that makes sense. That was just what he had to do to protect you."

"Precisely. Marcus had seen so much bloodshed, pain, and misery caused by witches he had no desire to see another life needlessly lost."

"That's something he and I have in common. I understand that sentiment all too well." Fenrald somberly raised his cup in salute before taking a drink.

"He had also seen too much to be disillusioned by false Ministry dogma and recognized the difference between good and evil. He didn't understand what I was, but he told me when he looked into my eyes, he saw the innocence of a child in them. That could not possibly exist in a creature of darkness.

"But even after he convinced them to let me live, The Ministry watched me like a hawk! If I made one step too far out of line or did anything proving to them I was dangerous, I was done, and Marcus wouldn't be able to stop them. Marcus adopted me and treated me like a son. When I was old enough, I began attending boarding school. It also so happened he was headmaster of the school."

Fenrald laughed, shaking his head. "Very fortuitous. I'm curious: what part did your mother play in all this?"

Hyroc's spirits dropped, and he gazed down at the floor somberly.

"Ah, I see." Fenrald reached over and squeezed Hyroc's shoulder comfortingly. "I had long feared as much."

Hyroc nodded his thanks, lifting his eyes to watch the flames within the fireplace.

"I'm sorry to hear that, my boy. She was a fine woman, and though I didn't know her nearly as well as your father, she will be missed." Fenrald raised his cup to her memory and took a drink."

"My father, does he still live?" Hyroc asked.

Fenrald sighed. "Afraid not, Hyroc."

Hyroc had always wondered if his birth father was out there somewhere, ready to whisk him out of Arnaira, but he had held little hope of this. If his father were still alive, Hyroc figured he would have come looking for him many years ago. But even losing this tiniest bit of hope still hurt.

Hyroc wiped his eyes on the back of his hand. "I think I wandered off topic. I went to the boarding school, and as you can imagine, the other kids and even the teachers treated me as if, at any moment, I would try to tear someone's face off. That made it difficult for me to make friends, but one boy didn't care about my appearance. He became my only friend." He thumbed toward the door. "That is until I met my friends, the Shackletons."

"Yes, I have also discovered in even the worst of conditions, there are always those who stand apart and see you for who you are," Fenrald noted. "That's one of the better qualities of people."

"There just never seems to be enough of them," Hyroc admitted.

Fenrald nodded his agreement. "Unfortunately."

"Then, when I was nine," Hyroc continued. "And…and Marcus… took a fever and died." Hyroc blew out a breath. The conversation had stirred up some emotions about Marcus he had almost forgotten.

"You don't need to tell me any more about it if you don't want to," Fenrald suggested. "I don't want to cause you to think about anything painful merely to satisfy my curiosity."

"No, it's fine, but thanks. So Marcus died, and he was headmaster. And because he was also my father, he was able to protect me from any serious bullying. When he was gone, that ended. Bullies now had access to me, and none of the teachers cared to pay any attention to my situation or stop anyone from having at me. I learned to fight back. The only problem was nobody at the school would tolerate me doing so. I mean, other than June."

"June?" Fenrald asked. "Who is she?"

Hyroc was suddenly struck by the memory of the monster that the man named Keller had turned June into. The Hand of Death she became. Keller had corrupted her with an infusion of shadow demon essence, twisting his beloved aunt into that horrid form. Hyroc was taken back to the memory of her bearing down on him with a dagger pointed at his chest, begging for him to end her suffering. He sharply jerked his head, forcing the memories to the back of his mind, focusing on his good times with her.

"You okay?" Fenrald asked.

"It's nothing," Hyroc said. "June, she was Marcus' sister. After he passed, she looked after me."

"Did she care about you despite–" Fenrald motioned toward his face.

Hyroc nodded. "She was very caring. My appearance didn't matter to her one bit. She was the closest thing to a mother I ever had. She was unable to have children. But I believe she thought of me as one of her own. She did everything she could to help me, but…but it wasn't enough. I know it hurt her to be unable to protect me from the bullying and the enmity of everyone else. There was nothing she could do to stop it. Her words of encouragement were the only thing she could offer me." Hyroc felt his eyes misting and wiped them on his sleeve.

"You chose the bear," Fenrald interjected. "You thought it was big enough to frighten off most would-be attackers and strong enough to fight off anyone who wanted to hurt you. Is that correct?"

"Yes, that's spot on," Hyroc said, taken aback. "I guess my story made that pretty obvious."

"A little," Fenrald agreed.

"I've done a lot of the talking," Hyroc said. "I should take a break and let you tell me your story."

"I think it would be better to give it a rest for the night."

"You do? There's still a lot I haven't told you."

"It's all right. There's plenty of time for us to talk. We don't need to be in a hurry to reveal everything about each other. We can take our time. Besides, it's getting late, and I've got an energetic youngster to put to bed. We must also figure out the sleeping arrangements for you and your friends."

Chapter 13

Wol'dger Walkabout

Hyroc sat on the wooden porch steps at his uncle's home, eating a strip of smoked venison for breakfast with his three friends. It was a crisp, clear morning with infrequent clouds drifting overhead. Fenrald had departed at first light, having errands to attend to in the village and would be back later this afternoon. The only condition he asked was they look after Elizabeth in his stead and take her with them if the four of them went into the village.

"What do the three of you think about my uncle?" Hyroc asked conversationally before tearing off another piece of venison with his sharp Wol'dger teeth.

"He seems nice enough," Elsa said. "From what I've seen of him so far, I don't think we have anything to worry about." She indicated Fenrald's home, where Elizabeth was still sleeping inside. "His taking such good care of Elizabeth, who also happens to be human, seems a good indication."

"Yeah, he seems to be a decent enough person," Donovan agreed. "But I think he's also hiding something."

"I thought the same thing," Curtis noted.

"I get that impression, too," Hyroc said. "But we did just meet him the other day. We have no idea what's happening here or what things of concern are a regular occurrence in this area."

"Discovering the particulars here should be our top priority," Elsa said.

"Well, the best way to discover more about our situation here," Hyroc suggested, "will be to learn it from the Wol'dgers who live in the village. They don't appear outwardly hostile. Yesterday, they were more curious than anything, so I assume they're not a threat."

"Also, don't forget we still need to find work or some way to earn some coin," Elsa said. "It's not an urgent need, but we still have to be on the lookout for opportunities."

"We need to wait until –" tiny footsteps behind Hyroc interrupted his thought.

He turned his head to see Elizabeth shyly peeking out the front door. She clutched a dark brown sackcloth doll with stitched eyes and mouth. Hyroc retrieved a biscuit from his pocket and offered it to her.

"Good morning," he said in greeting. "This is your breakfast."

She looked at him uncertainly, remaining where she was. "Where's Fem?" she asked quietly.

"Fenrald?" Hyroc questioned. "Oh, he went into the village to take care of something. He'll be back later. He told me to give you this roll for your breakfast when you woke up."

She studied him thoughtfully before approaching him to receive the bread he generously offered. Hyroc invitingly patted the porch next to him. She sat, casting an inquisitive gaze at everyone as she ate.

She looked up at Hyroc. "Where's big kitty?"

"Kit? He's…" Hyroc trailed off as he scanned their surroundings. "There, right over there," Hyroc said, pointing at Kit, who lay in the shade of a tree, sleeping with his head on his paws. "You want to see him?"

Elizabeth nodded eagerly. Kit's head popped up when Hyroc called his name. The big cat stood and walked over. He greeted Hyroc with his usual face rub across the hand. "Elizabeth wants to see you," Hyroc said. "You need to be gentle with her. Understood? Nothing rough."

His feline companion regarded him attentively before moving over to Elizabeth. He warily sniffed at her, softly pushing against her hand, wanting to be pet. She obliged his request with a few strokes across his head; Kit sprawled out beside her and rumbled happily.

"That's a good boy."

"We were waiting for her to get up so we could leave," Donovan noted. "So now, we have to interrupt this cute little moment."

"Right," Hyroc agreed.

"I could stay here and watch her and Kit," Elsa suggested. "While the three of you investigate the village."

"I'll also stay," Curtis volunteered.

"Okay, the two of us can look into the village," Hyroc said.

"It's probably better this way," Donovan said. "I wasn't entirely comfortable leaving you and Elizabeth alone here anyway. No offense to your uncle, Hyroc, but we don't know how safe or unsafe this place is."

"Some caution is probably prudent," Hyroc concurred. "Something is less likely to happen with a lightning mage around."

Curtis beamed.

Elsa leaned in and spoke quietly. "I may decide to look at Fenrald's things to try learning something about him." She tapped the side of her nose as she leaned away.

Hyroc gazed at her, considering the idea. "Just don't get caught. I don't want to complicate things even more between my uncle and me if it could be helped. But don't dig too deeply into anything personal."

"I'll be respectful. I just wanted to take a peek is all." She reassuringly patted his shoulder.

Hyroc and Donovan approached the outer edge of the village. Few villagers were out and about, as it was relatively early morning. They caught glimpses of Wol'dgers patrolling the area armed with spears. They wore no armor or uniforms indicative of guards; in fact, they all had various articles of clothing and differing styles. Perhaps they were Glacial militia?

"What should we start with?" Hyroc asked Donovan, turning his attention from the group.

"I didn't think about how early it was," Donovan said. "There's not a lot going on at the moment, so ..."

"A tavern," the two of them said simultaneously.

"Good place to hear what's going on," Hyroc said.

"It's also a good place to hear drunken babble."

Hyroc rolled his eyes and laughed.

They found The Mongrel, a small tavern wedged between two houses on a path branching off the main track. Inside, they found a heavy-set male Wol'dger with mostly black fur wearing a brown short-sleeved tunic behind a counter cleaning the inside of a mug with a rag. Another male with dark brown fur sat at a table, resting his clawed hand against a mug as he read a piece of parchment, and a white-brown-speckled female smoked a pipe in the corner.

The heavyset Wol'dger shot them a quizzical look. "What can I get for you two this fine morning?" he jovially greeted them in a rumbling voice reminiscent of a growling bear. This bearish quality of his tone sounded both gentle and threatening. He radiated an aura that strangely instilled security within his establishment and warned against getting on his bad side. He narrowed his hazel eyes; his gaze darted between Donovan and Hyroc. "Hey, aren't you that Anamagi traveling with those humans who came through yesterday?" His question drew the intrigue of the other patrons.

"That I am," Hyroc said, taken aback. He had only arrived yesterday, and word of him had already percolated through the village. It felt remarkable to him the villagers were enthralled by his presence and did not want to be rid of him for fear of him raining cataclysm down upon them.

"If I may ask, can you show me the azure?"

Hyroc lifted his hand and lit a blue flame in it.

The Wol'dger smiled in awe. "Well, I'll be, it is true."

Hyroc extinguished the flames.

The female Wol'dger came over and shook his hand. "It's a pleasure to meet you," she said. "May I have your name?"

"Hyroc."

"I'm Shile. You made my day with this meeting, Hyroc."

"This is fantastic news," the male patron said, shaking Hyroc's hand. "I didn't think there were any of you left."

"Whatever you and your friend want, it's on the house. The name's Halvic." Hyroc and Donovan introduced themselves. "Great to make your acquaintances."

"Yours as well," Hyroc said. He shot Donovan an enticed look at Halvic's free drink offer. "We'll take whatever's on tap as long as it's nothing too strong this early in the morning."

"Coming right up." He filled two mugs from a keg behind the counter and handed them to Hyroc and Donovan. "Enjoy."

Hyroc took a swig and nodded his satisfaction before speaking. "With us being newcomers here, your tavern seemed the best place to start learning more about the village."

"Ah," Halvic said, comprehending. He leaned on the counter, bracing thick, hairy arms against it. "What would you like to know?"

"What is this village? Why did you choose to build it in Mastgar?"

"Well, we wouldn't have lasted long if we had chosen the east now, would we," Halvic said sarcastically. Hyroc and Donovan cracked a gallows smile before taking a drink. "There wasn't an awful lot of what you would consider as *choosing* involved in our decision to build our village here. It was the best we were offered and the most expedient location."

Hyroc cocked an eyebrow. "This place was forced upon you by Mastgar?"

"In a fashion, yes."

"Then, why not look for a better place?"

Halvic looked somewhat perplexed. "We didn't have many good choices after we were forced out of Wulfren...."

"Hold on," Hyroc interrupted. "Forced out of Wulfren? Why were you forced out?"

His eyes widened with disbelief. "You truly *don't know*?"

"I don't know *what*? Why is everyone here vexed by me not knowing this?"

Halvic stood straight and dismissively pushed his hands toward Hyroc, urging him to stop speaking about it. His reassuring manner was interrupted by apprehension. "It would be best if your uncle explained this rather than I."

Hyroc looked at him, perplexed. "What?"

"Ask me about this no more," Halvic said, almost pleading. He looked at the tavern's front door, checking to make sure no one unwanted overheard him. "Ask me anything but *that*, and I promise I will answer as best as I can."

"I wasn't trying to cause any trouble."

Hyroc and Donovan exchanged a quick, baffled glance. Halvic's reaction was disconcerting. He acted concerned that the wrong person would hear him talking about it to Hyroc, and there might be repercussions. If everyone knew about this *thing* that happened, why did his uncle have to be the one to tell it to him? But it seemed best to avoid pushing for an explanation. He would refrain from asking about it though he would pose the question to Fenrald.

"Getting back to my friend and me being new here," Hyroc said, slightly irritated. "Do you know what there is to do around here, what kind of work we might find, and those types of things?"

Halvic thoughtfully rubbed his furry chin. "There are good places for trapping all over here, hunting, too. There's fishing, and timber for building is always needed. If you're strong and sound with an ax, you could make some good Coin. You may have trouble finding payment since our little community isn't blessed with riches." Halvic glanced down at the sword on Hyroc's hip and Donovan's spear, which rested against the counter. "If you're skilled with a blade, there's always something to be had fighting Fer ..." He abruptly stopped talking. "It would be better if I didn't finish that sentence. Come find me after talking with your uncle if you want to know the rest."

Hyroc blew out an annoyed sigh. His patience with the secrecy of *that event*, which he was ignorant of, was wearing thin. It was becoming increasingly difficult for him to keep his frustration from flying out his mouth.

"What you find to do around here may also depend on your animal form," Halvic continued. "If you have a bird, plenty of things need to be delivered here and there, and I hear it's well worth it. But that's about all I can think of." He indicated Hyroc. "Oh, and that azure Anamagi flame magic of yours; I imagine it has many uses."

"I'll keep that in mind," Hyroc said. "Thank you for the ale and your time."

Halvic nodded his acknowledgment. "Glad I could be of service."

Hyroc and Donovan turned to leave.

"One last thing," Halvic called to them. "When you're outside the village, it's best not to let your guard down. Animals are not the only things stalking these woods, especially to the northeast."

"I will. I appreciate the warning."

They stepped out of the tavern into the cool morning air, the door shutting behind them.

"Well, that was odd," Donovan said.

"Very odd," Hyroc agreed.

"The reluctance everyone has about discussing that *thing* with you is unnerving."

"I know. What on earth happened to these people?"

"Whatever it is, your uncle must tell us as soon as possible. I don't want us to get caught flat-footed again after what happened with that witch in Elswood and that blood werewolf commanded to destroy our village."

"I agree. We don't want a repeat of *that*."

Donovan pointed a thumb toward the tavern. "And what was that warning the bartender gave us just now as we walked out the door? What's around here and to the northeast we need to watch out for?"

"I bet it has something to do with those crazy Ferals."

"Maybe," Donovan agreed. "But it can't be nearly as bad as that mad Watcher tree, and those constructs made out of forest refuse, constantly trying to dismember us. Can it?"

Hyroc shrugged. "I don't think so. But don't say that too loudly and jinx it. Let's just be careful around here."

"Yes, good idea."

"Where to now?"

Donovan glanced around. "Why don't we go and check out the market to see what everyone is selling?" he said, pointing.

Hyroc nodded.

Activity in the village was slowly increasing, but there still weren't many bodies walking around on either two legs or four. Hyroc and Donovan found a stand selling pelts. They were familiar with most of the animals through trapping and hunting, but neither recognized a few.

"What's this?" Hyroc asked, pointing to one of the unknown pelts. It was rough and scaly.

"Frost snake," responded a dark brown female Wol'dger who wore a hat made from the pelt of a red fox; a green leather jerkin, and brown pants. Hyroc and Donovan cocked an eyebrow.

"Did you say 'frost snake?'"

She nodded. "Indeed, I did. They are plentiful northward in Wulfren but rarer around here. They are most active in winter but less so during summer. In the summer, they congregate near pools of water, where it's cool. I found this one resting beside a lake to the west. But you have to be careful around them; they can spit icicles, and they are sharp. I used a wooden shield to take the brunt of the icicles as I came at it. With ice shattering against my shield, I moved forward until I was close enough to stick it with my knife. Its skin will fetch a kingly sum. Are either of you interested?"

Hyroc and Donovan waved a dismissive hand.

The Wol'dger was crestfallen with their response.

"We absolutely couldn't afford it," Donovan said.

She nodded her understanding.

"That's interesting," Donovan said as they walked away. "A snake that prefers the cold over warmth. I guess nothing at this point should surprise me."

"Well, my people are supposed to be incredible hunters," Hyroc said. "So I guess going after icicle-spitting snake tracks."

"No kidding," Donovan agreed. "I don't think I would have done that."

"You helped kill a Werewolf; a frost snake, by comparison, should be nothing."

Donovan laughed. "True. That's very true. But I swear, if I find out there are dragons around here, I'm going to lose my mind!"

"I make no promises," Hyroc said smugly with a smile.

They moved from the Wol'dger toward another selling pelts. On their way over, Hyroc noticed a deer with pelts tied to its back. It was the same deer form Wol'dger they had met yesterday when they went to get Elizabeth. The Wol'dger's older brother, Shawnren, was haggling the merchant's price for their goods.

"Isn't that the Wol'dger we saw plowing the field yesterday?" Donovan asked.

"I believe so," Hyroc answered. "Why don't you see what that merchant offers while I say hello? I want to ask him something."

Donovan nodded, and they separated.

"Hello there," Hyroc said conversationally.

The deer popped his head up and said, "Hello."

"You're Iskall, right?"

"I am."

"I'm still trying to learn everyone's names; forgive me if I get yours wrong."

"It's okay if you do."

Hyroc nodded his appreciation. "This is your animal form. I'm curious to know what made you choose –"

"I'd stay away from him," a voice warned.

Hyroc turned to see two Wol'dger boys close to his age standing nearby.

"You don't want him to muddy your clothes," the other boy scoffed.

Hyroc saw Iskall's head droop, and dejection seeped into his eyes. It was a feeling Hyroc was well acquainted with. It was anticipating something unpleasant and knowing all you could do was withstand it and wait for it to disappear. Those two boys were bullies. Based on Iskall's behavior, this was not the first time. Hyroc felt his face warm. Unlike his time at the Forna boarding school and Elswood, he *could* do something about it.

"What's that supposed to mean?" Hyroc said, doing his best to maintain a level tone. To correctly resolve the situation, he needed to figure out what kind of bullying he was dealing with before acting. Was it physical bullying, or did it simply involve words?

The first boy to speak indicated Iskall. "You're new here, so I should tell you you're better off not talking to a *work mule*. He even plows fields. Can you believe that? A Wol'dger using their choice of animal form to become a *plow horse*! He's a disgrace."

"A complete disgrace," the second boy added. "What a waste."

"What animal did you choose?"

The first boy proudly puffed out his chest. "I chose a bear! A real animal, not a useless deer."

"Deer are only good for other animals to eat," the second boy said.

"Yeah, I'm a bear. Bears eat deer. You shouldn't waste your time on *him*."

"That's enough of that," Hyroc said.

The two boys were surprised by his words.

"It's no better than what he deserves for squandering his choice," the first boy said indignantly.

"I don't care what he deserves," Hyroc said coolly. "He doesn't deserve hurtful words – not around me."

The first boy stepped forward. Hyroc made a fist so the boy could see it and raised it partway, indicating how far he would go on this. This gave the boy pause. He studied Hyroc's fist briefly before looking back at his face.

"Let's go," the second boy said to the first, pulling his shoulder. "I hear he's an Anamagi."

"Yeah, let him waste his time with the *workhorse*. We've got better things to do."

The boys departed.

"You made them leave?" Iskall said, seeming grateful yet bemused. "Thank you."

"You're welcome," Hyroc said.

"But why?"

Hyroc looked astonished. "What do you mean, why?" The reason seemed blatantly obvious.

"It's just, apart from my big brother and my family, no one's ever stepped in on my behalf to stop me being made fun of. Don't you think my choosing a deer makes me a laughingstock? Everyone thinks it has hardly any uses, and it's demeaning for me to be used as a work animal."

"No, I don't," Hyroc said, baffled. "When choosing your animal form at the Tree of Memories, you're supposed to go with whichever one feels right. That's what my Guardian told me. Isn't that what you did?"

"Yes. This is the form that felt right."

"I, too, was presented with the option of a stag. It was appealing, but that's not what I chose. It wasn't because I was embarrassed by the idea of becoming a stag, it was just not what I wanted. Unless there's something seriously different about that animal I don't understand?"

Iskall appeared more interested. "I don't think there's anything much different about it than the other animals. But when it comes to the other forms, such as a bear or cat, what use in a fight is a deer?"

"Honestly, I've never contemplated that, but your antlers come to mind." Hyroc held his hand out, indicating he wanted to touch Iskall's horns. "Let me feel them." Iskall obligingly lowered his head. Hyroc rubbed a thumb across the end of one antler. "That feels fairly sharp, and they seem to have a good shape for ramming. If you could build up some speed, they could seriously hurt anything you hit. Am I right in assuming the Guardian that trained you instructed you on how to use them?"

Iskall nodded. "He did some, though he only showed me how they were used in sparring with another buck. His instructions never involved using them in a life or death fight."

"That could have been because it was something you needed to learn on your own. My Guardian indicated some things are best taught in that manner. I think, with practice, you would be proficient at it."

"Apart from my training, I guess I really haven't pushed myself much to learn how to use them."

"I'm sure you can do it."

"But beyond my headgear, this form can't have many uses."

"I've hunted deer for years and missed my fair share of them. I've seen how swiftly and gracefully they can move. They are swift runners, capable of quickly covering significant distances. If there's a decent-sized patch of open ground, you could get a good pace going. You are a lot more than a plow horse. If you think about it, you're more like a racehorse."

"Racehorse?" Iskall said, excitedly testing the feel of the word in his mouth. "But a racehorse also with horns."

"Exactly."

"What animal did you choose, if you don't mind my asking?"

"A bear."

"Why?"

"Well, believe it or not, I also had a problem with bullies." Iskall was instantly engrossed at hearing this. "The only difference, unless I'm assuming incorrectly, is that mine went further than just using words. I chose the bear because they are big, mean, brutish animals. I thought no one would ever bother me again if I were big, strong, and tough enough. And I was partially correct in that regard. But I also learned being big and brutish isn't necessarily bad. Those brutish qualities can be used to protect others. Protecting those weaker than yourself is one of the most noble causes."

"Do you think I could use my form to protect others?"

"Of course, you could. Though probably not in the same manner as I would in bear form, I'm certain you could do it."

"Thank you."

Hyroc patted him on his broad shoulder. "You don't need to thank me for standing up for you," he said.

Donovan moved away from the merchant to join them.

"See anything?" Hyroc asked.

Donovan shook his head. "Nah," he said. "They're selling more of the same: fox pelts, bear pelts, and mink." He turned his attention to Iskall. "Hello again."

"Hello," Iskall responded.

"All right, let's keep going," Hyroc said. "Until next time, Iskall."

Iskall nodded a horned farewell.

Donovan and Hyroc continued further into the village. The smell of fresh bread drew them to a bakery. The baker was a male Wol'dger with light brown and black fur. He wore a sleeveless tunic and a white apron lightly dusted with flour. Talking with the man was a young female, Wol'dger Hyroc's age, who had dark brown fur and was wearing a dark blue dress with a fluffy white liner.

"Oh, excuse me," she said, politely making way for Hyroc when she noticed him reading a sign hanging from the ceiling in front of her, listing the bakery's available products.

Hyroc and Donovan nodded their thanks.

"You must be the newcomer, the Anamagi."

"That I am," Hyroc said. He introduced himself and Donovan.

Donovan reached forward and shook her hand.

After shaking it, she made a slight curtsy. "And I'm Freija."

"Nice to meet you."

As Hyroc finished speaking, he feelt strange. His face warmed, and his heart beat faster.

"How do you find our village, Hyroc and Donovan?"

"This is my first Wol'dger village," Donovan said. "But so far, I think this is a fine place."

She nodded happily.

"I agree," Hyroc said hastily. "This be a good bear nest – I mean, a good place." He was having a tough time composing his words, and he could feel them coming out of his mouth all jumbled up. His face warmed more, and his heart thumped even quicker in his chest. Freija pushed the back of her wrist against her mouth and laughed. This made Hyroc feel like his face was about to burst into flames. He was overcome with the urge to flee and rushed out of the bakery. Rounding the corner of the closest building, he put it between him and the bakery, resting his back against it. He breathed heavily. What was going on with him? Why couldn't he seem to speak? Then it dawned on him. She was a witch! Though she appeared to have no interest in harming him or Donovan, she must have been trying to cast a charm on him. That was the only thing that made any sense. The use of witchcraft must not have any taboos associated with it among his people. Maybe to them, there's nothing wrong with using it. They could treat it the same as any other school of magic. *Did his people even have mages*, he wondered? What if they didn't even know magic existed? How could they recognize it if they were oblivious to it?

"Are you okay?" Donovan said as he caught back up to Hyroc. "Why did you run out of the bakery?"

Hyroc urgently waved him closer. With a confused expression, Donovan did as instructed. Hyroc peeked toward the bakery, covertly pointing at it.

"That girl in there; I think she's a witch," he said.

Donovan cocked an eyebrow. “She is?” He leaned forward to get a better look. “How can you tell?”

“I started feeling odd when she talked to us. She must have been trying to put an enchantment on me.”

Donovan looked from Hyroc to the bakery and back again. He narrowed his eyes as if concentrating on a sudden idea. A foxish grin spread across his face.

“What? Why are you smiling?” Hyroc asked uncertainly.

“I don’t think she’s a witch,” Donovan said smugly. He lightly swatted Hyroc’s shoulder. “You like her,” he said.

Hyroc looked gobsmacked. “What. No. Of course not! I know more about spotting a witch than you do. I’m telling you, she is a *witch*.”

“No, she’s not,” Donovan teased. He pointed an accusatory finger at him. “You like her. You’re in trouble now, my friend.”

“That’s ridiculous. *I met her two minutes ago*!”

“Doesn’t matter.”

“And how do you know this anyway? I’ve never seen you with a girl!”

He sniffed knowingly. “Well, I may or may not have had a girlfriend in Elswood. Just because you never saw it doesn’t mean it didn’t happen.”

“What? You had a girlfriend in Elswood?” He shook his head dismissively. “No, you’re making stuff up.”

Donovan shot him a stoic look.

“WHAT?”

Donovan nodded triumphantly.

Hyroc’s mouth fell partly open. “I can’t believe it; I never noticed.”

“Do you think I would lie to you?”

Hyroc nodded. “Yeah, you would.”

Donovan looked devilishly amused. “Go talk to her.” He playfully grabbed Hyroc, trying to force him closer to the bakery.

Hyroc twisted out of his grip and shoved Donovan away. “You’re such a jerk,” he said jokingly. He softly punched Donovan in the shoulder, garnering a laugh from his friend. “I’m not going over there, all right?”

"Okay, fine," Donovan conceded. "You're no fun."

"I could turn into a bear; then you'll see how much fun I can be."

"Uh-huh, Grumpy Bear is unamused."

"And don't you forget it."

The shadow of a large bird passed over them. Hyroc looked up to see the broad wings and talons of a bird of prey. It was too large to be one of the native species. It had to be a Wol'dger in bird form. The bird was low, indicating it was coming in for a landing. This piqued Hyroc's interest. He was curious to see how they handled this delicate procedure.

They followed the bird's direction, arriving at a small clearing. The Wol'dger had already transformed into their natural form and was talking to another Wol'dger on the ground. Behind the Wol'dger was a species of tree Hyroc didn't recognize. It was tall and had a thick trunk with dirt-colored bark. Its branches were wider than the trees in the surrounding forest. There was a considerable gap between each limb. The rungs of a ladder were nailed into the trunk, going up to a specific branch. The tree's shape was intended to give bird-form-Wol'dgers a safe perch to land on free of obstacles during their approach.

When he returned his attention to the Wol'dgers, he noticed one was Fenrald. The bird-Wol'dger pulled a scroll from a tube on his leg and handed it to Fenrald. They conversed a moment longer before the bird-Wol'dger held out a coin sack. Fenrald accepted it, but from his body posture, Hyroc could tell he was unhappy to take it. The Wol'dger clapped a comforting hand on his shoulder. With a nod, the bird-Wol'dger headed in Hyroc's direction to the trail leading to the village. He moved out briskly, seemingly unaware Hyroc and Donovan were standing there.

As Hyroc and Donovan headed over, Fenrald acted even more aggravated. Still not noticing them, he leaned against the nearest tree with the arm that held the coin sack curved over his head, touching the trunk. He seemed grieved by whatever the other Wol'dger had said.

"Fenrald?" Hyroc called out.

Fenrald turned, but his eyes were distant. Something weighed heavily on his mind.

"Uncle, is everything okay?"

An awkwardly long silence passed between them.

"You're a bear, correct?" Fenrald asked. "That's your animal form?"

"It is."

Fenrald nodded, bouncing the coin sack up and down in his hand. He was considering something. "There's something important I need to ask for your help with. I think it's time you learned of our peril here."

Chapter 14
Ferals

Hyroc used his Flame Claw to ignite a blaze in the firepit outside the house of Fenrald. His uncle hadn't talked to Hyroc or Donovan since they left the clearing where they saw the bird-Wol'dger. The whole time, he seemed preoccupied with something. What was this peril he mentioned? The village appeared peaceful and idyllic. What could it be?

"Uncle, what do you need to tell me?" Hyroc said, growing impatient as Fenrald stoked the fire with a stick.

Fenrald spoke, staring into the growing flames. "This is a complicated matter," he said. "There are certain things I must tell you first. This will also serve your friends if they intend to make a home in Mastgar. You remember what I told you about the Ferals and why their animal marks are red?"

"You said they were red because they didn't complete their animal form training."

"There's a bit more to it. Why they didn't complete their training is key. They didn't simply fail to complete it; they refused to do it entirely."

"Refused? Why would they refuse? Don't they understand they will become dangerous to everyone around them if they don't know how to cope with the tendencies of their animal form? Not to mention, they will act like the animal they chose."

"They understand this perfectly, but it isn't viewed as a bad thing. They desire for that very thing to happen. They think of succumbing to the tendencies of their animal form as strength."

"What madness makes them think that?" Hyroc said, befuddled.

"That's why that group of Wol'dgers we ran into in town were so unreasonably aggressive," Donovan interjected.

Fenrald nodded. "Succumbing to their animal form tendencies makes them especially quarrelsome. They are prone to acts of incredible violence over even the slightest provocation. Something as simple as accidentally bumping into one can have deadly consequences. That's why they are called Ferals. They are quite literally Feral Wol'dgers. They also don't care too much for humans."

"If they dislike humans, then why reside in a human kingdom where humans live?" Hyroc asked.

"Because we're here, or instead because we're Guidance Wol'dgers. Guidance refers to us obeying the teachings of the Guardians, or in other words, we are guided by the instructions they laid down for us. Because of our dedication, we are the sworn enemy of the Ferals. They have vowed our destruction. But to understand why, we must go back in history to when the Wol'dger curse struck Wulfren. Hyroc, I assume you have informed your friends about the events surrounding the Wol'dger curse?"

"Yes, sir, he has," Elsa confirmed.

Fenrald nodded. "Many Wol'dgers saw the curse as punishment for their misdeeds," he continued. "They stepped from the disobedient path that had led to our cursing, but some viewed their scourge as a gift. They realized this affliction increased their capabilities, giving them an advantage over their human form. We Wol'dgers have superior night vision, a better sense of smell, extra resistance to the cold, a slight increase in strength, and other such improvements. They wished to utilize their newfound edge to continue plundering from those they saw as weaker than themselves. But when they proposed this, those who saw it as a curse rejected it outright, fearing even further repercussions from the Guardians if they pursued this ill-advised proposition. This created a schism between the two sides. But those who saw it as a malady far outnumbered those who perceived to utilize it. Those in the minority sequestered themselves in fringe communities where they could hide themselves and practice and experiment with their ideology. This schism culminated with the emergence of Guidance and Feral Wol'dger centuries later."

"So the Ferals became the Wol'dger equivalent of a witch in Arnaira," Elsa said. "The real ones, not just people who simply use magic."

Fenrald nodded. "Yes, I believe that gets the point across. Now we arrive at something closer," he continued. "About twenty years ago, there was a renewed fervor toward considering the curse as a gift. But unlike before, the ideological schism leaned heavily in favor of the Ferals. At this time, the taboo of this view had waned. Many Wol'dgers thought the beliefs of the Ferals were nothing more than a harmless curiosity. The Ferals also held a deep disdain for the Guardians. They saw all the past actions taken by the Guardians as an attempt to maintain control over all Wol'dgers. In the minds of the Ferals, the Guardian Wearla gave them the gift of transformation during the first North Lander invasion because defeating them served their agenda. But, according to the Ferals, after the North Lander threat was ended and more Guardians arrived to teach about the transformation gift, this was done merely to advance this perceived control over them. Thus, this gift was established as part of a secret Guardian scheme. Similarly, when Wearla cursed us, that, too, was a means of controlling us, a punishment that rebuked us for behavior the Guardians disapproved of. But the Ferals believe they found a way to circumvent these suspected Guardian control methods."

"How can they believe something so ridiculous?" Hyroc asked. "Especially when it comes to the animal form. How can they think a Guardian instructing them on the importance of coping with the tendencies of whatever animal they chose is a method of control? Those tendencies will overcome you if you don't learn how to deal with them. I felt only the slightest influence of those tendencies when I received the transformation gift. And the mere notion of the brutal creature they would turn me into scared the hell out of me. I came face-to-face with that *bear* and wanted absolutely no part."

"Because they think even those precautionary instructions are a method of control," Fenrald continued. "To them, everything the Guardians have ever said or taught is a lie. They do not believe what those tendencies will do to them. They think the whole idea is a Guardian fabrication. The red animal mark they receive from refusing the animal form training is meant to warn others they are dangerous."

"I can't comprehend how anyone could think what the Guardians say is a lie," Hyroc said.

"Trying to understand their way of thinking is no easy task," Fenrald agreed. "I know from much experience. Even after years, I do not fully understand them. But the Ferals' disbelief toward anything Guardian-related caused another serious problem for the Anamagi. Since the Anamagi had never strayed from the teachings or instructions of the Guardians and willingly chose to be affected by the Wol'dger curse, they were unfavorably looked upon by the Ferals. They saw them as quislings, traitors loyal to the Guardians solely because they desired power over their fellow Wulfreners. The Anamagi accepting the Sentinel Flame, or Flame Claw, was used as further evidence against them. The Ferals hated them. However, the fact the Anamagi possessed Guardian powers through the Flame Claw kept the Ferals at bay. But the Ferals knew they could overcome this advantage if they persuaded enough Wol'dgers to side with them to oppose the Anamagi. Even as powerful as the Flame Claw made the Anamagi, the Ferals knew they could balance the odds if they gathered enough support. They could overwhelm the Anamagi if they threw enough bodies at them. They would deplete their individual Quintessence reserves with a ceaseless flow of attackers. But the grievous losses they would incur from such a head-on assault made them hesitant. This staved off their attack for a time. Then a Wol'dger named Eagle arose as their leader."

"Eagle?" Hyroc questioned. "I've heard that name before. The dying words of a witch we killed in Elswood referred to someone named Eagle."

Fenrald nodded. "I've reviled him for nigh twenty years. He's a ruthless, cunning, and honorless fiend." Fenrald indicated his eye patch. "He took my eye." Fenrald smiled remorselessly. "But I returned the favor by taking his. He bears four scars across his face and one eye. I gave him those *souvenirs* with my own claws in cat form. I was aiming for more permanent harm if you catch my meaning.

"Eagle stoked the fires of rebellion and stirred up trouble for the Anamagi anywhere he could. What drove him was a deep loathing he held toward the Guardians. He did not receive the transformation gift and felt it was a betrayal from the Guardians. This made him want to destroy everything they had influenced, especially the Anamagi. He saw the Anamagi as a threat to the freedom of all Wol'dgers, and this obstacle needed to be removed. And one day, he made his move.

"Without warning, he and the Ferals struck. Their first target in our city of Malrand was the Anamagi sanctuary. After they killed all at the sanctuary, they swept through the rest of the city, looking for any remaining Anamagi and those still loyal to their ways. The Ferals and their supporters far outnumbered the loyal Wol'dgers, making any meaningful resistance impossible. Fleeing the city was their only chance of survival.

"The sanctuary got word to our family, me, and others before it fell. As discreetly as they could, they made for the city gates. A small number of loyal guards assisted in the escape." Fenrald paused, his expression turning distant and sorrowful. "I wish I could tell you they made a successful and daring escape, but that's not what happened. The Ferals found them out. I don't know what happened. Perhaps the Ferals had gotten word from one of their supporters, or a Feral lookout in bird form flying above the city saw them? But it doesn't matter; knowing the answer doesn't change anything. The Ferals surrounded them just outside the city gates. There was no hope of escape. All of them fought valiantly though they knew their doom was assured. You and your mother were only saved by her bird form."

"No, only I was," Hyroc noted gloomily. "Marcus found me in her arms, but she was already dead. She had a fatal arrow wound in her side."

"Protecting you was all that mattered to her," Fenral said."Even more than life itself."

Hyroc wiped away a tear. "Why weren't you with them?" he asked, sharper than he had intended, sounding accusatory.

Fenrald reached up, absentmindedly grasping a small heart-shaped necklace with a tiny green emerald set in the center, which hung around his neck. He studied Hyroc thoughtfully. "I was away. I was with… someone. They had already left when I realized how dire the situation was. I intended to catch up to them, but I was too late. I came upon them after – after *it* was finished. I buried my brother, your father, and the rest of our family there."

"Then, you swore to avenge them," Hyroc added. Fenrald gazed at him, mystified, wondering how he could have known that. "I saw you in a vision the Tree of Memories showed me when I chose my bear form."

"I had heard stories of it doing such things, but I had never met anyone who had experienced a vision from it. Yes, that's when I vowed to avenge them. From there, I set out to find you and your mother. I thought the best way to honor my brother was for me to ensure the two of you were taken care of. I followed your trails for days but lost you in the southern mountains. And in my cat form, I could go no further without the proficiency a wolf or bear has with tracking by scent.

"When the two of you were lost to me, I turned my attention to hunting down the Ferals. An ironic twist of fate aided me. After purging the Anamagi from the city, support for Eagle and the Ferals abated. Many of those who had initially supported their efforts were under the impression that *casting off the shackles of the Anamagi* entailed less bloodshed and would not spread to non-Anamagi Wol'dgers. They were deluded by the idea of a more peaceful affair." He laughed humorlessly. "Or they had gotten a real taste of how inhumanly vicious a red-marked Feral could be. Eagle and his followers were exiled and chased out of the kingdom. I have been fighting him and his followers ever since.

"Slowly, the surviving loyal Wol'dgers found sanctuary in this village. Eventually, I found my way here as well. But so, too, did the Ferals. Unbeknownst to the survivors here, they had established their base to the north. Whether its proximity to us was intentional or an unfortunate coincidence, we do not know.

"But now we arrive at the current dilemma. While you were in Forestgold, did you happen to notice all the Mastgarien soldiers?"

Hyroc nodded. "Yes," he said. "They came to our rescue when we angered the Ferals."

"And just so you know," Donovan added. "I was not expecting the entire group to want to rip our faces off."

"You're not the first to have made that mistake, but you were lucky it didn't go any farther. Well, the size of the garrison there has increased lately. And there is a grave reason for this. You see, the Mastgar royal court has been gracious enough to let us settle the area here, and beyond us paying a tax to them, they have left us in peace. But that peace is predicated upon us not becoming a thorn in the side of or otherwise causing problems for the kingdom. The Ferals have disrupted this arrangement ever since they arrived. There have been kidnappings plaguing the areas to the south and west, and Ferals are responsible."

"I don't understand," Hyroc said. "What's to be gained by them kidnapping people?"

"Because they're slavers."

Everyone shot Fenrald an abhorrent look.

"Slavers?" Hyroc said in disbelief. "They're kidnapping people and turning them into slaves!"

"I'm afraid so. But it gets worse still."

"Worse?" Elsa interjected in disbelief. "*How can it get worse than that*?"

"The ones being kidnapped are children."

Elsa gaped. "Oh, wow, it did get worse."

"What reason do they have for doing that?" Donovan asked.

"We believe they're taking children to turn them into servants. It's much easier to break children and train them for whatever task you want them to do than, say, an adult. Adults are bigger, stronger, and more resilient, making things much more challenging for the Ferals. To say nothing of the added headache of keeping them under control. The tendencies to dominate the weak all predatory animal forms exert upon those using them are likely, in part, to blame for this callous behavior, but there's another element. Remember what I said about the advantages a Wol'dger has over a human. Granted, our benefits are minor, but Ferals think humans are inferior. Deceived by their believed superiority, it's easy for them to justify their kidnappings. Some may even deem their actions as a benefit to those they are enslaving, thinking such actions are elevating their victims.

"Returning to the Mastgar soldiers, they are being moved to Forestgold because the Crown's patience is running lethally thin."

"And they're preparing to cast every Wol'dger out of their kingdom," Hyroc speculated.

Fenrald nodded unhappily. "Yes. They'll cast out any Wol'dger they find, regardless of their ideology. And it won't be through asking *politely,* either. You see, the royal court in this kingdom does not understand the feud between our two sides. We've only been here for a few years, so it's far too short a time for Mastgar to acquire much knowledge about us. To them, a Wol'dger is a Wol'dger. They have not acquired any distinction between Ferals and Glacials. We're all the same and nothing but trouble. Trouble that needs to be done away with.

"But I've managed to maintain a tenuous armistice. I am known among the royal court through years of services rendered, which has earned me a certain amount of respect. My word carries weight among them. I have a reputation for resolving these particular situations. So long as I'm able to return the kidnapped children, no action is taken against us."

"That's what the sack you received from that Wol'dger was," Hyroc realized. "It was a coin purse, payment to help you facilitate rescuing the kidnapped children."

Fenrald nodded. "Right, you are. He is our envoy to the royal court, ensuring communication between us and them continues uninterrupted. So long as they're talking to us, any action against us is unlikely."

"So all we have to do is rescue those children, and everything will be fine."

Fenrald's expression darkened. "In practice, yes, but the execution has been more challenging. Rescuing them is no simple matter. The slaver caravans are always guarded. I've managed to poach a caravan from the Ferals here and there, but more often than not, the guards are too many for me to overcome, and all I can do is watch them pass me by. And my efforts are not nearly enough to buy the village any meaningful amount of time. I'm making us die slower but die nonetheless." His expression turned hopeful. "But that's where you and your friends will make a difference. Working together enough of us can tip the odds in our favor."

"If the slavers outnumber you, why don't you ask the other villagers for help?"

Fenrald's hopeful expression faded. "Because I can't. You know how I was with someone when your parents and the rest of my family fled the city. Not everyone in the village is accepting of my story that day. They are suspicious about my actions."

"They think you were involved."

Fenrald nodded.

Hyroc indicated himself and his friends: "We've had our own experience with distrustfulness. In Elswood – the village the four of us lived in – there was a situation where giant spiders killed their parents. Rumors and distrust permanently stained us because I succeeded only in saving my friends and not their parents."

"Everyone in the village thought we were all involved in some ridiculous secret plot to murder our parents," Elsa added. "They also didn't believe us about the spiders, which didn't help, either."

"We're no stranger to what distrust can make people do," Hyroc added.

"You have my sympathy," Fenrald said. "I'm sorry you had to go through that." Fenrald resumed his explanation after a brief respectful pause. "And because of their suspicion, it's hard for me to convince anyone to help. Or on the rare occasion I get someone to help, it doesn't happen often enough to make a difference."

"But it's clearly in their best interests," Hyroc said, perplexed. "If this kidnapping situation continues, they'll be cast out of Mastgar."

"It's mainly due to them thinking I'm exaggerating the danger or seriously misunderstanding the situation. They believe the royal court understands this village has nothing to do with the kidnappings. With this lack of involvement, they think there is no threat to them and they are seen as innocent. Then, to further enforce this fallacy, the villagers are emphatically trying to avoid any involvement whatsoever with the Ferals. This even includes rescuing those kidnapped children. But, in actuality, they are hastening their own demise.

"I also suspect they do not fully grasp how we Wol'dgers are seen. They have spent too much time with others of their kin and not enough time with humans. They've lost their perspective on this matter. Humans –" he indicated Elsa, Donovan, and Curtis "– I'm excluding you three; I'm positive what I'm about to say does not apply to any of you, so please don't take this personally. Humans can be very accepting, but our appearance puts them on edge. They see us as some strange creature that will try eating them. But once this misconception is dispelled, they learn we can peacefully coexist. We have to demonstrate we are not dangerous. Once this is done, they will generally be civil to us. But they do not tolerate danger among them. As soon as fear takes root, this established understanding vanishes, and that fear of the unknown takes control. This is when there's trouble. This is what the other villagers have forgotten."

"And their ignorance will destroy them," Donovan noted bleakly.

Fenrald jabbed a finger at Donovan in agreement. "Precisely." He sighed. "But fear is affecting their decisions as well. Remember, they have – all of us here— have escaped something truly terrible. These Wol'dgers were being purged and wiped out because of their beliefs. Most of them have lost someone or their entire family. Can you blame them for wanting to stay out of the fight, avoid taking a side, and remain in isolation where it's safe?"

Hyroc shook his head. "No, I guess I really can't. But regardless of their pain, inaction will end them."

"Therein lies the problem," Fenrald agreed. "Recognizing their pain is not enough. Something must be done regardless, or there will not be a village for much longer. Will you and your friends help me keep them safe? You will receive payment for your services. I know the four of you are destitute; your payment will remedy that. This will give you enough to get back on your feet. What say you?"

Hyroc, Donovan, Curtis, and Elsa looked at each other thoughtfully.

"We'll help you," the four said in turn.

"We need the money," Elsa said. "But we're doing it for those children."

Fenrald smiled eagerly. "I thought nothing else. I'm honored for your assistance."

"What do you need us to do?" Donovan asked.

Chapter 15

Father's Sword

Hyroc peered over Fenrald's shoulder at a piece of parchment his uncle was reading. The parchment detailed the suspected strength of the Feral guards traveling with the kidnapper's caravan. The Wol'dger envoy acquired this information with a flyover of the area where they were supposed to be while returning from Vettenfelth. It was helpful information, but its reliability was questionable. The Ferals were in a forested area, so trees would have obscured his view, and there was much he could have missed.

"From what I can tell," Fenrald said, "he counted no less than twelve Ferals."

"So there could be twelve or thirty," Hyroc noted bleakly.

"Which is why I need you and your friends to help ambush them. Despite them outnumbering us, we still have the advantage if we catch them by surprise." He indicated his eye patch. "With one eye, I obviously have some difficulties with depth perception. Unless I'm exceptionally lucky, hitting my intended target with a bow is beyond me. I have to get up close to fight while you and your friends can pick off targets from a distance. And since arrows are nearly silent, locating an archer amongst the trees is challenging. The only exception is a Wol'dger in a cat or wolf form, but it will still take their sharpened hearing vital seconds to do so. Nonetheless, you can likely take out a sizable chunk of their number before anyone knows you're there."

"That reminds me," Hyroc said. "Did the envoy report anything about Ferals with the transformation gift?"

Fenrald paused as he scanned the parchment. "Nothing about wolves or cats, just two bears. Bears are tremendous obstacles I've run into on many occasions when attempting to rescue kidnapped children. I can't take a bear head-on, even in my animal form." He affectionately patted Hyroc on the shoulder. "But you'll be a big help with that. Pardon the pun. I assume you were taught how to fight in your animal form."

Hyroc smirked. "I most definitely was. My Guardian made me go out and fight for a fish at a river against the biggest brown bears I've ever seen! But bears are nothing. I fought a werewolf before coming here. I'll take a bear any day over *that*."

"As would we," Elsa agreed.

"I'll take your word on that," Fenrald said with a hint of praise. "But can you handle two bears at once?"

"Not without help. I can fight them for a bit, but there's no way I can win alone without leaning heavily on my Flame Claw. But if it can be helped, I should use my Quintessence sparingly in case of any surprises. I don't want to blow it all on two bears only to need it for something worse."

Fenrald tapped his finger on the table as he mulled this over. "I'm just trying to figure out how I'm going to work that into our strategy. I guess I could – no, that wouldn't work, never mind."

"But whatever you're planning only works if there are only about twelve Ferals," Donovan said. "And only two of them are bears. Like Hyroc said, there could be more than that. Also, there could be more of them that can transform than just those two bears."

"That's a possibility," Fenrald said. "But this information is the best we're going to get." He quietly growled his dissatisfaction with the situation. "I would feel a whole lot better if we had a few more bodies. But I can make it work, even with as questionable as this information is. Just give me a bit."

An idea came to Hyroc. Maybe he could recruit another party member by convincing Iskall to join their venture. He seemed somewhat of an outcast from choosing a stag for his animal form and might not be restrained by the distrust that kept the other villagers from helping Fernald. Hyroc had chased away the bullies who were ridiculing Iskall, which may have ingratiated the young Wol'dger to him. Because of his choice of animal form, his family may have avoided entrusting him with responsibilities, and he could be eager to prove himself. Hyroc was unsure how much a deer-form-Wol'dger could contribute to their task, but he was sure he would find something useful that didn't include the indignity of carrying supplies. Hyroc hated doing that with his bear form and assumed Iskall did as well with his animal form. Iskall's horns could be a potent weapon. They were straighter and pointier than any buck Hyroc had hunted, making them better for goring.

"I'll be right back," Hyroc said, throwing on a dark gray jacket and rushing out the door before anyone inquired or followed.

He jogged through the village, heading toward the market where he had last seen Iskall and his brother. After combing through the vendors and coming up short, he headed for the Wol'dger's home. When he arrived, two of Iskall's younger brothers were sword fighting with sticks out front. They briefly paused their game and indicated around the side of the house. Hyroc arrived to find a single male, Wol'dger, who wore a white tunic and black pants around Hyroc's age, sharpening a reaping tool.

"Hello," the Wol'dger said.

"Hello," Hyroc responded. "I'm looking for Iskall. Is he here?"

The Wol'dger gave him a perplexed stare.

Hyroc felt embarrassed when he recognized the Wol'dger's dirty white fur with black patches. This *was* Iskall. "I'm sorry," Hyroc apologized. "This is my first time seeing you in your natural form. I need to pay more attention to people's markings in their animal form."

"It's okay," Iskall said with an understanding grin. "I am in my deer form a lot. Is there something I can help you with?"

"Maybe, yes. How much do you know about the kidnappings?"

"The kidnappings of human children? Not much. I know the Ferals are behind it, but no more than that. I've heard your uncle goes out and tries to rescue them. But everyone wants us to stay out of it. They say the Mastgarians will deal with the Ferals soon enough, and it's best if we don't get involved."

"The Mastgarians are tired of their citizens getting kidnapped and are preparing to take action against the Ferals. But I need to tell you their plans to eliminate them also include the destruction of this village."

Iskall's eyes widened with shock. "But why?" he asked with a startled tone. "We have nothing to do with those kidnappings!"

"Because the Mastgarians don't know that. They think we're all the same because we look the same as the Ferals. To them, we are more trouble than we are worth, and it's best to get rid of the lot of us."

"Is there anything we can do to convince the Mastgarians we are not a threat?"

"Yes. That's the good news. There is something *we can do.* If my uncle rescues those children and returns them to their families, we can keep the Mastgarians at bay. There's a slaver caravan passing close by, and we're going to head it off. But a lot of Ferals are guarding those kidnapped children. I've got my uncle and my friends to help deal with them, but –" he sighed, "– but I don't know if there's enough of us to do it. We could use your help."

"You want me to help?" Iskall said, taken aback.

"To help us fight, yes."

He shifted uncertainly onto his other foot. "I don't know; I'm not sure how much help I can be in a fight."

"Remember what I said about your horns yesterday? You could inflict some serious damage with them."

Iskall shook his head dismissively. "No, no, you won't want me."

"I'm sure you can –"

"No, you won't," he insisted, cutting in.

Hyroc shot him a sympathetic look. "Are you sure?"

Iskall nodded. "Yes. Yes, I'm sure. Thank you for the offer."

Hyroc sighed, defeated. "All right. But if you change your mind, we'll be at my uncle's cabin the next day or two while we prepare."

Iskall nodded, resuming his sharpening of the reaping tool.

Deflated, Hyroc turned away and headed back to Fenrald's home. He had been confident Iskall would want to help them, but the villagers' disappointment had browbeaten the Wol'dger too much for him to help them.

"What did you need to get to so urgently?" Elsa asked when Hyroc returned.

Hyroc blew out a breath. "Oh, it was nothing," he admitted. "It was just an idea that didn't pan out."

She nodded.

"Did I miss anything?"

"Just more strategizing with your uncle."

Fenrald stepped out of the cabin with a piece of parchment in front of his face. He approached Elsa and held it out to her as he spoke. "Elsa, I have a list of supplies we'll need. Can you and your brothers take care of this?"

"Yes, this is no problem," she said, receiving the parchment and reviewing the list.

"Let me come with you," Hyroc said.

"No, I need you to stay," Fenrald said. "There's something I want to show you."

"We can take care of this," Donovan said. "It's no problem; go ahead and stay."

Hyroc nodded.

Fenrald walked back to the cabin, beckoning Hyroc to follow. He led him to a room with several small wooden chests. "I've got something for you," he said, crouching to open one. He removed a dusty bundle of cloth wrapped around something. After blowing the dust off, he offered it to Hyroc.

Hyroc took it, removing the cloth to reveal a sheathed Hand-and-a-half-sword within a scabbard. Slipping the scabbard off, Hyroc saw the sword's blade had a uniform triangular shape with a rectangular guard and an opal set into a circular pommel. It was longer than his falchion, and though it felt lighter, it was no less sturdy, skillfully forged from high-quality steel.

Fenrald indicated it eagerly. "That sword belonged to your father."

A sense of reverence and awe washed over Hyroc. He held something the hands of his father had touched. He suddenly had a connection to a man he had no memory of and had always wanted to meet. The sword felt like the most precious thing he had ever touched.

"I know he would have wanted you to have it, and by right of inheritance, that belongs to you. I forged that myself. It was a wedding present when he married your mother. It's longer than your chopper, but I don't think it will take much getting used to. And it comes to a sharper point, making it better for thrusting. I made it so it could be wielded with one hand or two; that way, if the need presented itself, your mother could use it one-handed with her Flame Claw. You will be able to do the same."

"You made this?" Hyroc asked.

Fenrald nodded. He pulled back his sleeve on one arm and flexed, exposing a larger-than-average bicep. "You only get arms like these from working a forge," he said proudly. He put his arm down and drew his sword. It mirrored the appearance of the sword Hyroc held. "His sword was part of a set. My blade is its twin. They are both made from the same batch of steel. I had intended to make your mother a nice dagger as an anniversary present, but I never got to it." Fenrald pointed to his sword, indicating Hyroc should look closer at his own. "And if you look here, I etched something into the metal." Hyroc looked, finding a line of runes running toward the tip. "It says, 'The bonds of brotherhood can never be broken.'"

Hyroc smiled; it was a good saying. It was something only a loving brother would imprint on their work. He felt his eyes misting and wiped them before a tear formed.

"That's really nice," Hyroc said sincerely.

"Your father thought so, too. It hasn't been used in a long time, but I've tried my best to keep it in working order. Though it might need some sharpening. But enough of that. Go ahead, put it on."

Hyroc eagerly unbelted his falchion, replacing it with his father's sword. He happily turned to display it for his uncle. "What do you think?"

"You look magnificent," Fenrald said. "Let me put some wood on the stump outback for you to practice. We're not leaving until the day after tomorrow, which should be plenty of time for you to get a good feel for that sword."

Hyroc couldn't help hugging his uncle. "Thank you, uncle! This is the best gift I've ever gotten."

Fenrald laughed. "I'm flattered you appreciate it." He affectionately pushed Hyroc away, grabbing the sides of his shoulders to hold him in place for a moment. "All right, all right, enough of this. Let's go out and see what that old blade can do."

Chapter 16

Heading out

All right, let's run through that drill again," Fenrald told Hyroc.

They stood in front of Fenrald's home, swords in their hands. Hyroc held his father's sword, and his uncle was helping him practice with the new blade. The cool morning was warming toward noon.

Hyroc stepped forward, tapping his weapon on Fenrald's sword. Their steel sang with a metallic hum. Fenrald moved his blade to the side in a practiced motion, and Hyroc tapped it again. They repeated these motions in multiple directions.

Fenrald nodded satisfactorily. "Good," he said happily. "I think you've got the hang of it. Let's do a quick run-through of all the moves. Show me a one-handed strike, down and up." Hyroc slashed downward and upward. "Now, with two hands," Hyroc grasped the hilt with both hands and sliced with more force. "A one-handed and two-handed thrust." Hyroc drove his blade forward as instructed. "And a block." Hyroc slanted his sword as if blocking an imaginary strike. "Good, very good. That's enough for now." Hyroc nodded his acknowledgment, then slid his new sword into its scabbard.

Fenrald swept his eyes through his surroundings, taking stock of things. Elsa, Donovan, and Curtis were finishing securing their supplies and equipment onto their donkey and a mule Fenrald had rented from the village. Their donkey alone was sufficient for carrying everything they needed, but the mule had additional supplies for feeding and treating any potential injuries inflicted upon the kidnapped children. Also, as a secondary precaution, the mule could carry anyone unable to walk due to wounds.

"I think we're ready," Hyroc said.

Fenrald nodded his agreement, walking towards the pack animals.

As his uncle moved away, Hyroc saw Iskall's young sister approaching. She playfully skipped toward him.

"Is Elizabeth ready?" she asked in a sweet, innocent tone. She was here to escort Elizabeth back to her family, so they could care for her while the group carried out the rescue.

"Let me see," Hyroc answered. "Elizabeth," he called out.

Elizabeth stood near the donkey and mule as she turned to face them. She perked up happily, noticing the girl. They both waved excitedly at each other. Elizabeth rushed over to the front of the cabin to retrieve a doll on the porch before coming over.

"Be good!" Fenrald called to her. "I love you."

She waved a farewell back. With that, the two girls held hands and headed out. The Wol'dger girl happily chatted with Elizabeth.

As they disappeared, he spotted Iskall and his older brother, Shawnren, approaching. Iskall was in his natural form, with a knapsack slung over his shoulder and a dagger on his belt. Shawnren also had a knapsack but carried a round wooden shield on his back. Hanging from his waist were throwing hatchets and a war axe of the North Lander style.

"Iskall, what's going on?" Hyroc asked. "I thought you weren't coming."

"Well, I gave it some thought and decided I was being selfish," he said, a hint of shame in his voice. "Those kids have been taken from their families. How would I feel if someone had taken one of my siblings? Helping rescue them is the honorable thing to do. And from what you said, you, your uncle, and your friends need a helping hand to ensure everyone comes home."

"I'm glad you're here," Hyroc said eagerly. He shook Iskall's clawed hand. "We've got a plan, and your big showy antlers will come in handy."

Iskall gave him a toothy smile. He indicated Shawnren. "And my brother also decided to come."

Hyroc nodded happily. "Even better," he said. "The more we have, the easier this will be." He indicated the pack animals. "We're pretty much ready to go. You can head over and tell my uncle and friends what you're doing." Iskall nodded his understanding and walked away. Hyroc turned to Shawnren, reaching out to shake his hand. "I'm so glad you decided to accompany your brother. Thank –" Hyroc started to say before Shawnren cut him off.

"I'm not here for you, your flat-face friends, and definitely not for your uncle!" he said in a biting tone. "I'm only here because you filled my brother's head with all those noble ideals and convinced him to join this reckless venture to go off and fight Ferals. I'm here for *him*! I'm here to make sure he comes home *alive*. You don't know your uncle like we do. I don't trust him, and neither should you. He's not the saint he makes himself out to be."

With that, he shoved past Hyroc, purposely bumping shoulders with him. Hyroc shot him an indignant glare. That was unexpected and incredibly unkind to his uncle.

Fenrald approached Hyroc from the pack animals. "You look like you smashed your face into a tree branch you didn't see," he noted.

"That's not far from the truth," Hyroc said sourly.

"Did you invite Iskall?"

"Yes."

Fenrald let out an exasperated sigh. "If anything happens to either of those boys, I'll have to answer to *their mother*. Their family is the only one in the village who will take in Elizabeth when I go out. If they incur any grievances because of me, I'm the one who is ultimately responsible for anything that happens, regardless of what happens. You just put that arrangement in danger. What am I to do if I can no longer rely on them? Am I supposed to bring Elizabeth along with me and take care of her while I'm fighting Ferals?"

"I'm sorry. I didn't consider that," Hyroc said. "You were unsure if there were enough of us to get this done, so I found someone."

"I appreciate your effort, but this has put me in a bind."

"Should I tell them not to come?"

"If you want to end your friendship with him, that's a sure way to do it. No, you gave that boy a chance to make a difference, an opportunity he has never gotten. If you tell him to go home, that will crush his spirit, and he'll never try to help anyone again. It would do more harm than good to make them leave. He stays. But you need to ensure nothing happens to either of them. We'll both be in trouble if any harm comes to them."

Hyroc gave him a downtrodden nod.

Fenrald patted him on the shoulder. "So long as we're careful, I don't think anything will happen to them. Now, it's time for us to get going. Stay focused on our task."

Chapter 17

Pathfinders

HYROC WALKED ALONGSIDE FENRALD AS they led the group through the forest outside the Glacial village. They had abandoned the road for uncut terrain, following a path only Hyroc's uncle knew. The caravan they hunted would avoid roads or well-traveled areas to help it go unnoticed. The group moved beneath an overcast sky, but a dark patch to the south indicated rain later as the day wore on toward night. Even at this distance, Hyroc could smell the moisture-laden air that carried the storm. He enjoyed the scent of the ground and how clean everything smelled after a good rain had cleansed the air. He didn't quite know the words to describe it to anyone. The only thing he hated was the rainstorm part, especially when there was nothing to shelter beneath. He had experienced more than enough of that when his mentor Ursa was training him on his bear form. "A little rain wouldn't stop a bear," she had said when he had got beneath a tree during a heavy downpour. Hyroc smirked in a mixture of disdain and humor at the memory. A sense of longing struck him. Where was she right now, he wondered? Was she on some mysterious Guardian mission killing shadow demons? Did she ever think about him? He shrugged off the feeling. Now wasn't the best time to venture into his memories. They would engage the caravan guards in two days. That demanded his full attention.

"Fenrald," Hyroc asked. "What's the story with you and Elizabeth? How did the two of you meet?"

The Wol'dger slowed to match Hyroc's pace, sweeping his eyes through the trees to ensure it was safe to focus on his nephew.

"It's been a while since anyone has asked me about that," he said.

"I mean, unless that's something you would rather not talk about. I understand if you don't."

"It's okay. I think you're owed that, as we now live together. It was a few years ago. I was returning to the village after completing a mission for the Mastgar crown. I usually travel in cat form when I'm alone, as the increased agility of that form allows me to cover ground faster. My increased night vision, in that form, prevents me from having to stop after dark. I also carry my blades strapped to my back.

"One moonlit night, while moving east, something off the side of the road caught my attention. I don't know if it was a sound or a smell, but it stopped me dead. As I came away from the road, there was the unmistakable smell of blood lingering in the air. The first thing I found was the carcass of a pack mule. The sacks it carried had been ripped open, and their contents strewn about. Large gashes covered its body, any of which could have easily been the killing blow. The blood was sticky, not fully coagulated, suggesting the poor creature had been killed less than an hour prior. Past the mule were the bodies of a man, a woman, and a teenage boy. All human." He thumbed over his shoulder. "The boy was about the same age as your young lightning mage friend. Their bodies bore grave wounds. Since they were all beyond help, it seemed best to leave before I risked attracting the attention of whatever or whoever had done this. But as I turned to go, I became aware of a baby's crying. Coming to the sound behind a tree, I saw a basket for carrying a baby. It was tucked into some bushes as if someone had seen the attacker coming and tried to hide the basket. Within it, I found a girl human child. That's when I got the feeling I was suddenly being watched. I instinctively gripped the basket's handle with my jaws and retreated as fast as I could.

"There's not much else to tell after that. I brought her to Forestgold to see if anyone recognized her, but without success. No one there was willing to take her, so I brought her back. It was intended to be a temporary arrangement until I could track down any of her relatives. But that was never meant to be. So our paths merged." He smiled happily. "Little did I know yet another happy surprise awaited me." He patted Hyroc on the shoulder.

"Was it a Feral that took her family?" Hyroc asked.

The happiness faded from Fenrald's eyes. "I'm certain of it," he said gloomily. "I've seen enough victims of the brutality of Ferals to identify them, clear as day. Not even animals kill in that manner."

"What's it like to fight one of them?" Hyroc asked. He wasn't seeking to be awed by the knowledge; he wanted to know what awaited him and his friends.

"It's like nothing you've ever seen!" Fenrald said with such intensity it sent a shiver up Hyroc's back. "They're brutal. Yes, they can talk and have a person's intelligence but don't make the mistake of thinking about them as *someone. Something* is more accurate. Their minds are possessed by whatever creature they have chosen to take the form of. They exist in a realm that is neither human, Wol'dger, nor beast. When they attack, it is without restraint or morality. They fight with a fury like nothing else. Do not expect mercy from them, for they give none. When you fight them, fight with all the ferocity you can muster. You must hold nothing back! It is kill them or be killed. Plain and simple."

"It seems they act an awful lot like a werewolf," Hyroc noted.

Fenrald nodded. "But a werewolf has rules," he stated sourly. "They're only dangerous when there's a full moon. About once a month. The rest of the time, they're human and behave as one. Ferals pose the same dangers as a werewolf at full moon – or at least all the dangers I'm aware of; I've never had the misfortune of facing one – but it's a constant threat."

"My friends and I have killed a blood werewolf at full moon. We can kill them as well. We're used to dealing with monsters."

Fenrald grunted a half-humored laugh. "Is that so? Sometime, you and I must trade stories. I'm sure the two of us have quite the tales to tell." He cleared his throat to signal the return to the previous, more serious topic. "When you're fighting Ferals, do not look upon them as a person; look upon them as whatever animal they appear to be and treat them accordingly. But *do not* underestimate them. They are much smarter than any animal. Your ability to think does not give you an edge over them. They can feint an attack, trick you, draw you into a trap, or come at you in unexpected ways. You must be watchful for any hint of deception on their part. But *the beast* is also their greatest weakness. The unrestrained power they access through it blinds them, and they cannot react accordingly to that same deception. They are easily tricked. And the longer you fight with them, the less they can discern. Exploiting this vulnerability is the key. But the beast can make them unpredictable, and it's challenging to be certain how they'll react to whatever you do."

"I assume those animalistic qualities only apply to the Ferals with the transformation ability?" Hyroc asked.

"Yes, but even the ones that cannot shift out of their natural state behave similarly to the ones that can transform, only to a lesser degree. The beast cannot consume them, but they are just as deadly and vicious. *Do not treat them any differently*. They will be just as eager to *end* you and your friends as those in animal form."

"I'll keep that in mind."

"Make sure your friends do as well."

"We've dealt with our fair share of ruthless enemies intent on taking our lives and come out the other side alive. The four of us will do the same here."

The mottled shade of the forest gave way to a green grassy plain covered in all manner of wild weeds. They passed through the area quickly, returning to the forest by midafternoon. Past the tree line, the ground roughened considerably. A spider web of shallow roots spread in all directions, making walking especially troublesome. Lines of clustered trees formed walls of bark that prevented the group from going in straight lines. But despite the difficulty, Fenrald deftly led them through the labyrinth of tree trunks without backtracking once. He consulted no map and proceeded with efficiency that came only from years of familiarity with the path. Hyroc couldn't identify any distinguishing marks that might determine what his uncle followed, but he seemed to know where they were going. How many times had Fenrald traveled this direction to intercept a caravan, Hyroc wondered? How many kidnapped children had he brought back through it?

Then, a haunting thought occurred to him. How many had he failed to rescue? How many times had he come back empty-handed, unable to assist the innocent victims of the Ferals? Hyroc couldn't imagine how awful defeat would feel, knowing the families were probably never going to see their sons or daughters again. He didn't think he could look them in the eye and break the bad news to them. He had been the bearer of terrible news to his friends once before, and he couldn't bear it again. How had his uncle been able to fail and carry on, only to repeat the entire nightmare? It felt as if Fenrald was doing something impossible. Hyroc gained a new level of admiration for his uncle because of what he was willingly putting himself through.

The forest darkened noticeably. The air cooled, and a thunderclap boomed overhead.

"And here I was hoping we could do this without also being wet," Donovan said, downtrodden.

"Look on the bright side," Hyroc answered. "The rain could work in our favor. A downpour will deaden the sound of our approach and make it easier for us to sneak up on the caravan."

"I had considered that." His voice became jovial. "I just wasn't looking forward to the smell of wet Wol'dger."

Hyroc used his Flame Claw to harvest moisture from the air, making his fingertips wet. He mockingly flicked them at Donovan, who jerked his head back in surprise. Elsa, Curtis, and Iskall snickered. Then, as if his play had insulted the storm, it started raining. Everyone drew up the hoods on their cloaks and pulled together their clothing to keep out water.

"This is going to be a long, cold night," Donovan said unhappily. "Comfortable sleep, who needs it anyway," he stated sarcastically.

"No need to worry," Iskall said smugly. He indicated the pack he carried. "I brought a tarp. We'll be dry when we sleep at least."

Donovan shot him an appreciative smile. "Hey, Hyroc," he said. "Have I ever told you how much I like your new friend?"

Iskall returned a toothy smile.

It rained harder in the fading light.

Chapter 18

The Raven's Call

Something drew Hyroc from his sleep. It was dark when he opened his eyes. He lay on a hide beneath the tarp Iskall had brought, and the embers of their dying fire glowed dimly at its edge. It sounded like someone was arguing, but the source wasn't obvious when he swept his eyes through his surroundings. Everyone else was also starting to wake. The only person not moving was Fenrald. Hyroc rose from his sleeping mat and went to where his uncle lay. Fenrald was rolling on his sleeping mat with his eyes closed, speaking loudly as if having a heated argument. He was having a nightmare, and a terrible one at that. Hyroc crouched beside him and shook him. The instant his hand made contact, Fenrald's hand shot up and seized his arm, and Hyroc was on the ground before he knew what happened. Fenrald raised a dagger, a crazed look in his eyes. His expression calmed, turning to shock. Fenrald pulled away from Hyroc and dropped the dagger. The rest of the group looked astonished, unsure if they needed to draw a weapon and assist him.

"Forgive me!" Fenrald gasped. He stood and staggered away.

With a startled growl, Kit flew down the trunk of the tree he had slept in and darted to Hyroc's side. The big cat stood protectively over him; his ears pointed in opposite directions as he stared after Fenrald.

When the danger had passed, he turned his attention to Hyroc and sniffed him feverishly.

Elsa was next to rush over to Hyroc. “Are you all right?” she said, alarmed, looking him over.

“Yeah, yeah, I’m fine,” Hyroc said, pushing himself into a sitting position.

Donovan reached out and helped Hyroc to his feet. “What in the *shadow* was that!” he asked anxiously. “He was about to plunge that dagger into your chest.”

“Yes, *I know, I was the one on the ground,*” Hyroc said sharply. “He was having a nightmare when I tried to wake him.”

“Must have been an awful one,” Elsa noted. “I’ve never had one that made me want to stab somebody.”

“I should try talking to him to figure out what all that was about.”

“You sure you want to be alone with him?”

“Yes, I’m sure. I’m positive he wasn’t trying to hurt me on purpose. When he snapped out of it, he looked pretty shook up about what he had almost done.”

They nodded their acknowledgment.

Hyroc turned from them and headed after his uncle. Kit followed him cautiously. They found Fenrald leaning against the trunk of a cottonwood. He held the locket around his neck in one hand as he stared forward.

“I think it would be best if you stayed back,” Hyroc whispered to the agitated mountain lion. Kit groaned his displeasure at the request before sitting as Hyroc walked away.

“Uncle,” Hyroc said tentatively.

Fenrald acknowledged him with a side glance before continuing to look forward.

Hyroc stepped next to Fenrald and held out the dagger his uncle had dropped. Fenrald accepted it, slipping the blade back into its sheath.

He was silent a long moment before speaking, his hand grasping the locket. “All men have their demons,” he said sadly. “Mine are sometimes just louder.” He looked toward Hyroc thoughtfully. “I didn’t hurt you, did I?”

Hyroc shook his head. “I’m fine; just a little dirt on my clothes.”

"That's a relief."

"But I think Elsa was about to put an arrow in you."

Fenrald grunted a laugh. "I'm glad you've got such trustworthy friends to watch your back. Cherish that. When I was as young as you, I thought your father would always be there to watch mine. He was good about that." He let out a quiet sigh of longing. "But, one day, he was gone." He indicated back in the direction he had been lying. "What happened back there – I'm not used to having anyone with me when I go after Ferals, and I have to keep a sharp listen for the slightest sound. That might be the only warning I get before someone tries to put a knife in me."

"I understand," Hyroc said. "When I left Forna on my way to Elswood, I was alone. At night, every strange and unfamiliar sound startled me. I don't think I got any sleep for the first week. I remember getting so tired." Hyroc paused. "When I went to wake you, you were having a nightmare."

Fenrald nodded his understanding. "Ah, I was wondering," he said in a tone indicating he was uncertain if that was what had happened but not entirely surprised by the confirmation.

"I have to ask, does that happen to you a lot? So I can avoid another *incident*."

"From time to time, but not for a while."

Hyroc nodded. He indicated with his chin the locket Fenrald was fingering. "Who was she? If you want to tell me, I mean."

"That's very considerate. Thank you. She was very near to my heart. I would have done anything to keep her safe. You should go back to sleep. You don't need to worry about this grizzled wolf and his night terror. Go ahead. Go sleep."

Hyroc nodded. "Okay. I'll just be more careful about waking you."

"Good thinking."

"Night," Hyroc said before leaving.

Fenrald didn't respond.

Diffused gray morning light filtered through the trees as the group journeyed onward. A light mist of rain dampened the trees and ground. The roughness of the terrain remained unchanged, but they were now heading uphill, which only compounded the issue. They led their pack animals through the area, picking their path carefully to reduce the risk of one slipping and getting injured. A broken leg would not only be a death sentence for either animal but also reduce the group's ability to transport anyone who endured a wound from them executing their ambush. Such a setback would potentially force them to leave someone behind.

Gaps formed amid the trees, and the ground became rocky. The rain made the shelf slippery, and maintaining their footing became challenging. Iskall slipped while stepping over a boulder and stumbled backward. Luckily, Hyroc was next to him and caught him with a hand.

"You okay?" Hyroc asked.

"Yes, I'm fine," Iskall said gratefully. "Thank you."

Donovan, who was ahead of them, indicated a safer path around the rock.

"Can I ask you something?" Iskall said to Hyroc. "Why did you want me to join you and your friends on this?"

"Because we needed a few more people –" Hyroc started to say before Iskall interrupted him.

"No, no, I mean, why did you want *me* to come when …" he fluttered his fingers, unsure how to phrase what he wanted to say. "When no one trusts me to do, well, anything."

"Well, it seemed like you weren't given a chance to prove yourself – to show what you can do. I thought maybe I could give you that chance and you could give us something valuable with your skills. You see, Elsa is extraordinary with a bow. Donovan can also use one pretty well, but he's got that boar spear and can deal with anything big that gets too close. Curtis is also a lightning mage. Do you see what I'm getting at?"

"I think so. But what exactly do I give to the group?"

Hyroc scratched the back of his head and let out a nervous laugh. "I'm not entirely sure; I just know it's something. We were also very thankful you brought your brother."

Iskall laughed, nodding his understanding. "Well, whatever it is, I'll do my best not to disappoint."

"I know you won't."

The group reached a broad, bald hill atop the incline. Fenrald put both hands above his eyes to block out the cool gray light. He slowly surveyed the surrounding area in a broad sweep. He lowered his hands and unhappily shook his head.

"What's wrong?" Hyroc asked.

"I can't see any smoke haze from any fires the Ferals might have lit during the night," Fenrald said. "The rain has dissipated all of it. I know the caravan is out there, but not precisely where. They'd need to take this path because this hill, and the line of hills that run through here, allows them to travel unseen until they're too far away for me to do anything about them." He drummed his fingers on the hilt of his sword. The flapping of wings caught his attention. He looked toward Shimmer, perched on Elsa's shoulder, flailing his ebony wings to shed the rainwater. Fenrald indicated the raven. "You said that bird is a Guardian servant, correct?"

"Yes, he is."

"I wonder. Have you ever used him as a scout?"

Hyroc nodded. "Yeah, we used him to guide us through the north wilds of Arnaira. He'll tell you whatever you need to know."

"Elsa," Fenrald said. "I need your friend. I can't spot the caravan below us. Can you have him look for it?"

She nodded, moving her face closer to Shimmer and whispering instructions to him. She assisted Shimmer into flight by throwing her hand skyward. He floated down along the hill's decline, skimming the treetops before he was lost from sight.

"The other thing that worries me about not being able to see the caravan is we might have missed it. I don't know how old this information is or how long it has been since the envoy received word of it. There's no way of knowing how many days have passed since then. We can't ambush it if it's already gone past. Some of my rescue attempts ended after I spent days wandering through the forest without any sign of them. Or, I was wrong about their path, and this venture was doomed to fail from the start."

"Well, I'm sure Shimmer will find it," Hyroc said more to reassure himself than his uncle. Fenrald glanced at him as if aware of Hyroc's uncertainty.

"In any case," Fenrald continued. "Everyone might as well get comfortable; we'll be here a while."

Hyroc and Donovan sat in the shade of a bundle of birch trees, playing a game of dice. They had nothing of worth to stake on the game, so they used pinecones as a stand-in. It was Hyroc's turn to shake. He jiggled the dice in his hand before dropping them on the ground. They both landed skull-side up.

Hyroc smacked his hand on his knee in annoyance. "Oh, I don't believe it," he said with disbelief.

"Yes!" Donovan exclaimed. He made a beckoning motion with his hand. "You asked for a three and a five. Cough it up." Hyroc slid half his pile into Donovan's.

"I'll raise you my half against yours and do double threes."

"That's a little gutsy, but okay," Hyroc said jokingly, skeptical.

After receiving the dice for his turn, Donovan made his shake. It came up double threes. "Yes!" Donovan said, celebratory.

"And I'm out," Hyroc said, giving Donovan the remainder of his pile.

"You want a turn, Iskall?" Donovan asked.

"Sure," Iskall answered eagerly, switching places with Hyroc.

"I'll play the winner," Shawnren said, who was sharpening his axe with a whetstone.

Iskall shook for a two and a six.

Hyroc stealthily used his Flame Claw to make the dice come up on the intended number.

"Hey!" Donovan said, thrusting an accusatory finger at him. "I saw *that.*" Hyroc turned and feigned innocence by pretending to examine a pine needle-covered branch. "That didn't count. Go again."

Hyroc moved away from the branch to Fenrald and Elsa, who were pouring over a map to determine alternate routes the caravan may have taken.

"...that's what I was wondering," Elsa said. She pointed at the map. "What about over there to the north? Could they have gone around these hills? They would still be obscured from being seen by anyone from the settlements."

"Rarely have they gone that way," Fenrald said dismissively. "Yes, it brings them into the Northlands by skirting the edge of Mastgar territory, giving them some added protection, but the terrain is rough, rougher than what we went through here. There's also a bog on that path, which comes right up to the far side of these hills. The only caravans to attempt it were small, three to four slavers, nothing as big as the one we're hunting."

Elsa nodded.

"So how's it going?" Hyroc asked.

"Not great," Elsa admitted. She lightly smacked the map with the back of her hand. "Where we are is the likeliest path for them to take. So where are they?"

"That is the dilemma," Fenrald agreed. "And until your feathery friend returns, there's no way of knowing. But if he doesn't find them, they're not here. Which would definitely mean the end of our endeavor." He let out a quiet sigh of resignation. "And leaving another group of innocent souls to their doom."

"We shouldn't give up hope yet," Hyroc said. "Not before Shimmer returns with his report. He's only been gone a few hours. Even with wings, it always takes him some time to find what we're looking for."

"Nephew, I wish I shared your optimism, but I've been at this too long to dare to hope. It only makes the knife cut more painful."

"Who said I was being optimistic?" Hyroc said in a weak attempt to bring humor to his uncle's gallows mood.

Most of the day had passed, and the sky shifted toward the amber of dusk when Shimmer glided up on the thermals of air rising above the incline. He alighted onto the ground in front of Elsa and Hyroc. After a squawk of greeting, he turned toward the northwest and began hopping up into the air and fluttering. He stopped, looking at everyone expectantly.

"Is that him telling us something?" Fenrald asked.

Elsa and Hyroc nodded happily.

"Yes, that is," Elsa said. She pointed behind Shimmer. "That way?" He bobbed his head as a confirmation. "Good, that's good, " she said, stroking his head. He cooed at the praise.

Fenrald pointed in the same direction. "That way? You're sure?"

"Yes, I'm sure."

He made an excited snatching motion as if grabbing the moment to keep it from escaping. "I know exactly where they are," he exclaimed. Hastily, he gathered materials to construct an improvised map. He made a line of pinecones to form the rough top left of a square, and bridging the top and left side of the square, he put down a line of broken twigs. "The pinecones are a creek; the sticks are the caravan. The Ferals will be tucked into that bend in the stream – the top left corner. It's a formation I've seen them use many times in this area. And this close to dark, they'll be getting ready to settle down for the night. The creek acts as a defensive wall because not only will the water impede the movement of an attacker, but they will hear anyone trying to sneak in from that direction. So they will have their backs to it, facing forward, with the kidnapped behind and any carts or wagons they brought. We can turn the protection of the creek against them. The same qualities of the stream protecting them make escape far more difficult." He indicated the open bottom right of the map. "We're going to come at them through here and drive them into the water."

Donovan raised his hand. "Wait, your plan is for us to come at them head-on," he stated. "How many Ferals will we be facing?"

"Probably close to twenty."

"Twenty! That's almost two to one."

"The numbers are not in our favor," Shawnren agreed. "No, I'm not letting my brother go on your suicide mission. I'm not letting you sacrifice him on an ill-advised plan!"

"I have to agree," Hyroc said. "Even with my Flame Claw and Curtis' lightning magic, this is seriously dangerous. And that's just if there's twenty of them. The odds only get worse from there. I also want to help those children, but not like this."

"Yes, being dead seems like a bit of a problem," Donovan said.

"I have more of a plan than that," Fenrald said reassuringly. "I'm going to wait until nightfall before I scout out the caravan to see what we're dealing with. If it turns out this is beyond our ability to handle and there's too many of them, trust me, I will call this off."

"I'm holding you to *that*," Shawnren threatened. "I swear, if anything happens to my brother, I'll –"

"Shawnren, please relax," Elsa intervened. "I give you my word. If I think we can't do this, I assure you, I will personally call this off."

"You had better."

"Shawnren!" Iskall said, uncharacteristically passionate. "I am the one who willingly agreed to come. It's my decision if I want to leave, not yours."

"But you don't –"

"I certainly do know what I'm getting into," Iskall interrupted. "Enough discussion."

Shawnren closed his mouth, taken aback.

"Well, if we're all in agreement," Fenrald said. "We need to go see what we're dealing with before we make any decisions."

No one objected, and they headed off quietly. The group crept through the rapidly darkening forest, and the cool air gained the faint smell of smoke. If they listened carefully, they could now hear the distant voices of the caravan guards. They had found their quarry, but as near as they were to their target, it might be as close as they got.

"All right, what's the plan now?" Hyroc whispered.

"Now, now we wait until night," Fenrald said quietly. "Find a good spot to wait."

Hyroc jolted awake at the sound of rustling bushes. It was dark when he opened his eyes, and he could barely make out everyone's features. He didn't even remember starting to fall asleep. He was in his bear form, lying on his side. His much larger body took up most of the space where everyone waited. Kit laid beside himand groggily lifting his head to give Hyroc a dirty look. Elsa had her back pressed against Hyroc's. He couldn't tell if she was awake or asleep. Hyroc wondered with alarm if he had fallen asleep at a critical moment when he was supposed to do something? A large black feline strolled out of the bushes. It was only Fenrald in animal form. Hyroc relaxed.

"What news do you have," Elsa said.

"Do you know how many of them there are?" Donovan asked.

"I counted twenty-five," Fenrald said, dropping his hind legs into a sitting position.

"Twenty-five!" Donovan exclaimed, unintentionally raising his voice.

"Keep your voice down!" Fenrald hissed.

"Twenty-five," Donovan repeated much quieter. "We'll be fighting with roughly a four-to-one disadvantage. Do you have a trick we don't know about that will allow the donkey and mule to wield a sword? We can't win against that."

"I'm well aware of that, boy."

Donovan shot him an indignant look. "Did you just call me 'boy?'"

"Donovan, stop it," Elsa interjected. "Let's hear him out."

"Don't underestimate the element of surprise," Fenrald continued. "They have no idea we're coming, and from what I saw, at least a third of them are asleep. So only about fourteen of them are awake and ready to fight."

"Okay, now we're down slightly over two to one."

"If we're careful, we can easily turn the odds in our favor."

"How many bears did you see?" Hyroc asked, carefully rising into a sitting position on his thick haunches as quietly as he could manage.

"Three, but we went into this suspecting that. Hyroc, you said you could handle two. What about three bears?"

"I can hold their attention for a bit without getting murdered, but that's pushing it. I won't win on my own."

"That's all right; you won't be alone."

"Yeah, we'll be with him," Donovan noted. "But if all six of us go in there and attack them head-on, it's going to wake the third who are asleep, and we're going to be outnumbered once again."

"I'm counting on that."

"See, that's what I – wait, what?" Donovan said, baffled.

"I need a couple of you to create a distraction. We're going to split up. Hyroc, I'll have Iskall and Shawnren accompany you. Those three bears are together on the east side of the camp. I need you three to get their attention. And while you're doing that, we'll come up from the south, near the right side of the creek. All their attention will be focused on you to the east, and we'll come up on them from behind. The advantage they have in numbers won't last very long at all in that situation."

"But we'll have the attention of all twenty-five!" Hyroc warned. "That many will easily overwhelm us on the east. And, assuming we can do the first thing, how do you know we'll be able to draw their attention for long enough? What prevents them from turning around, coming after the rest of you, and killing us all?"

"Because they're Ferals. They don't think or even behave the way you're used to. Well, most of them, anyway. I noticed a few North Landers among them; their horned helmets gave them away. I don't know what idiot decided to put horns on their helmets. You're not supposed to purposely go out of your way to give your opponent something to grab onto and use the leverage against you in a fight."

"Wait, did you just say North Landers?" Elsa asked, confused. "I thought Ferals hated humans, that we were inferior beings. Why would they be working together?"

"It's an odd contradiction, I know. From what I've gathered, it's a union of necessity. They're North Lander mercenaries hired by interested Jarls who wish to buy the *merchandise*." Fenrald spat as if referring to the kidnapped children so filled his mouth with a foul taste. "Every time the Ferals deliver a shipment, they are paid in supplies or whatever else they require. They still depend on Forestgold to the south for provisions but can't rely too heavily on it. If the townsfolk got wise, they would immediately withhold their food and starve them out.

"Another thorn in my side is the corrupt sheriff in that town. Wallace, I believe, is his name. The Ferals pay him off with a sizable payment of gold or silver in exchange for his silence and for him to look the other way and let them procure whatever they need from the town. I've tried to get him ousted, but I've been unable to find any concrete evidence of his shady dealings, and I can do nothing about it. At least, nothing in a *peaceful* manner.

"Some North Landers also seem to think they can obtain what they see as the powers of the Ferals. They admire the unbridled animal savagery brought on by the Ferals abandoning the teachings of the Guardians toward the transformation gift. They see it as power, but it is no such thing. They think by working with them, the Ferals will be grateful and give them what they seek. It is almost a fanatical devotion some of them have toward it."

"Do you mean they worship it?" Hyroc asked.

Fenrald nodded. "I think some do just that."

Hyroc's expression turned disgusted.

"Excuse me for wandering off the topic. The minds of the Feral's is akin to a dog flying after a rabbit that it spooked. The dog moves without regard for what lies ahead or if it's moving toward danger. Its sole focus is catching that rabbit. So, when you get the attention of a Feral, nothing else exists to them. They will have no idea the rest of us are behind them, working our way through their numbers and doing our grim work. I assure you, I know how they behave in this instant. I would stake my life on it. But I speak as one who will not be jumping into the furnace. The choice rests with you three. If you believe you truly cannot do this, I will not ask you to do it. I would think not an iota less of any of you if you choose to turn around and leave."

Hyroc, Iskall, and Shawnren regarded each other for a long moment. "I'll do it," each of them said in turn.

Fenrald gave them a proud look.

"Let's go save these kids," Iskall said.

"Iskall, I need you to bring out your antlers; I need you to do something," Fenrald said. He smiled mischievously.

Iskall gave Hyroc an anxious sideways glance, seemingly asking, "What did I just agree to?"

Chapter 19

Spear Thrust

THIS IS DEMEANING," ISKALL SAID. "I can't believe this is part of your plan." He stood on all fours in deer form. Fenrald hung tiny servant bells on the Wol'dger's antlers. Each bell had a wad of cloth stuck in to keep the clapper from striking and giving away their position to the Ferals.

"Oh, it's not so bad," Shawnren joked. "I've always thought about hanging decorations from your antlers. Give you a little more *personality*."

Hyroc and Donovan snickered.

"That's not funny!" Iskall said in a sharp whisper. "You're not helping."

"Okay, that should do it," Fenrald said, leaning back from Iskall and appraising his handiwork. He turned to Hyroc. "Now it's your turn."

Hyroc's jovial expression evaporated. "Wha – what do you mean, *my turn*?" he asked indignantly. "You're not seriously going to put those on me?"

Fenrald nodded. "I most certainly am. I've got two bells left, and there is a lot of space on you, so we might as well use them."

"Yes, they will give you a little more *personality*," Iskall mocked.

Hyroc rolled his eyes, knowing he deserved that dig.

"I think we're ready," Fenrald said. "Everybody understand the plan?" Everyone nodded. "Hyroc, make sure your group doesn't pull the cloth out of those bells until you are certain you're close enough to the camp. I don't want the guards hearing you from too far out and potentially waking everyone up early. We need the delay from the confusion of you making a ruckus right next to them. If they hear you too soon they'll immediately throw an overwhelming force at you and you won't stand a chance. I'll try to send your raven your way to help coordinate our attacks but use your best judgment when getting their attention. Just don't do it too early, either. They'll all come after you as soon as they know you're there. Keep moving; don't let them encircle you when you fight them. If they surround you, *they will overpower you*. Remember, the three of you are just the distraction. Do what you can to them, but do not try to win; you'll lose."

The three nodded, and then everyone split into their respective groups.

"Elsa, wait," Hyroc said as she walked away. "You should take my sword." Hyroc picked up his sheathed sword with his jaws, offering it to her. Elsa accepted it. "That way, you have a backup weapon in case they get too close for your bow."

"Good idea," Elsa said as she belted on his sword. "Thanks. Stay safe." She hurried after Donovan.

"Kit, you also need to go with Elsa," Hyroc said. The mountain lion regarded him with a confounded expression. "You don't need to worry about me; I'll be fine. I know she has my sword, but she's still vulnerable if any of those men get close or a wolf rushes her. Don't go after anything, only dangerous things coming close to her, but you can't make any noise until then. Now, I need you to go." Kit followed Elsa. Fenrald slipped throwing knives into his belt before turning to leave. "Oh, and Fenrald," Hyroc said to his uncle with sincerity. "Take care of yourself out there. I don't want to lose what's left of my family."

Fenrald nodded his comprehension. "That fact was not lost on me," he said. "But you should worry more about yourself. You've got the dangerous job. Happy hunting."

Hyroc, Iskall, and Shawnren stealthily moved off to spring the trap.

Shawnren removed the cloth stopper from the servant bells. "So we just start making noise?" he asked.

"I guess so," Hyroc agreed. "I haven't seen Shimmer yet, but I think it's been long enough for everyone to get into position."

"Yeah, let's be annoying as hell," Iskall said energetically.

Hyroc let out the loudest roar he could muster and shook his head to ring the bells. Iskall shook his head with a wild flourish of his horns, unleashing a clamorous din.

Shawnren banged the back of his axe against his shield. "Wakey, wakey, you stupid wretches!" he yelled. "Come and get us, you child snatching filth."

"Here we are," Hyroc said. "Or are the bunch of you too big of cowards to face us? I've heard Ferals are nothing but chickens."

Angry roars answered him. Two brown bears and a North Lander with a sword and shield emerged from the foliage. The North Lander, with his horned helmet, was easy to identify. One bear was a deep brownish-red color, and the other was black with broken streaks of white across the body. The black bear was close to Hyroc's size, but the brown one was much larger. Its wide, rotund belly reminded Hyroc of a fat fall bear just before winter. That bear had an undeniable weight advantage over Hyroc and was a severe problem. If that bear got him on the ground he was finished.

The large bear licked his lips in a showy attempt at intimidation. "So you brought us a midnight snack," he said, fixing his gaze on Iskall. "It's been a while since I've eaten fresh venison. Why don't you step aside, little bear, and let us have that walking feast."

The North Lander pointed his sword at Shawnren. "That's a nice shield you've got there," he said with a cold eagerness. "I wouldn't mind taking that off you."

"Well, you'll have to come and take it!" Shawnren said fiercely.

"I bet you're too fat to catch me," Iskall mockingly told the giant bear. "You're probably too lazy even to make the attempt."

"You think so, huh?" the bear said. "Why don't we test *that*?"

The brown bear charged Iskall, while the black one rushed Hyroc. The brown bear was utterly fixated on Iskall. He flew at a frightening speed that almost seemed impossibly fast for something so big to move. Iskall darted away, leading the bear away as it pursued him. That was only a temporary strategy, as the bear could not maintain that pace for long, and when it tired, it would return its attention to Hyroc. But this provided Hyroc an opening to deal with the black bear without fighting two opponents simultaneously.

Shawnren took out the North Lander by surprising them with a throwing axe to the chest. Hyroc and the black bear slammed into each other with a momentous impact. The bear ferociously clawed and boxed Hyroc's upper body. Despite the brutality of its unrestrained attack, its technique was sloppy and primarily ineffective. It was singularly intent on hurting Hyroc instead of defeating him. The pain it inflicted was hardly a challenge for him to withstand. He had dealt with far worse from a werewolf. This revealed this Feral didn't know how to fight an evenly-matched opponent. With its rejection of the bear from training, it had never learned how to fight another bear properly. It was accustomed to using its size and strength to dominate adversaries which could not match its abilities. This could have been the first time this bear fought another of its kind. Now, it would pay for its disregard.

Hyroc steadily backpedaled on two legs as he grappled with the bear to maintain his balance under its relentless assault while he waited for an opening. The bear gave him a hard shove and revealed the opportunity Hyroc needed. Hyroc tightened the grip of his paws around the bear's shoulders and yanked its body sideways to unbalance it. The bear stumbled, allowing Hyroc to lean into it and use his body weight to press down on it. The bear struggled to regain its footing as Hyroc exerted a tremendous amount of force. The left side of its neck was vulnerable, and Hyroc buried his teeth into it. The bear roared in pain as Hyroc mauled it, staining his muzzle red with blood. The pain was too much for his adversary. The bear's legs buckled, and it fell to the ground. Hyroc's opponent fought to get free, but he had the floundering bear firmly pinned beneath him.

Shawnren darted over to him with the dead North Lander's sword in hand. He struggled to find an opening to deliver a killing blow as he shuffled through a flurry of blindly swiping broad paws that could seriously injure him if one hit. An opportunity presented itself, and he drove the blade into the bear's chest. He stabbed repeatedly until the bear stopped moving.

Shawnren released his grip from the blade and retrieved his ax from his belt as he stepped away. "HYROC, LOOK OUT!" Shawnren yelled.

Hyroc broke from the dead bear to see a Feral charging him with a spear. He scrambled out of the way of a thrust. He rapidly backpedaled as he jerked his body out of the way of numerous strikes. The Feral attacked too swiftly for Hyroc to retaliate without getting stabbed. He feigned pulling one way, catching the Wol'dger by surprise when he dodged in the opposite direction. Before his opponent recovered, he immobilized the spear's shaft by clamping it in his jaws. The Feral desperately yanked on the spear to no avail. Hyroc pivoted and swatted the Wol'dger in the head with his paw. With a snap of bone, the Feral collapsed lifelessly to the ground.

Shawnren stood nearby, exchanging blows with a North Lander. Hyroc moved to assist him, but the thumping of large paws and heavy panting suddenly drew his focus. He saw the large bear. It had finally grown tired of pursuing Iskall and had returned. It rushed toward Shawnren, seemingly oblivious to Hyroc. Hyroc flew to intercept the returning Feral. It was like hitting a brick wall of fat and fur. The bear hardly seemed to stop despite the amount of force behind Hyroc's impact. Hyroc threw himself onto the bear to knock his enemy to the ground. The bear shrugged off his attack and dumped him off with a firm shove of its shoulders into him. Hyroc regained his footing before feeling a thrill of fear as the goliath bear rose on his back legs to tower over him. "Now it's my turn, little bear!" the bear snarled.

The bear crashed into him. It boxed his upper body savagely; each hit felt like a hammer blow. Hyroc pushed against the bear with all his might as he futilely tried to resist his adversary. He couldn't get the pudgy Feral to budge no matter how hard he pushed. The Feral was so strong! A flare of pain shot across Hyroc's chest as the bear's claws laid open a gash in his flesh. Several more bolts of pain materialized on his upper body. He was being torn apart! He struggled to keep his neck protected. It was all over if the bear got its teeth to his throat. Black spots popped into Hyroc's vision as the bear cracked him in the head with a mighty paw strike. Hyroc braced one paw against the bear's neck to hold its face back as he pulled the other paw away from his opponent. The paw glowed blue as Hyroc infused it with an enchantment enhancing the strength it struck with. He slammed it into the bear's face. The bear's head snapped back, and its body lurched away a little but remained standing. The bear's tremendous padding dampened the blow, severely reducing its effectiveness.

Working its jaw irritably with a bead of blood on the end of its nose, the bear turned its head to fix a murderous glare on Hyroc. "You are weak," the bear derisively scoffed. "You didn't stand a chance from the beginning, little bear. Just give in; it will hurt less."

Hyroc heard the ringing of bells and the thundering of hooves coming up behind him, and the bear looked up, astonishment forming in its expression. Hyroc turned his head just enough to see Iskall charging toward him. A thrill of fear surged through him when he thought of his friend impaling his back with those sharp horns. The deer Wol'dger leaped over Hyroc with his antlers pointed forward, slamming them into the enormous Feral bear's face. The bear toppled backward while Iskall's body ricocheted back from the opposing force of the impact, landing on Hyroc's head and shoulders. Hyroc took a sharp hoof to the head, splitting his lip as he collapsed beneath the deer's sudden weight.

Hyroc and Iskall hastily disentangled their limbs to pounce on the larger bear. Iskall stomped and gored the bear. Hyroc went to take a chunk out of the bear's neck, but all he got was a mouthful of blubber. The bear's neck was so thick he couldn't open his mouth wide enough to take a meaningful bite. The bear growled wrathfully. Despite their barrage of attacks, they couldn't cause any lethal damage. They were merely causing the bear to bleed, but minor injuries were useless. Arduously, the bear pushed back against Hyroc and Iskall to regain its footing. Their combined weight still wasn't enough to hold it down! It swiped Iskall with a paw to throw him back. Iskall dodged the strike, thrashing his horns at the bear's legs. Its legs were too thickly padded for him to wound the lumbering beast.

"You're mine, weaklings!" the bear snarled. "I'm going to enjoy ripping both of you to shreds."

Shawnren darted to the bear's side with his ax and started hacking into its shoulder. The bear roared in pain, fiercely trying to cast Hyroc out of its way. Hyroc felt the strength fade from the bear's paw on the side of its body where Shawnren attacked. The tables were now turned in their favor. Hyroc pushed against the bear, which was like trying to move a boulder. Iskall drove his horns into the bear's chest to assist Hyroc in pinning the bear to the ground. As soon as they got the bear down, Shawnren chopped into its neck with his ax. With a weak groan of pain, the bear went still. Everyone pulled away from the bear's lifeless body, heavily breathing a collective sigh of relief.

"Good job – everyone," Hyroc said, panting.

Before anyone could respond, an arrow whistled past.

"Move now!" Iskall said.

"Head toward the river," Hyroc advised. "And keep making noise."

They heard the flapping of wings and cawing overhead. It was Shimmer; the rest of the attack was well underway.

"I think there might be a few more than what your uncle told us," Iskall said.

"I agree," Hyroc said.

"What do you think we're dealing with?" Shawnren asked.

"Let me check," Hyroc said. He took a deep whiff through his nose, utilizing his enhanced sense of smell granted by his bear form. Hyroc coughed, catching a whiff of the bear they had just killed. It seriously stunk! It smelled like a wild animal bear. Bathing had obviously not been a high priority for that Feral. Hyroc slid a paw over his nose to help block out the stink and sniffed again. What he found startled him. "Brace yourselves; there are four wolves almost on top of us! There's one human …" Hyroc took another sniff. "– Wait, no, there's at least two. There's a smell I don't recognize. I assume that's Wol'dger scent. So there are also three Wol'dgers. Those are the closest to us. We can't handle nine of them at the same time. Wait, I know what we need to do. You saw how that big bear fixated on Iskall. Well, dogs are essentially wolves, and they love to chase things, especially things that run. One thing they tell you not to do with wolves and feral dogs is to run because they'll run you down. But we don't need to get away. We need to buy time. So let's give them something to chase."

"You know that's how wolves kill elk, right?" Iskall questioned. "They run them to death. The wolves push them until they're exhausted and move in for the kill."

"Well, just don't let them catch you! You only have to run them in circles to give us enough time to deal with those other guards. Then, you return to us, and we kill those wolves."

"Yeah, and what happens if he trips and they catch him?" Shawnren questioned angrily. "He'll be too far away for us to help him. That's my brother you're talking about. They'll eat him alive!"

"If we don't do something, we'll all die!" Hyroc roared.

"Hey, they're not going to catch me, all right," Iskall reassured. "Don't worry, I've got this. I'm going to give those wolves something incredible to chase!" He trotted around, shaking his head to ring the bells. "Here I am, *stupides*; here I am," Iskall shouted.

Four wolves burst through the foliage. One of the wolves turned out to be a hunting hound.

"I'm going to see what your flanks taste like, *meat*," one wolf threatened Iskall.

"You have to catch me first," Iskall taunted. "Come and get me!" Iskall bolted off into the trees. The wolves shot after him.

"Get back here, coward!" one wolf shouted, their voice fading into the distance.

"Okay, Shawnren," Hyroc said, speaking quickly. "They're coming, so I need you to head out to the south, away from me, circle around, and come up from behind the group coming this way. But make sure you don't run into any of the slavers who might be fanning out to search for us." Shawnren nodded, running off as instructed. Hyroc shook, ringing the bells to draw the attention of anyone nearby. Then, just for good measure, he let out a roar. He darted a short distance away, so they wouldn't know his exact location before crouching down, ready to attack. He stayed completely still to avoid ringing the bells tied to him.

Five figures materialized from the foliage. Three held torches and axes, while the other two held bows with nocked arrows ready to fly.

"Where are those wretched wolves we sent ahead of us?" one North Lander human growled. "I do not enjoy wandering through the dark without knowing if someone is coming up behind me."

"I can't believe how weak you *flat-faces* are at night," a Wol'dger archer said irritably. "The light from your torches is blinding my night eyes. We might as well advertise our location."

"And who in the sunless plains attacks a caravan while ringing bells," another North Lander said, who wore a thick leather band around their head.

"What's that over there?"

Hyroc charged, garnering a wave of swearing from the group. When the archers aimed at him, he swiped a paw in front of him to form a barrier with his Flame Claw. The arrows whistled into the barrier, shattering on impact like they had struck a rock face. Hyroc slammed into a Wol'dger, throwing them to the ground and grabbing them between his jaws by the neck. He snapped their neck with a sharp twisting motion. A North Lander rushed toward Hyroc, swinging an ax. Hyroc dodged backward, answering the strike by swatting them with his paw. It was a non-killing blow that flung the human off their feet.

Hyroc saw the archers leveling another volley of arrows at him. He prepared to form another barrier, but one archer was hit with a throwing hatchet before they could fire. The still-living Wol'dger archer dropped their bow and reached for a dagger, but it was already too late for them. Shawnren exploded out of the foliage and hit them with a lethal strike from his axe.

Hyroc jolted sideways when another caravan guard swung a sword at him in a flurry. He lifted off his front legs while backpedaling to avoid a second strike. After ducking a third, he used a paw to sweep the guard's feet out from under them. But before he could move in for the kill, a shield slammed into his nose from the other guard he had yet to deal with. Hyroc felt a line of warm blood run out of a nostril. He dove into his attacker, throwing them to the ground. When he brought his open mouth down to bite the guard, they still held the shield and shoved it into his mouth. Shawnren dispatched the other guard. The guard with the shield drew a knife and stabbed Hyroc in the shoulder. Luckily, the blade nicked him, which made him bleed, but it didn't inflict any serious harm. Hyroc clenched his teeth around the shield and wrenched it out of the guard's grip, then used it to flick the knife out of their hand. Shawnren delivered the killing blow with his ax.

"Are you okay?" Shawnren asked, indicating the patch of bloodied fur on Hyroc's shoulder.

Hyroc nodded. "I'm good; it was just a glancing hit," he said. They heard the faint sound of ringing bells. The sound was rapidly approaching. "And here comes your brother. Get ready!"

He felt the painful bite of something hitting his left flank. When he wheeled around, he saw a new archer reaching for another arrow. Shawnren dashed toward them, blocking a second shot with his shield. Hyroc glanced back to see the feather-studded shaft of an arrow sticking out of his hindquarters. The wound wasn't within reach of his paws, so he couldn't use his Flame Claw to heal it until he transformed back into his natural form. Unable to attend to it, he had to push through the pain. It hurt tremendously when he moved his left back leg, and he could only endure the pain enough to achieve a slow, laborious limp.

Iskall surged through the foliage toward Hyroc, the bells on his antlers ringing wildly. "I HOPE YOU TWO ARE READY!" he yelled as he thundered toward them. "That's all I can run without a breather. Here they come!" He slowed his pace with a circular trot. The three wolves and the hunting hound immediately followed.

One wolf released a startled yelp when they spotted Hyroc, and the dog started barking. The wolves pushed their noses upward as an enticing smell captured their attention.

"What's this?" the leader said excitedly. "Is that blood we smell? Looks like this bear isn't having a *good night*. We should go ahead and make it worse! We'll deal with you before bringing down your winded meat-deer."

The wolves barreled toward Hyroc. Hyroc swiped a paw to create a wall of blue fire to obstruct the path of the wolves. The wolves hardly slowed as they tore around the fire. One wolf lunged at Hyroc, and he tortuously reared up on his back legs to swat it out of the air. He wasn't fast enough, and the wolf sprang into him. Hyroc reeled from the hit, and a second wolf threw itself into him, sending him the rest of the way over. A storm of pain shot through Hyroc's leg when he hit the ground. The wolves went into a frenzy, attacking any part of his body within reach.

Hyroc frantically swatted his paws at his attackers, but the wolves moved too quickly with erratic swarming motions for him to smack hard enough to do anything. He was strong, but the combined weight of all three wolves was beyond what he could lift, preventing him from regaining his feet. Hyroc used his Flame Claw to envelop his paws in a fiery enchantment. He started swiping his paws wildly, simply trying to clip the wolves. The fire on his paws flared and hissed, throwing out a whoosh of sparks. One wolf howled in pain as their fur ignited with blue fire, followed by a second. The two flaming wolves leaped away, frantically rolling on the ground, trying to extinguish themselves. The last remaining wolf was petrified, realizing he no longer held the advantage.

Hyroc dismissed the enchantment, seizing the wolf with both his paws. He gave his enemy a wrathful glare. "My turn, filth!" he said malevolently. He grabbed the wolf with his teeth and mauled it viciously. His opponent's whole body shook as Hyroc made several savage wrenching motions. Within a few seconds, life left its body. Hyroc got back on all fours, grabbed the wolf's carcass with his teeth, and flung it into the nearest wolf. The impact knocked the wolf off its feet. Hyroc turned from that one and charged toward the other. The wolf had doused the fire and was horrified to see Hyroc on the offense. Before Hyroc could reach it, Iskall blitzed the wolf with his antlers. His horns speared the wolf to a tree, but none of the resulting lacerations were lethal. The wolf squirmed fiercely but couldn't escape. With it immobilized, it was temporarily out of the fight.

When Hyroc returned his attention to the wolf he had struck, he saw a glimpse of its tail as it scurried away for its life. He rushed over and finished off the one Iskall had pinned.

"YOU THREE MUTTS WILL NOT BE THE CURS TO SEND ME TO VALHALLA!" a man's voice bellowed. A tall, burly, baldheaded North Lander appeared with a massive claymore sword. He wore hardened leather armor with dark brown animal skin around the shoulders. Shawnren was his nearest target. Shawnren backpedaled out of the way of a series of strikes from the longsword.

Hyroc moved to assist, but the arrow protruding from his leg restricted him to a sluggish and painful limp. The pain became too much, forcing him to halt, and he struggled to stay standing. He watched Shawnren block a downward sword strike. He heard the shield's wood cracking and splintering under the pummeling. Hyroc formed a fireball and threw it at the North Lander. The fire struck with a bright blue flare, igniting the man's shoulder. He paused his assault to regard his burning shoulder with mild surprise, then continued as if it were a mere annoyance. Hyroc realized the man was a Berzerker. These fierce North Lander warriors were known for taking substances before going into battle that prevented them from feeling pain. Nothing short of death would even slow him down.

Iskall came at the man from behind and jammed his antlers into his back, making him stumble. The man stabbed backward with his sword. Iskall bounded sideways. The man made a wide lateral slice. Iskall ducked the blow, but his antlers didn't clear it. The blade chipped and severed a branch of horn with a loud crack. Iskall darted out of reach before the North Lander struck again.

"Iskall, stay back!" Shawnren yelled. "You can't do anything against that blade." He banged his ax on his shield to draw the North Lander's attention. "Over here, you big ogre."

"I'm going to rip your legs off!" a voice roared. Another black bear with brownish stripes, slightly larger than the first, emerged from the trees. The side of the bear's head and shoulder were marred with scars.

The bear charged straight at Hyroc. Hyroc formed a barrier which the bear crashed into. His quintessence reserve took a sizable hit from absorbing the impact. Using his Flame Claw, mixed with fighting through immense pain, had nearly exhausted his strength.

Hyroc reared on his back legs to meet the attack the bear was doling out. The pain from doing so was excruciating. It was almost more than he could handle.

Two arrows whistled into the bear's back. The bear tensed and grunted at the sudden pain but continued attacking unperturbed. Hyroc wrenched the bear's upper body sideways to prevent his enemy from sinking their teeth into him. Two more arrows hit the bear. This time, the bear was unable to ignore the wounds. Hyroc felt the bear's grip slackening and pressed his advantage. He forced the bear's head down, exposing the back of their neck, and sank his teeth into it. The bear writhed as it futilely tried to break free of his grip.

From the corner of his eye, Hyroc saw an arrow strike the North Lander in the back. Then, Donovan appeared, running toward the North Lander with his spear. He drove his spear into the North Lander's back. This immediately caught the man's attention while a fire still burned on his shoulder. Donovan twisted out of the way of a retaliatory sword swing before delivering another thrust. Shawnren dashed forward with his ax to aid Donovan. They delivered multiple strikes before they finally brought down their obstinate opponent. Even without feeling pain, there was only so much the body could withstand.

Donovan surveyed their surroundings for additional enemies. "Is everybody still alive?" he called out. He focused on Hyroc. "Shadow! You look like hell."

"No, I'm doing swimmingly," Hyroc said sarcastically.

Donovan indicated Hyroc's back end, looking nauseated as he spoke. "Is that – is that an *arrow* sticking out of your butt?"

"*Yes, thanks for noticing,*" Hyroc said crossly.

"Are you sure you're okay?"

Hyroc cringed, speaking through gritted teeth. "I'm fine."

"Do you want me to –"

"WHAT DO YOU THINK!" Hyroc interrupted impatiently.

"I assume everything on your side was successful," Shawnren said. He held his ribs with pain scrawled across his face as he walked.

"Yes, my sister, brother, and Fenrald are back there securing the camp as we speak."

Hyroc roared as Donovan pulled the arrow out, but he was relieved to be free of it. Since the arrowhead was made of metal and stuck in the flesh of his leg, he couldn't transform to heal himself until it was removed. Hyroc dropped down on all fours and transformed. The instant he was in his natural form, he put his hand on his thigh and used his Flame Claw to heal it. He moved on to healing his remaining somewhat serious injuries. That took almost everything he had, so he siphoned a small amount of Quintessence energy from his power gem necklace to maintain his waning strength.

"Shawnren, you good?" Hyroc asked as he got to his feet.

"Yeah, I'll live," he answered. "I got nicked by the tip of that monster of a sword."

"If you're sure, but when I get my strength back, I can take care of that for you."

Hyroc and Donovan took each of Shawnren's shoulders and helped him toward the caravan, with Iskall leading the way. Small campfires came into sight scattered throughout the area, their light illuminating carts, wagons, and tents. Bodies of humans and Ferals littered the area. Here and there, some were smoldering from a large blackened wound, indicative of a lightning bolt from Curtis.

The clang of steel on steel got their attention. The camp wasn't as secure as Donovan had indicated. Hyroc and Donovan unencumbered themselves with Shawnren before moving away to investigate the sound. Hyroc snatched a dagger off one of the bodies. On the other side of a tent, they saw Fenrald using his sword to block a strike from an ax before parrying with a dagger. In a flash of blades, he dispatched his opponent. The body had scarcely hit the ground before he engaged two more guards. Fenrald took care of them so quickly and efficiently that Hyroc had never imagined you could kill someone so fast without magic. Hyroc gaped in astonishment.

"Oh, I should tell you that your uncle is terrifyingly good at killing people," Donovan noted.

"I can see that," Hyroc said, shaking out of his stupor.

"I'm glad he's on our side."

Fenrald turned to receive the attack of a North Lander, but an arrow hit his opponent in the chest first, knocking him onto his back. Fenrald snapped his attention on Hyroc and Donovan. For an instant, Hyroc saw an icy, dispassionate look in his eye and knew his uncle was assessing the best way to eliminate him as a threat if he were one. Fenrald was far more dangerous than Hyroc had possibly imagined. He would be a tremendous adversary if he ever became one. It was indeed a good thing he was on their side. Hyroc would doubly make sure he never got on his bad side.

"Fenrald," Hyroc said with a raised hand to announce they weren't Ferals. Fenrald nodded his acknowledgment before disappearing around a tent. Hyroc and Donovan returned to Iskall to help bring Shawnren to the rest of the group.

There, they found fifteen human children of a wide range of ages shackled to a chain driven into a tree. Two of the oldest were around sixteen, a boy and a girl, with the youngest children being about seven. They wore clothing caked with dried mud. All of them were bruised and scraped and had sores around their wrists and ankles from the abrasive shackles rubbing ceaselessly on their skin. Elsa stood next to the chain anchor, hacking at the tree with a hatchet to release it.

"Wol'dgers!" several children screamed when Hyroc and his companions were close.

Elsa turned, instinctively reaching for her bow. She relaxed, bobbing her head in relief upon recognizing them. Curtis stood near the children and gave them a gentle, reassuring shush to quiet the younger ones. "No, no, those are my friends," he said. "Those are good Wol'dgers. Those are my brothers Donovan and Hyroc. The other Wol'dger is Shawnren, and the deer with the big horns is Iskall."

"Hello," Hyroc, Donovan, and Shawnren said with a friendly wave. Iskall waved a front leg in a motion that looked bizarre for a deer.

"You got him?" Donovan asked, indicating Shawnren. "I should help my sister with that anchor so we can get out of here."

"Yeah, I've got him," Hyroc said. He helped Shawnren sit by the children. Shawnren stripped off his bloodied tunic to assess the extent of his injury. Hyroc located a bucket of water and brought it to the children. He couldn't find any containers, so he had to settle for a wooden spoon for them to share.

"Give that here," the older boy said. Hyroc gave it to him, and as soon as he had taken a drink, he started passing it around the group.

"You're hurt," a young girl beside Shawnren said in an innocent voice. She ripped away the cleanest chunk of her clothing and held it out as an offer to him.

Shawnren looked at her, confounded as if this were the first time he had imagined humans were capable of such acts of compassion. "Thank you," he said, accepting the improvised rag to dab the blood around his wound. "Don't worry; it's not bad; it just looks that way."

Fenrald came to the group. "All right, everything looks clear," he announced. "For the time being, at least, the camp is ours. But I don't want to spend more time here than is needed. I don't know if there are more of them out there we missed."

"Fenrald!" the eldest girl said eagerly. She had blonde hair, blue eyes, and a tall, slender figure.

"Sandra?" Fenrald said with surprised recognition. "What are you doing here?"

"I'm so glad you're here."

"Everyone, this is Sandra. She is the niece of a baron I've worked with on occasion. I'm sure your uncle will be happy to have you safely back at your home. We'll have all of you safe and sound in no time, don't you worry." He turned his attention back to his instructions. "Stay alert while you grab anything we need, especially pack animals; round up any you find. Stay together."

Iskall rooted around with his nose in several containers in a cart. Hyroc investigated inside a tent with pieces of parchment laid across animal skins on the ground. He found a map of the area with important-looking markings inside a leather tube and slung it over his shoulder. The rest of the parchment consisted of messages warning the caravan guards of potential threats and what looked to be delivery instructions for the children, but nothing of interest.

When Hyroc returned to the children, the anchor was free, and Elsa, Curtis, and Fenrald were working feverishly to remove the shackles. Hyroc moved over to assist.

"Anything I can do to help?" Hyroc asked, coming next to Fenrald.

"No, I think …" Fenrald trailed off, looking at Hyroc with sudden inspiration. "Your Flame Claw; is there any spell or such you can use on these chains?"

"Probably; let me see what I can do." He grabbed the chain to examine it closely. He could melt and deform the shackles – no, that would require burning someone's hand off. Why was he even thinking about that? What if he simply cast a spell to release the manacles? That shouldn't take a whole lot of Quintessence. He could spare it.

Suddenly, the children looked behind Hyroc with horrified expressions. Then, he heard growling.

"HYROC," Fenrald yelled, grabbing his arm and yanking him sideways.

The gaping jaws of a wolf flew through where Hyroc had been sitting an instant prior. But without Hyroc there, that now put the oldest kidnapped boy directly in its path. The mistaken target made no difference to the Feral. The wolf slammed into the boy and savaged him with its teeth. Kit was the first one to react by hurling himself into the wolf. Hyroc, Elsa, and Fenrald ripped the big cat away from the wolf before each of them drove a blade into it, stabbing repeatedly. As soon as the wolf died, they pulled the carcass aside to check on the boy.

Fenrald cursed. The boy bled profusely from the neck. It was a mortal wound. Fenrald stooped to grab the tunic Shawnren had taken off and pressed it against the boy's neck. This slowed the bleeding, but not enough. Elsa could do nothing beyond comforting the boy with a hand on his head.

"Hyroc!" Fenrald said frantically. "Your mother could use her Flame Claw to heal. Are you able to heal?"

"Yes," Hyroc said.

"Good. I need you to heal him."

Hyroc felt a thrill of apprehension. "I don't know …"

"Hyroc, *heal* him," Fenrald urged more sternly.

"I've never done anything that deep. I've only done shallow things like sores, scrapes, and cuts. Never anything this serious."

Fenrald grabbed Hyroc's shoulder and turned him so he could look into his eyes. "Dammit! If we don't try something *now*, he will *die*."

Hyroc felt a surge of fear from the intensity with which his uncle spoke. The fire in Fenrald's eyes almost sent him into a panic. Disappointing him was a terrible thought. Suddenly, Hyroc wondered what would happen if he disappointed his uncle. Would failure cause Fenrald to hurt him or do something more severe? Hyroc pushed aside his shock. His concerns were ridiculous. His uncle would never do anything to him. Hyroc held someone's life in his hands; for the moment, his feelings meant nothing. Saving them took precedence over anything he felt.

Fenrald released him. Hyroc removed the blood-soaked tunic and placed his hand over the wound. Warm blood flowed over his hand. He focused on molding his Quintessence into a potent healing spell. A blue glow moved from his hand, fading as it sank into the wound. Hyroc felt the drain on his diminished Quintessence, and the accompanying fatigue, but blood continued to issue out of the wound.

"Did it work?" Fenrald impatiently asked.

"I – I don't," Hyroc said uncertainly. "I felt the Quintessence leave me when I cast the spell."

"But he's still bleeding. It must not have worked. You did something wrong. Try again."

"I don't know if I can. That took a lot out of me, and I don't think I have enough Quintessence to try again."

"Here, take this," Curtis said. He offered his emerald necklace to Hyroc.

Gratefully, Hyroc placed a hand over the gem and siphoned off the required energy. Then, he made another healing attempt. The energy left him, but as before, it made no difference with the boy's wound.

"It's not working," Hyroc said in frustration.

"He doesn't have any time left. Try again!"

"There's one more thing I can try. I need to modify the spell." He reached for Curtis's necklace again.

"Hyroc," Elsa said.

"It's a small modification; I know what to do."

She grabbed his hand. "No, Hyroc, it's too late. He's gone."

Hyroc looked at the boy's face to see his eyes staring off, unmoving, and he was no longer breathing. Hyroc slumped back, grabbing the back of his head.

Elsa comfortingly squeezed his shoulder. "You tried your best, but there was nothing you could have done," she said gently.

Fenrald rose to his feet, walked over to the closest tree, and angrily smacked it with the palm of his hand. The youngest children began crying. Elsa and Curtis worked to console them.

"Donovan, Elsa," Fenrald said in a calm, somber voice. "You remember where we left the pack mule and donkey." They nodded. "Bring them here, if you would." He indicated the boy. "I've got something to wrap him in. Keep an eye out for more Ferals in case they're out there." They headed off.

Fenrald returned to the boy and covered his body with Shawnren's bloodied tunic. He reached out and put a comforting hand on Hyroc's shoulder. Hyroc barely noticed. "I'm sorry for how I treated you just now," he said. "I let the situation get the better of me. Can you forgive me for that?" Hyroc didn't respond. "We lost one, but the other fourteen get to go home. You still did well. Take solace in that. Now, let's get you taken care of. It looks like they tore you up something fierce. I'm sorry about that and that it couldn't be avoided. None of your injuries are too bad, but they need tending. But it was still a decent night."

Chapter 20

A Surprising Gift

Hyroc followed Fenrald through the forest, where streamers of sunlight shone through the canopy. They were at the head of the group, making sure the way was safe. Hyroc stepped aside and stopped, making sure no one lagged behind. Sandra passed him first, giving him a friendly wave. He nodded his appreciation at the gesture. Iskall trotted past in his stag form with four of the youngest children on his back. They all smiled broadly, clearly enjoying riding such an unusual mount. Elsa was in the middle, watching the rest of the rescued captives. Shawnren was at the back of the group riding their pack mule with Donovan on foot beside him. Attached to Shawnren's mule with a lead were their donkey and two horses they had found with the Feral caravan. Shawnren's injury, though not life-threatening, caused him considerable pain and discomfort when he walked, and he was slowing them down. They also couldn't put him on one of the horses because he was a Wol'dger, and neither animal would permit him on their back. That relegated him to the mule. Unlike the horses, the mule had been raised by Wol'dger's from a foal and had no fear of their kind riding it.

But the very last horse carried the body of the slain boy to keep it as far from the other children as possible. The body was wrapped in white cloth, reminding Hyroc of someone wrapped in a spider web. He averted his gaze from the body. That brought back too many bad memories. It had been about two days since they left the Feral caravan, but he was reminded of his uncle yelling in his face every time he looked at it. That was a side of his uncle he didn't want to see again. The intensity of it all made him rethink how much he knew Fenrald. They were still trying to get a grasp on each other's personalities. He didn't think anything bad about his uncle from the situation. It was a life and death moment, which made emotions run high, but something he saw in his uncle made him uneasy.

Hyroc turned with Shawnren to continue moving alongside him. "How's the side?" he asked.

"Good," Shawnren answered. "But it will be doing a whole lot better once I get off this damn mule." Hyroc nodded his sympathy. "But at least all my pain and suffering was for a good cause. I also got a pretty nice reward for my trouble." He patted the hilt of a sheathed claymore secured across the donkey's hindquarters. It had belonged to the massive North Lander they had killed with the Ferals. Shawnren was trying to decide whether to keep it as a weapon or sell it. It was forged from high-quality steel and would go for a hefty sum in Forestgold. He was unsure about using it as a weapon because it might simply be too large and cumbersome of a blade for him to wield proficiently. It could be more dangerous for him than any adversary.

"Well, there's not much further we need to go," Hyroc said reassuringly. With that, he worked his way to the front of the group.

Soon, the company moved from the rough, uneven terrain of the uncut forest onto the road toward the Glacial village. They passed baffled onlookers. The presence of human children in a place where their kind seldom ventured was quite the spectacle. A dark brown Wol'dger in wolf form passed them, going in the other direction. The children riding Iskall pointed excitedly at the wolf, laughing happily. The wolf stopped, lifting a paw to ensure it hadn't stepped in something, seemingly confused about what made it so interesting. Then, they arrived at Fenrald's cabin.

Fenrald deposited a load of firewood from his stockpile in a fire pit outside. Curtis ignited it with a tight shower of white sparks. Next, Fenrald retrieved blankets from his cabin and laid them on the ground to give the children a place to sit. Kit excitedly jumped on the roof, scanning his surroundings to ensure some monster wasn't sneaking up on them. Once the children were comfortable, everyone started unloading the supplies. Fenrald led the horse with the body behind the cabin so it was entirely out of sight of the children.

"If there isn't anything else," Shawnren said. "My brother and I would really like to get home."

"That's fine," Fenrald said. "We're pretty much done here. And I'll get both your portions of the reward as soon as I have it."

They nodded their agreement.

"I'll come with you," Elsa said. "You'll need somebody to bring that mule back, and I can get Elizabeth at the same time. Iskall, may I ride you?"

"You certainly may, madam," he said. He graciously lowered himself so she could easily climb on his back before trotting off.

Hyroc and Fenrald moved inside the cabin to examine their recovered map. Fenrald unrolled it on a table and leaned over it. Hyroc came close on the side.

"So what do we have?" Hyroc asked expectantly.

Fenrald rubbed his chin. "It looks like a slaver map," he said. "It's got marked the best paths the caravan could take, the easiest places to kidnap, and delivery locations."

"Is that useful?"

"Yes, a little bit. There are a few paths here I've never seen on any of their other maps." He retrieved a map from a basket full of rolled-up parchment and laid it next to the current one to compare the two. He leaned back and was silent a moment. "This could have been disastrous," he said without taking his eye off the map.

"Disastrous?" Hyroc asked uncertainly. "You mean for the children?"

"Oh, yes, of course, but not just for them. For all of us." He moved to the cabin's doorway. "You see that girl, Sandra?"

Hyroc saw Sandra braiding another girl's hair. "Yeah, she is the niece of a baron you worked for once."

"Yes, and can you imagine what the consequences would have been if we hadn't been able to rescue her, the relative of someone who has sway with the King? That baron would have been outraged when he learned his niece had been kidnapped by the Ferals and sold to the North Landers. He would have cried for retribution. And that would have almost certainly brought down the wrath of the Mastgar Crown. They do not understand the distinction between the ideology of us Glacials and the Ferals. Since we are heaped together, they would drive us out all the same."

He shook his head in disbelief. "This is the first time they've been bold enough to go after someone from the upper crust. Whether that was intentional or purely by accident I do not know. Despite the unstable animalistic behavior of his followers, Eagle has always avoided such recklessness. His restraint all these years indicates his awareness of the danger to them and us in antagonizing the Mastgariens. He and his followers have no less desire to live than we do. On the off chance this was intentional, and I'm not simply reading too much into this, what caused their newfound hubris? We'll have to ponder that enigma. In any event, we can celebrate rescuing those children. But, remember, our victory only bought us time. Things are still falling apart."

"But now you have *me*," Hyroc said sternly. "I don't like bullies picking on defenseless children. I want to help; I want to get in on this fight. You have my Flame Claw." He created a blue fire in his palm to emphasize his point. "We don't have to wait for another caravan, hoping we don't miss one that will lead to our destruction before acting. We can take the fight to them. Maybe end this for good."

Fenrald cracked a tiny, hopeful smile. He squeezed Hyroc's shoulder. "Your enthusiasm heartens me," he said gratefully. "It's been a long time since I've been graced with a modicum of hope. I almost forgot it existed. I am grateful you once again reminded me of its light. But before we get lost thinking about anything else, we must focus on reuniting those children with their families. There's a bunch of worried parents out there. Then… then we make the Ferals pay."

Elsa returned, riding the mule with Elizabeth sitting on her lap. She handed Elizabeth down into Fenrald's waiting arms before dismounting.

Elizabeth clung close to Fenrald, casting an uncertain gaze at the young strangers in front of her home.

"Have you seen what's going on in the village?" Elsa asked. She made a beckoning motion, bidding Hyroc and Fenral to follow. She led them to the road beyond the cabin. Pulling back the edge of a clump of bushes, she revealed a sizable crowd of gawking Wol'dgers looking eagerly in their direction.

"It looks like rescuing those children has caused quite a stir with the villagers," she said.

"I'm not sure why," Fenrald admitted. "This isn't the first time I've had a successful rescue, and it's not the first time they've seen human children at my home."

"You seriously don't know the reason?" Donovan said as if nothing were plainer to see.

"If you know, please enlighten us," Fenrald said, sounding slightly indignant.

Donovan leaned close to Hyroc and gave his shoulders a quick squeeze. "It's because an Anamagi helped with the rescue."

"Me?" Hyroc asked, pushing away one of Donovan's hands. "No, that can't be it."

Fenrald's face filled with comprehension. "You know, I think you're right. An Anamagi did help me. I think that is what caught their attention."

"So what are we supposed to do about it?" Hyroc said.

"There's only one thing to do," Fenrald said. He surprised Hyroc with a hand on his back and shoved him from the concealment of the bushes.

The group of Wol'dgers stopped a quiet conversation upon spotting Hyroc. They all regarded him with marveling, eager expressions. One of the older Wol'dgers, a brown and dark gray male, wearing a black tunic and pants, stepped forward with an authoritative presence; the village leader, Hyroc, assumed.

"We heard what you did," he said eagerly. "And it is an honor to meet you, Anamagi." He reached forward with a clawed hand, grabbing Hyroc's forearm to shake it. "I thought all of your bloodline had been slain." He shook his head as if embarrassed. "Please excuse me; I haven't even given you my name. I am Sanoc of the Icebane clan."

"I'm Hyroc Foxclaw," Hyroc said.

"I'm so glad to be able to meet you, Hyroc. "And what of your companions? The human? It's quite the spectacle to see humans venturing into the village, let alone traveling with a Wol'dger and fighting alongside our kind. I should very much like to meet them as well."

Hyroc waved his friends over. When they emerged, Sanoc grabbed their forearm to shake, grabbing there because his claws wouldn't accidentally scratch anyone.

"It's such a pleasure to meet all of you, Elsa, Donovan, and Curtis," he said. The crowd meandered over to offer their greetings.

"What an amazing accomplishment," one Wol'dger said.

"How many Ferals did you face?" asked another.

"I hope that will learn those Ferals a lesson," a third said.

"That's a story you must tell us more of," a fourth said.

"We wanted to celebrate this heroic occasion with you," Sanoc said. "It's been such a long time since we've had anything joyous to celebrate." He made a beckoning motion. "Come, we prepared something special for everyone."

"We will absolutely come!" Donovan said excitedly.

With a sharp-toothed smile, Sanoc led them toward the village.

"A celebration?" a voice said. Hyroc turned to see Sandra peeking out from behind the bush. "Can I come?"

Hyroc looked to his uncle. "I don't know," he said. "It's up to Fenrald."

"I don't see why not," Fenrald said. "It will take me a while to get everything together for these kids' return journey. So her joining the celebration won't cause any problems. Just keep a close eye on her. Remember our *important talk earlier*?"

Hyroc nodded. "Wait, aren't you coming?" he asked.

Fenrald shook his head. "Nah, I have no interest in the praise for what I did as I know it was the right thing. Besides, you and your companions did most of the work. To say nothing of the thrashing you endured. The six of you are the real heroes. You deserve this more than I. Go, go enjoy yourselves."

Hyroc nodded his understanding and headed to the village with his friends, Sandra, and the crowd of excited onlookers.

"I want to see more of what you nice Wol'dgers are like," Sandra said as they walked. "Why is that, by the way? Why are you so much nicer than the ones you saved us from?"

"Because they're Feral Wol'dgers," Hyroc answered. "And we, everyone in this village, are Guidance Wol'dger. Or call us Glacials for short."

"But why are you here, all you Guidance Wol'dgers?"

"First, I need to show you something, so this makes sense." Hyroc opened the chest of his jerkin to expose the glowing blue bear paw print on his shoulder. He tapped it. "You see this blue tattoo-looking thing here. This is my animal mark. It lets me turn into a bear." He did his jerkin back up.

"A bear? Really?" she said in awe.

Hyroc nodded. "We – my kind – can turn into many different animals, depending on the person. But not all of us have the chance to get a mark. So most of us are just like you, like humans. We just look a little different."

"I saw those marks on some of the Wol'dgers that kidnapped us. But their's were red."

"Their marks were red because there are specific rules with our animal form. If you don't follow those rules, the mark turns red."

"And yours is blue because you follow the rules?"

Hyroc nodded. "And if we don't follow the rules, we are afflicted with some nasty tendencies, which is why those rules exist."

"Is that why the Ferals act like animals?"

"Mostly, yes. But it's also partly due to the way they think. They think they are superior to humans and view becoming more animal-like as a strength."

"If they despise humans, why are they allied with the North Landers?"

"It's an alliance of necessity. The Ferals need the North Landers for supplies and such. And the North Landers are getting …" Hyroc paused, thinking it might not be wise to tell her the North Landers were receiving slaves so soon after rescuing her from their clutches.

"They're getting *us*," Sandra finished his words. "That's why they kidnapped us, isn't it?"

Hyroc sighed dejectedly. "Yeah. They were getting you and the other children."

They were quiet for a long moment before Sandra broke the silence. "The village leader referred to you as an Anamagi. I've never heard that word before. What does it mean? They regard you with esteem. Are you a Wol'dger Prince?"

"No, nothing as prestigious as that," Hyroc said. "But it does mean I am someone special among us Glacial Wol'dgers. It's because of this." Hyroc lifted his hand and summoned a blue ball of fire. "This represents a promise and a willing sacrifice of loyalty long ago. Only the bloodline of the Anamagi possess it."

"So you're a Wol'dger mage?"

"Maybe think of me as a powerful special kind of Wol'dger mage."

By now, they had arrived at the center of the village. It was nearing dusk, and the dull orange light of the setting sun had settled on the village, casting long shadows. A bonfire burned in the center, and pairs of Wol'dgers danced nearby at a relaxed pace. Some Wol'dgers sat on chairs playing instruments. The tune was slow but festive. A cart was drawn up with a sizable wooden keg. Tables had been lined up near the keg, each with mugs spread over them. Signs had been erected with the spiral symbol often seen on Guardians to honor them and act as decorations.

Iskall and Shawnren stood near one of the tables, each talking to a female Wol'dger. They acknowledged Hyroc with a raised mug of ale.

"I know it's not much, but it's the least we could do to commemorate your success against the Ferals," Sanoc said with his hands together. "Please, enjoy." He ushered everyone past with a grand gesture. The already festive atmosphere became even livelier. Excited conversations filled the air.

Hyroc was at the center of attention, but Elsa, Donovan, and Curtis also received a fair amount of interest. For the first few minutes, Hyroc was wholly inundated with praise before things turned more conversational. A female Wol'dger he judged to be close to his age grabbed his arm. Not wanting to be rude, he submitted to her leading him over to sit on a bench at one of the tables. When he reached for a mug, it was whisked away by another female Wol'dger. She was also young. She obligingly filled the mug for him. When it was in his hand, Hyroc raised it in thanks to her.

"I can't believe you took on all those Ferals and North Landers to rescue those human children," the original young Wol'dger female said to him. "That must have been frightening."

"It truly was," Hyroc said. "But we had a plan …" he paused distractedly when the Wol'dger lightly rubbed his arm. "We had a plan," he said, regaining his composure. "Me, Shawnren, and Iskall were going to …" The other Wol'dger sat beside him. Having lost his train of thought, he took a drink of his ale as he attempted to regain it. The third Wol'dger scooted closer so her hip was against his. She snuggled under his arm and lay her head on his. Seemingly threatened by this gesture, the other Wol'dger attempted the same maneuver. Then Hyroc felt two arms from behind, rubbing his shoulders. Suddenly, he felt like a hunted animal and had an overwhelming urge to flee. He darted out of the grip of the three Wol'dgers with a mortified expression. They regarded him with confusion and started to come off the bench to join him.

Then he felt a hand tapping him on the shoulder. He glanced over his shoulder and recognized the female Wol'dger Freija he had mistaken for a witch the other day. She wore a dress, a slightly darker shade of blue than during their first meeting, with a similar soft white inner lining.

"May I have this dance?" Freija asked politely.

"I – I don't know, I haven't –" Hyroc said until she interrupted, leaning closer to him.

"You can dance with me," she whispered. "Or I can give you back to *them*." She discreetly indicated with her chin the three Wol'dgers who regarded him with jealous eyes.

"I see your point," Hyroc agreed. He said the next part unnecessarily loud to ensure the three Wol'dgers heard him and hopefully make them look elsewhere for prey. "Yes, *I absolutely will dance with you*!"

"Put a hand on my hip," she politely instructed. "Then, grab my raised hand. Okay, now, shuffle your feet as you lead me in a circle."

Hyroc stepped awkwardly and caught her foot with the edge of his, causing her to stumble slightly. "Sorry," Hyroc apologized, his face warming with embarrassment. "I understand the irony. I can kill Ferals, but I can't dance." She laughed, and they resumed dancing. Hyroc had now gotten a feel for the movements.

"So you and your friends rescued all those children?" she asked.

"We did," he answered.

"It must have been terrible fighting those Ferals. I've heard they are ruthless and cruel. I can only imagine what that must have been like."

"Yes, they were vicious. They didn't want just to kill me; they wanted to tear me to pieces, and they were going to make it hurt as much as possible."

She pulled her lip back on one side of her mouth, revealing teeth in a displeased, empathetic sneer. "That sounds awful."

"Especially the Wol'dgers in bear form," Hyroc continued. "The bears were the worst. They are far more aggressive than any animal I've had to fight. They don't hold anything back and are much faster than they look. When you fight them, you know it's going to hurt."

"I can only wonder how dangerous an animal that can think like a person would be."

Hyroc nodded his agreement. "But they have one weakness." He stopped dancing to tap the side of his head for emphasis. "Their minds." After another couple nearly tripped over them, they stepped out of the dancing area. "You see," he continued, "if you can whip them into a fury, you can turn the *beast* against them. The *beast* usually makes them dangerous and unpredictable, but they don't see things clearly when you make them mad. When you do this, they're not so smart anymore. It's easy to trick them, lead them into a trap, or cause them to make a mistake you can exploit."

"I see," she said. "You blind them with rage. But by making them so angry, doesn't it make them want to rip you apart even more? What happens if you make a mistake when they're in that frenzy, and they unleash all their rage upon you? Isn't it also risky to do that?"

Hyroc bobbed his head. "Yes, I guess it's also dangerous doing that. But if you fight them head-on, there's a good chance you'll lose. They mainly rely on overpowering you. Pain also doesn't affect them as much. So if you want to hurt them enough to drive them away, you have to hurt them *a lot*."

"Makes sense. So, I hear you are an Anamagi."

"You've already heard that?"

She nodded. "Of course. It's not every day such a regal bloodline returns from oblivion. Am I correct in assuming your Flame Claw helped defeat those Ferals?"

"I don't think we would have succeeded without it."

She nodded her understanding. "I won't ask you to give me a demonstration –" she indicated everyone around her "– and draw any more unwanted attention to you."

Hyroc nodded his thanks. "But, maybe sometime in the future, and in a less crowded place, I could give you a demonstration."

"I would like that."

The band played a faster, more energetic tune.

"You have to give me another dance," she said excitedly. Before Hyroc could respond, she grabbed his arm and yanked him back into the dancing area.

After they had their fill of dancing, Hyroc and Freija found a seat at one of the tables next to Iskall. Iskall regaled three young Wol'dger boys with the description of his harrowing rescue of the human children. Hyroc appreciated his friend embellishing how he had fought in his bear form. However, he was unsure if this was premeditated or if his friend had hit the keg too much. Hyroc got a mug of ale for him and Freija while Iskall finished up his telling of the violent portion of the rescue.

"And how are you enjoying this evening?" Iskall said.

"I'm enjoying it a lot," Hyroc said.

"You as well, Freija?"

"Yes, me as well," Freija said before taking a draught of her ale.

Iskall nodded and laughed before speaking. "I saw how you rescued my friend –" he smugly indicated Hyroc "– from those overly interested ladies."

"I saw an opportunity, and I took it." Freija squeezed Hyroc's arm and leaned against it for emphasis.

Hyroc smiled before taking another drink of his ale. A thought came to him. "So, Iskall, that North Lander took off a sizable portion of your rack with his sword. What does that do, with it being in animal form and all?"

"Oh, it will grow back," Iskall said. "That's not the first time I've had pieces of it break off."

"Does it just pop out of nowhere as if nothing happened next time you transform?"

"No, it will take some time before I get it back. I have to do all the velvet fuzzy stuff again like a rutting buck. When I'm in that form, I hate how itchy it gets toward the end when it falls off. The dried blood on my horns from shedding the velvet makes me appear to be some kind of demon deer."

Hyroc and Freija let out a mildly disturbed laugh.

"But at least your brother got a nice sword out of that ordeal," Hyroc said.

"True, very true," Iskall agreed.

"Friends, may I have everyone's attention?" Sanoc announced with a clap of his hands. He gestured toward several Wol'dgers standing in a line beside him, who had large trays of food held in their arms. "Now, let us feast."

Chapter 21

A Good Deed

…*He* can shoot lightning?" Sandra said in amazement.

Hyroc nodded. "He sure can," he said. "That's come in handy on many occasions."

"I never knew there were such magic casters."

The morning was overcast, a white film of wispy clouds across the sky. Hyroc and Donovan walked beside a horse-drawn cart carrying the rescued fourteen children. Fenrald drove the cart, with Curtis sitting beside him, ready to blast with lightning anything foolish enough to attempt blocking their path. They escorted the children across the road connecting the Glacial village to Forestgold. Awaiting them at the town was an entourage of Mastgar knights. The knights would accompany the children the rest of the way to where they had initially been kidnapped. Elsa had opted out of the trip to hunt because housing the fourteen children had depleted Fenrald's food stores, and she wanted to help replenish them. Joining them also seemed overkill to her since Hyroc and Curtis alone could protect the children from any threat.

"Well, technically," Hyroc continued. "I could create lightning as well, I'm just not very good at it. We magic users are typically best at a single school of magic. Fire mages are best at fire; ice mages are best at ice; and so forth. But using those other schools of magic is more taxing."

"Why is your fire blue? I've never seen that before. "

Because –" Hyroc abruptly paused, gazing at the trail behind them. He thought he saw something. Fenrald had advised the group to keep a sharp eye out for signs of pursuit from Ferals. Even traversing the short distance from the Glacial village to Forestgold created an opening for the Ferals to try to recover their lost prize. But once the knights took over guarding the children, they would be too well protected for retrieval by the Ferals.

Hyroc studied the trail but nothing was out of place. He walked backward several steps before returning to his position beside the cart.

"See something?" Donovan called back.

Hyroc raised a hand and waved Donovan off. "No, we're good," Hyroc said.

Donovan nodded.

"Is it true you grew up in Arnaira to the east?" Sandra asked. Hyroc nodded. "I've heard The Ministry of the Silver Scythe is fanatically anti-magic. That they label all magic, even beneficial kinds, as witchcraft and put to death anyone they catch using it?"

"They do indeed," Hyroc said. "We just refer to them as The Ministry. It's less of a mouthful. You're wondering how I managed to survive?" Sandra nodded with intrigue. "That is usually the first thing people ask. I was wise and cautious about staying hidden from The Ministry. My good friends, Donovan, Curtis, and Elsa, also played a big part in that." Hyroc looked distant as the memory of June washed over him. "But even as careful as I was, I couldn't hide from them forever."

"And you came here?"

"Pretty much. It was about –" Hyroc halted, swiveling as his hand flew to the hilt of his sword. This time, he had undeniably seen something out of the corner of his eye. It was something walking on four legs. Donovan ran over to Hyroc, his spear at the ready.

"Did you see it?" Hyroc said, scanning his surroundings.

Donovan shook his head. "No, sorry, just your reaction," he apologized. "Did you see a Feral?"

"There is a good chance it was one in animal form. It walked on all fours."

"Hyroc, Donovan!" Fenrald yelled over his shoulder while he steered the horses from the driving position. "Jump on. I'm going to pick up the pace. We're almost to the gate; I don't want to take any chances." The two of them hopped on the back of the cart. With a crack of the reins, the horses quickened their pace. Hyroc held one hand up, ready to summon a barrier in case an arrow came flying their way. One of the younger children, a brown-haired boy curiously lifted his head to peer over his shoulder.

"You need to stay down," Hyroc urged while reaching over and easing him down.

The cart rounded a corner. They saw the town through the leaves of a clump of alders. Hyroc swept his eyes through their surroundings. All was clear. As they drew close to the gate, guards flanked the road, shields at the ready, and hands on swords. Fenrald waited as long as possible before yanking on the reins to slow the horses and trot them through the gate's portcullis.

Hyroc and Donovan let out a collective relieved sigh. A couple of the children gave them an appreciative smile. Their visages wrapped Hyroc in a warm, happy sensation. Because of him, Fenrald, and his friends, they got to go home.

The horses pulled the cart through the streets, their hooves clip-clopping against the cobblestone as they arrived at the town center near the fountain. Except for Hyroc and Fenrald, the square was devoid of Wol'dgers. The area contained dozens of guards, making any attack by the Ferals suicide. Guards formed in front of the cart, with at least a dozen heavily armed Knights on horseback behind them.

Hyroc and Donovan dismounted first.

"Fenrald?" a guard captain, distinguished by black feathers on their shoulder, asked, coming around the side of the cart.

"Yes," Fenrald said with a nod, handing the reins off to Curtis. He dismounted, leading the guard to the back of the cart. "And here they are."

The guard nodded, looking over the side of the cart to count the children. He gave Fenrald a perplexed look. "I counted only fourteen, I thought …"

Fenrald interrupted him with a sharp movement of his hand, indicating the guard should lower their voice. He guided the guard to a tarp laid across something behind the children. Discreetly, he pulled open a corner, revealing the white cloth wrapped around the body of the boy who had been killed. That somberly reminded everybody one family was in for a horrific message. The guard gave him a pained look before nodding his acknowledgment. "And no, that's not the Baron's niece."

"That's good," the guard said. "It just doesn't mean anything for the family about to hear the worst."

Fenrald nodded sadly.

"Do you require anything?"

"Only some provisions for the children."

The captain waved over a group of guards. They loaded two sacks of bread into the cart. Then, the captain informed the knights they were departing momentarily.

Fenrald indicated Curtis should climb off the cart. "All right, boys," he said. "This is where you get off. I can take care of the rest from here." He shook Curtis and Donovan's hands. "Thank you for all of your help."

"You're welcome," Curtis said.

"Glad to help," Donovan said.

Fenrald clapped Hyroc on the shoulder. "I especially couldn't have done this without you." Hyroc nodded proudly. Fenrald gazed at him with supreme satisfaction. "Your parents would have been proud of you. You honor your family well."

Hyroc beamed. He opened his mouth to speak, but none of the words he wanted to say seemed sufficient to capture his feelings.

"It's okay. I know," Fenrald said happily.

"Stay – stay safe," Hyroc settled on.

"We've got a lot of work to do once I return. Until then."

"Wol'dger Hyroc," Sandra said, leaning over the side of the cart.

"I should like to hear more about you and your people. If you find yourself in my uncle's region, please visit me. He might also take interest in some of what you have to say. And – and thank you for rescuing us. I shan't forget it."

"You're very welcome," he said. "Take care."

With a crack of the reins, the cart rolled forward. Fenrald gave a final wave. Half of the knights formed in front of the cart and the other half at the back.

Hyroc, Donovan, and Curtis watched until the column disappeared through the other gate.

Chapter 22
Retribution

...Why do I feel like I'm forgetting something?" Hyroc said. He stared at Fenrald's cabin with his arms crossed as he racked his brain. Elsa was inside cooking some fish she had caught at a nearby stream. Donovan chopped firewood while Curtis played with Elizabeth on the porch. Three days had passed since Fenrald departed to accompany the rescued children back home. He wasn't expected back for at least another week. But in the meantime, it was up to the four of them to take care of things until his return. Fenrald had left a list of bare minimum chores that needed doing, and Hyroc was sure he had taken care of everything, but he felt like something was missing.

"Don't you need to return the mule Fenrald had rented?" Curtis suggested.

"That's what it was," Hyroc said excitedly, pointing at him. "Thank you, Curtis." He was supposed to return the mule to avoid the owner charging his uncle extra for using the animal beyond their initial contract. The owner had required Fenrald to give a sizable deposit of Flecks as collateral in case the animal was injured or killed while he used it. His uncle needed that deposit back. The group also had no money, so the amount would carry them over with the essentials until Fenrald returned with his payment for completing the task.

Hyroc secured the reins to the animal and led it toward town. "I'll be right back," he said.

"Remember, Fenrald said to go to the village center and take a left," Curtis called out. "He said the stable was pretty easy to spot." Hyroc waved his acknowledgment.

Several Glacials he passed gave him a friendly wave; he returned the gestures. The village had gained a friendlier air since he and his friends had liberated the children from the Ferals. Even though the children were humans, the group's efforts earned them momentous respect from the villagers. When he came to the village center, he spotted Freija carrying a basket of bread with another female Wol'dger whom he didn't recognize. She waved at him happily, and he returned the gesture. The other Wol'dger's mouth fell open in astonishment when she saw Hyroc. She shot Freija an envious look. Envy? That was something new to Hyroc. There wasn't a whole lot in his life to envy. Everyone in Arnaira thought he was some hairy demon, which had caused him all kinds of unpleasant problems. He wondered what could be so enticing about him. Was it because he was an Anamagi? It made sense his prestigious lineage would instill a sense of fame upon him among the villagers. Or could it be from him rescuing those children from the slavers? Hyroc felt a burst of gladness from the thought. He resisted approaching her because they were going in opposite directions. That would have to wait another day.

"Hyroc," a familiar voice called to him. He saw Iskall's mother walking toward him with one of her youngest children. "I hope this day finds you well," Silka said. "I didn't get to thank you during the celebration for keeping my oldest sons safe when you went after those children. Thank you; you have our sincerest gratitude." She placed a comforting hand on his arm. "There's been such a change with Iskall since he's returned. He used to be so timid and reserved. Now, he seems so confident, happy, and full of energy. It's almost like he's a whole different person."

"I'm glad," Hyroc said.

"He thinks so highly of you. I thought it would be good for you to hear that."

"I appreciate that very much. And I'm glad to call him my friend."

"Be safe." She gently patted his hand before walking off.

Hyroc turned left at the village center. He scrutinized his surroundings, looking for any structures with a stable. Off one of the side paths, he caught sight of a group of gathered citizens. He stopped to investigate. Two villagers lay on the ground. A brown and dark gray male and a whitish-gray female, Glacial, were on their knees next to them. Hyroc thought he heard crying. When he came closer, he recognized the male as the village leader, Sanoc. Sanoc removed a black jacket he wore and laid it across one villager on the ground, followed by another onlooker doing the same for the second. Then, it struck Hyroc; the ones on the ground were bodies. Two people had been killed. The crying female was mourning their passing. Sanoc put a consoling hand on her shoulder.

"Sanoc?" Hyroc asked in a low, respectful voice. "What happened?"

Sanoc shook his head gloomily. "It's a sad day," he said. He indicated the woman. "Her husband and daughter have been slain."

"Slain? It wasn't an accident?"

"I'm afraid not. They were set upon by Ferals this morning."

Hyroc shot him a stunned look. "Ferals? They were inside the village?"

He nodded. "Yes, not even inside this village are we entirely safe from surprise attacks."

"So this isn't the first time?"

"We try to do what we can to prevent this, but we cannot avoid them claiming lives. But, no, this isn't the first time. However, as of late, their attacks have become less frequent. Maybe they are tiring of such actions."

Hyroc looked to the grieving widow but couldn't help seething with rage. *This had to stop*!

Chapter 23
Lynx

Hyroc and Donovan passed beneath the teeth of the raised gate of Forestgold. Kit sauntered close behind them, casting a wary gaze at the throng of passersby going about their business. The cougar was uncomfortable being forced into close proximity to so many strangers. Those who were not preoccupied with their errands noticed him with cautious expressions. Hyroc thought it prudent to bring his feline companion along for protection. After their raid on the slaver caravan, he was uncertain whether the Ferals would attempt to exact retribution upon them. Contending with a temperamental mountain lion should dissuade them from such actions.

Divided amongst Hyroc and Donovan, they carried the pelts of two foxes, three pine martins, and two river otters. The area around Fenrald's cabin was a prolific trapping area. Since Hyroc's uncle wasn't actively trapping there, fur-bearing animals populated the region considerably. It was close to a week since Fenrald had left. He was expected to return any day.

They came to the town center.

"We need to pick up arrows while we're here," Hyroc stated, glancing off to the side.

"I can sell the pelts while you head to the Fletcher if you want," Donovan suggested.

"Do you think you can handle carrying all those pelts yourself? They're going to be heavy."

"I can manage."

"All right."

Hyroc passed the pelts to him, and then they separated to attend to their errands. At the Fletcher, Hyroc absentmindedly perused their wares. Finding nothing that interested him, he proceeded to buy the arrows.

"I need a dozen blunt-head arrows," he instructed. "And two dozen razor heads."

"I can get you the twelve blunt-head," said an older man wearing a dark brown tunic and a scruffy U-shaped mustache on his face. "But I've only got twenty of the razor-heads."

"Twenty's fine."

The man disappeared into the shop's back room. He re-emerged carrying two bundles of arrows, each tip with a piece of cork stuck on the end to make them safer to handle. After slapping down the necessary payment of Flecks on the counter, Hyroc stuffed the bundles into a knapsack.

"Pleasure doing business with you, Wol'dger," the man said as Hyroc exited the shop. Hyroc waved his thanks.

From the shop, Hyroc headed to the market area where the furriers were. When he arrived, he swept his eyes through the area but didn't see Donovan. "Excuse me," Hyroc said to a merchant in a red leather jerkin that was over a white tunic, and they wore brown pants and matching boots. "Have you seen a young man, a human, with brown hair and a spear strapped to his back? He would have been carrying animal pelts in his arms."

The merchant shook his head. "No, can't say I have," he said. "Sorry."

"Okay, thanks," Hyroc said before moving to another merchant and repeating his question. They hadn't seen anyone like that, either, nor did the following several merchants he asked.

Hyroc rubbed his chin thoughtfully. Where was Donovan? His friend said he was taking care of the pelts, and this was the appropriate place. Had he got sidetracked? Hyroc nodded to himself. That's what had to have happened. Something grabbed his attention, and he had lost track of time. They needed to conclude their business before it got too late in the day if they wanted to avoid traveling at night.

"Looking for someone?" a young woman's voice asked. Hyroc turned to see a female Wol'dger with green eyes and black-gray striped fur leaning her back against a tree trunk. She wore a green, short-sleeved-leather jerkin, and dark brown leather pants, but was barefoot. Around her neck was a necklace of polished, sharp animal teeth. Thin stripes of red paint ran across her face, and her hair was disheveled, giving her a mildly wild look. She held an apple in one hand and used a knife to slice pieces off it to eat. Despite her feminine figure, she had strong, toned arms that gave her a surprisingly muscular appearance. She appeared to do something rigorous with her arms regularly to make them muscular. Perhaps it was related to her animal form. Wrestling bears had given Hyroc strong arms, so maybe it was something along those lines. Hyroc didn't recognize her, but she was fetching, though he was still not entirely sure how Wol'dgers distinguished beauty.

"Ye – yeah," Hyroc said. "I was looking for my friend. He had a spear on his back and carried some animal pelts."

She used her knife to slide a piece of apple into her mouth before answering. "No, sorry. I haven't seen them."

"I'm just wondering where he could be."

"I'm Lynx, by the way," she said, holding her hand out.

"And I'm Hyroc," he said, grasping her fingers and greeting her. He thought he saw a flash of excitement in her eyes for a split second.

Kit let out a low growl, slightly startling Lynx, who at that instant had not known the big cat was there.

Hyroc nudged, his companion, with his boot. "Stop that!" he commanded disapprovingly. "That's no way to treat her. She's friendly." Kit obstinately continued to growl. "Hey, *knock it off*." Kit stopped but irritably glared back at him. "Sorry about that," Hyroc apologized to Lynx. "He doesn't like being surrounded by people he doesn't know."

"It's quite all right," Lynx said. "It's more than understandable for a *cat*. It's in our nature."

Our nature, Hyroc wondered to himself. *That was an odd way of phrasing that. She must have just misspoken.*

"Anyway, you're free to wait for your friend here with me, Hyroc."

Hyroc knew he should prioritize finding Donovan but couldn't resist the invitation. He could spend a minute talking to her. This wasn't going to hurt anything. It was probably a good idea if he took advantage of this opportunity to meet a pretty girl. There was a wild air about her, and he didn't know why, but he found it enticing.

"Yeah, I'll wait here a minute in case he's just taking his time," Hyroc agreed. He slipped off his knapsack and set it on the ground. Kit settled on his haunches, begrudgingly flicking his tail from Hyroc's earlier rebuke. "I've never seen you around here."

"I've never seen you around here, either," she noted, taking another slice of apple.

Hyroc felt his face warm a little. That was true. This was only his third time venturing into Forestgold, so she would be more aware of this than he was. That was a dumb question.

"I've never seen you in the village."

"I live here in town, but head to the village whenever possible." She indicated the frostbite on one of Hyroc's ears by tapping the tip of one of her own. "What's that?"

"Oh, that's nothing," Hyroc said dismissively. "It's just the scar left from frostbite when I was little." She nodded. "What brings you out here, under this tree?"

She indicated the merchants with the wave of her knife. "I'm waiting on one of those flat-faced merchants to finish appraising a wolf pelt I gave them. And I figured I'd wait here in the shade while I eat my apple." She took another bite.

"As good a spot as any to get out of the hot sun," Hyroc agreed.

"And with such appealing company," she said.

Hyroc blushed. "What animal can you turn into?" He winced, realizing he just made an embarrassing assumption. "You can turn into an animal, right?"

She laughed. Despite feeling embarrassed, he found her laugh an enjoyable sound.

"Yes, I can turn into an animal," she assured him. "I can turn into a big cat. Is there something I should be made aware of with that?"

"No, no, I was just making conversation."

She nodded. "What animal can you turn into?" she mirrored back at him playfully. "You *can* turn into an animal, right?"

Touché, Hyroc thought to himself. "Yes, a bear. I can turn into a brown bear."

"Ah, a big boy, I see. How like you the strength of a bear?"

"I like it a lot. I can use it to protect the people I care about."

"Protect?" she said as if it were a foreign word. "Why protect when you can lead?"

Hyroc thought that an unusual question. He dismissed it, assuming she had again misspoken.

"I don't know," Hyroc said. "Leading has never really been my strong suit."

His answers seemed to confound her for an instant. "Do you see your friend anywhere?"

Hyroc surveyed the area but still no Donovan. Hyroc was now getting concerned. Even as much as he wanted to continue talking to Lynx, he needed to see what was delaying his friends.

"Lynx, it was nice talking to you, but I should probably find my companion."

"Mind if I come with you?"

That caught Hyroc off guard, and he barely prevented himself from instantly agreeing. "I thought you were waiting on that furrier to finish your pelt?"

"I can spare a few minutes to help you locate your friend," she said dismissively.

"Well, I don't see why not."

She tossed the apple's core aside, then wiped her knife off on the tree's trunk before slipping it back into its sheath. She motioned for Hyroc to lead the way.

Hyroc backtracked in the direction he assumed Donovan would have gone. The main path curved around a T-shaped alleyway.

Hyroc motioned toward the path. "Lynx, would you mind continuing along the main path to see if he's there?" he asked. "Look for somebody with a boar spear."

She nodded, walking past him.

The alleyway was narrower than the main path, making it difficult for carts to pass. An orange tabby was crouched on the roof's edge above him, watching him curiously as it flicked its striped tail. Hyroc checked behind a line of barrels and a stack of wooden crates. No Donovan in either place. He glanced around the corner of the T, a dead end, and saw nothing. As he moved past, out of the corner of his eye, he spotted a booted foot sticking out behind a couple of barrels. Then he saw what appeared to be animal skins strewn about. He rushed toward the foot, feeling a burst of apprehension. The foot belonged to Donovan!

His companion was alive, with his back against the alleyway wall, but he had a black eye almost completely swollen shut. He had purplish bruises and spots of blood across his face. Thankfully, Donovan's nose was unbroken. He held his side with a sore expression scrawled across his face.

"Oh, hey, Hyroc," Donovan said dizzily.

"Donovan!" Hyroc yelled, rushing to his friend's side. "What happened?"

"That's a good question. I'll tell you when my head stops ringing.

"Kit, roof," Hyroc ordered. "Keep watch, be ready to pounce on attackers." Kit leaped onto the roof. The shadow of the top of his head on the opposite wall of the alley was all that revealed his deadly presence.

Hyroc quickly assessed Donovan's injuries to ensure none were of immediate concern. Donovan winced and drew in a sharp breath when Hyroc touched his ribs. Hyroc knew one or more of his ribs were cracked. Mending bone was beyond his ability to heal with his Flame Claw. He needed to get his friend to someone more experienced; otherwise, Donovan would have to endure the long and painful process of his body healing itself unassisted. To say nothing of how unpleasant moving him was going to be.

"So I had the pelts in my hands," Donovan said. "And I was on my way to sell them to the furriers. Then, I saw the path curving to the side and decided to continue through the alley because it went straight through. And because I'm an idiot, I wasn't even thinking about it being a good place for an ambush. I'm about halfway through when two Wol'dgers come around the corner. That's when I noticed the third one coming up behind me. I dropped the pelts and went for my spear, but they were on me before I could do anything. Then –" he spit out a mouthful of blood "– then they proceeded to beat the ever-living crap out of me."

"They were Wol'dgers. Did any of them have an animal mark?"

Donovan thought for a moment before nodding. "Yes, now that I think it, one of them had an animal mark. And with our luck, *of course, it was red*, shaped like a wolf's paw."

Hyroc quietly cursed under his breath. "Ferals," he said. "Probably also members of The Pack."

"Yep, Ferals. They really hold a grudge."

"Well, you did smash one of them in the face with the shaft of your spear," Hyroc noted. "Not that he didn't deserve it. I'm just saying."

Kit chuffed a warning, and Hyroc heard footsteps behind him. Hyroc wheeled around, grasping the hilt of his sword. He relaxed, seeing Lynx. "Calm, friendly," he said to Kit.

"Well, it looks like you've found him," Lynx said, glancing up at the roof.

Donovan gave her a startled look.

"No, it's okay. She's not a threat," Hyroc said, placing a comforting hand on his friend's shoulder. "Donovan, Lynx. Lynx, Donovan."

"Forgive me if I want to skip the pleasantries. You'll have to introduce yourself again when I can see from both eyes, so I actually know what you look like."

Hyroc looked at Lynx apologetically. Then he noticed her holding a dagger. She glanced around nervously, clearly fearing Donovan's attackers would return.

"Hey, hey," Hyroc said to her gently and calmly. "It's okay; they're not going to hurt you. I promise I'm not going to let them."

She stared at him in astonishment as if he had said the most bizarre thing she had ever heard. Hyroc reassuringly cuffed his hand around hers, guiding her blade back into its sheath.

Donovan glared at him irritably. "*Oh, I see,*" he said accusingly. "While I was getting my teeth kicked in, you were busy talking to *a girl.*"

"Oh, come off it," Hyroc said. "I wasn't talking to her *that* long. It wouldn't have made any difference. They still would have gotten you even if I hadn't stopped to talk to her."

"You would have found me a lot sooner."

Hyroc opened his mouth to retort before realizing that was true. "Okay, I'll give you that one. But we need to get you out of here. Do you think you can stand?" Donovan nodded, and Hyroc gingerly helped him to his feet.

"Also, while I was enduring blunt-force trauma to my fragile skull, I realized Wol'dgers are *strong.*"

"And you just now realized that?" Hyroc questioned.

"I always thought *you were,* not that *all of you were like that.* I tried fighting back with my fists when they jumped me, but they overpowered me like it was nothing."

"There were three of them. So the odds weren't in your favor."

"I understand that, but I've been in fights before. It was like I was a fly they flicked away."

"Well, if you had gotten to your spear, their extra strength probably wouldn't have made any difference."

"Stop trying to make me feel better; it's annoying."

"Would you rather I say you're a wuss?"

"Okay, no, I wouldn't, but …"

"But nothing. Just shut up, okay."

Donovan grumbled something inaudible under his breath.

Lynx laughed. "Are the two of you always like this?" she asked. "You bicker like brothers."

"That's because he *is* my brother," Donovan corrected. "Or like one. It's hard to remember a time before I met him."

"His dad caught me in a net and threatened to turn me into a rug," Hyroc said dryly.

Lynx laughed again. "Okay, it sounds like there's an interesting story behind that. You'll have to tell that to me when you're not in agony."

"Sounds good," Donovan agreed.

"Do you know where we might find a healer?" Hyroc asked.

Lynx looked thoughtful. "Yes, but I think they're on the other side of town," she said. "And your friend won't enjoy *that*."

"There's a tavern not far from here, the Wheezing Cottonwood," Hyroc advised. "We can bring him there, then one of us could fetch the healer."

"Yes, I like this plan," Donovan agreed. "And since we're at a tavern, I'll be able to consume a certain liquid that will make my brain work less good and help make the pain go away for a bit."

Hyroc and Lynx shook their heads, trying not to laugh.

"Yes, you can do that, *too*, while we're there," Hyroc agreed.

Hyroc pointed to the pelts lying on the ground. "Lynx, if you wouldn't mind, could you hold those for my friend and me while I carry him?

She nodded, doing as requested.

"Kit, follow," Hyroc called out. The big cat dropped off the roof, landing nearly soundlessly.

The group moved out of the alleyway. The only problem with going to the tavern was the quickest way to reach it would take them past the fountain, the main haunt for The Pack, Ferals, who spent most of their time in wolf form. Hyroc wondered if they would let them pass unmolested, even with guards around. He didn't know how much of a detour avoiding them would entail and gambled going through there wouldn't be a problem so long as they avoided drawing attention to themselves.

When they reached the fountain, Hyroc saw The Pack lounging around it. None of them faced Hyroc, and a cluster of guards was between them. They should be safe. A guard leaning against the wall while he ate something regarded them curiously but did nothing beyond that.

A glint of sunlight on something metallic caught Hyroc's attention. When he turned his head to get a better look at it, the glint came off the tip of a spear. It was Donovan's spear! Hyroc felt a molten swell of anger, and something snapped inside him that hadn't snapped for a long time. They had not only hurt Donovan; they had stolen his spear. Donovan had acquired it from a destroyed town in the heart of The Devouring

Thicket, a nightmarishly twisted forest that an insane Warding tree had altered. The weapon symbolized the tremendous hardships he and his friends had endured to reach this place, and he wasn't about to let Ferals defile it.

"Donovan, I need to let go of you for a second," Hyroc said, disentangling himself from his friend's arm and giving him the wall for support. "Kit, stay, no assist." Kit quietly chuffed his protest as he sat.

Donovan grabbed Hyroc's shoulder as he turned to walk away. "Hyroc, don't," Donovan urged. "It's not worth it. *It's just a spear.*"

"*It's about more than the spear*!" Hyroc said fiercely. He shook off Donovan's grip, making a beeline for the spear.

A natural form Wol'dger held the spear, proudly displaying it to another in natural form and one wolf form as they boasted about their accomplishment. The rest of The Pack lay nearby, uninterested. Hyroc was sure they were about to become incredibly *interested.* The three Wol'dgers around the spear had their backs to Hyroc as he rushed towards them.

"...yeah, I can't believe how easy it was," bragged the Wol'dger holding the spear.

"Hey, *thief*, I need a word with you," Hyroc called out coolly. The Wol'dger turned to receive a solid haymaker to the face. The Wol'dger and spear fell to the ground with a clatter. Hyroc was on the other natural form Wol'dger before they reacted. He kicked the side of their leg to unbalance them and nailed them with an uppercut, lifting their feet off the ground for an instant. The first Wol'dger was starting to stand, and Hyroc spun around with a kick that sent him unconscious. Then Hyroc drew his sword.

A wall of snarling and gnashing teeth, fangs, and ferociously wrinkled muzzles had materialized before him.

"NOW YOU DIE, ANAMAGI!" one wolf yelled.

"You just made the last mistake you'll ever make," another yelled.

Hyroc ignited a blue flame on the tip of his sword and swept it across the ground between him and The Pack. A wave of blue fire and sparks flared in front of him. This gave the group pause, and several members instinctually pulled away from the fire.

“You might be able to overwhelm me!” Hyroc roared. “But I swear, I’ll take half of you with me before I go down. NOW, WHOSE FIRST?” The wolves looked at each other uncertainly, and there was even a hint of fear in their expressions.

“STOP,” a male voice ordered. The group turned their attention to a massive black wolf approaching Hyroc. Lines of scars covered the wolf’s snout and face. It had orange eyes, and the glowing red animal mark on its shoulder showed angrily against its dark coat. This was the alpha.

The wolf’s head was level with Hyroc’s chest. The wolf regarded Hyroc with a slow and methodical appraising look. “What do you want?” he said malevolently. Hyroc saw the blazing hate in its eyes. This wolf very much wanted to rip his throat out here and now but knew doing so would exact a heavy toll on his marauders.

Hyroc indicated the spear with his chin. “That spear doesn’t belong to you,” he said without looking away from the wolf. “It was stolen from a friend of mine. *I want it back*.”

The wolf let out a derisive laugh. “Very well,” he said, speaking in a frigid tone. “Collect your *prize*, then leave!” The wolf jerked his head to signal for one of its followers to pick up Donovan’s spear. That wolf carried the spear shaft in its jaws, offering it to Hyroc. Hyroc lowered himself toward the unconscious Wol’dger without turning his back to the wolf. He cut away a coin sack using the tip of his sword. Hyroc had noticed Donovan was missing his coin purse and was recovering it. He sheathed his sword before snatching the spear. Hyroc backed away from the group, only turning around after the alpha had done so first.

Hyroc saw guards with their weapons drawn coming his way. The guards halted, looking with astonishment between him and The Pack. They expected everything to go straight to The Sunless Plains and couldn’t comprehend how it had been averted.

Lynx, Donovan, and Kit were similarly bewildered. Lynx was gobsmacked, with her mouth hanging open, unsure whether to smile or gasp. Donovan was laughing in amazement.

“Okay, I’m not going to lie, I think I peed a little,” Donovan admitted. “*Are you suicidal*? I cannot believe you’re still alive.” He laughed, then winced. “Oh, ow, don’t make me laugh.”

Kit worriedly sniffed at Hyroc, checking him for injuries.

"It's okay. I'm fine," Hyroc assured the mountain lion. He returned his attention to Donovan. "I got your coin purse back," he said, handing it to Donovan, who secured it to his belt.

"Is there something wrong with your head?" Lynx praised. "I don't know if that was the most courageous thing I have ever seen or the most moronic. I thought for sure they were going to tear you limb from limb. And that was all over a *spear*?"

"I didn't do it for the spear," Hyroc admitted. "Well, I did it a little bit for the spear. That spear represents overcoming a particularly hazardous situation, and I despise bullies. I couldn't stand to see that Feral gloating about stealing the spear and hurting my friend – no, for hurting my *brother*."

"Okay, now, before you pick a fight with a troll or something else nasty, can you take care of me and get me to the tavern already?"

"Didn't I tell you to shut up?"

Donovan gave him an indignant look. "Oh, ha, ha."

They moved from the fountain, finally arriving at the tavern. Surprised stares welcomed them as they pushed their way into the building. The patrons were baffled by Donovan's condition and the fact two Wol'dgers and a mountain lion had entered the establishment to help him. Hyroc found the nearest table and eased Donovan into a seat. Lynx deposited the armload of pelts onto the table. She glanced around uncertainly at the faces of the strangers. This appeared to be the first time so many humans had surrounded her.

At an adjacent table sat Darius Ashfin, with an open leather-bound book in front of him. "Is he okay?" he asked, indicating Donovan, bewildered.

"Not really," Hyroc answered. "He needs a healer. I think he has a cracked rib."

"Mind if I take a look?"

"Go right ahead."

The mage pulled up a chair beside Donovan. "I need to take a look under your tunic." He gently pulled up Donovan's shirt, revealing a dark purple bruise on his side. When he touched it, Donovan winced. "Very painful to the touch," he noted. "Yep, you've definitely got a broken rib."

"Wouldn't it have been easier for me to tell you where it hurts?" Donovan said indignantly.

"I'm not qualified enough with healing to do anything about this."

The barkeep set a mug of ale in front of Donovan. "Your friend could probably use this," he said kindly. "It's on the house."

"Could I trouble you by asking if one of your servers could fetch a healer?" Darius Ashfin asked.

He reached into a coin sack on his hip and laid the required amount of Flecks in their hand. The barkeep nodded before walking away.

"Donovan, I've got something to show you," Hyroc said happily. He set the coin purse on the table and splayed it open. Within was a significant amount of Fleck coins. "I don't think this is your coin sack," he said in surprise. "There wasn't nearly that much in yours. So I accidentally nicked a coin sack from one of those Ferals I knocked unconscious." Hyroc laughed. "Well, that's a good thing for us. I think it's only proper if those Ferals at least pay for your room."

Donovan grabbed the mug and downed its contents. He burped as his eyes glazed over. "Ahh, that hit the spot," he said, relieved. "I feel a little better now."

"I bet you do," Hyroc agreed flatly. "Now, how about we take you to the room so you'll get more privacy?

"That's a good idea," Donovan agreed, slurring slightly.

"Let me give you a hand with that," Darius Ashfin offered, grabbing one of Donovan's arms. Carefully, they carried Donovan up the stairs and lay him on the bed in the room.

"This is a very comfortable bed," Donovan said distantly.

The mage and Hyroc exchanged a confused look. No, the beds here were very uncomfortable!

"Hyroc, you're an excellent friend," Donovan said. "And I do like your girlfriend." Hyroc felt his face warm. "She's – she's not my girlfriend. I literally just met her." He glanced toward Lynx and noticed she was staring at him with admiration. It was the type of stare that only came from someone who was very much enjoying spending time with someone. She liked him. No, whether he wanted to accept it, she was his girlfriend.

"All right, I'll send the healer your way as soon as they arrive," Darius Ashfin said before leaving. Lynx found an out-of-the-way corner of the room and deposited the pelts there.

"Thank you for helping my friend and me," Hyroc said to Lynx gratefully. "I hope I didn't stress you out too much."

"Are you kidding? I haven't had this much fun in a long time," she said excitedly.

Hyroc shot her a look of surprise. "Really? You had fun?"

"Yes, *a lot of fun.*"

He smiled, nervously tracing a circle on the floor with his foot. "My friend and I will probably be stuck in town for another day. Would you like to do something again tomorrow?"

"I would very much like that."

"I should probably let you get going so you can check on the pelt you left at the furrier."

"Pelt? Oh, right, right, that pelt. I was waiting for them to finish appraising. Yes, I should go check in on that. I'll meet you outside this tavern in the morning."

"That sounds great. Enjoy the rest of your day."

"I'd wish you the same, but I have a feeling your friend is not going to enjoy it so much," she called over her shoulder as she left.

"That's okay. I need to pour more ale into him, and I'm sure he'll *enjoy* things just fine.

She signaled her departure with a raised hand before disappearing down the stairs.

"Did you tell her that you *liked her*," Donovan called from the room, obnoxiously loud. Hyroc buried his face in his hands.

"Yes, and I appreciate you sharing that with the rest of the tavern," Hyroc said sarcastically.

Chapter 24
Blight

...AND THAT SPELL SHOULD mend the bone," the healer said. She was a slender older woman wearing a gray cloth dress with her hair done up in a bun. She stood beside Donovan's bed. Hyroc sat in a chair next to the door with his arms crossed. Kit was sprawled out on the floor beside him half asleep.

"But that will still take time," she continued. "The bone will be fragile until it has finished healing your ribs. You must avoid anything strenuous and move as little as possible."

"So I'm guessing I won't be able to make the trip back to my friend's home outside of town."

"No."

"And how long will the spell take?"

"No longer than a day as long as you follow my instructions."

"Which means I'm stuck here until tomorrow."

"Thank you," Hyroc said. "We really appreciate your doing this."

She nodded her thanks. "Helping others is what I'm best at."

Hyroc held out a hand with the required payment of Flecks. She accepted it, and Hyroc held the door open for her.

"I thought healing with magic was supposed to be immediate," Donovan questioned. "That's how it is when you use your Flame Claw to treat scrapes and cuts."

"I think it's because she's healing bone," Hyroc suggested. "Pretty much any broken bone is a serious injury. Beyond infection, scrapes and cuts are minor wounds. So it only makes sense for it to take longer than the other and probably requires more Quintessence. But you should be glad it only takes a day. Usually, an injury like yours would take weeks to heal before you can breathe again without pain."

"Uh huh," Donovan said mildly. "But I'm going to be bored out of my skull until then."

"That's not my fault."

"You just want to get rid of me so you can go on that date with your *girlfriend*."

"She's not my girlfriend," Hyroc retorted. Kit grumbled his skepticism, seemingly in agreement with Donovan. "Oh, shush you."

Donovan nodded, looking unconvinced. "You could have fooled me."

"We're just going to do something today since I'm not going to leave you behind injured in town, and I've got time to kill. Besides, I still need to try to sell those pelts. I might as well do it with company."

"You mean kind of like A DATE!" Donovan said smugly.

Hyroc rolled his eyes as he gathered the pelts. "I'll see you later," he said, annoyed, turning and opening the door. Kit made no move to follow him. "Are you coming?" he impatiently asked the big cat. Kit chuffed, indicating an emphatic *no*. "Well, the two of you have fun together," Hyroc scoffed, mildly annoyed. "Enjoy Kit driving you nuts when he starts scratching the door to be let out."

"And when you're done with your *date*," Donovan called out through the door. "Be sure to bring me something potent to drink." He mockingly hurled his boot at the door as Hyroc pulled it shut with his foot. Hyroc paid the barkeep to bring Donovan something to eat later before leaving the tavern.

He found Lynx outside wearing a sturdier-looking green jerkin than yesterday and gray pants with her back against the building. "Is your human friend doing better?" she asked.

"Yes, the healer cast a mending spell on his ribs, but fixing bone takes a while. He can't leave until tomorrow when it finishes."

She nodded. "So the whole day is ours?"

"Yep. Oh, wait –" he raised and lowered his armload of pelts. "I need to take care of these first. But I don't expect that to take long. Then, the whole day is ours. Do you have anything in mind for us to do?"

She studied him thoughtfully before answering. "How are you at hunting?"

"Oh, you want to go hunting? Uh, yeah, we absolutely can do that. I don't know any of the hunting grounds around here."

"That's all right; I know them quite well. I can show you."

"I would love for you to show them to me," he said eagerly. "Just need to take care of these real quick."

Hyroc and Lynx departed from the town a few hours later, following a game trail into the forest.

"This should be far enough," she said, stopping.

Hyroc slung a leather tube off his shoulder and slipped a hunting bow out of it. The bow belonged to Donovan, and Hyroc was borrowing it for the day. As he strung the bowstring, he noticed Lynx wasn't carrying a bow or any other hunting weapon. She regarded him inquisitively, seemingly unsure as to what he was doing.

"You hunt with a bow?" she asked as if doing so was the most absurd thing she had ever seen.

"Usually, yes."

"You said you could turn into a bear."

"I don't use my animal form while hunting unless I really need to." She regarded him with a strange expression. "Am I right in assuming you will use your animal form?"

She gave him a flat look. "Of course."

"If we're both in our animal forms, neither of us will have hands, and it will be difficult for us to dress the carcass or cook some of it, won't it?"

She shot him another confused look. "Who said anything about doing any of *that*," she said with a wicked smile.

Hyroc gaped in astonishment. "You want to eat the meat raw, *on purpose*?"

"You don't?"

"No!" Hyroc said emphatically. "No, I don't eat it raw. I cook it." He now wondered if this hunting excursion was such a good idea.

"If you get to the meat right after a kill, it's hot right off the bone as if you just cooked it. There's nothing else like eating it that way."

There's nothing like it because it's disgusting, and that's why nobody likes eating it that way, Hyroc wondered sourly.

"I'm going to have to pass on that," Hyroc said. "And I must tell you right now, I'm going to cook it."

She looked at him displeased. "Okay, fine," she agreed. "You can cook it if that's really what you want." Hyroc nodded triumphantly. "Now, unless there's some other way you want to ruin our fun, I'm going into my animal form." She dropped onto her hands and knees to begin the process. Hyroc looked on inquisitively. The way her body shape began changing, Hyroc thought he had misheard her earlier and she had the animal form of a bear instead of a cat. Her clothing faded to reveal a black coat of fur with stripes of gray. She grew larger than he had anticipated. There was enough slack in her tooth necklace to avoid interrupting the process. Her animal form had a robust, burly build with long, powerfully muscled limbs and mighty jaws. But despite her form's exotic nature, he still recognized the sleek familiarity of a large feline. Hyroc gazed in amazement, sure she had to weigh nearly as much as him in bear form.

"What do you think?" she said, turning toward him expectantly.

Hyroc was so captivated he struggled to respond: "You, uh – you, uh – you look gorgeous." She regarded him with a pleased look. "The cat you saw when you chose this, was it an orange one with black stripes?"

She looked surprised. "Yes, that's how it looked. How'd you know?"

"I also saw one of these during the Choosing Ritual."

"And you still decided on a fat bear?" she said mockingly.

"Hey, *I like bears*. And just so you know, I am at a perfectly healthy weight. It's right where it's supposed to be."

"Uh, huh, that's what all *fat bears* say," she joked.

Hyroc held his hand toward her head as if wanting to pet her. "May I?" he asked politely. She shot him a dirty look, and he realized his mistake too late. She rammed her head into his chest, unbalancing him, and swiped his legs out from under him. He landed on his back, and the world turned to blue sky through the treetops. She pinned him down with a paw pressing on his chest. Then, she pinched one of his ears between her teeth. It wasn't painful, as she intentionally avoided causing him any lasting harm.

"Ahh, sorry, I'm sorry, I'm sorry," Hyroc yelled frantically.

She released his ear but continued pressing down on him. She looked at him disapprovingly. "Never ask to *pet me*," she said, with exasperation but still somewhat playfully.

"I got it, sorry."

"Do you ask people to give your head a nice petting? Maybe you allow that with your flat-faced human companions, but I don't. And they had better not try it."

"Duly noted."

"And don't you forget it." She removed her paw. Hyroc dusted himself off. When he turned his attention back to her, he felt the urge to engage her in a sparring match. She was big enough for it to be an even bout or, at the very least, fun for the both of them. He pushed the thought aside but would keep her in mind as a possible sparring partner for him in his bear form.

Then, the mark on her shoulder alarmed him. It was the animal mark of a big cat's paw, *but it was red.* She was a Feral! Hyroc froze, a sense of danger rapidly rising inside him. Lynx was currently big enough to easily be a lethal threat to him, even with the advantage of his Flame Claw. The whole forest suddenly seemed to turn against him. Was this animal trail destined to become his tomb? He was all alone, here with a Feral! This was a trap, and he had walked headlong into it. How could he have been so stupid? He had survived shadow demons, witches, the Ministry, and a werewolf, and *a girl had undone him.* The irony of that was unbelievably humiliating.

He tossed his bow aside, drawing his sword as quietly as possible, but it wasn't quiet enough. Lynx's ears rotated in his direction, and she snapped her head toward him. She regarded him baffled.

"Is that what your plan was?" Hyroc said accusingly, tightly grasping the hilt of his sword with both hands. "Get me out here *alone, away from my friends*, and then you were going to strike?"

"Hyroc?" she asked. "What are you talking about? Why do you have your sword out?"

Hyroc indicated her animal mark with his chin. "Your mark is *red.* YOU'RE A FERAL."

She turned her head as if she had forgotten the mark, straining to look at her shoulder with her peripheral vision. "Oh," she acknowledged. "Yes, I'm a Feral. I thought you already knew."

"Do you expect me to believe it simply slipped your mind?"

"Yes, *because that's the truth.* And if I wanted to hurt you, why didn't I attack you when I had you on the ground a moment ago? I had the perfect opportunity then and had at least a dozen others since we left the town. Why wait?"

Hyroc couldn't think of a reason. Unless her mind was unhinged like every other Feral he had met, and there wasn't a logical explanation. But there was something different about her behavior compared to them. The other Ferals were incredibly aggressive and bloodthirsty, with a robust violent propensity. She sounded reasonable when she spoke and was quite polite and agreeable. It was a little counterintuitive she might want to rip his throat out. She spoke like a Glacial. Or was that a ploy, and she was trying to get him to lower his guard so he was easier prey? That was the tactic the witch in Elswood had attempted to employ against him. Erode his morale, so he didn't have the will to fight.

"That's a good question," Hyroc answered. "But every time I've run into a Feral, they've tried to kill me. So, tell me, why are you different? Why haven't you tried that?"

"Because I don't want to do you any harm. Not all Ferals are the same. Some of us are not all that different from you Glacials. Some of us don't want to hurt anyone."

"But the only way for the animal mark to turn red is you have to refuse the training process. And without that training, you are vulnerable to succumbing to the tendencies of whatever animal form you possess. That's what makes Ferals so dangerous. You are essentially animals – no, those tendencies make you act worse than animals. Why are you different? Why are you not like that?"

"Yes, I did that, but just because I refused the training doesn't mean I enjoy causing needless pain. And those tendencies you are referring to mainly affect wolves and bears. I am a cat, so I am not afflicted with those tendencies, and the ones I experience are easy to manage. I am affected by them no more than you are affected by yours. You're a bear, so, in all likelihood, you feel them more than I do. How do I know they're not making you dangerous?"

"That's a good point."

"Do you have any more questions, or can you please put away your sword so we can return to hunting?" she said, mildly indignant.

Hyroc studied her, looking for signs of deception. He found none. Cautiously and slowly, he slipped his sword back into its scabbard. Then, while keeping a close watch on her, retrieved his bow. He motioned forward. "Lead the way," he said.

She turned, sauntering away. "There is a hollow up ahead," she said. "I usually follow alongside it until I come to a flat area. Around there is normally where I find prey."

The game trail curved down an incline. At the bottom was a shallow trench with a small stream flowing through it. Hyroc readied an arrow when Lynx started walking along the edge of the hollow. She halted abruptly, one paw suspended in the air, and her ears rotated alertly. Hyroc jerked to a stop, scanning their surroundings for a target.

"Never mind, I thought I heard something," she said before continuing.

The hollow gently bent down toward a depression, which widened and flattened. The stream pooled in the depression but remained shallow enough for Hyroc to cross without getting his legs wet. Further ahead, the hollow curved around a parcel of raised ground.

Lynx moved along the pool's edge, her head low and nose hovering above the ground as she sniffed for a scent. She stopped, something catching her attention. She bobbed her head curiously as she investigated the scents around her.

"And what is this?" she said to herself eagerly.

"Got something?" Hyroc asked, coming closer.

"Yes, it's a scythe horn." She used her paw to point toward a hoof print in a patch of mud. The edges of the print maintained its shape, indicating it was fresh. "I bet we could get a good price for its pelt, but its horns are the real prize. Every merchant in town always asks me if I have any, so we will get a decent amount from selling them."

"I came face to face with one of those," Hyroc said as he crouched down to get a better look at the print. "And it seemed pretty mean. Are you certain we can take one down with just the two of us?"

She nodded. "Have you ever hunted moose?"

"Yes, a few times."

"They're like a moose. All their vitals are in the same places, so you should know where to place your arrows. But I need to get onto its back, and I can easily bring it down. Getting there is just a bit of a challenge."

"What about its horns? It would hurt a lot to get hit with them."

She gave him a playful look. "Yes, so don't get hit," she said. Hyroc shot her a flat look. "Besides, you've got that blue fire magic stuff. I'm sure we'll be fine." She turned toward Hyroc, rubbing her feline face against his. Hyroc had to catch himself with an outstretched hand behind him to keep from toppling over and plunging the back of his head into the pool. He couldn't tell if getting him wet had been intentional or a mere oversight on her part. She gracefully bounded across the pool, heading into the trees.

Hyroc followed, keeping a close eye on their surroundings. Away from the hollow, the ground sloped with a modest incline. Spruce trees covered the slope with patches of purplish fireweed. Then, the ground evened out, giving way to birch trees interspersed with pines. Lynx stopped mid-step, and Hyroc did the same. He had to restrain himself from inquiring what had made her stop and risk alerting game to their presence. She stepped backward to come closer to Hyroc.

"It's just ahead of us," she whispered, indicating the direction with her chin. "Don't make a sound." She entered a low crouch, her belly almost scraping the ground, and silently pushed onward. She moved so swiftly Hyroc struggled to keep up. Then, he noticed an unusual change in the trees. The birch trees ahead of him had black bark instead of the usual papery white, and their leaves were a sickly yellow. Several pine trees had patches of brown needles amongst the green ones and appeared unhealthy. There was a dead cottonwood tree, but he couldn't tell what had killed it. Much of the foliage had pale yellow and brown leaves. The look of everything was familiar. He had very recently passed through a forest in a similar condition. There couldn't be another mad Warding tree here, could there? What could be causing this?

"That's very odd," Lynx said, indicating the dead plants. "I've never seen a die-off of plants this big. I wonder what's causing it." She stepped closer to take a whiff. "These don't smell of any blight or rot that I've ever encountered." She took another sniff. "These have a strong smokey odor, but nothing is burnt or burning. It's the strangest thing."

"Wait, did you say they smell like smoke?" An epiphany suddenly struck Hyroc.

"Yes, everything smells like smoke, but there isn't any smoke or ash in the air."

"You know what also smells like smoke? Shadow demons."

"Did you just say *shadow demons*?" she asked with dismay. "How – how do you know that?"

"Because I've killed a bunch of them. They smell heavily of smoke and turn to ash when you cut their heads off."

"We should probably leave then."

"That's definitely a good idea. Let a Guardian handle this."

"Guardian? They take care of these kinds of things."

Hyroc opened his mouth to answer as he backed away from the die-off but heard dead leaves crackling beneath heavy hooves. Glancing toward the sound, he saw the black horns and a scythe horn's large, wide, dark body. The scythe horn's nostrils flared angrily, and its eyes glowed purple. It had been corrupted! Hyroc and Lynx's enjoyable hunting trip had now turned into a fight for survival.

"Lynx!" was all Hyroc could yell before the animal reacted.

The scythe horn lowered its head to position its horns at a better goring angle and charged toward Hyroc. Hyroc dove out of the way, feeling through the ground the animal's mammoth hooves pounding the loam frighteningly close. The animal aimed for Lynx, but with her feline reflexes, she leaped out of the way long before it reached her. While on his side, Hyroc sent an arrow whistling into the scythe horn. The arrow struck but was a nonvital hit. He pushed himself into a sitting position, hastily drawing another arrow, running it through the side of his mouth to smooth out the tail and make it fly straighter. The scythe horn wheeled around and primed another run at Hyroc. Hyroc cast an enchantment on his arrow that would cause it to hit with substantially increased force before sending it flying. The exhilaration of the encounter threw his aim off, causing him to miss, and the arrow struck one of the animal's antlers. The arrow shattered a section of its antler, causing the animal to lose a sizable chunk of horn. His adversary stumbled sideways from the impact, wrenching its head. With a shake of its head, it shrugged off the concussive force and continued at full speed.

Hyroc tossed his bow aside and hooked an arm in front of him to form a translucent blue shimmering barrier with his Flame Claw. The scythe horn's heavy serrated antlers plowed into it. With a reverberating crack, the tips of several antlers busted off while one was ripped from the pedicle skin at the base of the horn. The barrier arrested the scythe horn's tremendous momentum, and Hyroc felt the mighty thump through his feet. The crash of completely stopping something as large as a moose drained a substantial amount of Quintessence from him. He couldn't do that again. The scythe horn dropped to the ground, dazed with a stream of crimson flowing from the torn flesh on its head. Hyroc had hoped the force of hitting an unyielding barrier at that speed would break the animal's neck.

Lynx threw herself onto the animal's back. She anchored her massive claws into its shoulders and viciously bit at the back of its neck. The animal gave an aggravated snort as it stood. Doing so was strenuous for the animal because of Lynx's added weight. It jerked and bucked erratically as it tried to knock her off, but her claws held firm.

Hyroc scrambled to his feet and drew his sword. He danced through a flurry of agitated motions from the animal before he could get into position to strike. He slashed its flank, trying to sever tendons in its back leg. His sword rent open a deep gash, but it didn't cut anything vital. The animal turned unexpectedly and nailed him with an errant hoof. It was a glancing blow that merely knocked him off his feet. He rolled away from a storm of stomping feet as the scythe horn shifted in his direction. He regained his footing and came in for a second strike. The animal sharply twisted, finally shedding its feline attacker. Lynx landed on her side but was out of the way before the scythe horn could take advantage. The animal scoured the ground with a swipe of its battered antlers where she had been an instant earlier.

Hyroc slashed into its other flank. The blade hit a tendon, going all the way to the bone. With a grunt, the animal's rear end dropped as its leg could no longer support its weight. Lynx dove on its head, clamping her jaws around its throat to disrupt its breathing. The animal thrashed and swung its front legs at Lynx, but she was at an angle where it couldn't get a hit. Hyroc took a deep, relieved breath before sheathing his sword. He wrapped his arms around the animal's front legs to immobilize them and eliminate the risk of them hurting someone. The animal's writhing slowed and weakened. Then, it went still and closed its eyes. Just for good measure, Hyroc drove a knife into its heart.

When Hyroc removed his knife, the blade was coated in blood much darker than it should have been. He wiped the blade off on the animal's fur before returning it to its sheath. Lynx released her grip and stood up on all fours. She stared at the lifeless animal, trying to make sense of what had just happened.

"Are you okay?" Hyroc asked.

Lynx answered after a long moment. "Yes. I'm fine. And you?"

Hyroc nodded. "Yes, I'm also good. I'm only going to have a little bit of a bruise from a hoof clipping me." He noticed a small wound on her side. It was likely caused by her landing on a stick or something on the ground when the animal had thrown her off. It was by no means of concern, but Hyroc could easily take care of it and spare her its annoyance. He cast a healing spell on his hand and reached over to heal it. "Hold on, let me take care of that real quick," he said.

Lynx caught sight of his glowing hand about to touch her side and jumped away, startled. She shot him an accusatory glare. "*What are you doing*!" she asked as more of a demand than a question.

Hyroc indicated her side. "You have a scrape right there," he answered, perplexed. "I was trying to heal it for you."

"No, *don't touch me with that Flame Claw*. It will heal just fine on its own without your help, thanks."

Hyroc cocked an eyebrow but dismissed the spell without speaking about his confusion. If she didn't want him to take care of it, he wasn't going to force the issue over a minor injury. He figured the last few minutes were probably enough for her to handle without him adding to it.

"Was – was that a *shadow demon* that attacked us?" she asked.

"No," Hyroc said. "That was a scythe horn corrupted by shadow demon essence. It makes animals incredibly aggressive, and infected animals also spread corruption." He indicated the nearby die-off. "That's probably what was killing those plants." The lively green plants near the carcass were starting to turn a rust-brown color as the life was being drained from them.

"Is the pelt safe to harvest?"

Hyroc shook his head. "No, every part of this animal has been contaminated. We need to burn its carcass to keep the corruption from spreading. Gather some firewood and …"

"I apologize for not getting here sooner," a female voice said, interrupting him.

Hyroc recognized that voice though it had been years since he last heard it.

"Ursa?"

Chapter 25

Burden of the Anamagi

HYROCSAWALARGEWHITEbearwithpalegrayish-blueeyessaunteringtowardhim.Itwashis mentor, Ursa! She had thoroughly trained him on the use of his animal form as well as his Flame Claw. This was the first time he had seen her since her departure from Elswood more than two years ago. She had dark blue spiral markings on her shoulders and hips. Wrapped around her wrists and ankles, she had circles of silver adorned with markings similar to those on her body and a silver necklace with a ruby spike hung around her neck.

"Ursa!" Hyroc called in greeting as he rushed toward her.

She wrapped an enormous white paw around him in a welcoming embrace. This warmth was akin to a mother bear and a long-lost cub being reunited. "It's good to again see my favorite pupil," she said before releasing her grip.

"Likewise. What have you been doing all this time?"

"I appreciate the pleasantries, but we must take care of the shadow-contamination before it spreads further."

Hyroc nodded, reining in his emotions and returning focus to the situation. Disposing of the scythe horn carcass was more critical than him catching up with a friend.

"Hyroc?" Lynx asked cautiously, giving Ursa a suspicious look.

"Oh, by the way, this is my friend, Lynx," Hyroc said, indicating her.

Ursa stopped, her eyes narrowing fiercely as she looked at Lynx as if suddenly noticing something appalling. "I will not suffer the presence of an *oath breaker*," she sharply commanded in a threatening tone. "Leave before you kindle my wrath!"

Her harsh words toward Lynx startled Hyroc and stirred up some anger. Lynx had helped him tremendously with killing the scythe horn. She didn't deserve this treatment.

Hyroc stepped in front of Ursa so he was between her and Lynx. "Ursa, come on," he said defensively. "She helped me kill the scythe horn, you don't need –"

"No, Hyroc, it's all right," Lynx interrupted. "There's no need for you to argue with her. Really. I'll leave." She sounded uncomfortable as if simultaneously dealing with shadow demons and Guardians was more than she could handle. She severely wanted to leave, to have this situation be someone else's problem. She departed.

"Wait, no, Lynx, you don't need to ..." Hyroc called after her. He trailed off, unable to think of anything else to say. He threw up a hand in frustration as she disappeared down the incline. Hyroc bowed his head in defeat. Great, he had found a girl he liked, and his old mentor and a fight with a corrupted animal had scared her off. He wasn't optimistic about the possibility of her wanting to be around him ever again. That was yet another failed relationship for him.

"Yes, *thank you for that*, Ursa," Hyroc said scathingly. "I'm *not* going to see her again."

"You would do well to keep better companions than those *oath breakers*," Ursa said unapologetically.

"By *oath breaker*, you mean because she refused to undergo training on how to use her animal form and resist its tendencies," Hyroc said. "By the way, we call them Ferals."

"Your name for them is irrelevant, but their choices are not."

"Well, she's different from the other Ferals. She has been kind and I like spending time with her. She also hasn't tried to kill me, which I think is a pretty good indication she's a decent person. You're telling her to leave was uncalled for!"

"Or that is simply what she wants you to think, and she is deceiving you."

"I haven't known her long enough to figure any of that out, but I doubt that's going to be a problem with her anymore," he said with an indignant sigh.

"Enough! There is important work that needs doing."

Ursa stepped over to the scythe horn and slowly wiped an ursine paw across the animal's side. Ripples of blue fire radiated over the body from where she touched, igniting the animal. The acrid smell of burnt hair and burning flesh filled the air as the azure flames consumed the body. The carcass was rapidly reduced to ash with a purplish tint. Ursa slapped the ground with her paw and swiped across it. The ash dissipated into the air.

"You truly never stop amazing me," Ursa said, looking at Hyroc proudly.

Hyroc regarding her quizzically. "What are you talking about?" That was an unexpected change of tone, considering his chiding.

She laughed. "How you handled the mad Warding tree in the wounded forest."

"Oh, *that*. I wasn't trying to handle anything. My friends and I were trying to escape The Ministry. We accidentally ran into *that* forest."

"Ah, I see," she said comprehendingly. "That's the same as any animal caught in a trap."

"That was one hellish trap! It was like trying to walk through a mirror."

"That Warding tree created an incredibly potent and dangerous trap. It was too dangerous for a loan Guardian to attempt to eliminate it. We left it alone because the Warding tree was protecting itself from further harm and not expanding its influence."

"Was ignoring something that incredibly dangerous really the best solution?" Hyroc scoffed. "If you find an old abandoned trap, *you're supposed to dismantle it* to avoid it hurting any people or animals. You're not supposed to leave it there for someone to blunder into!"

"For the most part, the inhabitants of the surrounding towns and villages in that region avoided it."

Hyroc cocked an eyebrow. "What does 'for the most part' mean?" he asked suspiciously.

Ursa's broad, stoic face gained an uncharacteristically sheepish expression. "Well, occasionally, someone lacking in intelligence would test the authenticity of any prohibition against traveling through those woods. Those foolish enough to enter the forest were never heard from again. That only contributed to the threatening nature of the forest. And not that I revel in the loss of lives, it may also have had the unintentional benefit of strengthening the bloodlines of those villages and towns, if you catch my meaning."

Hyroc laughed darkly, unable to contain his disbelief.

"By burning down that poor tortured tree, you not only ended its suffering, you did us and those villages a great service."

"There's now no need to avoid that forest or the need for any stories that have cropped up regarding its danger," Hyroc said smugly.

Ursa nodded. "Precisely. The cleansing fire you ignited will bring new life to that area and return balance. You have earned the greatest admiration of the Guardians. You honor your forbearers well." Hyroc beamed.

"A question is weighing on my mind," Hyroc said. "Where did this corruption come from that infected the scythe horn? Do you know?"

"It originated from the same place as the Shade Hunter that ambushed you and your human companions years ago. It's from the same adversary that has always sought your end."

"The Ferals?"

"Yes, the Ferals, as you call them. They are responsible. They control a shadow demon."

Hyroc nodded his understanding. "Good. I'm glad you're here to destroy them. They need to be stopped."

She looked at him curiously. "No, I'm afraid I won't."

"WHAT?" Hyroc yelled incredulously, his face heating with anger. "What do you mean *you won't*? The Ferals have dominated a shadow demon and are on the verge of wiping out the Guidance Wol'dgers, *what's left of my people*. Guardians destroy shadow demons and punish anyone using black magic."

"Normally, yes, but this situation is *unique*."

"How is this unique? Is it because we're Wol'dgers, cursed and beneath receiving your assistance."

"You go too far!" Ursa roared fiercely, startling Hyroc. "You understand nothing of this situation, Anamagi. Justice demands I do nothing to intervene in the feud between your two ideologies, even concerning shadow demons. I am only allowed to contain their rot and keep it from spreading. But I will, with extreme prejudice, destroy any dark creature and anyone who tries to wield the powers of darkness."

"And why does justice stay your wrath if the Ferals are more than deserving of it?"

"Because of you."

Hyroc indicated himself, baffled when he spoke. "Me? I just got here! All I've done is help my uncle rescue a group of kidnapped children. Human children. I haven't done anything of consequence since arriving."

"Because a Guardian is required to resolve it."

Hyroc shot her a strange look. "Yes, that's *you*," he said pointedly, indicating her with both hands.

Ursa shook her head. She indicated him with a raised paw. "No, you misunderstand; so long as any Anamagi lives, they are the only ones allowed to intercede in this conflict. And yes, you are a Guardian."

"So, that *is* why the Warding tree referred to me as a Guardian. I possess a portion of your power with my Flame Claw."

"Correct. We Guardians stay out of human affairs beyond shadow demon incursions and significant disruptions to the balance."

"And we Wol'dgers are still technically considered humans."

"This was the deal struck with your ancestors. When the people of Wulfren began attacking the Guardians, a substantial loss of life was inevitable. Any violence directed toward a Guardian with the express purpose of taking their lives demanded a lethal response. But desperate to avert this, those loyal Wulfreners who would later become the Anamagi took on the responsibilities of the Guardians in exchange for their departure. They would teach the people in their stead, maintain the balance, and deal with shadow intrusions wherever Wulfren was concerned. And this bargain continued even after the cursing of the kingdom that created the Wol'dger. That was so long as the Anamagi bloodline remained."

"Because I'm the last of the Anamagi, that responsibility falls on me," Hyroc said.

"Yes. But if you were to be killed, though it is a rather morbid line of thinking, the contract would be void. Then, we would swiftly pour our wrath upon their heads for their transgressions."

"But the Ferals want to kill everyone in the Glacial village. Can't you break the contract or alter it so you can intervene and save them?"

"I'm afraid not. The covenant they swore to was never to be broken, save for the Anamagi are no more, or they fall into darkness. They knew the price. They went into it willingly. And it was the only way it could function. It is not much different from weaving an enchantment. Certain rules and specific instructions must be followed to accomplish your aim properly. This holds the same for the contract with us. If you truly wish for an outcome where the Glacials survive, either they must end this, or you must."

"How?" Hyroc asked. "How do I end this? It's just me, my uncle, and my friends. And frankly, I'm not even sure I feel right about dragging them into this. Is this their fight?" Hyroc squeezed his eyes shut in a painful expression and clenched his fists. "And – and I don't know if I could forgive myself if anything happened to them. They're my family. I love them."

Ursa regarded him compassionately. "I can give you no easy solution. I wish I could. Truly. This is a trial I wish I could whisk away from you, sparing you from it. I do not wish to see you suffer it. But I cannot without creating consequences that will affect many more lives than yours and the villagers. That is not something I can condone, even for you. I am sorry."

Hyroc opened his eyes. "I will have to make hard choices, won't I?"

"Undoubtedly." A tear ran out of the corner of her eye, darkening her white fur with moisture. That was the first time Hyroc had ever seen her cry. This was tearing her up on the inside. He meant to her as much as she meant to him, and she didn't want to see him hurt.

"I can only offer you this: be vigilant. Your recent actions have not gone unnoticed by your enemy. His plans are already in motion even as we speak. Trust yourself. And as I've always taught you, strike hard when you have an opening."

Hyroc nodded his thanks. "Will I be able to come see you again?"

"Maybe. I am uncertain. I will be somewhere in the vicinity to cleanse any shadow corruption that spreads into my purview, but I do not know if circumstances will align and our paths will cross again before all this is over. But no matter what happens, it is not goodbye forever."

Hyroc gazed at her fondly. "Thank you for telling me the truth."

"The truth is all that should be spoken."

"Can I ask you one last thing before I go that will put my mind at ease?"

"Always. Name it?"

"The man from The Ministry named Keller, does he still pursue me?"

"No. He has already drawn his last breath. An acquaintance whom you met briefly dealt the final blow for Keller dabbling in the dark arts. You no more need fear him."

Hyroc nodded. "Good."

Hyroc used his back to push open the door to Donovan's room, with a piece of bread and cheese on a plate in one hand and a mug of ale in the other. Donovan sat in a chair near the bed, his arms folded behind his head. The healing spell seemed to have finished because he appeared to be in no pain. Kit was still sprawled out on the floor, hardly seeming to have moved since Hyroc had left.

"So, how did it go?" Donovan asked conversationally.

Hyroc sighed, setting the plate on the bed before sitting on its edge. "Not good," he said dryly. He tossed Kit a piece of jerky from his pocket, which scarcely had landed before the big cat snapped it up.

Hyroc quickly recounted the day's events, mentioning Ursa minus any of her explanations.

Donovan shot him a sympathetic look. "So are you saying it was less than ideal?" he asked half-humoredly.

"What do you think?" Hyroc answered indignantly.

"And what about your girlfriend? How'd she take all of this?"

Hyroc blew out an exasperated breath. "Well, let me put it this way: I'm positive I won't be seeing her again."

"*Shadow*, I'm sorry. She seemed to like you."

"Tell me about it," Hyroc agreed before taking a drink of his ale.

Donovan slapped him reassuringly with the back of his hand. "Hey, there's still another Wol'dger woman back at the village who seemed to like you. You should try talking to her when we get back. I bet the two of you would hit it off."

"Oh, now you're a matchmaker," Hyroc said sarcastically. "That rib of yours has given you way too much time for your mind to run away."

"I'm just trying to help. But you never know; what if I am an excellent matchmaker?"

"Then, I'll eat my boot."

Donovan pointed at him excitedly. "I'm holding you to *that.* You've got the teeth for it."

Hyroc rolled his eyes. "Just shut up, you," he said irritably, slugging his friend in the shoulder. "I'm ready to leave this town and return to the village."

"Sounds good, but we still have to wait until morning. Oh – oh," Donovan said excitedly. "And since we've got a lot of time to kill, I've come up with a bunch of Wol'dger jokes I wanted to test out on you."

Hyroc bowed his head and groaned miserably.

Chapter 26

A Glimmer

ALL RIGHT, I’M READY TO get out of here,” Donovan said as he and Hyroc walked down the stairs of the Wheezing Cottonwood tavern. Kit excitedly bounced down the stairs past them, nearly tripping someone coming up. “Elsa’s probably wondering why we’re not back yet. We wouldn’t want to worry her that the Ferals found us and ripped us limb from limb.”

Hyroc nodded his agreement. “But you’re going to be the one to explain what happened to *you*,” he noted.

“Oh, sure, put that responsibility on me, the guy who got his head caved in, and his ribs snapped like twigs,” Donovan said, mildly indignant.

“Yes, what other use are you?” Hyroc joked.

“Hey, that’s not funny. And what about your girlfriend?”

Hyroc sighed. “Well, seeing as I scared her off, no thanks to a surprise attack from a corrupted scythe horn, I wasn’t going to say anything.”

Donovan nodded.

“Hold up,” Darius Ashfin said. “Are the two of you heading back to the Wol’dger village?” Hyroc and Donovan nodded. “I do not wish to impose, but might I accompany you?”

“I don’t see why not,” Hyroc answered. “I assume it’s for your research.”

“That’s correct. I finally got things in order to begin my study of your village, your culture, those sorts of things, so we can better understand how to –" he waved his hand in a circular motion, trying to find the best word "– interact. To help avoid harmful misunderstandings."

"If you think it will benefit our relationship with Mastgar, let's go."

He hurriedly gathered his equipment, including a travel pack.

"But I can't speak about how the villagers will receive you," Hyroc said as they waited patiently. "I barely arrived there myself, so I don't know them well." Kit impatiently scratched at the tavern's door, wanting to be released outside. Hyroc gave the big cat a disapproving nudge with his boot, making him stop. "I'll let you out in just a second, Mr. Impatient," Hyroc whispered.

"I don't think that will be a problem," Darius continued. "I'm positive I can handle whatever comes up. So long as nobody tries to make a stew out of my head, that is." He gave Hyroc a friendly wink. Hyroc gave the man a flat look, unsure if he should laugh or be offended. The man slipped on his pack and looked around curiously. "Where's that female I saw you with the other day?"

"Oh, it didn't work out," Hyroc admitted, subdued.

"Ah, I see. I was interested in learning about the Wol'dger courting habits, but I'm sure I'll have other opportunities."

Donovan stifled a laugh. Hyroc shot him a wide-eyed look. He felt warmth flood his face as he embarrassingly started scratching the back of his head. Unable to respond, he wheeled around and quickly exited the tavern.

"Why don't we *not* talk about *that*," Hyroc heard Donovan sternly suggest while trying not to laugh.

"…That's why there's been such a discrepancy," Darius said comprehendingly to Hyroc.

The three rode on an ox-drawn cart with rectangular bundles of golden hay. The driver, an older man wearing a wide-brimmed hat, happened to have business to the southeast, leading him in the same direction as the Wol'dger village. He would take them as far as he could before their paths diverged.

They bumped along the dirt roadway beneath a blue sky, where intermittent puffy white clouds obscured the sun. The mage had a piece of brownish parchment across his lap while swishing a finger around to magically manipulate a writing quill floating before him. In his other hand, he held his inkwell. Hyroc didn't mind talking, but he was more interested in observing this magical technique so he could replicate it. Learning it seemed especially beneficial. It would save him considerable time and effort when it came to writing.

"So you're saying the Wol'dgers with the red mark on their shoulder are called Ferals," Darius continued. "And they're the hostile ones." Hyroc nodded, and the writing quill inscribed this on the parchment. "And, your side – the friendlier Wol'dgers with the blue marks – are called Glacials." Hyroc nodded again, and the quill jotted it down. The mage scratched his chin, and the quill mirrored the movement with a back-and-forth motion as if scratching an unseen face. "But what is the cause of this feud between your two sides? Why do you behave so differently?"

"I'm not certain of the specifics, but it's because the Ferals think we, Glacials, are following false ideals installed in us by Guardians. They believe the Guardians are tyrannical beings that want to control all Wol'dgers, preventing our kind from reaching their highest potential."

"So it's ideological."

Hyroc nodded. "I guess, mostly, yes."

"And what about this I hear about their particular grievance regarding your being an Anamagi. Why is that?"

"It's because, according to them, my Anamagi bloodline is, or was, knowingly in league with the Guardians. We are complicit with the designs holding all Wol'dgers down to maintain power or something or another. And because the Glacials follow the teachings of the Guardians and the Anamagi, continuing what the Ferals claim are lies, they, too, must be destroyed."

"I see. But why do you, as they say, hold them down? Why do you continue this way of thinking?"

"Our animal form exerts some pretty bad tendencies upon us. If not held in check, they will control us."

"It makes them violent and crazy, like a rabid dog," Donovan interjected.

Hyroc waggled his head in moderate agreement. "Okay, if you want to put it bluntly, yes. They act a lot like a rabid dog or a wild animal."

"That makes sense. So what do you do to prevent this? You do something because you don't seem, as your friend put it, violent and crazy?"

"That's because I finished my animal form training. After the Choosing ritual – where we choose our animal form, my Guardian mentor Ur ..." Hyroc paused when Darius gave him a puzzled look.

"Wait, wait, please back up," he said, holding up a halting hand that caused his writing quill to mimic the movement by abruptly thrusting upward. "What's this you say about a Guardian?"

Hyroc felt a thrill of apprehension. Had he accidentally alluded to something that maybe he shouldn't have? He was already well into it, and regardless of what may come, he needed to respond lest he appear to be hiding something, thus worsening tensions between the Glacials and the Mastgar Crown.

"After we choose our animal form," Hyroc said. "A Guardian trains us on how to use whatever animal form we chose."

"Interesting," Darius said. "We've had infrequent dealings with them, but no such interactions as what you're describing. They mainly keep to themselves and seem wholly uninterested in our affairs. The only situation I know where they intervene is where a shadow demon is involved."

"*Yes*, they don't like *those*," Hyroc agreed.

"Not that I much blame them; nasty creatures, those shadow demons. So a Guardian trained you to resist these animal form tendencies you speak of?" Hyroc nodded. "And this *Choosing ritual* for your animal form is the first I've heard of it. Tell me more about that."

Hyroc scratched the back of his head nervously. "There's a lot to tell. It's no simple matter."

The cart jolted to a stop. "This is where you get off," the driver called over his shoulder. "Git, I've got places to go, animals to feed, livelihoods to maintain."

Darius' writing quill dropped lifelessly to the parchment. He placed it and the inkwell in his pack before rolling up the parchment and stowing it away. The three of them hopped off the cart. With a snap of the reins, their ride rolled away.

"You'll have to tell me more about this Choosing ritual while I'm here," Darius said.

Hyroc nodded his acknowledgment before walking off, taking advantage of the opportunity to avoid further discussion. At least until he figured out what he should and shouldn't talk about with the mage. Everything he disclosed would end up in front of someone within the royal court or potentially the Mastgar king. He needed to be careful. Discussing the more sensitive Wol'dger information might have dire consequences. It also seemed best to avoid discussing the dominated Shade Hunter at the Feral settlement. Supplying Darius with knowledge of dangers associated with either Wol'dger group could easily result in the obliteration of the Ferals and the Glacials.

The three moved off the main track onto the smaller path leading to the Glacial village. Then, by late afternoon, they arrived at Fenrald's cabin. They found Elsa dressing a couple of rabbit carcasses while the female Wol'dger Freija aassisted. Curtis stood nearby, entertaining Elizabeth with lightning animals that ran through the air.

"There you two are!" Elsa said in greeting, bloodied, filleting knife still in her hand. "You're almost two days late. What took you so long? I was starting to wonder if I should go looking for you two."

She snagged Kit's collar with her empty hand when he tried to dart past her to investigate the skinned rabbits and potentially run off with one. He chuffed in protest, trying to escape her grasp. Hyroc jumped in to assist her with restraining the big cat. Defeated, Kit dropped into a low crouch, giving them a homicidal glare.

"Sorry," Donovan apologized. "An unexpected situation delayed us."

"That's pretty obvious, but what kind of *unexpected situation*?"

"The kind that gives you a black eye and a ton of bruises all over your body."

"You got into a fight?"

"Calling it a fight is kind of pushing it."

"He got jumped by Ferals, and we fought them off," Hyroc interjected. He gave Donovan a quick wink.

"Yeah – yeah, we fought them off," Donovan said, catching on and going along with it. "Fists were flying, but they were no match for us."

Elsa nodded her acknowledgment before returning to the rabbits. "You fought off those Ferals. That's quite impressive."

"Truly," Freija agreed.

Hyroc and Donovan greeted her, having almost forgotten she was there.

Hyroc indicated Darius while his other hand pressed down between Kit's shoulders. "This is Darius," he introduced. "Darius, you've already met Elsa and Curtis, and this is Freija, and that's Elizabeth."

The two exchanged a polite "Nice to meet you" and shook hands.

"Darius is here to learn about our village."

"Yes, I am here to help the king of Mastgar understand you, so we can avoid misunderstanding between our peoples."

"Really?" Freija said eagerly. "That's fantastic news. Oh, while we're on the topic, that reminds me, Hyroc, we heard back from your uncle from the envoy. He is fine, and the children arrived safe and sound at home. He'll be back any day now."

"That's great to hear, thank you," Hyroc said.

Freija nodded satisfactorily. "Okay," she continued. "I assume you'll need a place to stay. Let me show you to the tavern."

"Yes, that would be lovely," the mage said.

"Have a good evening, Hyroc," Freija said before turning and guiding Darius toward the village.

"You, too," Hyroc called after her before focusing on Elsa.

She wore a baffled expression, and Donovan seemed almost irritated.

"Hyroc, *go with her*," Elsa said.

"Go with her?" Hyroc questioned, mildly confused. "What for? I'm sure she's –" He was interrupted when Donovan grabbed him with both arms, spun him around, placed a boot against his back, and shoved him after Freija. Hyroc barely had enough time to realize he was walking. Freija regarded him with a happy expression that made Hyroc feel good.

"… I'll also need to arrange a meeting with your elders or whoever is in charge of the village," Darius explained. "Where might I find them?"

The three of them were now at the center of the village

"We've got the tavern, a stable on the left, a few shops, but mostly houses behind us and in front. Sanoc's house – he's the village leader – is straight ahead. This way."

"Thank you so much for helping me."

"You're very much welcome."

Iskall trotted past in his stag form with two of his younger brothers riding on his back. Hyroc waved, and they returned the gesture. Iskall acknowledged him with an antler flourish.

Hyroc, Freija, and Darius garnered curious glances from the villagers they passed. They arrived at a small cottage with a thatched roof and brick chimney. The door was open, and Sanoc was inside, sitting on a stool at a table, reading a piece of parchment. Hyroc made the introduction.

"Yes, yes, please come sit, let us speak," Sanoc said eagerly. "I'm happy to assist you in any way you need."

"That is greatly appreciated," Darius said thankfully. The two of them then began discussing various topics.

"This is exciting!" Freija said as she and Hyroc ducked outside to avoid disturbing the conversation. "Do you think this will finally lead to something being done about those Ferals?"

"Maybe," Hyroc suggested. "If this leads to the Mastgar royal court understanding the difference between our two sides, they might move against the Ferals."

"I need to notify my family about this news!" She took a few steps before turning back toward Hyroc. "I have a wonderful idea. Why don't you come to have supper with us tonight? I know they would be happy to make your acquaintance. What do you say?"

Hyroc felt a surge of apprehension at her request. Although he liked her, he was *not* prepared for that encounter.

"I – I appreciate the request, but – but I needed to get back to take care of something important before my uncle returns. Maybe some other time."

Freija nodded, seeming downtrodden, before continuing on her way. Hyroc hurried off in the opposite direction to ensure he avoided her trying to make another attempt. *Maybe in the future, just not right now,* Hyroc thought.

They were running low on firewood the next day, so Hyroc and Donovan got to work felling a tree at the edge of the clearing around Fenrald's home. Hyroc was up first with the ax.

"Couldn't you bring it down with magic?" Donovan asked after Hyroc got a couple of swings in on the tree's trunk.

"I could," Hyroc agreed. "But that will take a lot out of me." He took another swing.

"More than the strenuous effort it will take for you to chop it down?"

"Yes."

"Are you planning on doing something later you need to save your strength for?"

"No, but you never know when something might come up." Hyroc continued chopping.

"Nothing will happen here, this close to the village, that tiring yourself out would be a disaster. You'll be fine."

"Okay, and what happens when I bring the trees down? Would you want me to divide the tree into rounds and split them into firewood?"

"Well, I wasn't thinking about asking that, but now that you mention it, yes, that would be a great idea. It would save us a bunch of time, time we could then spend hunting and fishing."

"Do you know how much Quintessence it would take for me to do all of that? I would be exhausted even if I had a large enough reserve to do that. The only thing I would be good for afterward would be taking a nap. So no."

Donovan snapped his finger as an idea came to him. "Oh, I know! We could have Curtis do it. He's pretty *useless*, and it won't matter how tired he gets."

Curtis shot him a dirty look. "I AM NOT," he retorted. "You're just trying to get out of it."

"*Of course, I'm trying to get out of it*; it's hard work. Okay, Hyroc, maybe only use a little magic, nothing big, just enough to speed things up."

"You know what non-magic thing *will* speed this up?"

"What?"

"*If you stop talking*!" Donovan glared at him indignantly. "Besides, now it's your turn with the ax." Hyroc handed it to him.

"Just a little mag –" Donovan said, turning to Hyroc.

"No!" Hyroc interrupted.

"Yes, me, Lord," Donovan said sourly as he started chopping.

Hyroc raised his eyes and watched the tree to see which way it would fall. "Curtis, go ahead and move back, and also make sure Elizabeth stays away until it falls." Curtis nodded, doing as instructed. The tree leaned toward the clearing. It wasn't going to hit anything. With a loud crack, the tree snapped from its base where it had been chipped away.

"Coming down!" Donovan yelled, stepping out of the way.

The tree swayed to the ground, landing with a whooshing thud. A shower of leaves followed, and fine bits of bark flashed in the sunlight as they rained down. Hyroc, Donovan, and Curtis removed the branches and limbs to make the log easier to split into smaller, more manageable pieces.

As they finished with the branches, Hyroc noticed Elsa on the other side of the clearing abruptly stop preparing fish on a smoking rack because of something that caught her attention. She moved over to a patch of underbrush. Then, it appeared as if she was talking to some unseen person. The fact that whomever she spoke to hadn't used the road greatly concerned him. They wished to remain concealed, clearly indicating some deception, and typically, anyone who did that was dangerous.

"Donovan, Curtis," Hyroc said, jerking his head in Elsa's direction when they gave him an inquiring look. Donovan carried the wood ax. Though the blade was blunted from use, it was still deadly. Silently, the three of them rushed toward her. Hyroc snatched up his sword, which was propped against the outside of the cabin, while Curtis readied a lightning attack.

"…I can – I can go get him," Elsa said to the unseen figure.

"He's already here," a female voice said. Hyroc recognized that voice.

With a start, Elsa noticed Hyroc and her brothers. "It's okay, everything is fine!" Elsa shouted, waving her hands in a placating up-and-down motion.

"Show yourself," Hyroc demanded.

A large four-legged feline body with a glowing red paw print on its shoulder and gray-striped fur emerged from the foliage. It was Lynx. "You can relax, Hyroc, it's me."

"Lynx?" Hyroc questioned in bewilderment.

"Oh, it's you?" Donovan asked, embarrassed. "There's nothing to worry about."

"Everyone, this is Lynx," Hyroc said, introducing her. Everyone gave her a quick hello.

"Why don't we give these two a minute," Donovan suggested before ushering everyone away.

"What – what are you doing here?" Hyroc asked as he propped his sword against the trunk of the nearest tree.

Lynx looked perplexed. "I'm here to see you," she said.

Hyroc cocked a confounded eyebrow. "See me?" he repeated back. "I thought that corrupted scythe horn was enough for you."

She laughed softly. "It will take more than that to scare me off."

"I would have stuck around the town longer if I had known *that*. I'm sorry."

"No, that's okay. I didn't mind the trip."

Hyroc shook his head, suddenly realizing a new problem glared him in the face. She was a Feral! She was associated with the Wol'dgers responsible for tormenting and even killing the villagers. They wouldn't take kindly to the presence of their enemy. And the fiery crimson paw print on her shoulder would surely give her away. She could pass as a Glacial if nobody looked too closely if her mark was covered.

He swept his eyes through their surroundings, and the area was clear. "Lynx, you need to transform!" Hyroc said. "If someone sees your animal mark – well – just transform before someone sees *that*."

She looked sheepish and let out a mildly embarrassed laugh. "Oh, oops, I didn't even think about that. I'm so used to being around humans who don't care one way or the other that it completely slipped my mind." She spread her limbs, putting equal pressure on each before closing her eyes and beginning the transformation process.

Hyroc felt a flood of warmth across his face when a thought came to him. She was wearing clothing, right? He hadn't even considered that possibility. She was a Feral, and since they were more animal-like behaviorally, he didn't know if they shared the same dogmatic view on wearing clothes. Being naked before going into animal form might be perfectly normal to them. He would never hear the end of that from his companions.

Hyroc breathed a silent sigh of relief as her transformation concluded. She was indeed clothed. Her green jerkin covered her animal mark entirely; no one would know it was there.

"That better?" she asked as she got to her feet.

Hyroc nodded emphatically. "Yes," he said. "Yes, that's much better. Thank you."

"So what are you up to?"

Hyroc indicated the fallen tree. "Not much," he admitted. "Just chopping up that tree."

"You chop it, as in with an ax?"

"Yes," he said, slightly confused. "What else would I use?"

"I thought you would have some sort of magic spell or something to do that for you."

"No, I could, but it would take a tone of Quintessence, and I would be exhausted for the rest of the day. I know it's counterintuitive, but it's easier for me to chop it up like everyone else without magic."

"I see, but what's Quintessence? I've never heard that word before."

"Oh. Quintessence is the name for what you might call magical energy."

"Interesting." She looked thoughtful. "We should go do something."

"Sure. What do you want to do?"

"I don't know, this is *your* village. You had better choose."

Hyroc felt a surge of apprehension. *Oh, no, she wants to do something; what was there to do in the village*, he wondered. He needed help.

"Hold that thought," Hyroc asked. "Give me one second." He turned and walked over to Donovan, ensuring he didn't move too rapidly and potentially giving away what was happening inside his head.

"Donovan," Hyroc hissed, trying not to speak loudly enough for Lynx to overhear. "Donovan. Come here. I need your help."

"I thought you would never ask," Donovan said gleefully, his wide grin almost making Hyroc want to smack him.

"She wants to *do something with me*. I have no idea what I could do with her. What do I do?"

Donovan looked thoughtful before answering. "Here's what you're going to do…."

"It's pretty," Lynx said happily.

"I'm glad you think so," Hyroc said thankfully. Though he was doing his best to maintain a calm facade, a storm of anxiety raged within him.

The two of them stood beside a burbling stream of clear shallow water. The stream flowed into a pool with a current so gentle it was hard to discern its presence. Hyroc dropped into a crouch, laying out a quilt. After smoothing it out, the two of them sat. Hyroc slid a basket onto the quilt that contained some cheese and a round of bread.

"Let's see," Hyroc said, reaching toward the basket. "We've got cheese. We've got bread. Which would you –"

He was interrupted when Lynx reached into the basket, collected what she wanted, and began to eat. Hyroc resisted the urge to laugh. *Right, she's a Feral,* Hyroc reminded himself. With her being more animalistic, lady-like manners are probably not a high priority. Jovially, Hyroc joined in on the meal. He paused, noticing Lynx devouring the bread like a starving wolf after a kill.

"Whoa, slow down. You're going to choke," Hyroc noted. "There's no rush."

Lynx was abashed. "Oh, sorry," she said half-humoredly, wiping her mouth on the back of her hand. "Habit."

"No need to apologize. I was just concerned."

"Thank you for the thought." She resumed eating, but slower. Hyroc took a bite of bread. "This is nice. I really appreciate it."

"I'm glad you like it."

"So I saw you yesterday with *her*."

"Freija?" Hyroc asked tentatively.

"Is that her name? Yes, with Freija."

"She's a friend. She once saved me from a group of over-exuberant Glacial girls. I don't know if they were just excited, but it felt like they were gazing upon me like a piece of meat."

"Ah, so nothing serious?"

"No, no, I met her a couple of days ago."

Lynx nodded. "She seemed nice. Nice if you like the tame, polite, and boring type."

Was that a hint of jealousy in her voice, Hyroc wondered? Was she worried Freija would poach him away from her? He hadn't even considered the possibility of jealousy sparking a fight between the two girls. Getting caught in the middle of a competition over him was not at all appealing. And if he wasn't careful, he could easily anger either of them or turn both of them against him. But he may have to choose one of them at a certain point and inevitably draw one's wrath. Or he might not choose either of them. But he needed to be cautious.

"Wait," Hyroc said, realizing something. "How did you know I was with Freija? Were you – were you spying on me?"

She looked guilty. "Well –"

Hyroc interrupted her by jabbing an accusing finger at her. "You were!" he said with a laugh. "You were spying on me."

"Yes, yes I was. My animal form is a cat; you should already know cats are great at being sneaky. I was only using my talents."

"I assume so. And nobody saw you?"

"None that I'm aware of."

"That's very impressive."

"You couldn't ever hope to do the same with that lumbering bear body of yours."

"I wouldn't expect so," Hyroc agreed. "I assume you were being so stealthy because you're a Feral."

"Of course. I had no idea and still don't know how the villagers would have reacted to me.

"That's understandable. I know exactly what that feels like."

"You do?"

Hyroc nodded. "Yes. When I first arrived at Elswood – a human village in Arnaira – I had no idea how the villagers would react to me.

Would they offer me refuge, cast me out, or would they try and kill me? Luckily, my friend's family took me in."

"Sounds tough."

"Yes, it was very tough. So you tracked me from Forestgold?" She nodded. "I was certain you were gone for good because of the corrupted scythe horn and the saltiness of my old mentor dismissing you in a less-than-polite manner."

"To tell the truth, it *was* a jarring occurrence. The thought of staying away from you did cross my mind, but I don't know why. I just thought I should give you a second chance."

"Even after all that?"

"Yes, even after all that happened."

Hyroc leaned back into a more comfortable position. Then, he noticed it was a clear night, and the stars were out. Almost purely out of habit, he began tracing the constellations with his eyes. The thought to share his knowledge popped into his head. Maybe she would like that.

"Lynx, look here, I want you to see something," Hyroc said, pointing at the sky. Curiously, Lynx leaned back to gaze at the stars. "You see that line of uneven stars right above us?" After a moment of searching, Lynx found it. "That's Ferma, the serpent." Hyroc swept his eyes across the sky, searching for his next target. "Oh, look here, that's Kaska the hawk. It's usually hard to see. And that's Anol, the wolf.

Lynx gently took hold of Hyroc's hand. Happily, he glanced at their hands, then looked into her eyes. Her eyes were like finely cut emeralds, and he felt as if they were the most beautiful things he had ever laid eyes upon.

The idea to kiss her suddenly appeared in his head. That seemed the appropriate display of affection. He really liked her. The possibility hadn't crossed his mind until that instant. He felt his face moving toward hers like an invisible hand was easing his head forward. Then, he was mortified by a disastrous concept.

He pulled his head back, garnering a baffled look from Lynx. With a finger, he made an embarrassed back-and-forth motion, indicating both of their faces, and nervously scratched the back of his head.

"I – uh – I don't – how do we – I don't know how we – Wol'dgers, I mean – how do we – umm – you know – kiss?" Hyroc stammered. He tapped the end of his snout. "I don't know how to do it with *these*. I've seen how humans do it. Just not Wol'dgers."

She softly laughed her understanding, but it wasn't a mocking laugh. It was simply finding humor in the situation. "I see. Well, there's only one way to remedy that. Let me show you."

Chapter 27

Fenrald's Success

HYROC STIRRED A POT OF hot bubbling porridge in the cool morning air. He stood beside the fire pit outside of Fenrald's cabin with the pot suspended above the fire by a stick tripod. A sleepy-eyed Elizabeth sat on a log bench, waiting patiently as she played with her doll. Hyroc had opted to cook outside to avoid waking his friends, who slept inside his uncle's home.

He spooned porridge into a bowl but paused, suddenly inspired to make the meal more entertaining for his adopted cousin. "Elizabeth, you want to see something?" Hyroc said invitingly.

She looked on, instantly excited like a cat springing on a mouse. Hyroc activated his Flame Claw, cupped his hand, and made a tall scooping motion. A steaming cream-colored porridge erupted out of the pot, spiraling through the air in a figure-eight shape before flowing into a bowl. Elizabeth's eyes were wide with captivation as she giggled and happily clapped her applause.

"Want me to do it *again*?" he teased.

Elizabeth nodded emphatically. This time, Hyroc animated the porridge into a rabbit, which galloped through the air into a second bowl with a sloppy splat. Some of it sloshed out onto his hand.

"This is fun!" she squealed. Hyroc was overjoyed at her mirthful outburst and couldn't resist giving her a sharp-toothed smile. "Again, again."

"No, that's enough for now," Hyroc said apologetically. "I shouldn't waste any more Quintessence on breakfast." This dampened Elizabeth's delight.

Hyroc slid his mouth across his hand to slurp the spot of porridge on it before serving Elizabeth's and sitting down beside her with a bowl of his own. Almost without realizing it, he hummed happily as he ate.

"Someone's in a good mood," Elsa said from the cabin's porch, yawning as she stretched her arms.

"Yes, I am," Hyroc agreed, continuing to hum.

Elsa incredulously cocked her head. "Wait, are you *humming*?"

Hyroc paused, his eyes widening, suddenly aware of the noise rattling through his throat. "I – uh – guess I am."

"That's the first time *I've ever* heard you hum." She filled a bowl with porridge.

"I can stop if it's annoying."

"No, it's not annoying. It's a delightful change. I enjoy seeing you happy after everything we've been through lately." Before joining them, she tapped off the wooden serving spoon on the pot's rim. "So what filled you with so much joy?"

Hyroc absentmindedly poked the contents of his bowl with his spoon. He shyly glanced over at her when he spoke. "You know, last night when Lynx showed up. Well –" he bashfully waggled his head as he answered, "I – umm – I kissed her."

Elsa's mouth fell open in astonishment. "No, *you did*!" she said excitedly.

Hyroc nodded. "I sure did," he agreed.

"Wow!" She clapped his shoulder and gave it a congratulatory shake. "Good for you."

Donovan put on his boots, followed by Curtis. Groggily, Curtis went to the porridge, wholly oblivious to the monumental occurrence Hyroc had admitted, wanting to get to his breakfast as soon as possible.

Elsa fished a Fleck coin out of her pocket and flipped it to Donovan when he got close enough. Caught by surprise, he fumbled for the coin, seizing it before it slipped to the ground.

"What's this for?" Donovan asked, holding up the Fleck.

She pointed at Hyroc. "You were right, they kissed."

Donovan chuckled. "See, I told you."

Hyroc and Curtis gave them a quizzical look.

"What are you two talking about?" Hyroc asked, feeling like they had made a joke about him he didn't understand.

"Oh, the two of us made a bet you were going to kiss her last night," Donovan said.

"You two seriously bet on *that*?" Hyroc said, mildly indignant, feeling a mixture of insult and flattery.

Donovan shrugged. "Why not?"

Hyroc couldn't think of an answer. "But yes, I absolutely kissed her last night," he said satisfactorily. "And it was fantastic! And her eyes. Oh, her eyes. I could have stared into those beautiful emeralds all night."

"Oh, you are dreadfully in love, mate."

"I know," Hyroc sighed ecstatically.

"So when are you going to meet with her again?" Elsa asked.

"In three days."

"You should give her something special for next time," Donovan suggested, taking a bite of porridge.

"You're right!" Hyroc agreed. "I should make her something."

"Oh, and you could use that Flame Claw of yours to make her something exceptional."

"That's a great idea. What should I make?"

"Well, that's for you to figure out. She's *your* girlfriend." Donovan paused, becoming humorously indignant when he spoke. "Oh, and by the way, I saw that little *show* of yours with the porridge. So you can use your Quintessence to entertain your cousin with breakfast but not to split up a log. Now, I see!"

Hyroc's expression turned sheepish. He had no way of defending himself against *that*. "Well, there's lots of things for me to get to, so I had better get to them," he said evasively before abandoning his bowl and walking away.

"Yeah, you had better run," Donovan jested.

Hyroc headed from the cabin to check the traps Elsa and Donovan had set. Only a trap near a creek had snared a beaver. The animal's meat was not enticing, but he went through the process of dressing the carcass purely out of habit of not having enough food. Hyroc gutted it, careful to avoid damaging its pelt because it would fetch a reasonable price in Forestgold. He disposed of its innards in the river to prevent the scent from attracting unwanted scavengers. He secured the animal carcass to his belt to skin later.

"Hey, Hyroc!" Elsa called to him.

Hyroc waved his acknowledgment. "I already got all the traps," he said. "I was just now heading back."

"That's what I figured." She thumbed over her shoulder. "I passed some deer tracks back there and wanted to know if you're up for hunting?"

Hyroc noticed the fully stocked quiver on her back and the bow she carried. She didn't have an extra of either, so Hyroc knew what that meant.

"You want me in bear form, I presume," he asked.

"If you wouldn't mind, yes. I don't know the area well, and you being in bear form to scent it would be our best bet at getting something."

"All right," Hyroc agreed. "But if my clothes get dirty, you're washing them."

"Well, if we manage to kill something, I'll gladly wash your clothes as long as you don't decide to wallow in mud."

"Oh, if you insist," Hyroc said sarcastically, feigning being downtrodden. "You know me, always seeking an opportunity to get myself as filthy as possible. I can't resist."

Elsa chuckled. "That's not like a true bear at all," she commented playfully.

Hyroc spoke as he handed her the beaver carcass. "Well, I would exude the true fragrance of a bear if I didn't bathe." He removed his sword, knife, and his jerkin.

"True, very true." Elsa stashed his gear beneath the low branches of a spruce tree near one of their traps, ensuring they wouldn't forget its location.

Then, Hyroc dropped onto all fours. "And apparently, neither do bear-Ferals. Be glad you didn't have the stink of those bloated brutes

I had to face at that caravan invading your beak. My face was right there in their noxious musk." Hyroc's expression turned to disgust at the memory.

"And with your enhanced sense of smell, that must have been an especially grody encounter."

"Yeah," he agreed. "It was *incredibly* unpleasant. It took me the better half of a week to wash the stench out of my nose." He paused to transform into bear form. "Just thinking about it gives me a shiver," Hyroc continued when the transformation concluded. "It will be nice to have a more agreeable *bouquet* flowing through my sniffer. Where were those tracks?" He pointed with a raised paw in the direction she had indicated. "That way, right?"

"Yes," Elsa agreed.

Hyroc nodded, sauntering ahead of her. The tracks were fresh, no more than an hour old. Hyroc dropped his nose to the ground and discovered the deer's scent. It had the pungent smell of a buck, which would yield a large amount of meat. That was excellent; they were running low on food, and their quarry would remedy that. He deftly followed the scent trail; years of practice aided him. His movements were smooth and precise, and he avoided unnecessary noise. He and Elsa were so accustomed to hunting this way that little verbal communication was necessary between them. Hyroc led the way, and she followed with an arrow at the ready. After following the trail through the chaotic meandering of a hungry animal looking for food, they eventually found their target.

The rutting season was not yet underway, and the buck's antlers, not fully formed, were covered in fuzzy brown velvet. The animal was looking away from them, and Hyroc angled toward its rear end while Elsa came in for a shot. When it noticed Hyroc's heavy footfall, it was already too late. Elsa sent an arrow whistling into its chest. It was a fatal shot into its heart. Their prey's fate was sealed. The doomed animal attempted to flee. With the swipe of his broad paw, Hyroc knocked the deer's back legs out from under it. Then, he threw himself onto its back to immobilize it and waited for the end. Though the animal would perish regardless of his actions, enough life remained in its body to put an annoying distance between them before it expired. Hyroc figured he might as well save himself the task of tracking down the creature. The deer struggled vigorously, but its strength hastily disappeared. Its breathing became labored until it ceased drawing breath. Hyroc climbed off the carcass to examine their kill.

"Good job," she said. "That was a nice takedown, but tackling it might have been a tad unnecessary."

"Probably," Hyroc agreed. "But I didn't want to have to track it down."

"Yes, track it down the five yards it might have traveled," she joked. Hyroc humoredly rolled his eyes. "Now, we must drag it back to your uncle's place, then we can safely butcher it."

Utilizing his enhanced strength to haul away an animal at least one hundred pounds was an efficient use of his ability. It was tiring work, but beyond this, the only downside of doing so was it incorporated more dirt and forest debris into the meat. Luckily, they weren't far from Fenrald's cabin.

Hyroc clamped his jaws around the animal's neck; its hairy flesh was still warm when the inside of his mouth touched it. He carefully chose his course to avoid the buck's protruding antlers getting hung up on branches or any semi-stiff plant matter in his path. Rigor had also set in, which stiffened the animal's limbs, turning the limber body into a mass of immobile legs and hooves. It was as if the animal fought them from beyond the grave, its spirit tormenting them with the remnants of its fleeting ghostly will. It became so difficult to move the animal that, to avoid an irritating detour around a clump of spruce trees with branches that grew too close together, they broke the animal's stiff legs to get it through. Breaking bone was no obstacle for Hyroc's bear form. They eventually arrived at their destination.

Hyroc slumped into a prone position, tired and thankful his arduous task was concluded.

"About time you two go back," Donovan said, feigning indignity. "I wanted to eat hours ago."

"Shut up," Hyroc growled. "Next time, you're going to drag the carcass through the forest."

"Well, when I can transform into a frumpy bear, I will."

Elsa removed her boot and playfully threw it at him. He dodged it with a swift sidestep, but with the wave of a paw, Hyroc used his Flame Claw to redirect it and whacked his friend in the back of the head with it.

"Ow," Donovan said flatly, his voice baffled. He rubbed the back of his head, bewildered by the inexplicable occurrence. "You used your Flame Claw to do that, didn't you?"

Hyroc looked around innocently. "I know not what you speak of," he said with a sarcastic sniff.

"That's not fair." As Donovan turned his attention to the carcass, Elsa's boot levitated off the ground, flipped so the bottom faced toward him and sailed into his rear. Dazed by the impact, Donovan stumbled forward with a wrathful expression.

"That wasn't *me*," Hyroc pleaded. He pointed an accusatory paw at Curtis. "It was *him* this time. Honest."

"Oh, you think that's funny," Donovan said playfully angry as he rushed toward his younger brother.

"Wait, no!" Curtis yelled with a laugh as Donovan grabbed him and proceeded to rough him up.

Elsa shook her head humorously before getting to work removing the hide from the carcass. Donovan and Curtis joined the work when they finished horsing around. While in bear form, Hyroc was incapable of helping, so he took a nap on the porch while waiting for the required amount of time to remain in bear form to elapse.

He awoke to the sound of Shimmer squawking and excited yelling. When he opened his eyes, he saw Fenrald arriving at the cabin.

"Fenrald!" Hyroc called out in greeting as he rose on all fours. "Fenrald, welcome back." His companions gave their greetings as well.

"I'm glad to be back," Fenrald said, relieved.

"Papa!" Elizabeth yelled excitedly as she rushed toward him with her doll in hand.

Fenrald dropped onto one knee and spread his arms to accept her lovingly. "I'm so delighted to see you again, my love," he said happily.

"Were you good for your cousin and his friends while I was gone?" Elizabeth nodded emphatically. "Good, good."

Hyroc came in to embrace him in a welcoming gesture but stopped when his uncle shot him a strange look. "Hyroc, if you're trying to welcome me back, aren't you forgetting something? It's going to be somewhat awkward if you do it like *that*."

Hyroc regarded him, perplexed. "Like what?" he said. "What are –" His situation suddenly dawned on him. He felt mortified he had forgotten he was in his bear form. In his current oafish body, trying to welcome his uncle using anything beyond words would be complicated and unmanageable. Though extremely unlikely, Hyroc could also hurt someone in this form if he wasn't careful.

"Oh, right," Hyroc said, subdued. He took a step back before dropping to the ground and transforming. Once in his natural form, he gave his uncle a proper welcoming embrace.

"Did you have any trouble with the Ferals or North Landers?" Donovan asked.

Fenrald shook his head. "No, they didn't cause any problems bringing those kids home. Apart from some rain, it was smooth sailing from the time I left Forestgold."

"Glad to hear."

"I'm sure the parents were happy to have their children back," Elsa said.

"Oh, yes, they most definitely were," Fenrald agreed. "I wish you could have been there to see the grateful looks on their faces. The feeling it gives me is indescribable. That tiny ray of sunshine always reminds me why I keep fighting to stop the Ferals." The happiness vanished from his face, replaced by sorrow. "And the ones I cannot save, they remind me this must stop." He clenched his fists angrily. "It tears you apart on the inside when you have to tell a parent they will never hear their child's voice again."

Hyroc laid a comforting hand on his uncle's shoulder. This diffused Fenrald's rage. "Maybe this will have been the last time you have to do it," Hyroc said reassuringly. "Now that we're together, and with my friends' help, maybe we can permanently stop this madness."

"Maybe," Fenrald agreed, heartened by Hyroc's words. "Maybe, yes. We can implement our plans as soon as I have recovered from my trip. Maybe we can stop this." With that, Fenrald walked through the front door of his home to remove his travel gear. Hyroc followed him inside. "Did I miss anything happening here while I was gone?" he asked.

"No, not really," Hyroc said. "It stayed pretty quiet here. Oh, yeah, I think I –" He trailed off, his courage to talk about Lynx failing him. She was a Feral, and as agitated as his uncle was talking about the terrible pain Ferals were responsible for, now wasn't the best time to tell him. He would wait for a better opportunity. "Yes," Hyroc said, trying to sound believable without revealing his mistake. "I think I found the tracks of a – uh, of a bear – that, uh – that was close to the village, and yeah – yeah, it might become a problem, so we should probably keep an eye on it."

Fenrald removed a dark blue cloak and stowed it away while he spoke. "Yes, definitely," he agreed. "It could become a problem if it comes near anyone with livestock. You'll have to show it to me later, so I can have a look."

"Will do," Hyroc said, hoping that *later* Fenrald would have forgotten his innocuous white lie before it turned into a hindrance.

"Oh, that reminds me," Fenrald said, reaching into a knapsack and removing two coin sacks. He placed one in each of Hyroc's hands. "The one in your left hand is payment for services rendered by your friends helping us rescue those children, and the one in your right is for Iskall and Shawnren. Would you mind getting it to them?"

"Not at all." Hyroc exited the cabin. He gave the sack to his friends, letting them decide how to divide it, while he headed to Iskall's home. There, he found Iskall and his younger brothers putting in a new post for their fence.

They accepted the payment with looks of awe as if they had never seen so many Flecks.

"Thank you so very much," Iskall said graciously. He jerked the sack out of reach when one of his brothers tried grabbing it. "Anything happen to your uncle while he took those kids back to their home?"

Hyroc shook his head. "No, he said everything went well. There were no Ferals or North Landers."

"That's good. I'm glad to hear it."

"And to what do we owe the honor of your visit, Anamagi, Hyroc?" said Iskall's father, Unresh, ambling toward them.

"We got paid!" one of Iskall's brothers blurted out.

"Ah, I see," the man said warmly.

"Shush, you, loud mouth," Iskall hissed. "But, yeah, we got paid." He went to hand the sack to his father but was stopped by a dismissive wave.

"No, that belongs to you and your brother and is to be split among you," Unresh said. "The two of you more than earned it; you keep it."

Iskall nodded, awestruck, retracting his hand. "Well, I'll be right back to finish that fence post," he said. "I need to put this down somewhere more secure." He walked off toward his family's home.

"I heard you and my brothers killed more than a hundred Ferals," one of the youngest boys said to Hyroc.

Hyroc was dumbfounded, unable to formulate a response to the child's wild exaggeration.

"Stop pestering our guest," the boy's father ordered. "Get back to that fence. It's getting late, and you won't want to be working when it's dark." They nodded, complying. "I'm sorry about that, but you must admit, it was quite impressive for the lot of you and your uncle to have accomplished what you did for those children."

"Thank you."

"You're welcome. Well, I'm sure you have other things to get to. Have a Guardian blessed day."

As he hobbled away, his arduous movement became more apparent to Hyroc. His sympathy sparked a question in his mind. "Wait," Hyroc said. The Wol'dger turned back, regarding him with a quizzical expression. Hyroc indicated his walking stick. "If you don't mind my asking, how did your leg get hurt?"

The man leaned on his stick, looking distant. "It happened a while ago, in Wulfren, while we fled the Feral Purge. Thankfully, I could walk without difficulty back then. I was even well-practiced in swordsmanship. My family and I fled with neighbors. Ferals fell upon us at night. The sentries on watch barely saw them coming before they were slain. It was pure chaos! I saw friends hewn down as they unknowingly rushed straight into the enemy. My brother and I slew two Ferals as we cleared a path through the carnage for our family. But before we reached safety, we were set upon by a murderous Feral in the form of a bear. My brother was the bear's first target. He didn't stand a chance! He was gone in the blink of an eye. Then, the bear came after me. It knocked me down and bit into my leg. The pain was unbearable, but I battled through it. The lives of my wife and children were at stake. I drove my sword into the bear's neck. It took two more thrusts to finish it off. My leg was in bad shape, and I fully expected the wounds to take my life. But, almost miraculously, we managed to stop the bleeding. Infection didn't take hold, and it eventually healed. But even as fortuitous as my recovery was, I never regained full use of that leg. And that's pretty much the whole story."

"I'm sorry to hear that," Hyroc said sympathetically. "Thank – thank you for telling me."

The man nodded his appreciation for Hyroc listening to his despairing story, then moved away, looking as if his mind was still elsewhere.

Hyroc felt a sickening weight in the pit of his stomach. Just thinking about the man recounting his Feral bear attack disturbed Hyroc. He was more than acquainted with the fact that a bear's jaws were powerful enough to crush bone with barely any effort. He had used his bear-form teeth to do just that more times than he could count. But he couldn't comprehend using them on innocent people. That was monstrous! No, that was beyond monstrous. *That was evil.*

Hyroc restrained himself from exploring that insidious darkness further. He turned his thoughts from that to wondering if he could heal the man's injury with his Flame Claw. The root of the debilitating injury was further in than the subcutaneous tissue of the leg. The cause lay deeper, within the bone and sinew. He didn't know how to repair anything occupying that realm. The healer in Forestgold had cast a spell that healed Donovan's broken ribs, so he didn't see why it wouldn't be possible. He could probably learn to do it one day, but who knew how distant that day was? Maybe through Darius, he could arrange a visit from a healer if money were a problem for the family. Where was their new visitor anyway?

Chapter 28
Spiderbane

"Now, we need to figure out where to focus," Fenrald said as he leaned over a map across the table in his cabin.

Hyroc sat across the room on a stool, using a whetstone to sharpen his falchion. He hadn't used his old battle-worn blade since receiving his father's hand and a half-sword, but he kept it sharp in case the need for an extra weapon arose. It was like a close friend who had seen him through tough times and stood at his side during the fray of numerous fights. Letting it rust, forgotten in a closet, would be a dishonorable repayment for its unwavering service.

"We cannot directly assail the main Feral settlement to the north," Fenrald continued. "Not with only the two of us and your friends. I would wager there are no less than one hundred Ferals at any one time and probably an equal number of North Landers."

"So likely around two hundred enemies in total," Hyroc added.

"I think it's safe to assume that. I would err on the side of caution and assume three hundred."

Hyroc sighed irritably. "There's what, two or three times that number of villagers living here?"

"Yes, I think it's about that."

"It's so stupid the villagers won't help us deal with the Ferals. If everyone joined us, we could crush them *right now* and permanently end their threat." Fenrald grunted a laugh of agreement. "Practically everyone who lives here has lost someone or experienced the brutality of the Ferals. They continue to kill people here. Not that long ago, while you were gone, some Ferals snuck in and murdered somebody. These people – our people, are being terrorized. They could stop all of that. Aren't they tired of being afraid and constantly looking over their shoulders?"

"Wiping out the Feral threat would ensure their safety and end this bloody feud," Fenrald agreed. "But have you considered how many lives would be lost in the endeavor? How would you convince them to go willingly through the resulting painful loss of loved ones?"

"I have no idea," Hyroc said, frustrated. "But something I learned from my Guardian mentor, Ursa, is sometimes you have to go through a lot of pain to get to something good at the end."

"How did she teach you that?"

Hyroc blew out a breath. "She made me crack open a beehive."

Fenrald turned from the map to regard him with an astonished expression. "Really! Wow, that had to hurt."

"Yes, *extremely*. But the honey I got afterward was delicious."

"And was it worth the pain?"

"Oh, absolutely not! It was nowhere near worth the agony of all those stingers. But what I'm getting at is I went through something incredibly unpleasant and was rewarded at the end. It's the same thing with the villagers. Their pain will lead to something much better."

"That's a rational proposition. But trying to persuade people with tremendous pain is not a great selling point. No one wants to experience pain, usually, no matter what is waiting for them after. They won't do it even if it's in their best interests."

Hyroc cut through hairs on his arm to test the falchion's sharpness. The blade sailed through them cleanly. It was sharp. He slid the sword back into its sheath.

"Oh, and," Hyroc continued, "apparently, because I got stung by that swarm of angry bees, it gave me a very high pain tolerance."

Fenrald cocked an eyebrow. "That's interesting," he said. "But it seems to me maybe your mentor was just a masochist."

Hyroc laughed half-humoredly. "Yes, I had also considered that possibility. But, still, something good *did* come out of all that."

"Makes me glad I didn't choose a bear."

"Didn't your mentor put you through anything like that?"

Fenrald shook his head. "He put me through some unpleasant things, yes, but nothing remotely close to making me shove my delicate schnoz inside a beehive."

"Huh," Hyroc said, perplexed.

A long, awkward silence ensued and was broken by Fenrald returning to his original point. "All right. Hitting the Feral settlement is out of the question, so we must look for other targets. What can we attack that will still hurt them? Where are they vulnerable?" He beckoned Hyroc over to the map. "Getting supplies, such as food, is rather difficult for them. As far as I know, they have nowhere to farm, and because of their unruly activities, they are not welcome to openly trade anywhere in Mastgar. They get some food through their cooperation with the North Landers, but that region is not known for its abundant farmland, so the food is either in short supply or of relatively lower quality. They need more than what they get through that associate. If you remember the corrupt official in Forestgold, the Ferals pay him off in exchange for allowing them to purchase food safely. If we sabotage or disrupt this activity, it will harm their settlement. This is their weak point."

"You want to attack the Ferals coming to and from Forestgold?" Hyroc asked.

"Precisely."

"And what about the guards? I wouldn't expect them to take kindly to us harrying Ferals in their town, causing a ruckus and otherwise disturbing the peace. To say nothing of the corrupt official reacting to us threatening his *cut*."

"We won't hit them in town – at least not openly, but that's a discussion for later. For now, we should only think about disrupting this supply line. We are open to attacking them when they leave sight of the town's guards." He indicated the distance on the map by running a finger from Forestgold's symbology to the Feral village's symbology. "From *here* to *here*, they are exposed to ambush." He lightly smacked Hyroc with the back of his hand, wearing a wiry expression. "You and your friends are hunters and trappers. Why don't we give the lot of you something to hunt? What do you say?"

"Sounds good," Hyroc said eagerly.

"Just remember, these animals can think and are more dangerous than anything you've hunted."

"Well, I don't know about that. We've hunted some pretty dangerous quarry and managed to survive. So I'm sure we can handle them."

"That's good to hear."

"Is there anything I need to do right now to help you prepare, or am I free to take care of some chores?"

"No, you can go. I've got to think on this before I put anything into motion." Hyroc nodded and turned to leave. "Wait, Hyroc. I saw how carefully you maintained that falchion. I can tell it's special to you and has got you through difficulties. Do you, by chance, have a name for it?"

"Have I named it?" Hyroc repeated back. "No."

"Well, there's this tradition of naming weapons that have seen service. I think it's because it's supposed to bring its owner luck and whatnot. But I'm sure with everything it's got you through, it's more than deserving of a name."

"What's the name of your sword?"

"Wildcat. The name should be something related to whatever it's been used for or what it's fought for. Something special to you."

Hyroc paused, contemplating the subject. "It's named Spiderbane."

Fenrald nodded congratulatory. "That's a good name. Thank you for entertaining me with that."

"I wanted to ask you one last thing before I headed out," Hyroc said. He indicated the locket around Fenrald's neck. "Would you mind if I had a look at your locket?"

Fenrald regarded him quizzically. "Yes, you may." Fenrald handed it to him.

Hyroc rolled it between his thumb and a finger, watching the light dance across the locket's cool metallic surface.

"What's her name?" Fenrald asked.

Hyroc shot him a startled look. "What's whose name?" he said evasively.

"You can't hide it. I can tell by how interested you are looking at my locket. You found someone."

Hyroc shyly nodded, handing the necklace back to his uncle. "Yes, I think I have met someone special."

Fenrald gave him a congratulatory pat on the shoulder. "I'm truly happy for you. I thought the two of you would make a good couple."

"Really?" Hyroc said, astonished. Lynx was a Feral. He didn't think in his wildest dreams his uncle would be so cavalier about such a relationship."You already know who it is?"

"I have a good inkling."

"And you're okay with it?"

"Of course. Remember, I was also once a young man who fell in love."

Hyroc beamed. "Thank you, uncle."

Fenrald nodded his appreciation. "Just remember, don't ever take her for granted."

"Don't worry, I won't." He paused. "I wanted to make her something special for the next time we're together, but I'm not sure what to make. What would a woman want?"

"It depends on the woman. What does she like? What's something she might find pretty? Women love their trinkets. Flowers are always nice. It's hard to go wrong with a nice handful of flowers. Give it some thought, and you'll think of something. But you're not going to figure it out here. Go on out."

With a nod, Hyroc eagerly headed out. Outside, Elsa, Donovan, and Curtis were attending to a couple of animal pelts.

"Anything new to report from your uncle?" Donovan asked.

"No, he's still trying to figure something out," Hyroc said.

"And what did your uncle say about Lynx," Elsa prodded. "Did you tell him about her?"

"He already figured it out for himself," Hyroc said.

"And he's okay with that?"

"Yes."

"You're sure?"

"Positive."

"Okay."

"I just need to figure out what to make for her when I see her tomorrow night."

Donovan excitedly pointed as an idea came to him. "Oh, oh, flowers! Get her some pretty flowers. Women love flowers."

"No, don't get her flowers," Elsa said disapprovingly. "She already knows about your Flame Claw and that you can use magic. If you do flowers when she knows *that*, she'll think you're a stingy tightwad or that you're just plain lazy. Suppose she thinks any of that about you. That'll probably make tomorrow night the last time she wants to see you. You have to figure out something to make with magic."

"But what can I make?"

"Wait," Donovan said again as another idea came. "You like her eyes. They were green, right? Make something green like her eyes."

"Good idea," Hyroc agreed. "Emeralds would be a good choice, but those are way too expensive and aren't just lying around the forest."

"Can you use your magic to make one appear?"

"No, remember, I can't use Quintessence to conjure objects out of thin air. I can only form things from materials already in the area, meaning I can make rocks and make them as shiny as silver."

Donovan jabbed a finger at him. "Wait! That gives me an idea. Follow me." He rushed off toward the creek. Everyone followed, unable to figure out what he could be referring to. He led them to a shallow stretch of clear flowing water where the bottom was covered in rocks rounded by the unending flow of current. Donovan rolled up his pant legs before trudging out into the creek, his eyes fixed on the bottom. He grabbed a fist-sized rock with a white line of quartz and set it on the shore before Hyroc.

"Break that in half," Donovan said. "Just trust me. You'll understand why."

Hyroc drew a wood hatchet, turning it so the flat back of the head faced down. He dropped onto one knee, and the flat part of the hatchet glowed blue. When he struck the rock, there was a loud grinding crack as it split. Quartz crystals with a reddish hue lined the inside of both halves.

"See those crystals?" Donovan said. "Can you do anything with those?"

"Yes, I think I can," Hyroc said eagerly. "But you need to bring me more."

Hyroc's friends brought him rocks, placing them in a pile in front of him. Hyroc used his Flame Claw to crack them open. Next, with his palms glowing blue, he raised both hands, straining as if he fought against unseen ropes. Tiny crystals separated from the rocks, appearing as a dusting of large sparkling grains of sand suspended in the air. Hyroc clapped his hands together, and the crystal dust cloud condensed into a solid mass. The translucent glass took on the form of a small crystalline feline. Hyroc held out his palm, and the crystal cat settled on it. He held his other hand above the cat and wiggled his fingers. The pellucid animal took on a dark greenish hue. Its color was that of the finest cut emerald.

"What do you think?" Hyroc said, holding it out for inspection.

"I think that will work," Donovan said.

"She'll love that," Elsa said. "I know I would. And, well, if she doesn't, I don't think she's the one for you."

"Great!" Hyroc said. He suddenly looked fatigued. "Now, if you'll excuse me, I need to take a nap. Doing that sapped all my strength."

When they returned to the cabin, they found Fenrald on the porch talking to Darius.

"Here they come now," Fenrald announced. "Donovan, Elsa, and Curtis, there's someone here to see you."

"Hello again," the mage said conversationally. Everyone greeted him. "I believe I have something for you. A courier arrived with a letter this morning." He rifled through his knapsack, removing an envelope with a crimson seal and handing it to Elsa. "Here you are."

Elsa used her knife to break the seal, revealing the letter within. Everyone peered over her shoulder curiously, trying to read what it said.

"On behalf of the Mastgar Arcane Society," Darius said formally. "We hereby accept the admission of Curtis Burk into our school of magical advancement to hone his skills and knowledge. Congratulations, you are now an official pupil of magic."

Chapter 29
Departure

Elsa stared at the mage; her eyes widened excitedly. She, Hyroc, Donovan, and Curtis exchanged an energetic look. "HE'S IN!" she exclaimed. "HE GOT IN. Oh, thank you, thank you." She lunged at the mage, embraced and kissed him on the cheek. The mage's cheeks flushed, and his expression turned startled but appreciative of the praise. Elsa jumped back, covering her mouth, mortified. "I – I am so sorry."

Darius coughed a laugh. "All is forgiven," he said cheerfully. "I'll admit, I wish everyone reacted so gleefully to my presence as you."

"So – uh – what do you need from us? You know, to get him there and such."

From his knapsack, the mage removed a map from a protruding leather tube he laid on the ground. The map showed the Mastgar region, including the towns and other notable points of interest. Reddish lines showed the course the group should take to get Curtis to his destination.

Darius pointed at the Glacial village. "We are here," he said. "The red lines are the course to follow to reach Vettenfelth, the Mastgar capital. You are to leave as soon as possible for Forestgold. Travel lightly, bringing only necessary supplies, and whatever you require for the journey will be provided upon your arrival. There will be horses waiting for you to expedite your arrival."

He produced an amulet with the Mastgar Magical Society's sigil from his knapsack. "A colleague of mine awaits you at the Wheezing Cottonwood tavern. Show him this sigil. He will get the three of you prepared and headed on your way with further instructions. Just stick to the map, and you'll safely get to Vettenfelth." He rolled the map and stuffed it back into its tube before handing it to Elsa along with the sigil.

"What happens after we have got my brother to the school?" Donovan asked. "I hope your colleagues will also help us with a return journey here."

"If that is your wish, yes, they will assist you," Darius assured them. "But the school is prepared to pay in full for your housing within the city. Unless the situation demands it, we are not in the habit of splitting up families if it can be avoided. We find the performance of our younger students is enhanced by their having easy and continued access to their family relations. Do either of you have any more questions for me?"

"No," Elsa and Donovan said.

"Very good. Also, keep that letter with you in case of any difficulties." He extended a welcoming hand to Curtis, speaking as they shook. "Welcome to the fold, Curtis. I sincerely look forward to working with you when I finish my research here. I'll let you get to it. Safe journey to all of you." The mage headed off.

Everyone beamed.

"I've got some smoked venison you're welcome to," Fenrald volunteered. "Should be enough to get you to town without you having to go hungry for the better part of a day."

"Thank you," Elsa said gratefully. "We have to get our things together and take down our tarp, and we'll be on our way."

Hyroc and Fenrald assembled the venison while the rest collected their things. It didn't take everyone long to finish.

"All right, that's everything," Donovan announced.

"Okay, just let me get my swords," Hyroc said, heading toward the cabin.

"Hyroc, wait, we need to tell you something," Elsa said.

Hyroc froze, feeling like a weight had just dropped into his stomach.

"Sorry, what?" Hyroc asked anxiously.

"We were talking just now and decided you won't be coming with us."

Hyroc was so astonished it almost hurt. "What – what do you mean I won't be?" he asked, incredulous.

She indicated everything around them with a sweeping motion of her hand. "We're not going to take you away from all *this*," Elsa said. She indicated Fenrald. "Especially not away from your family. You've looked for this your whole life. A place where you've started to reconnect with your past, a place where you truly belong. You found it. We won't ask you to leave all that behind for us. It wouldn't be right."

Hyroc gave her a pained look. "But – but the three of you, you're *still* my family. I care about you, and I love you, all of you. You are my brothers and my sister. I need to make sure you're safe. I vowed I would always do this. I saved you from the spiders and am responsible for you – I am honor-bound to ensure nothing happens to you. And I willingly and gladly accept this burden. You don't have to feel bad about asking me."

"I know," she said, clearly holding back emotions. "We know you would. But you did what you promised you would for us. You kept us safe. You helped the three of us get out of Arnaira to safety. We set out to find a place where Curtis would be safe from The Ministry, and we've done that. We're in Mastgar. The Ministry can't get to us here. We hold your vow fulfilled and release you from your obligation."

It felt as if a hammer had struck him in the stomach. Her decree pained him, and sorrow overcame him. For so long, his close relationship with them had been the only thing in the world that had mattered to him. He had grown to love his service to them. Now, it was gone. The most important thing in his life was suddenly whisked away from him. It felt as if he had lost an essential part of his identity. What was he supposed to do without them?

"No, you don't mean that," Hyroc pleaded. "Please, take it back. I need you to take it *back*."

"We're not going to do that," Elsa said, rubbing his shoulder. "It is done." Hyroc felt a tear in his eye, and Elsa wiped it away. "We will always remember everything you've done for us. We wholeheartedly thank you for helping us, Hyroc. Goodbye." She stepped back. Next, Donovan and Curtis said their goodbyes. With an anxious chuff, Kit sauntered over to them. Elsa crouched and affectionately stroked the cougar's head. "And I am especially grateful for your help as well. You've also been a good friend. I will miss you."

"Wait," Hyroc said, pulling out of his sadness. "There's something I wanted to give you." He retrieved his falchion sword from inside Fenrald's cabin. "I want you to have Spiderbane." Elsa gave him a confused look. "That's what I named the sword, Spiderbane. I know you understand the reference."

"No, I couldn't," Elsa said dismissively. "It's your –"

"I'm giving it to you," Hyroc interrupted insistently. "I want you to have it. It's now yours. Besides, it wasn't mine to begin with. I took it off a witch hunter's body." He gave her an ironic smile. "He didn't need it anymore."

Defeated, she smiled gladly, accepting it. "Thank you. I'll take good care of it."

Hyroc turned to Curtis. "I will come see you at that school as soon as possible. Okay?"

"Yes, you should," Curtis agreed eagerly.

Hyroc turned to Donovan. "I'm going to miss you, my sarcastic, smart-ass friend who has courageously always had my back no matter the danger."

Donovan smiled. "I'm also going to miss you, *Grumpy Bear*," he said sincerely. He held his hand out for Hyroc to shake.

"You're not getting off that easy." Hyroc embraced Donovan, jarring him.

"I – well, I," Donovan said, fighting back emasculating tears. He patted Hyroc on the back. "Farewell, my Wol'dger brother."

"Goodbye," Hyroc said, taking a step back. With that, the three of them headed out. Hyroc and they waved at each other. "*This is not goodbye forever*!" Hyroc called after them. "I'm going to find the three of you again," he promised as he said farewell to his old family.

All he had now was Kit, Fenrald, and his adopted cousin, Elizabeth.

Chapter 30

Unexpected Change

...Hyroc," Fenrald said to his nephew. "Hyroc, is this the last trap your friends set?"

Hyroc was jolted from his thoughts. He was resetting one of Elsa's traps when his thoughts drew him away into daydreaming. He resumed his work.

"Hyroc? Are you okay?"

"Fine," Hyroc answered. "I'm fine."

"Are you sure? You seem distracted."

Hyroc nodded, completing the trap. "I already said yes. And that's the last trap."

"You miss them?"

Hyroc didn't want to discuss the departure of his friends, but he couldn't help voicing his frustration. "Yes," he answered gloomily. "I very much miss my friends. The four of us have been together for years, and this is the first time I have been without them for more than a few days. I almost can't remember a time before I met them. It was us against everything. Nobody helped us. We solely relied on each other. We always had each other's backs. We even managed to kill a blood werewolf and an insane Warding tree. Now – now, my friends are just *gone.* It's off-putting knowing they aren't around. I feel like a wolf without a pack."

"I went through the same adjustment after your father, my brother, Jasok, was killed," Fenrald said. "For so much of my life, I had him watching my back; then, he simply wasn't there anymore. I felt vulnerable, as if enemies would spring out of the shadows to strike at me. Nobody was there to watch my back, so I learned to do it all myself. It wasn't easy to exist without him, but I learned to lock away my grief and put it in a box. The bite of what you feel now will diminish. Don't worry. Just give it time." Fenrald placed a comforting hand on his shoulder. "But no matter how you feel, remember, you're not alone. You still have me. I know we are practically strangers, but I dearly care about you. You'll make new friends. You made quite an impression on Iskall."

"I know," Hyroc agreed, glumly. "I know I'm not alone. Not like I was before. I know you care about me. It just feels like there's –"

"Like there's a hole inside of you that wasn't there before?" Fenrald finished.

Hyroc nodded. "Yes, like there's now a hole inside me. I told my friends this wasn't goodbye, but I can't shake the feeling I will never see them again."

"Don't let those doubts get to you. Your friends may have left, but this isn't a permanent separation. You will see them again, but it may be on a different path from your current one. The best thing you can do until then is concentrate on building your life here and focus on doing the important tasks."

Hyroc nodded. His uncle was right. He needed to focus all his attention on the village and dealing with the Ferals threatening to destroy it. Elsa, Donovan, and Curtis were gone, but not permanently. After the Ferals were eliminated, he would be free to see them again.

"Oh, and I hope you didn't forget about *her* tonight," Fenrald said with a hopeful smile.

"Yes, that's right," Hyroc said energetically. "I had nearly forgotten. Thank you for reminding me." He reached into his pocket and pulled out the green cat figurine made from quartz crystals. "What do you think?" Hyroc asked, displaying his handiwork.

"I know she'll love it," Fenrald assured him. "But we've got things that must be taken care of before then."

When they returned to the cabin, Fenrald went inside to strategize further a plan to strike at the Feral supply lines. Hyroc got to work sharpening their blades in preparation for the attack. When he finished, he went to chop firewood, but Fenrald interrupted him.

"Okay, I'm considering striking the Ferals inside Forestgold," he said. "Though I can only do it at night. They won't see me coming if I'm in my cat form. I can find my target, take them out, and disappear before anyone notices me."

"Who are you thinking you'll go after?" Hyroc questioned as he examined the sharpness of the wood ax.

"That corrupt official is a prime target. The Ferals will no longer be protected in town if we can eliminate him. And without that protection, they lose a significant source of supplies. But I need to do more scouting and investigating before putting anything solid into motion."

"Getting rid of him would help us, but doing so is incredibly risky. If you leave behind any trace you were there or anything indicating a Wol'dger was involved, it will have dire consequences for *everyone*."

"The risk is not lost on me. But remember, if we do nothing, a severe outcome is guaranteed. If the situation is dire enough, we will have to take risks to survive this."

"I am aware, and if it comes down to it, I will be open to taking such a big risk. But, until then, I'm not sure about eliminating that official through assassination. It's just too dangerous. And I hope you weren't planning on killing any of the town guards while doing so. They have nothing to do with the situation and don't deserve to be dragged into it. Unless they attack us, I won't help you kill any of them."

Fenrald nodded, though his expression indicated he was irritated at Hyroc's reluctance. "All right, it was just a thought. So, if that official is off the table, we can directly hit the Ferals there. There's a good chance the town guards won't interfere; they are no allies of the Ferals who cause trouble for them and the citizens. Paying them off to look the other way may be an option. We'll need to collect information on them as well before planning anything. Maybe tomorrow we can –" He trailed off when he noticed Darius coming to them. "Heads up," he said under his breath, jerking his head toward the mage to warn Hyroc to cease their sensitive discussion.

"Hello there," Darius called out politely, but the quizzical look on his visage suggested something bothered him. "If I could have a moment of your time, I would be very grateful."

Fenrald waved him over. "What might we help you with?"

"I have questions I hope you can answer." He made several hand motions to magically pull a sheaf of parchment and a writing quill from his knapsack. Both objects floated beside him as if held by some phantom. The mage looked thoughtful for a long moment before speaking. "You Glacials are very curious."

"How so?" Hyroc asked, hoping for specificity.

"They seem *normal*," Darius said, sounding as if that were a bad thing.

"Normal?" Hyroc and Fenrald asked simultaneously, both confused.

"What I mean is –" He threw up a baffled hand gesture as if struggling to find the words to explain what he meant. "They seem no different from the citizens of our lands, Mastgar lands. Of course, they – you look different, but appearances aside, you might easily be mistaken for humans. You talk the same as us, and you act similarly to us. Everyone I've talked to has been helpful, and beyond my wildest imagining, everyone has attempted to be polite. It – it is most disturbing."

"That's disturbing?" Hyroc asked, dazzled. "Those all sound like good things. *Why on earth would that be disturbing*?"

Darius shook his head. "No, no, you misunderstand me," he hastily apologized. "That's the wrong word. I beg your forgiveness. A more accurate word would be astonishing. After all the stories of your kind being ruthless barbarians and doing terrible things, one would never expect us to share such similarities."

"That's because we're Glacials," Fenrald said. "You've noticed a number of my kin, myself and my nephew included, can transform our bodies into the form of an animal?" The mage nodded. "Well, that ability comes with certain side effects on our behavior. If not held in check, it will essentially make us behave like the animals we have transformed into, and we will usually become dangerous. But because we are Glacials, we constantly strive to keep those behaviors in check and not allow them any sway over us. But beyond this, as you have seen firsthand, we try to maintain a peaceful livelihood, or more simply, a living that any other citizen of Mastgar wishes for."

"I see," Darius said before making hand motions that caused the writing quill to jot down notes. "Then, from what you say, can I assume the Wol'dgers, referred to as Ferals, do the opposite as you Glacial Wol'dgers?"

"Yes, exactly," Fenrald said. "They let those dreadful tendencies from their animal form have complete control over them."

"Fascinating." The mage's quill wrote more notes. "That explains the vast contradictory behavior between your two groups. So, all this time, what we have taken as violent attacks from Wol'dgers were, in fact, these Ferals."

"Yes, and our village had nothing to do with those attacks."

"I understand now. We share a common enemy, and there's a straightforward way to restore order to this region."

Fenrald's eyes lit with hope, an expression Hyroc never expected to see with his uncle. "If you bring what you have learned here before the Mastgar crown, you could convince them to send us aid against the Ferals?"

"I sincerely believe so. It's in both of our best interests to eliminate their threat."

"Thank you!" Fenrald said as he jolted forward and embraced the mage in an uncharacteristic display of affection from the Wol'dger warrior. "Thank you." He released Darius, leaving his guest with a surprised and apprcciative expression before energetically shaking his hand. "You don't know the hope you have instilled in me."

"I'm glad to have given it to you. But I won't be taking this discovery to the king just yet. Before I leave, I still have questions and observations for my research. A few more days, I would say."

"Then, you'll bring our case to the royal court?" Fenrald interjected.

Darius nodded. "Yes. I assure you I'll bring your case to the royal court."

"All right. Well, you best be getting to those questions and observations. The sooner you finish, the sooner we can deal with our *common enemy*."

The mage nodded before heading out.

"Do you know what this means?" Fenrald said excitedly to Hyroc.

"Yes, yes I do," Hyroc said. "It means the Mastgar crown will know none of the villagers here are responsible for the kidnappings and we are not a danger. Then, he'll start openly moving on the Ferals to clear them out of their camp."

Fenrald nodded his agreement. "It means the situation will resolve itself without our intervention, or at least not nearly as much of our intervention as I anticipated." A shadow passed over his face as he realized something tremendous. "It also means if anything happens to the mage before he delivers his findings to the Mastgar Crown, we're back to square one. No, we're even worse off than that! If this mage, a researcher who answers to the Mastgar crown, is killed, the blame will certainly fall upon us, and will no doubt provoke them into wiping us out."

Hyroc and Fenrald looked at each other with deadly serious eyes. "We have to protect him!" they said simultaneously.

Fenrald massaged the side of his head as if a headache was forming there. "Okay, that mage is now the most important person in this village," he fiercely stated. "We must protect him *at all costs* and ensure his information safely reaches its destination." He paused, thinking. "All right. All right, you head into the village and get some food for tonight."

"Tonight?" Hyroc asked with astonishment. "You still think I will meet up with my girlfriend after I learned something that could save us or doom us all? No, I think we've got more important matters than my personal life."

Fenrald waved a dismissive hand. "I can keep an eye on that mage without you for one night. Don't worry, I've got this. Go, enjoy being with her. Show her that cat you made from crystals for her."

"If you're sure."

"Yes, I'm sure." Fenrald gave him a comforting pat on the shoulder. "Go find a nice meal for the both of you to share. Go on."

Hyroc nodded his thanks, turning away. "Kit," he called out. The big cat lay on the roof of Fenrald's dwelling with his head resting on his paws. Kit regarded him with intrigue, flicking his tail. "Kit, let's go." His companion remained where he was. "Are you coming?" Kit groaned with displeasure. Hyroc assumed that was a no. "All right, fine," he conceded before walking off. Kit groaned again. "It's okay; I'll be back later," Hyroc called over his shoulder as he rushed toward the village.

The smell coming off a large pot wafted toward Hyroc's nose. It smelled meaty and delicious. "Okay, I'll have some of this stew," he said. A portly Wol'dger woman wearing a light blue dress and a white apron spooned the hot stew into a small clay container. "Thank you," Hyroc said as he handed her the payment. She nodded her thanks.

Hyroc walked away from the woman, trying to ensure he hadn't overlooked anything he might need for tonight. No, everything seemed in order. Then, he heard Iskall calling his name. Hyroc waved as his friend came closer to talk.

"Hey, what's all this for?" Iskall asked. He was in his natural form.

"Wouldn't you like to know," Hyroc teased playfully before turning to leave.

"Is it for *her*?"

Hyroc paused, giving his friend a surprised look. He had never introduced Lynx to Iskall. How did he know about her?

"How did you –?"

"I saw her, the Feral with the gray stripes, sneaking around the village before she went to you."

"All right, yes, I'm going to see her tonight."

"But she's a *Feral*," Iskall warned.

"Yes, I know she's a Feral!" Hyroc said, an edge coming into his tone. "And I know Ferals are dangerous, but I'm telling you she's different."

"And how do you know?"

"Because she hasn't tried to kill me! That's how. A corrupted scythe horn attacked us, and she helped me kill it. Then, I was certain she wasn't coming back, *and she did.* She came back. Only someone who saw something special in me would do that. And I like her, and she likes me. That's proof enough for me."

"Are you certain she's not playing you?"

"Playing me?" Hyroc repeated back in a harsh tone. He felt his face warm with anger. "*You think she is playing me*? No, she is not! If she were deceiving me in any way, I would certainly have noticed by now."

"Would you? Okay, then, where are you meeting her?"

"At a lake off the main road, just before you reach the village."

"Outside the village?" Iskall said skeptically. "That's a good place for an ambush."

"That's enough!" Hyroc growled. "She isn't part of some elaborate plan to ambush me. Now drop it."

"All right, all right. How about I come with you? I can hang back, out of earshot, and be quiet. The two of you won't even know I am there."

"Absolutely not! This is none of your business. You need to stay out of this." With that, Hyroc wheeled around and stormed away.

"You're letting your feelings for her blind you," Iskall called after him. Hyroc acknowledged him with an angry wave-off motion.

Hyroc arrived at the lake around dusk. Just as he expected, Lynx waited for him. Hyroc unbelted his sword, setting it against the trunk of a white birch tree before he headed over to her. She sat on a quilted blanket at the grassy lake shore. To one side of her was a thicket of bushes and leafy foliage. Hyroc wondered why she sat so close to the thicket because, from that direction, it would be difficult to spot the approach of any potential predators. However, he supposed that between the two of them, they could easily handle any animal that came their way, so they need not worry.

"You look lovely this evening," Hyroc said graciously.

Lynx beamed at the compliment. "Why, thank you so very much, good sir," she said happily.

Hyroc settled beside her, opening the top of the clay container with the stew.

"Ahh, that smells wonderful," Lynx said.

"Thank you," Hyroc said. "I picked it up in the village, and I hope it tastes as good as it smells." He placed a hand beneath the container, using his Flame Claw to ignite a blue flame. The flame's heat seeped into the container, warming the cooled stew. When white vapor flowed from the container's mouth, he dismissed the flame before spooning the hot stew into bowls. He served her first. But as she accepted her bowl, she almost seemed uninterested in the meal, as if distracted by something bothering her.

"Is everything all right?" Hyroc asked politely.

She turned her attention to him as if he had startled her. "Huh, what?" she asked. "What was that again?"

"You seem distracted. Is something bothering you?"

"Oh, it's nothing. I just got a little lost in how pretty this lake is."

Hyroc could tell from her tone whatever was distracting her was, in fact, *something*, but he didn't want to pry. He was sure he would discover what she concealed when she was ready to tell him.

"Yes, the lake is wonderful," he said, letting her think he thought nothing of her reaction. "Oh, I made something for you." He pulled the green crystal cat from his pocket. The feline figure now featured a loop for attaching a necklace chain.

Her eyes lit joyfully. "That's beautiful!" she said with a mild gasp as she took it into her hand. "I love it. You – you shouldn't have." For an instant, Hyroc detected sadness in her voice. She also instantly sounded reluctant to accept his gift. He couldn't figure out why that would be and ignored it, figuring he was overthinking things.

Lynx stole a glance at the thicket.

Hyroc turned, looking in the same direction. He couldn't see anything of interest. "Did you see an animal moving in there?" he asked curiously.

"It was just a squirrel," she said dismissively before taking a bite of stew.

Hyroc's sight lingered there a moment longer before he did the same. He swallowed his bite, then spoke. "I heard something great today."

She spoke with a sarcastic tone. "I know. You were coming to see me. I'm glad you knew how great this was going to be." She playfully rubbed his hand. Hyroc gave her a humorous glare. "I couldn't help it. Continue."

"There's this human mage named Darius who came to our village," Hyroc said.

"A human?" she said, taken aback. "Why in the world would one of those lesser creatures be interested in your village?"

"It's because he's trying to –" Hyroc paused. "What did you just say?"

She shot him a confused look. "What?"

"You said,' lesser creatures?'"

"I don't think so."

"Yes, I believe you did. I've heard that from the Ferals threatening my village. My best friends are human. Please don't –" He trailed off as a horrifying realization struck him. She was part of those Ferals! The thicket seemed to close in around him.

Lynx's expression turned from happiness to sorrow. "I had hoped you wouldn't come," she said gloomily. "I'm sorry." She focused on something past Hyroc, and he could tell she was looking at someone.

Hyroc instinctively reached for his sword at his waist but immediately remembered he didn't have it. He ducked the swing of a cudgel from behind before scrambling to his feet and driving his fist into the face of his attacker. His knuckle impacted fur; it was a Feral. While the Wol'dger reeled from the hit, he did a leg sweep. But as he rose back up, something heavy bashed him in the side of the head. Enormous black spots sprouted across his vision as he collapsed to the ground. He knew he needed to return to his feet, but his body refused to respond. After a few seconds, he was able to roll onto his back. He caught a glimpse of a Feral standing over him before their foot slammed into his head, sending him into blackness.

Chapter 31

Eagle

...WHY DOES THE EAGLE SUFFER the presence of an Anamagi?" Hyroc heard an icy, malice-filled voice growl. "The azure flame threatens the shadows."

Hyroc lethargically seeped back into consciousness. The side of his head throbbed painfully as if somebody was knocking on it with a wooden mallet, and he felt something crusty stuck to it. It was difficult to form thoughts through the pain. He opened his eyes. The eye closest to the throbbing didn't open all the way. It felt puffy and impeded by swelling. He was outside in a village or a large camp. Surrounding him was an array of tents and structures similarly constructed to the ones in the Glacial village. Most figures he saw moving around him were Wol'dgers, but some were human, presumably North Landers. Above the smells of burning wood and cooking food, the air held the fetid odor of rotting plant matter. His first thought was he was in a swamp or bog, but the smell was different. It reminded him of the mad Warding tree's forest. Raising his eyes to the tree line, many of the trees were bare. Nearly all the spiny branches of any spruce and pine trees displayed a sickly yellowish-brown color. The forest around him was dying.

When he moved his hands, he realized they were immobilized in shackles chained to a tall post against his back. The shackles held his arms up and out at about the same level as his shoulders. A third shackle on one ankle was attached to a chain anchored into the ground. The shackles were metallic, preventing him from transforming into his animal form. No doubt that had not been lost on whoever had put them on him. He attempted to activate his Flame Claw to melt through his restraints, but nothing happened. He tried again without success. Something blocked his ability. His head hurt too much for him to consider how to get around this obstacle.

"The azure flame stirs," the icy voice said, sounding even more callous.

As much as Hyroc's bruised head bothered them, he wished whoever spoke would shut up! And why were they speaking so strangely? He was in no mood for riddles. Then, it occurred to him that it was familiar. Sweeping his eyes around as far as his restraints would allow, he found the speaker. He saw the flaming purple eyes and the spiny, roughly wolfish shape of a Shade Hunter. The shadow demon lay on its haunches no more than a few steps away, regarding him with what appeared to be severe disdain. Hyroc spotted purple-eyed wolves and some stags the creature had dominated.

"Yes, Anamagi *wretch*, you are a prisoner as I am!"

"Notify Eagle the prisoner is awake!" Hyroc heard someone announce.

All eyes within earshot focused on him. A male Feral approached. He had dark gray fur with stripes of white and a strong muscular build, wearing a short-sleeved blue tunic, brown pants, and supple brown leather boots. A sheathed sword in the North Lander style, with a hilt of gray antler wrapped in bands of metal and shaped like a sideways H, hung from his belt. This man was esteemed in the settlement. An entourage of hairy, snouted faces followed him. The distinguished Feral had a milky white blind eye and one green eye. Four enormous long scars covered his head, indicating something had attempted to tear his face off. Hyroc remembered Fenrald telling him about the scars he had left on his nemesis. This was Eagle, the leader of the Ferals.

Eagle crouched in front of Hyroc, giving him an appraising look. "I see you're awake," he said coldly. "You were out for a full day, and I worried they had been overzealous when they struck you and you would never wake up. That would have been quite regrettable, and it would have robbed us of this chance to finally speak face-to-face."

"I'm a bear, and I've got a *hard head*," Hyroc said sharply. "Why don't you let me out of these shackles so you can find out!"

Eagle laughed humorlessly. "Ah, I'm glad you noticed iron is handy for preventing animal transformations. But I'm afraid even if I was stupid enough to let you out, it wouldn't do you any good." He indicated a sizeable glowing rune on the ground beneath Hyroc. "You're sitting in what's called a Quintessence Void. I picked it up from a North Lander witch during my travels. I have found it effective for neutralizing the magical abilities of captives. It blocks magic from being cast within a small area, including animal transformation magic and Guardian magic, from which your Flame Claw is derived. So, you see, none of your abilities are of any use to you." He gave Hyroc an evil sharp-toothed smile. "I can do whatever I wish to you, and you can do nothing about it."

"As soon as my *uncle* finds out you took me, he's coming after me!" Hyroc shot back acidly. "You won't be able to stop him."

"Your uncle won't know you're gone for at least another day. That's more than enough time for me to finish my examination of you."

"You're lying. You're only telling me that to frighten me, but you'll have to try harder than that."

"Well, then, I best meet your expectations." The group behind Eagle chuckled. "Let me tell you a story. Once, there was this little girl and her father. The father loved his daughter more than anything in the world and would do anything to protect her. But, one night, the father had a terrible nightmare where he watched a bear kill his daughter – a big black bear with blue eyes and brown stripes on his head. Only, the nightmare wasn't a nightmare. It was a prediction about the future. The father had the gift of foresight. And since he would do anything to protect his daughter, he vowed to kill *that bear*. But there was a problem; he didn't know when or where this would happen, only that *it would happen*. Then, the father discovered a Wol'dger with a bear stamped into his silver necklace. So the father planned to kill the Wol'dger. Only the plan failed, and the father and daughter were cast out. When the girl was old enough, the father warned her about the bear and ordered her to stay away from it. Except, she didn't listen – as the young often don't. Then, one day, she found *that bear.* Don't worry; she came away from this encounter unscathed. She deceived this Wol'dger into having feelings for her. And in this, the father saw an opportunity. The father used the Wol'dger's feelings for his daughter against him, leading him unsuspectingly by the nose into a trap."

"Let me guess, I'm that Wol'dger, and you're the father," Hyroc impatiently interjected dryly.

Eagle regarded him with a predatory glare. "That's very good," he said coldly. "I figured you must have a cunning mind to have defeated all my plans."

Hyroc noticed Eagle was missing a pinky on one hand. The scar where the digit should have been was a clean, pale scar, indicating the finger had been severed with a blade. Raising his eyes a little, he saw the severed pinky suspended in a brownish liquid within a crystal vial hanging from his neck. To control a shadow demon, someone must sacrifice a small amount of their flesh and incorporate it into a magic-infused amulet. Then, so long as the amulet is intact, they can control the demon. But binding the demon will enrage it, and though it cannot act of its own will, should the amulet be destroyed, the creature will seek vengeance upon this person.

Eagle was the person who had sent the Shade Hunter after him in Elswood. He was also responsible for the shadow essence from that same creature infecting a spider brood, driving them into a frenzy to attack his friends and their family. He was responsible for the deaths of Helen, Svald, and Walter, the mother, father, and grandfather of his friends. And that was to say nothing of the damage caused by the witch and the werewolf and the resulting exposure forcing Hyroc and his friends to flee from The Ministry. This man was responsible for practically every bad thing that had happened to Hyroc after his arrival in Elswood.

"Now, the Seer wishes to harm the weak Anamagi," the Shade Hunter said eagerly.

"Can you do me a favor; tell your Shade Hunter to shut up over there?" Hyroc said bitterly.

Eagle regarded him with intrigue, glancing at the Shade Hunter. "I've heard tales that Anamagi could perceive the hidden speech of shadow demons, but I haven't believed it until now."

"Yes, I can hear them when they want to talk. And while you're at it, if you're going to talk me to death, why don't you smash that amulet and let your pet darkness monster put us both out of our misery?"

Eagle laughed half-humoredly. "That's pretty funny." He made a beckoning motion toward the group behind him. The nearest Feral stepped forward and struck Hyroc in the stomach with a painful punch. Hyroc gasped and coughed once he was able to breathe again. "Didn't anyone tell you insulting your host is bad form?"

Hyroc spoke as his coughing fit subsided. "That was – a good one," he choked out. "Maybe next time you should try hitting me *actually* hard." Hyroc was fully aware of the likely consequences of his saying this. The Wol'dger punched him again. Hyroc spoke again after a longer coughing fit. "Oh, did I already mention *I'm a bear*?" he said defiantly. "I'm well acquainted with pain. You're going to have to hit me much harder than that!"

"Enough," Eagles said with a sharply raised hand as the Feral prepared to kick Hyroc. The Wol'dger nodded his acknowledgment and spat before rejoining the others. "I must ask you to refrain from taunting the members of my entourage. I may not always be able to control them." He spoke conversationally, but his threatening intentions were clear, and his words were full of ice.

"I'm curious about something. If you're supposed to be a seer and see the future and whatnot, why didn't you stop us from attacking your caravan?"

"My ability is somewhat unpredictable and vague in what I can see. You merely caught me by surprise and got lucky. If I had witnessed what you were about to do, you, your uncle, your friends, and your beloved mountain lion pet would not have survived. And it still boggles my mind you would find friendship with lesser beings. Perhaps that is why we're going to emerge victorious."

Hyroc coughed out a laugh. "You, victorious?" he said with disbelief. "I think your ability is going to your head. You're not going to win. The Mastgariens are about to realize you, the Ferals, are their true enemy. We will strike a truce with them and help them end this bloody feud once and for all."

Eagle grinned wickedly, which made Hyroc's skin crawl. "Oh, yes, I'm well aware of *that development*. You brought this to the attention of that impotent, flat-faced ice mage – Darius, I believe, is his name – who came to investigate your precious village. He's there to learn about Glacial culture and customs, hoping our two societies coexist peacefully. Unfortunately, his discoveries will not come to fruition."

"What, are you planning on killing him?" Hyroc asked. "My uncle knows exactly how important what that mage has discovered, and he won't let anyone harm a single hair on his head. I would also wager that mage is capable of impaling his enemies with a spike of ice or something nasty along those lines. You're not going to get him."

"Yes, I imagine he possesses formidable powers, but no, his life is of little consequence. And this coming truce with the Mastgariens will surely bring about my end and that of all my cohorts. I would caution you about placing your hopes on such lofty things that have not yet come to be."

"You're insane," Hyroc said with disbelief. "Your band of bloodthirsty brigands won't stand a chance against the Mastgar Army when they turn their wrath on you. Even your shadow demon pet and the transformation gift of your followers won't make a difference against that large of a force. You can't win that fight!"

Eagle regarded him with cold, mocking eyes. "You poor misguided fool! I have no intention of fighting the Mastgar Army. But I will tell you *this*: they will serve my plans. My followers and I will survive this. Then, once your accursed bloodline and your people are no more, we will finally be free to start building our better world."

"You've lost your mind," Hyroc noted dismissively.

"I assure you I am quite in control of all my faculties."

"Okay, then, you're either incredibly arrogant or dumber than I thought if you believe you have control over the Mastgar Army."

"I do, in a way. You just don't see it *yet*." He paused. "In that story, I just told you, did you figure out the identity of my daughter?"

"No, I haven't met her yet, but I suspect that apple didn't fall far from the *loony tree.*"

Eagle regarded him with an eager expression. "Are you sure about that? I believe the two of you have already met?"

Hyroc cocked an eyebrow, confident he had never met or been introduced to Eagle's daughter. Unless....

A gray-striped female Feral stepped forward, and Hyroc was dumbfounded to see Lynx.

"This is my daughter, Lynx," Eagle said, evil enjoyment radiating from his tone.

Hyroc's mouth fell open, and he felt as if the kick of a moose had struck him. She was *his* daughter! Hyroc had been spending time with his enemy's daughter! Now everything made sense. From the start, his entire relationship with Lynx had been orchestrated by her father. His meeting her hadn't been a happy accident; it had been due to the machinations of Eagle. Every move she made, and every caring word she uttered was intended to drag him into a trap. And the most frustrating thing for Hyroc was knowing he had fallen for it. Why had he been so stupid to think she happened to be a good Feral? With everything he knew regarding how ruthless and dangerous Ferals were, she wasn't any different. She was cunning enough to come at him in a way he would never have imagined. The witch her father had sent to Elswood had similarly attempted to exploit his feelings for his friends to kill him, so why wouldn't she mimic this strategy?

He now understood why he had so quickly fallen for her. It was by design. She intentionally made herself irresistible to him, behaving to manipulate his interest and make him think they were developing a loving relationship. He felt she shared the same feelings for him as he had for her. But, no, it was all a lie. Now, he was paying the price for remaining ignorant of her deception. Iskall was correct in his concern about her! Hyroc chided himself for arguing with his friend. Iskall was a true friend to voice his distrust of her. Now, Hyroc wondered if he would ever see another friendly face.

Lynx remained silent, her expression impassive.

"You see, after the disruption of our caravan that transported the children for the North Landers," Eagle continued, "you and your uncle immediately drew my attention." He spoke with a flash of anger. "And my ire!" He paused, regaining a calmer tone. "After such a *setback*, I knew I needed to deal with the two of you. Your human friends were also part of my considerations, but unfortunately, they departed before I could set anything in motion against them. Your Flame Claw makes you a deadly adversary in a fight, and it occurred to me I needed to use more subtle and precise actions against you. I needed to avoid facing you in a fight. So I settled on attacking your heart. And here we are."

"You sent your daughter to execute your plan?" Hyroc questioned, finally snapping out of his stupor. "You told me a moment ago you feared that bear – me – killing your daughter. You saw that in a vision, so you sent her after me, putting her in danger. You don't care for her one bit."

Eagle punched Hyroc in the face with a strike so fast the fist was a blur. Hyroc's head snapped back, but the shackles around his hands kept him from falling back. He hung in shock with his head back as the world spun. When everything settled, he pulled against the shackles to sit up.

"I care for her quite a bit," Eagle growled. "Originally, I had no intentions of sending her anywhere near you, but the young are often disobedient." He shot an accusatory glance at Lynx, and she diverted her eyes shamefully. "My daughter got the idea to disregard my warnings and went to deal with you herself. But no harm befell her. It seemed you were far softer than I had realized. When I learned this, seeing as you wouldn't hurt her in any way, I decided to exploit this opportunity and let her continue with it. It was a grand opportunity to rid myself of the thorn in my side for nearly twenty years. I never imagined it would have been so easy."

"If your whole plan was to lure me into a trap because I'm too powerful to fight directly, why am I still alive?" Hyroc demanded. "I was unconscious and completely at your mercy. There is no better situation for ending someone. Why am I still alive? Why didn't you kill me? If all you're going to do is sit there and boast about the success of your master plan, I'd rather get this over with."

"Because you may yet prove to be useful," Eagle said. "But, I assure you, in due time –" His expression turned deadly serious "when you are no longer useful, I will take pleasure in snuffing your life out myself."

Chapter 32

The Betrayer

HYROC'S HEAD JERKED SIDEWAYS AS a fist plowed into it. His attacker was a muscular, broad-shouldered Wol'dger with dark fur. Behind him, Eagle sat on a stool, observing the interrogation as he calmly ate a bowl of soup. It was morning, wearing on toward noon beneath a cloudy sky. Hyroc's captors had left him outside during the cold night. His Wol'dger fur had insulated him from the main bite of the cold, but it was still unpleasant. Then, on top of the discomfort, they had also neglected to give him any food or drink. If not for the battering of his face dominating his attention, he would feel substantial hunger pangs. Undoubtedly, the lack of sustenance sapping his strength was an intentional part of Eagle's strategy to incentivize Hyroc to be forthcoming with the information.

Eagle scooped up a spoonful of soup, took a bite, and spoke after swallowing. "Let me ask you again," he said, his tone almost uninterested, as if it were just another typical day. "What weapons do the Glacials possess?"

Hyroc spit out a mouthful of blood, mildly surprised to find no teeth had come out. "I already told you I don't know," he answered. "I never went through the village looking for any."

Eagle nodded dispassionately, and the Wol'dger punched Hyroc again. His bruised face felt like one giant sore. The bruises were hidden beneath his fur, but they loudly announced their presence. One of his eyes was swollen shut, and the other was on its way toward that if his beating continued.

"All right, let's try this instead," Eagle continued. "How many Glacials live in the village, and how many can bear arms?"

"I don't know. I have barely lived in the village for two weeks."

Eagle's eyes bored into Hyroc. "Hazard a guess! *You have two intact eyes*. You will have seen something. Give me a number."

Hyroc had an estimate in mind, but he refused to reveal it. Whatever he said would certainly be used against the Glacial villagers, but he knew as soon as he gave his captors everything they asked for, they would kill him. So long as he held on to valuable information, he was useful and, therefore, not expendable. Only doing so would aggravate his interrogators and make his predicament much more miserable. But he was a *bear*! Enduring pain was what bears did best. Ursa had taught him how to withstand pain that would overwhelm the strongest person. He was prepared for this.

"It seems starving me and repeatedly hitting me in the head prevents me from doing math," Hyroc said defiantly. "Once I have had a hot meal and can fully see out of my eyes, I might be able to give you a number. Oh, you should also get someone who hits harder than a summer breeze."

The Feral lurched forward to hit Hyroc.

"Hold," Eagle ordered, mid-swing. The Feral nodded his acknowledgment, glaring hatefully at Hyroc as he stepped back. Eagle stood, empty soup bowl in hand. "I think that's enough *for now*. We can begin again tonight. Let hunger and thirst wear on him a bit more. That's sure to loosen his tongue."

"What if he still doesn't cooperate?" the Feral asked gruffly.

Eagle smirked malevolently at Hyroc. "Then, well – I guess we'll find out, won't we?"

The Feral chuckled coldly. "Yes, I believe we will," he said eagerly.

"Come, there are other matters to attend to." With that, they walked away, leaving Hyroc alone with his thoughts.

Hyroc reveled in the respite from the pain. He never expected peace to be so glorious. When the euphoria had faded, he reassessed his situation, looking for vulnerabilities or oversights with his restraints he could exploit. His hands were immobilized in shackles, and a third shackle on a chain restrained one leg. His other leg was free, but there wasn't anything within reach of his foot. He had spent the entire night devising strategies to escape his bonds without discovering anything useful, and his situation remained unchanged.

He slumped against the wooden post as much as his hand shackles allowed and blew out an exasperated breath. How was he going to get out of this? Was he going to get out of this? He banished the latter thought to the deepest recesses of his mind. If he dwelled on such a despairing idea, he would never escape. But, without food or drink, he suspected he wouldn't last much longer. Any time now, Fenrald should discover his absence, think the worst had happened, and come after him. But would his uncle know where to find him? Hyroc didn't even know how far from the village this encampment was. Would his uncle even be able to reach him in time? Was he prolonging the inevitable by keeping his mouth shut? Maybe it was best to give in, tell Eagle everything, and get this unpleasantness over with.

NO! He could not do that. What he told Eagle would be used against the Glacials, *his people*. More than his life was at stake if he submitted. He had to hold on, no matter the cost. His uncle *would* find him. He had to believe that.

In the meantime, he had to do everything he could to get free. But what? He scanned his surroundings, then focused on the chain anchor holding his leg shackle. He gave it a hard tug with his leg. The anchor wiggled an almost imperceptible amount. The movement was so tiny he had missed it during the night hours when he had tested the solidness of the chain. He could work it loose. That would free up his leg, and he could use the anchor as a makeshift tool to remove his hand shackles. But he wondered how he would manage that with only the use of his feet. He pushed the question aside. He would deal with it when he got there. If he got there. He repeatedly jiggled the chain. The exertion returned his hunger pangs with a vengeance. His stomach growled loudly, begging for food.

"You are a prisoner here, as am I," the Shade Hunter said. "We both seek escape, yet the same."

"We are most definitely *not* the same," Hyroc retorted.

"Is that so?"

"Yes! You're a shadow demon. I assume even one of your dark kind could recognize the difference."

"You dilute my meaning as you do yourself. Your bonds manifest in iron. My bonds are ephemeral and unseen but are no less restrictive."

Hyroc continued pulling on the chain as he spoke. "If you're trying to make me feel sympathy for you, you're wasting your time. One of you sent by Eagle tried to kill me and a dear friend of mine a couple of years ago. I killed it, but inadvertently, its lingering essence infected a clutch of spiders, and they killed the parents and grandfather of my friends. They were good people! So you might understand why I'm a tad unsympathetic to your predicament."

The Shade Hunter regarded him; the flaming purple orbs serving as its eyes revealed nothing of its thoughts. "Your past draws my interest but is pointless to my predicament. I draw out our similarities to propose a consolidation of efforts."

Hyroc paused from working on the chain. "A consolidation?" Hyroc repeated, perplexed. "You want us to work together?"

"Perceptive, Anamagi," the Shade Hunter said in acknowledgment, but Hyroc also suspected it had, in a shadow demon's way, suggested he was stupid for asking. "Our goals are shared. We have a common interest in this?"

That caught Hyroc's attention. Could this creature help him escape? As it was, he didn't have any viable options for escape. But what could it offer him? Since it was bound to Eagle, it couldn't take actions contrary to his will, such as killing him or doing anything negative that directly affected him. The instant Eagle discovered they had escaped, he could order the Shade Hunter to kill Hyroc, and it would immediately turn on him. They couldn't be together if he agreed. But there was something else to consider. He had read multiple tales about people who made pacts with shadow demons dying horribly once the creature got what it wanted. He could chalk most of those up to cautionary tales told to de-incentivize exploring the dark arts, but Marcus had given some of them credence. Besides, the shadow demon would undoubtedly seek to kill Eagle to free itself and exact revenge upon him. It couldn't so long as the amulet that controlled it was intact. So, if it helped him, destroying the amulet was its price. Then, with him being an Anamagi, he would probably be its next target. No, there were too many potential risks.

"That's tempting," Hyroc said. "But I'm going to have to pass. If you want out, *do it yourself*."

"A foolish choice, Anamagi," the Shade Hunter said sharply. "My master intends on killing you. His lips betrayed this. A certainty even if given what he desires. Our consolidation is your sole hope."

"It's still a no."

"So be it. You will suffer despair, pain, hunger, and thirst before the end. You shall see this, I swear it."

"If knowing that will make you shut up, I gladly accept it. I will get out of here without making any deals with you." Hyroc spoke under his breath before resuming pulling on the chain. "I hope."

Hyroc stopped in the middle of his routine when he saw someone approaching, feigning hopeless submission to keep his captors none the wiser. It was Lynx. Lynx! A surge of anger bubbled up inside him. He was *here* because of her!

"What do you want?" Hyroc asked acidly. "Here to rub in my face you managed to lead an Anamagi into a trap with your feminine wiles?"

"No, I'm not here for any of that."

"Good. Then you can leave! I've got nothing I want to say to you."

She gave Hyroc a saddened look. "When I found out what my father was planning, I hoped you wouldn't come."

"BUT I DID COME!" Hyroc snapped back. "You had three days to warn me, and you did *nothing*. You even had a chance to tell me that day and said *nothing*. You didn't even tell me when I walked into the trap. You would have said something if you cared even a bit about me. Our entire relationship was built on a lie. From the first day we met, it was all part of a plan hatched by your father to get past my guard." Hyroc saw a tear in her eye.

"No, not from the first day," she corrected. "Ever since I was a little girl, I had heard my father telling me about this vision he had about a bear killing me. He did what he did in Wulfren to keep me safe from that terrible beast. It was a monster that had consumed my every thought. I trained myself and did everything I could to be ready to fight and kill that bear when it eventually came for me. Then, one day, he tells me the bear is very near, and the fight I've been preparing for is here. But instead of waiting for the beast to come after me, against my father's wishes, I decided to go after it and take it on my terms. But, when I finally laid eyes on you, you didn't look like some monstrous, bloodthirsty creature; you were a young man. I thought you were a far less dangerous foe and would be easier to dispatch. I devised a plan to lure you into a trap using your human friend as bait. Everything unfolded as I had planned. I had you where I wanted you, and I drew my dagger to strike. Then – then something unexpected happened. You grabbed my hands and reassured me you would protect me. You thought I was afraid of being attacked, and you wanted to make me feel safe. I saw compassion and gentleness in your eyes. That shattered the terrible image instilled in me. This monster I had been told about all my life wasn't supposed to have such feelings. And beyond my wildest imagining, I put down the dagger. I even helped you carry your injured friend, a friend I had conspired to injure."

Hyroc shook his head in disbelief. "Wait, wait, when we met in Forestgold, you were planning to kill me?" he said, astonished. The events of that day suddenly made so much more sense. Their meeting had been arranged, but not in the way he thought. "So your father wasn't responsible for that?" Hyroc questioned.

"No, I had defied him," she admitted. "He only got involved when he learned of my actions."

"*And you still followed them*," Hyroc said, regaining an acidic tone. "Even after what you saw."

"I didn't know what to think. Nothing made sense. But my father told me what I saw was just a mask concealing your true form and intentions. That what I saw was merely what you wanted everyone to see."

"Then, why didn't I kill you right then and there?"

"He said you didn't know who I was, but as soon as I revealed it to you, you would turn on me."

"Don't you think that's a little convenient?"

"You have to understand; he's my father. He's always been there for me and has always been there to protect me. I had – I had to do what he said."

"*And what of my father*!" Hyroc shot back, her words rekindling his rage. "I didn't have a father because of *him*. And you still obey him?"

"I …," Lynx said, trailing off, a storm of emotions in her eyes. She spun around and stormed off.

Hyroc opened his mouth to shout something after her but closed it when no words came. Shaking his head, unsure how he should feel, he resumed pulling on the chain. He was making progress.

A little while later, Lynx returned carrying a cup. She glanced around, ensuring no one was watching, before crouching in front of Hyroc. She moved the cup toward his mouth, and he recoiled, confused about what she was doing.

"No, hurry, drink," she urged in a hushed tone. "While no one's looking."

Hyroc realized she was offering him water. Desperate to quench his need for the life-sustaining liquid, he pushed his face against the cup. Lynx tipped it into his mouth, and he gulped it down. The soothing water felt sublime as it flowed down his parched throat. It was the best water he had ever tasted! When he had drained the cup, she pulled a rag from her pocket, dumping the last remaining drops of water onto it. Then, she moved it to his face. Hyroc pulled back again, looking at her, puzzled.

"Why are you doing this?"

"Because I want to help you."

Hyroc cocked an eyebrow, baffled as to why she would do anything after leading him into a trap. "Why do you –" He trailed off. He saw a tremendous amount of conflict and sorrow in her eyes. But beneath that, he detected affection. That's when it dawned on him *she had* developed feelings for him despite her actions, feelings strong enough to be displeased with her father's treatment of him. Their false relationship hadn't been as one-sided as he had initially thought. That gave him a desperate idea. Maybe he could use those feelings to persuade her to help him escape if she cared for him strongly. It was his most promising opportunity.

He pulled back into his original position, letting her clean the dried blood from the fur on the side of his head. "Lynx," Hyroc said urgently. "Lynx, you have to help me get free of my bonds, okay? Before your father comes back. Help me escape."

"No, I can't," she said adamantly. "I'm already risking trouble just by doing this. It's all I can do."

"Lynx, listen to me! If you have ever cared for me even the slightest, you need to help me get free."

She shook her head. "No, this is all I can help you."

"Your father, *he's going to kill me when he's got all he can from me*," Hyroc pleaded. "I need to get out of here!"

"No, I know my father; I can make him see reason with sparing you. Trust me."

"He told me as much right to my face. He fully intends to keep his word and go through with it. You have to let me escape."

"No, you'll see. I –"

She was interrupted by a question from an inquiring Feral. "Lynx? What are you doing over there?"

She jerked away from Hyroc, discreetly stuffing the handkerchief back into her pocket and tossing the cup behind a bush. "I just had a few questions for the prisoner," Lynx answered. "But this Anamagi *scum* isn't talking," she said, solely to embellish her ruse. She shot Hyroc an apologetic look as she rose to her feet and turned toward the Feral.

"Lynx, you have to help me escape," Hyroc pleaded in a low voice. "Please, help me!"

Then he heard Eagle's voice, which stole his hope away. "Lynx, come out of there," he called to her with a beckoning motion. "You do not need to be here around the prisoner." With a nod, she obeyed.

Eagle and his interrogation lackey approached. Eagle grabbed the stool from earlier and set it down in front of Hyroc. After sitting, he gave Hyroc an appraising look without speaking for a long moment.

"You have your mother's eyes," Eagle said. He turned partway toward the other Feral. "Don't you think he has his mother's eyes?"

"Yes, I believe he does," the Wol'dger said uninterestedly.

"Yes, yes, it's true. You also seem to have her determination. Nothing ever got in her way once she had her mind set on something." He paused. "And it seems you also have your father's shoulders and stature. He always kept the bullies in check."

"And what would you know of them?" Hyroc asked pointedly.

Eagle grunted a laugh, speaking with a cold smile. "Because I killed them."

Hyroc felt something break inside him like a dam had burst its banks, unleashing a torrent of anger hotter than anything he had ever felt. From the look in Eagle's eyes and the tone of his voice, Hyroc knew his words to be true. He felt himself strain against his shackles, pulling with his arms as hard as he could to try and break free. The candor and the uncaring way Eagle spoke about the murder of his parents made Hyroc want to dig his claws into the Wol'dger's face. Try as he might, his restraints held firm. This Feral *animal* was responsible for so many of the terrible things Hyroc had to endure.

"I NEVER KNEW MY MOTHER AND FATHER BECAUSE OF YOU!" Hyroc yelled, funneling as much ferocity as possible into his words. "YOU KILLED THEM. Let me out of these restraints so I can have it out with you, or you're every bit the coward I know you to be."

Eagle chuckled again, further infuriating Hyroc. "Those are indeed mighty words. Calls of cowardice are a serious accusation. Many a fight has started with those words. But they mean *nothing to me*."

"Of course not. If they meant anything to you, you would have come after me yourself long ago instead of sending monsters and witches to do your dirty work. But they all failed! You didn't stop me from arriving here."

"Yes, that is true," Eagle admitted. "You defeated all of them. You are truly a mighty foe. And those humans you befriended, surprisingly, despite their *disadvantages*, they, too, are not to be underestimated. You chose your companions well. And I do not blame you for your fury with me. I imagine I, too, would share those strong feelings if someone took the lives of my parents. But you don't know I am merely the instrument, the blade that claimed their lives. I am, however, not the hand or the arm that wielded that blade."

"Enough with the metaphors!" Hyroc demanded. "I don't care if you're the sword, the hand, the arm, or the whole shadowed body. You killed my parents! The burden of your cold-blooded actions was your decision and yours alone. I promise I will have justice."

"No, not alone," Eagle disputed. "There is *another*. He is closer than you think."

"Of course others share the blame. Every Feral here played a part, but *you're* the one who instigated the purge, and *you* continue it."

"That may be true, but I refer to someone much closer."

"Then, who?"

"Do you know of your parent's fate while they tried to escape?"

"Yes, that's when you ambushed them!"

"A most unfortunate turn of events indeed *for you*. Well, for everyone. But have you ever wondered how we learned of their flight?"

"I don't know, from your spies? I don't care!"

"Oh, but you really *should care*. We learned of their escape from someone seeking our help. They were more than happy to divulge their escape route. Do you know who that might be?"

Hyroc rolled his eyes, weary of this charade. "I don't know," he said irritably. "Why don't you tell me."

"Your uncle, Fenrald."

Hyroc laughed. Fenrald, that was preposterous! "Fenrald?" he exclaimed. "You expect me to believe it was my uncle? You're insane. Why on earth would he help you? He wants you dead as much as I do. You took his family away for him as well."

"Once, we were quite close. Brothers, you might have considered us. But as soon as he heard I was purging the Anamagi influence from Wulfren, he was more than happy to assist."

"No, you're lying," Hyroc insisted. "Fenrald warned me about your deception with your speech. It's not going to work on me."

"He gave me detailed instructions about their escape plans," Eagle continued. "Then, when he had relayed everything he could tell me, we toasted to the success of our ambush."

"I don't believe you," Hyroc said, concern growing in his mind. "Why would he do that?"

"Why?" Eagle teased. "For a reason as old as time. He was jealous of his brother, your father. He wanted everything your father had for himself."

Hyroc shook his head dismissively, despairing beliefs slowly creeping into his mind. Reluctantly, everything was slowly making sense.

"And his jealousy didn't stop there," Eagle continued. "He also wanted everything your mother had. I believe her family possessed a considerable wealth of gold and silver. He wanted it all for himself."

"How do I know you're not making this all up? It could all be just a story, a horrific story. If my uncle wanted all this wealth, then, where is it? I didn't see any gold or silver lying around his cabin. What happened to it?"

"That's because he never got it. His scheme failed alongside mine. When the gutless rulers of Wulfren lost their appetite for doing what was necessary, I and all my followers were cast out of the kingdom under the pain of death. This included your uncle.

"Haven't you wondered why the Glacial villagers distrust him so? Why they won't heed any of his words or calls to action which are, in fact, in their best interest? They know of his betrayal, the part he played in the death of your parents and your entire family."

Hyroc shook his head. "No, no, that's not true," Hyroc said, hoping speaking those words would maintain his current reality where he had a caring uncle without the stain of betrayal and his parent's blood on his hands. "You're lying! That's what you do. You lie."

"Think about it; it all makes sense. You know this to be true. You're not an idiot."

"Then why has he been helping me all this time?"

"To hide his shame. You've seen the guilt in his eyes. He can't stand knowing his deeds are there for all to see. He's helped you to assist his own ends. He hopes if he does enough good by destroying us, the enemies of the Guidance Wol'dger, they will forget his transgressions. But there's no hiding it."

Hyroc bowed his head shamefully. He was so lost and confused. This revelation turned his world upside down. His uncle was a completely different person now. He was a dangerous betrayer, responsible for Hyroc not having a family throughout his life. So much of the pain and loneliness he had experienced was because of Fenrald. Hyroc's emotions were cast into so much turmoil he couldn't make sense of his feelings.

"Now, Hyroc, you know the truth. Fenrald was the one to bear responsibility for the deaths of your parents, not me." Eagle stood, picking up his stool. "I leave you now to consider where your true loyalties lie and whether or not it will loosen your tongue." He set the stool safely out of Hyroc's reach before turning to the other Wol'dger. "You may begin. Just be sure to be sparing with the shocks to his head. It might affect what he wants to tell us if you catch my meaning." The Wol'dger nodded eagerly.

Chapter 33

The Shadow Demon's Curse

LYNX PACED AROUND INSIDE HER father's dwelling in the Feral village. Eagle was hunched over a table as he studied a map. She tended to pace when something weighed heavily on her. She couldn't take her mind off her assurance to Hyroc she could convince her father to spare his life. He was an Anamagi, a puppet of the Guardians and a sworn enemy of her people, but despite all that, she still held feelings for him. She couldn't make sense of it. By drawing Hyroc into her father's trap, she got to know him better than planned. Despite their ideological differences, she had surprisingly found him to be someone she enjoyed being with. So much so that she found the idea of his life being extinguished distressing. She was sure she could convince her father to spare the Anamagi's life, but she couldn't figure out what to say.

"Something bothering you?" Eagle asked without looking up from his map. She was too deep in thought to notice him speaking. Eagle raised his eyes. "Lynx?" This time, she heard him.

"Sorry, what?" she said, pulling out of her thinking.

"You're pacing. Is something the matter?"

It took her a second to pluck up her courage enough to turn toward him and answer. "Yes," she said. "It's about Hyroc, the Anamagi. I – I think you should spare him."

Eagle looked at her skeptically. "Lynx, my darling, you know why I cannot," he said. "He's the last Anamagi, and their tainted bloodline will be no more once he's gone. But, beyond that, he's no longer a danger to you. We will have achieved the goal we have been chasing for nearly twenty years."

"Yes, I know, but why hasn't he tried to do anything to hurt me? He's had plenty of opportunities. I haven't even seen anything remotely mean-spirited from him besides the beating he gave those two boys who had helped me set up my trap. But I really can't blame him for that. They had hurt his friend and stolen their spear, and he got it back from them. Apart from that instance, he actually seemed quite nice."

"Lynx, that's because he didn't know who you were. If he had, we wouldn't be having this conversation. And now we've got him at our mercy, he's afraid. He knows his end is drawing near, and he will say anything to convince you to let him go."

"Do you know that for sure?"

Eagle shook his head. "I was afraid of this. I should not have let you get close to him again after you disobeyed my strict instructions to stay away from him. I shouldn't have let you risk yourself and instead made someone else take on this role."

"And there's what he said," she continued.

"All lies," Eagle interjected.

"Lies?" she questioned, sounding indignant. She walked to the entrance of the dwelling and indicated the Shade Hunter. "He warned me about the effects of shadow demon essence. Look out there. Every plant and tree around us is dying. That didn't start until you summoned that *thing*. Are you sure this is the best course of action? Maybe we should get rid of it."

"No," her father said adamantly. "It is an integral part of my plan. Besides, they're just flowers and some scrubby evergreens. They'll grow back as soon as the demon leaves the area. It's nothing to worry about."

Lynx shot him a defiant look. "There's something I never told you that happened the day after I tried to get him while his friend recuperated in Forestgold. The two of us went hunting and ran into a scythe horn. It had been corrupted by shadow demon essence and attacked us."

Eagle gave her a puzzled look. "It attacked you?" He shook his head. "No, the Shade Hunter's essence couldn't have gotten into any animals outside the camp besides the ones I specifically told it to dominate. The two of you probably spooked a buck; it was frightened and attacked. Sometimes, even deer do that."

"It had glowing purple eyes!" Lynx challenged.

"Perhaps it was a trick of the light," Eagle suggested.

Her expression turned astonished. "It was no trick of the light. I know –"

"LYNX," her father shouted, startling her. He placed a reassuring hand on her shoulders. "You know I love you more than anything, don't you?" She nodded. "You know that as your father, I would give my life to protect you, don't you?" She nodded again. "Then, trust me. That's all that I ask of you, to trust me. We are so close to accomplishing our goal and ending all this once and for all. I've already seen our success. We must stay the course a little longer, and that future will be ours. The Jarl we've been cooperating with has offered us refuge in his lands. So as soon as our task here is complete, we'll be safe there."

She nodded. "Yes, father, I understand."

"Good," Eagle said happily. "Good. We can't afford to get distracted now. Don't lose focus on the coming fight. I meticulously planned out every detail of what's to come, but do not underestimate our quarry. The Mastgariens may be human, but they are still dangerous."

Chapter 34

A Deer Friend

HYROC GAZED ABSENTMINDEDLY AT THE ground beneath him. Night had descended upon the camp, and the faint flickering orange light of torches illuminated his surroundings. Everything hurt. The pain centered around his face and abdomen. His interrogator had spent the preceding hours of dusk beating him like a dusty rug. The Feral did so with such exuberance he had to call over another to take over when his arms tired and his knuckles split. Hyroc's ribs were his primary concern. Despite the discomfort, he didn't think any of them were broken yet, but he figured that was on the way. He was so tired and weak from hunger. He didn't know if he could last much longer.

But he was beginning to wonder if holding out was worth it, though he knew what awaited him if he told the Ferals everything they wished to know. Not only had Lynx stabbed him through the heart with her betrayal, but now, he knew his uncle was nowhere near the man Hyroc thought he was. Coveting his brother's possessions – Hyroc's father – and his mother's wealth, Hyroc would never have guessed that was beneath Fenrald's caring and polite manner. Hyroc wasn't sure how to feel about that. But, gloomily, he figured it probably wouldn't be his problem if things kept up at the current pace.

Why hadn't he just listened to Iskall's warning about Lynx? He wouldn't be in this dire situation if he hadn't been so stubborn. Even Kit seemed to know something was wrong with Lynx from the big cat's reluctance to join them. How could he have been so blind to her deception when it was all right in front of him? Now, look where he was because of his stupidity. Part of him supposed he deserved this from being so oblivious. Even Fenrald had deceived him. Was anybody he met at the village the person they appeared to be? What else was he missing? Perhaps he wasn't nearly as bright as he thought if so much escaped his notice. Why had he let himself get separated from his true friends, Elsa, Donovan, and Curtis? This would never have happened if he had stuck with them. Then, he couldn't help but wonder what they were doing at that moment. They were traveling to Vettenfelth, blissfully unaware of his grim predicament. He was struck by a stab of forlorn sorrow at the realization they weren't going to see him again. This was likely his end, and a torturous one at that.

"– I heard all of these stories about the Anamagi," Hyroc's interrogator said as they sat on a stool with their back to him before biting something. From the tearing noise, Hyroc guessed they ate jerky or something else dry. "So I thought of you as this terrible monster, but look at you. You're pathetic. The world will be a better place without you."

A shadowed figure appeared out of nowhere, clocking his interrogator on the back of the head with a club. The Feral fell to the ground in a heap. The figure patted down the interrogator's body, returning with a key. When the assailant turned to Hyroc, he saw it was Iskall. Hyroc couldn't tell if he was hallucinating or if his friend were really there.

"I'll get you out of those right quick," Iskall said as he fiddled with the key and Hyroc's restraints.

"Iskall, is that you?" Hyroc asked deliriously.

"Yes, I'm really here. I wouldn't abandon you to the Ferals. What have they done to you?"

When his shackles released, Hyroc rotated and rubbed his stiff, sore wrists. "I'm sorry I didn't listen to you about *her*," Hyroc apologized.

"That's perfectly all right," Iskall answered, helping Hyroc. "I'm not going to put you down with your mistake. I think you've more than paid for it already."

Hyroc took a step before falling. His leg, unused to bearing weight, gave out when he tried to stand. His immobility was temporary. The time for this to wear off was time they didn't have. They could be noticed at any moment, and every passing second increased the likelihood. Thinking fast, Iskall dropped down on all fours just outside the Quintessence Void rune beneath Hyroc and transformed into his stag form. He lowered himself onto his haunches when he became a four-legged creature.

"Climb on my back," Iskall insisted. "That's the only way I can get you out of here."

Hyroc arduously pulled himself onto Iskall's back. He was so weak from his days of starvation that he barely managed. Hyroc wrapped his arms around his companion's neck, laying on his stomach upon their back. Iskall rose on all fours, careful to keep from knocking Hyroc off.

"Okay, hang on," Iskall said before charging away. Thankfully, the place where Hyroc was held captive was at the edge of the camp, allowing them to escape undetected. But they didn't expect that to last long. Aside from horses, the Ferals in wolf form were the only ones with any hope of catching them. Hopefully, by the time Hyroc's escape was discovered, they would be too far away for even the wolves to catch them.

"When did you learn of my capture?" Hyroc asked as they weaved through the darkened forest.

Iskall settled into a slower, more sustainable stride when he spoke. "I knew straight away when you didn't return that night. I would have freed you sooner, but I haven't got an opening with the Ferals guarding you until now."

"Good point," Hyroc agreed. "Did you have any food left you brought with you? By my reckoning, I haven't eaten in four days. *I'm famished.*"

"I'm sorry, but you'll have to wait a bit longer for a meal. I didn't bring any food with me."

Hyroc was crestfallen, and then the strangeness of the statement struck him. "Wait, you didn't?" he asked, confused. "You didn't bring any food? You mean to say you starved yourself while waiting for an opening?"

"Not at all. You do understand what kind of animal I can turn into, right? I didn't need to bring food. I'm a grazer."

"Seriously?" Hyroc asked in disbelief. "You've been eating forest plants the whole time I have been a prisoner of the Ferals?"

"That's exactly what I'm saying. During my animal form training, my mentor forced me to eat nothing but leaves and flowers to help me learn how to think like a deer. One lesson even involved me stripping the bark from a tree with my horns and teeth to get at the cambium layer beneath it. That capability is often overlooked in my animal form for the more predatory animals. Mine can subsist on the greenery in a pinch to stave off starvation. Utilizing that ability is not a very pleasant experience. So I hope you realize how good a friend I am for willingly sacrificing my comfort while I waited for the opening to rescue you."

"Yes, thank you. I very much recognize and appreciate what you did for me. You truly are a great friend."

"And I hope you'll remember that next time you find yourself held for days on end by ruffians."

"My mentor taught me the same foraging lesson during my bear form training since bears eat meat and plants. I doubt any Ferals who chose a bear had eating plants in mind when they selected it."

"Probably not," Iskall agreed.

"But I think you probably still had it easier with your training."

"How so?"

"My lesson included eating bugs and big fat grubs full of juice that tasted like moldy sawdust."

"Oh, *that's nasty*."

"I understand that a lot more than you. She also made me eat raw meat the entire time."

"All right, all right, I get the idea; you don't need to tell me any more," Iskall pleaded, sounding repulsed.

"I had never been so happy in my entire life than when I was reintroduced to hot cooked food."

"I can imagine. I bet your uncle will be relieved to have you back at his home. I bet he's figured out by now that something's wrong."

"No, don't take me to my uncle's," Hyroc demanded. "There's something I need to tell you."

Hyroc filled Iskall in on what he had learned about Fenrald from Eagle.

"No, you're kidding me," Iskall said, baffled when Hyroc had finished relaying his information.

"I'm dead serious," Hyroc assured him.

"That explains so much more about why so many villagers won't have anything to do with him. He's just been useful enough to keep some villagers on his side to avoid being exiled from the village."

"Precisely. I think he only saw my arrival as his means of wiping the slate clean of his past actions."

"Okay, if I shouldn't take you back to his home, I can stash you with my family until we figure something out."

"No, not with them either. I know your family wouldn't intentionally betray me, but it would be too easy for something to slip out accidentally, putting them in harm's way. Do you know of anywhere else you can take me while we figure this out?"

"Yes, I know a place just outside the village."

They arrived at a stony recess protruding into the side of a hill outside the Glacial village. Hyroc rested his back against a cool rock, moving as little as possible to avoid agitating his injuries.The cleft was barely big enough to accommodate two people, but it was concealed behind a clump of bushes. It was a good hiding spot. Iskall and his brothers had discovered the recess years ago. Still, they had kept it secret from anyone outside the family in case there was any trouble with the Ferals and they needed a temporary hiding place. Iskall had departed for the village to acquire food discreetly for Hyroc. He hadn't eaten for days and was ravenous. Then, once he had addressed his hunger, he would figure out his next course of action.

Hyroc drifted in and out of sleep until the sounds of footsteps outside drew him into wakefulness. He could only use his Flame Claw as a last resort because he was so weak even the tiniest spell would probably knock him unconscious. And if he missed his attacker, that was the end of him. A fist-sized rock was the only weapon he had access to.

"Iskall, is that you?" Hyroc called out, gripping the rock, readying himself for a potential fight.

"Yes, it's me."

Hyroc relaxed. "I'm glad you're back. *I'm starving.*" He poked his head out of the recess to see Iskall and his brother Shawnren picking through the bushes toward him. "Iskall," Hyroc said disapprovingly. "I told you not to bring anyone else into this for now."

"I know, but I thought he could help," Iskall said, handing Hyroc a hunk of bread.

"And I could also tell something was off," Shawnren noted. "My brother's been gone almost four days now without a word, and you suddenly show up in the village, so, of course, I figured something was wrong." He lightly smacked Iskall with the back of his hand. "That reminds me, brother of mine. Mother's been worried something has happened to you. You're on your own when you explain everything to her, and the longer you keep her waiting, the worse it'll get."

"Yes, thanks for the support," Iskall said sarcastically.

Hyroc ripped off a chunk of bread and stuffed it into his face. He bowed his head and sighed happily. This was the best-tasting bread he had ever eaten.

Shawnren indicated Hyroc's face. "Shadow, they did a number on you. What happened?"

Hyroc swallowed his mouthful before responding. "I didn't listen to your brother when I should have. That is what happened," he said before demolishing another piece.

"Yeah, some Feral woman he fancied stabbed him in the back," Iskall answered while Hyroc chewed.

"A Feral?" Shawnren questioned in surprise. "I could have told you she was going to do that."

Hyroc's mouth was partially full when he answered, "She sheemed nice." He paused to swallow after a sizable piece of spittle and bread flew out of his mouth, nearly landing on Shawnren's foot. "She appeared to be in charge of all of her faculties, despite ..."

"Despite being red-marked and murderous," Shawnren finished.

Hyroc waggled his head in agreement. "I guess that's one way to put it," he agreed. "She seemed different from the rest of them, and in a good way. Until she drove a knife into my back, she didn't seem all that dissimilar from us Glacials."

"Well, I hope you learned your lesson."

Hyroc refrained from answering. He polished off the remainder of the bread, washing it down with a prolonged drought from a water skin.

"What's with all this secrecy? I would assume after being held prisoner by the Ferals for so long, without food or drink, you would want to spread the word about your captivity. Then, maybe organize some retribution."

A shadow passed over Hyroc's visage. "Because there's something you don't know, *something serious*. But I'll get to that in a second. First, I need to get my thoughts together because I haven't had a chance until now." Some of the things Eagle had said were weighing on his mind. "Iskall, while you were waiting for an opening to rescue me, did you do any scouting of their camp?"

"A little, yes," Iskall said. "But it was mostly at night. That was the only time I could do so without revealing my presence."

"What did you see? Any weapon caches, carts, or wagons with provisions. Anything like that?"

Iskall nodded. "Yeah, I saw a lot of weapons. Bundles of arrows, swords, and axes. Some armor, too. I saw wagons, but I'm not sure if they were for transporting food or not. I couldn't get very close to checking them out, but people started taking down their tents as if preparing to break camp."

Breaking camp seemed odd. Where were they going? Did they assume Darius' insights would bring the Mastgar Crown down upon them? Had that spooked them, and they were fleeing to the North Lands? That was an enticing idea, but why did they need so many additional weapons? Stockpiling weapons usually preceded an attack. Were they arming to attack the village? If that were the case, why did Eagle repeatedly mention the Mastgariens? They had nothing to do with the conflict between the two groups of Wol'dgers. And an attack against them would result in assured destruction. The Mastgariens could muster a force to annihilate the Ferals easily. Sure, Eagle was unhinged, but he didn't seem stupid. He would know how idiotic such a course of action was. But Hyroc could not figure out what his adversary was planning for the life of him. Eagle was planning something, and he seemed plenty confident of its success. Hyroc knew whatever that plan was, it wouldn't be good for him or anyone else in the village. He needed to figure it out.

Hyroc cursed in frustration. "I don't know," he said. "I can't figure out his goal. Unless he's suicidal and doesn't care for his daughter nearly as much as he claims, it doesn't make sense."

"All right, you're safe," Iskall said. "Why don't you give yourself a few days to recuperate – you know better than I what you've been through – and just think on it. I'm sure it'll come to you."

"I don't think we've got a few days for me to spend getting better while I figure it out," Hyroc said indignantly.

"Well, why don't we go tell your uncle all of this so he can help you figure it out," Shawnren said. "Figuring these types of things out is what he's good at."

"No, we can't," Hyroc said sternly. "There's something I need to tell you about Fenrald." He clenched his fists, anger springing up within him. "He – he killed my parents. My mother and father! He was my father's brother, and he killed him."

Shawnren's mouth fell open. "No, you're kidding," he said.

"I'm dead serious."

"But he – but he invited you to live with him. I don't understand. He's been so nice to you."

"He hoped I would never find out the truth. He feels guilty for what he did."

"And what about the children he rescued?"

"I think he's trying to atone for his past actions. He wanted everything my father had, and he wanted the riches of my mother. He was jealous. Only his plan failed. It failed, but not before he took the lives of my parents. He can never atone for their blood on his hands, no matter how much good he does."

"Hold on," Shawnren said. "Where did you learn this? You've been gone for four days. You couldn't have heard it from him."

"A Feral named Eagle told me this while I was his prisoner."

"Eagle!" Shawnren said indignantly. "You heard it from him?"

"Yes, he and Fenrald were working together."

"How do you know he wasn't lying? You know, to get under your skin, to make you angry, rile you up because – I don't know – he enjoys that."

"No, I believe him because he knew things about what my uncle did that only Fenrald could have told him. I know Eagle's dangerous and a liar, but I believe him with this."

Shawnren shook his head in agreement and disbelief. "What are you going to do?"

Hyroc took a deep breath to help settle his nerves. "I'm going to avenge my parents," Hyroc said coldly. "*I'm going to kill Fenrald.*"

Chapter 35

A Kernel of Truth

HYROC CREPT THROUGH THE TREES outside Fenrald’s cabin. His sides throbbed angrily with pain. He had relieved the swelling around his eyes and the most painful bruising on his abdomen with his Flame Claw but could do nothing for his ribs. Iskall and Shawnren had offered to assist him in his mission of vengeance, but he refused. It was something he felt he should not involve them with. He needed to do this alone.

It seemed ironically fitting he wielded his father’s sword to avenge his parents. The blade had been meant as a gift to Jasok from Fenrald, a sign of endearment to symbolize an obviously false bond between brothers. Fenrald had forged the sword with his hand, given it to Jasok, and, by the rules of inheritance, passed the sword to Hyroc. Now, Hyroc would use that same blade to end his uncle’s traitorous life. It was as if fate wished him to deliver long-overdue justice upon his uncle. If not for his uncle’s betrayal of his family, they would all still be alive and together. So many bad things he experienced would never have happened.

Hyroc pressed toward the cabin, drawing his blade out of its scabbard. He had yet to spot his uncle. Shawnren had confirmed Fenrald was at the cabin this morning. Hyroc had to hurry, though, because, after his days-long imprisonment, Fenrald had become concerned about his absence and inquired around the village about his whereabouts. He was preparing to leave in search of his nephew. His uncle feigned concern for him to relieve his unbearable guilt, which enraged Hyroc. It was greed that had generated his guilt. He had coveted what Hyroc's parents had and wanted what others had worked hard to create for themselves. Now, he would pay the price for his selfish deed.

Hyroc heard Elizabeth's soft voice. It came from the front of the cabin, and Hyroc stealthily moved toward it. He pressed against the side of the cabin, moving along its smooth logs. He was startled by the sound of footfall behind him. He wheeled around, his sword raised to strike. It was Kit. Hyroc had almost forgotten his mountain lion companion was still here, having stayed behind when Lynx ambushed him. After four days, the big cat would be overjoyed by his return. But Kit's eagerness for attention would wreck catching Fenrald unaware if he made any noise. Hyroc desperately needed to get him to leave quickly and quietly. He crouched, silently setting his sword on the ground before allowing the big cat to push his head into his arms. Kit rumbled happily as Hyroc scratched behind his ears.

"Yes, I'm very glad to see you, too," Hyroc whispered. "Sorry I was gone for so long. Okay, buddy, I know you're happy to see me, but I don't have time to pet you right now." Kit stopped purring and gave him a contemptuous glare. "I've got something I need to take care of with Fenrald first. Go wait at your favorite tree, and I'll come get you when I'm done." Kit flicked his tail with displeasure before sauntering away.

Hyroc took a deep breath to calm his nerves before grabbing his sword and continuing. When he peered around the wooden corner of Fenrald's home, he saw Elizabeth playing with her doll a few steps from the open front door. Hyroc pulled back when Fenrald exited. He was garbed in travel gear and a black cloak. He knelt, fiddling with a knapsack on the ground, with his back to Hyroc. This was as good as any opportunity Hyroc would get to strike. That was no longer his uncle; he was a dangerous enemy. This Wol'dger was no better than the witches or shadow demons he had dealt with before. Hyroc was here to take Fenrald's life, and he expected his uncle to fight with all the intensity of a cornered animal. Hyroc needed to fight with no less ferocity or mercy.

"Fenrald!" Hyroc shouted as he stepped forward.

Startled, Fenrald bolted to his feet, wheeling around. He reached for a dagger but stopped his hand when he realized it was Hyroc. "There you are!" he said with great relief. "I've been looking –" He trailed off, noticing the fire in Hyroc's sapphire eyes and his raised sword. His relief dissipated, turning to confusion. "Hyroc?"

"I know what you did," Hyroc said sternly. "I know what you did *to my parents*. I know how you betrayed them. And it was all because you wanted what was theirs."

Cold comprehension filtered into Fenrald's expression. "So you now know the truth," he said.

"Yes, I know *everything*."

He grunted a humorless laugh. "It shouldn't surprise me you figured it out. You have your mother's wits. She was just as smart."

"Don't you dare talk about my mother or father!" Hyroc snarled. "Don't you dare talk about having any care at all for either of them. The only care you ever held for her was for her wealth and nothing else."

"Wealth?" Fenrald said, puzzled. "You think I was after her wealth?"

"Don't pretend you don't know what I'm talking about. I'm not stupid."

"Who told you about *her Wealth*?"

"Eagle, he told me everything."

"Ah, I see," Fenrald said. He took a long breath. "I'll tell you everything that happened. When we lived in Wulfren, Eagle and I were close. Close like you and your human friends. We grew up together and were like brothers to each other. Your father also counted him as a friend. Much less so as we came into adulthood but still friends. Then, one day, I heard word of the Ferals slaughtering anyone loyal to the ways of the Guardians. Then, I, your father, and your mother devised our escape." He paused, taking a deep breath as if stricken by a painful memory or, as Hyroc imagined, pretending grief. "Then – *then I was a fool*! My concern turned to my friend, Eagle. While your parents prepared to leave with the three of you, I headed out alone to warn him. In my ignorance, I delivered their escape plan to the one responsible for the killings. And my mistake cost me – us – dearly."

"You're lying!" Hyroc said. "You were after the riches of my parents. Why was it you were the one who lived? Eagle didn't think twice about slaughtering my family and countless others. He made no distinction between Anamagi and Wol'dger. Anyone touched by the Guardians or who obeyed their ways had to die. How is it he spared you when your brother's wife was an Anamagi? Eagle wouldn't have overlooked *that.*"

"He didn't spare me," Fenrald spat. "After I informed him about their escape plans, he drugged me. I was stupid to accept a drink of water he put something in. By the time I realized his deception, it was too late. When I came to, I was tied to a post. There were two Ferals with me. One held an executioner's ax." Fenrald lightly pounded a fist against the side of the cabin as if in anguish. "But – but I was not their only captive." He tightly grasped the locket around his neck. "My love, Shandshra, was there tied up beside me. The two Ferals had been ordered to remove our heads to serve as a warning to any followers of the Guardians or those who were still loyal to the Anamagi. I managed to get free and slay my captors, but I was unaware of a third nearby Feral. I turned my back for an instant to cut Shandshra free when our attacker struck. I slayed them, but in the process, I lost my eye and something unimaginably dear. Shandshra died in my arms. Then, I learned what had befallen your parents. A piece of me died that day, leaving behind a cruel void of emptiness. I had nothing to fill it. Broken and guilt-ridden, I had nothing left to live for and decided to join my brother. Right before the end, I realized your mother's body was not among the dead. She was alive, and so were you! I needed to find her. I could safeguard those whom my brother loved. That's what he would have wanted. I could save the last bit of my brother. I owed him that much. The rest – the rest, you know."

"No, you're lying!" Hyroc said. He had to force himself away from pondering the discrepancy between the two stories and deciding which one was the truth. "You didn't admit to wanting my father and mother's wealth. Tell me why you wanted their wealth."

"I never wanted to take what your father had," Fenrald said as if the mere thought was a vile proposition. "Your mother was Anamagi, and yes, she possessed considerable wealth because of her lineage, but I give you my word, on my father's grave, I never once thought about taking any of her riches. It was not mine to take."

"No, you know that's not true," Hyroc said. "Stop lying to my face!"

"The truth is the only thing I have spoken here."

"Then, why did you try hiding this from me? Innocent people don't hide the truth. Why haven't you told me any of this until now?"

Fenrald sighed. "Honestly, I don't know why I concealed this from you. Maybe I was fearful of bringing up the pain of those memories. Maybe I was afraid of inflicting pain on you with the truth. You were so happy to meet me finally, the last remnant of your family. I didn't want to diminish your joy. I thought it was better just to let it rest. We were going after Eagle, the true culprit of all this madness. We were going to avenge your parents. I didn't think telling you this was necessary or worth the anguish it would stir up in you. Maybe that was wrong of me? But I wasn't trying to hurt you. I loved my brother dearly, and you're the only piece of him I have left. I would die to protect you."

"No, no, you're just making this all up," Hyroc said defiantly. He wiped away a tear blurring his vision. "You know why I'm here, and you're trying to save your life. You'll say anything to make me spare you. You're a greedy, covetous liar! I can't believe anything you tell me."

Fenrald dropped to his knees. "If avenging your parents for my mistake is my penance, and it'll bring you a measure of peace, I gladly accept my punishment." He unbelted his dagger and tossed it aside before spreading his arms. "I won't resist you. Do what you came here to do."

"No, stand up!" Hyroc demanded. "Stand up and fight me. Shadows take you, coward. Get back on your feet and fight me!"

"I'm not going to fight you, Hyroc. This day has been a long time coming. I should never have survived that day. I should have died with my brother and the rest of our family. This is the least I can do for you." He indicated Elizabeth, who was staring at the scene wide-eyed with terror, her face tear-streaked. "I only ask you take care of Elizabeth or find her a good home. She is blameless of my wrongdoing. And Eagle.

Don't let him get inside your head. Put him in the ground." He closed his eyes. "I am here. End this for your parents."

Hyroc stepped forward, his father's sword at the ready. He needed to finish this before his will to strike crumbled. The betrayer of him, his parents, and many others was at his feet. Justice needed to be served. Hyroc raised the cold steel of his sword. It was time to strike. He was one sword stroke from avenging his family. But as he looked at Fenrald, the long scar across his face and eye patch showed prominently, and Hyroc couldn't help pitying him. His uncle had not come through that day unscathed. He had lost an eye and someone whom he dearly cared about, as evident from his treatment of her locket around his neck. And what if he was telling the truth about his mistake? He was trying to help a friend from getting killed, unaware his friend was the perpetrator who would stab him in the back. Hyroc had made a similar mistake with Lynx. His mistake hadn't killed anyone; it had caused him considerable pain and discomfort, but he had trusted Lynx, and she had turned on him. Their experiences weren't all that dissimilar. If nothing else, they shared this in common.

Or Fenrald was lying about the whole thing. This could be a desperate attempt by a man scared of death, but Fenrald's behavior didn't make sense. Why had he put himself in such a vulnerable position if he wanted to live? He should be fighting back tooth and claw. Why was he willing, almost eager, for Hyroc to slay him? This wasn't making sense.

Then, Hyroc wondered if Eagle was the one who was lying. He had once heard from Marcus every lie is built upon a kernel of truth. One story had Fenrald as a jealous brother who greedily wanted to kill his sibling's family and steal what they possessed. The other portrayed Fenrald as a loving brother who mistakenly revealed vital information to a villain he thought was a friend with dire consequences. Which one was the truth? With Fenrald's submissive behavior, he was inclined to believe the latter. What was gained from Eagle telling him the former version of the story? Was it an attempt to increase the pressure on him to make the starvation and interrogation break him? That's when something he had not considered popped into his mind.

Had Eagle fabricated his version specifically to make Hyroc kill his uncle for a completely unrelated reason other than fulfilling vengeance? Regardless of the validity of either version, Eagle and Fenrald were bitter enemies. This was evident from the myriad of claw marks on Eagle's head and a blind eye from Fenrald trying to kill him. What if Eagle saw an opportunity with Hyroc to eliminate a dangerous adversary? He was cunning and gravitated toward mind games, as Lynx had shown through her betrayal. The witch in Elswood had attempted to use the same tactic before Hyroc and Donovan killed him. Eagle had a pattern of using this tactic. Deceiving Hyroc with a false story would fit right into this. That's all this was; one gigantic mind game. Hyroc was sick of playing this game. Everything considered, Eagle was indeed the one deserving of his fury. Eagle was the one who, either by his hand or by his order, had killed his parents and forced him to deal with tremendous obstacles. *He was the enemy*, not Fenrald.

Fenrald was as much a victim as he was. Hyroc's uncle had made a mistake. That's what it all boiled down to. Fenrald had made a single mistake with drastic ramifications for him and his nephew. Hyroc had made plenty of mistakes. He had accidentally broken the leg of the other students at the boarding school. That event seemed a lifetime ago. That had been a grim accident. And what about the spiders in Elswood? Hyroc had kept the presence of the giant arachnids secret from the Shackletons for fear of appearing unhinged, resulting in him getting cast out of Elswood. If he had warned his friends, maybe their parents would have survived. Elsa, Donovan, and Curtis never sought to punish him. And why should they? Warning the family might have made no difference. It could have had the same outcome. Or it may have even made things worse. Mistakes happen, and that was a fact of life. Sometimes, people make mistakes that unintentionally hurt others, but people can forgive. Now, it was Hyroc's obligation.

The sword fell from Hyroc's hand, clattering on the cabin's evenly nailed wooden porch boards. Hyroc fell to his knees and embraced Fenrald.

"I forgive you," Hyroc said.

"I'm – so – sorry," Fenrald said through misting eyes, reverberating with twenty years of regret. "I'm sorry – for everything! I didn't mean to put you through all this. I didn't see him for who *he* was. I never would have done anything to hurt your parents or any of the others, especially not you. I made a mistake, a terrible, wretched mistake. Rarely a day goes by I don't think about what I might have done differently that day, how I might have saved them."

"I understand," Hyroc said. "It was out of your control. The fault rests with the holder of the sword. Not the one caught up in what it has wrought. I never should have believed Eagle's story. I'm so sorry I doubted you."

Fenrald laughed hesitantly. "I don't deserve your apology," he said. "Don't you dare apologize to me. I don't want to hear that out of your mouth again. I warned you he could worm his way inside of your mind. I don't know if that power of his is magic-driven or if he is immensely talented with words." Fenrald pulled Hyroc away for him. "Hyroc, are we square?"

"Yes, Fenrald, we are square."

Fenrald nodded happily, rising back to his feet. He helped Hyroc to his feet. Then, he turned his attention to Elizabeth. She clutched her doll tightly, holding it in front of her like a shield. She still wore a horrified expression.

"It's okay, my love," Fenrald said reassuringly and gently. He scooped her up into his arms, her distraught expression melting away. "Your cousin and I were just talking, nothing more. Everything is okay."

Hyroc retrieved his sword and slipped it back into its sheath on his hip.

Chapter 36

Hidden Agenda

...THEY ROUGHED ME UP PRETTY good," Hyroc said as he lay down inside Fenrald's home. It was the following day after Hyroc had forgiven his uncle's disastrous misstep. Fenrald listened to his nephew recount his imprisonment at the Feral camp while he reviewed a map at a table. "That went on for a while. Then Eagle convinced me to come after you. I still can't believe I trusted anything he said."

"You shouldn't feel bad you fell for his words," Fenrald advised without looking away from the map. He tapped the table with a clawed finger, deep in thought for a moment. "I know how convincing he can be. Why do you think he was able to attract so many Feral followers or strike a deal with the North Landers?"

"That's a good point," Hyroc agreed. "But I thought him being a seer would have drawn many of them to him."

"Yes, the mystique brought by him seeing the future was also very beneficial to his cause. That, in combination with his silver tongue, is a potent formula."

Hyroc shook his head in disbelief. "I never considered him using those together. No wonder he's such a dangerous adversary. He *even* made me think I needed to get vengeance against you."

"That's but one example of his cunning," Fenrald said. "When we were young, I remember him convincing your father and me to do some of the most foolhardy things. Things that, afterward, seemed utterly ridiculous. He once convinced us there were a couple of rabid wolves and we needed to put them down before they got into the city. We slayed them without difficulty, but when we wanted to help him dispose of the carcasses, he assured us he could do it himself. Then, come to find out, they weren't rabid; he just wanted the pelts and didn't want to share the profit of selling them with us. We only found this out because we saw them hanging up at a furrier a few days later. We both felt like idiots for being duped when his deception was so plainly obvious."

"Anyway, to finish off my capture," Hyroc said. "They had at me for a while before Iskall came and rescued me. Thank goodness he was paying attention. And you know the rest."

"I know this probably goes without saying," Fenrald said over his shoulder. "But that sounds like a thoroughly unpleasant experience, and I'm just glad it's now over for you."

"Yes, extremely unpleasant," Hyroc agreed. "And so am I." He absentmindedly rubbed his sore ribs. Overall, Hyroc's condition had vastly improved through his day of rest, but in a way that wounds often heal, everything ached more today. To say nothing about the whole ordeal with Lynx."

Fenrald laughed half humoredly. "I'm also a little embarrassed about that. I never once asked what her name was, and in hindsight, I should have made more of an attempt to find out. I must apologize for not doing so. If I had known it was *her*, I would have warned you." A shadow passed over his face as he spoke the last few words. "And I would have eliminated the danger."

Hyroc frowned, catching his uncle's dark meaning. Even though Lynx had stabbed him in the back, the thought of her death was displeasing. "You have nothing to apologize for," Hyroc said, hoping his comment would lead to another less disturbing topic. "It was my own stupidity for believing her absurd explanation about being a good Feral."

"That's odd," Fenrald said when Hyroc had finished. "I don't know what they are planning to attack. But you're right; with all those extra weapons, they certainly will attack *something*. And that Shade Hunter of his has me exceedingly concerned. Eagle could do a lot of damage with a shadow demon under his control. But there are no major targets or settlements anywhere near his camp. That has me – wait –" He trailed off. "OH, NO!" he exclaimed as a sudden burst of energy overtook him. "I know what *he's doing*. How did I NOT see this sooner? It's what *he's* been working toward all this time." He rushed into the other room, rummaging through a box of rolled-up scrolls.

"What?" Hyroc asked impatiently as he swung his legs off the bed. "What has Eagle been working toward? What did you see?"

Fenrald came away from the box with another map. He reviewed it briefly before returning his attention to the first map. "Okay, okay, come look at this," he said. Hyroc grimaced a little as the pain in his side intensified from the motions of standing. "Right here is our village." He pointed to it. "This is the Feral camp, and this is Forestgold. Eagle is absolutely planning an attack, but the question is, where? He wouldn't attack our village. Our numbers here are about three times larger than the force he can bring to bear. It would be bloody, presumably with many casualties, but against us in a head-on assault his defeat is very likely. The next closest target is Forestgold. Nothing is stopping him from doing so, but if he were to attack it, the Mastgariens would assuredly retaliate with a force he has no hope of standing against. They would route him, kill him, and do the same to us."

"But there's nothing else for him to go after," Hyroc noted. "Unless he heads westward where there are more towns, the Mastgariens would just as swiftly attack him if he hit any of them. Is there something I'm missing?"

"Here's the thing: he *is* going to attack Forestgold."

"What? Attack them? I seriously do not understand. You laid out all the reasons he would die if he did. Is he a lunatic, and I haven't figured that out yet or what?"

"No, no. He *is not* unstable. He's wicked smart. He always has been. This is part of a devious plan. You are completely right about your assessment. Any attack against the Mastgariens will provoke an overwhelming retaliation. He is more than aware of this. He's planning on using their retaliation to his advantage."

"I don't follow. How can he use that to his advantage? Him being dead isn't a good plan on his part."

"I assure you, he *is not* planning on dying. Listen to this carefully. By attacking the town, he will cause the Mastgariens to muster an army to destroy him. But he will pull back as soon as he successfully provokes that reaction. He knows they will come after him and he has no chance of victory against them. So he abandons his camp, and then he and the Ferals flee into Northlander territory. Remember, Eagle has curried favor with a North Lander Jarl. That is the same Jarl who has been contributing forces to Eagle's cause. We've killed several of the Jarl's warriors. He's also the one Eagle was kidnapping those children for."

"So not a nice guy," Hyroc said.

"No," Fenrald agreed. "I had the mind to pay him a visit but was never afforded that opportunity."

Hyroc couldn't help narrowing his eyes at the last statement.

"But kidnapping all those Mastgar children served another purpose I had missed. All this time, I thought he was kidnapping those children to trade for supplies and whatnot with the North Landers. This is part of a plan he has been slowly working towards for years. It's longer in scope than what I imagined him capable of. Eagle is patient, very patient. I told you how much those kidnappings angered the Mastgariens. That outrage is exactly what he is counting on. He's been purposely and steadily stoking their wrath. And his patience is now coming to fruition. Now, the ire of the Mastgariens is at its breaking point. Since the kidnappings have been perpetrated by Ferals, the Mastgariens associate us Wol'dgers with stealing away children and all sorts of nasty business. They do not understand the difference between our two groups. Red or blue marked, Feral or Glacial; it makes no difference. They see us as the same. To them, a Wol'dger is a Wol'dger; all of us are dangerous, and they feel it is better to get rid of the lot of us. And with them feeling as they do, once Eagle attacks Forestgold, Mastgar will assuredly wipe us out."

"All the while, Eagle flees to safety with that Jarl," Hyroc said, shaking his head in disbelief. "And he will once and for all have finished what he started all those years ago in Wulfren. The Glacials – probably me as well, the last Anamagi – will finally be purged from this earth. That's a diabolical strategy. Use the Mastgar Army to do the dirty work for him. No wonder you had never figured this out until now. I couldn't have figured this out."

"He's cunning," Fenrald agreed. "I will give him that. After all these years of trying to get him, it's hard to believe I still somehow managed to underestimate him."

Hyroc gave him a reassuring pat on the shoulder. "But I have a question," Hyroc said. "What about Darius? He discovered the difference between our two groups and will bring it to the Mastgar crown. When he does, they'll know the Ferals are their real enemy, not us."

"His discovery will make no difference when Eagle attacks Forestgold," Fenrald said cynically. "They won't listen after the town has been decimated and their citizens slain."

"When people get scared, they stop listening." Hyroc lightly pounded his fist on the table in frustration.

Fenrald nodded in grim agreement. "Besides, it's already too late for that."

"Too late?" Hyroc questioned.

"Yes, too late. From what you told me you saw in the camp, his attack is imminent. If it isn't underway already."

"Then we've got to try warning them."

"By the time we can get word to them, I doubt it would make any difference."

"Well, we've got to try something! There's got to be something we can do to stop him."

Fenrald blew out an exasperated breath. "I really don't know if there's anything the two of us can do. He might have already won."

"No, I don't believe that! I'm going to do something, and I'm going to stop him. Come on, I've got an idea!"

Chapter 37

The Only Chance

Hyroc, where are you going?" Fenrald called out.

"I think you know," Hyroc said over his shoulder. He quickly walked through the Glacial village. "We're going to spread the word about the Feral attack on Forestgold, and we're going to need help doing so."

"I've already been over this with you. The villagers are not going to help us. I've tried time after time without any meaningful success. You're wasting your time."

Hyroc wheeled around, speaking loudly, not caring if anyone heard their argument. "We've got to try! If Eagle provokes the Mastgariens, all of us will be finding a new home – if we even survive far enough to find a new one. Our choices are to find a place in the Northlands, where they'll probably kill us, Wulfren, where they *did* try to kill us all, or Arnaira to the east, where I came from, where I know from personal experience we won't live long there, and our ends will be *incendiary.* The only favorable option is to find some far-off land, but I doubt many of us will make it to the other side of Mastgar. And if every Wol'dger is banished from this kingdom and considered an enemy, I'll never see Elsa, Donovan, and Curtis again. They're also my family. I've known them for so long I barely remember what life was like before they came into my life. We've been through so much together that shadows be cursed if I'm going to let a one-eyed, nine-fingered, warmongering coward make me break my promise to my friends. Last of all, by killing a bunch of innocent people that have nothing to do with this."

"I admire your determination, I do," Fenrald said sympathetically. "But that's if any villagers here will even listen to you. You may not have a choice as much as it pains me to tell you this."

"I know they'll listen to me! I have one advantage you don't. I am an Anamagi. Now, come on! Every second we waste is another Eagle draws nearer to victory."

He rushed to the home of Iskall's family. His friend and Shawnren were the first family members he encountered; they were out front sharpening tools.

"Well, h …" Iskall barely managed to get out before Hyroc interrupted him.

"There's no time for pleasantries," Hyroc said curtly. "And you'll just have to trust me and do as I ask without question, no matter how absurd my request seems. I have a good reason for it, and you'll get an explanation, but not right now. Okay?"

The brothers glanced at each other uncertainly but nodded.

"What do you need?" Shawnren said.

"Okay, okay, something awful is about to happen, and I need to address everyone in the village. I need the two of you and as many of your family members you can get to spread the word that – uh – that the Anamagi, yeah, that's it, that the Anamagi has something vital to tell everyone. That'll get their attention. Tell them to meet in the village center. Now, go!"

"Iskall, transform; on four legs, you can fly through the village," Shawnren suggested. "I'll let the rest of the family know what to do. Get going!"

Iskall transformed, bolting off at full gallop as soon as he stood on nimble hooved feet.

Hyroc followed as fast as his two-legged form could carry him. When he reached the village center, a crowd of intrigued onlookers had gathered. He shoved down the nervousness he had always felt being in front of so many eyes. The feeling was amplified by the knowledge he was giving a speech. He turned away from the crowd, closing his eyes, calming his breathing, and organizing his thoughts. When a sufficiently large crowd had accumulated, he stepped on top of a wooden box Fenrald found for him. Villagers were still arriving. He hoped latecomers would hear enough of his words to get the gist. Fenrald gave him a look that said, "Look on the bright side; if you embarrass yourself, no one will be around to remember it." Hyroc took a deep breath.

"Can I have everyone's attention?" Hyroc called out. There was no going back now. The crowd quieted. "I have troubling news. I've learned that, at this very moment, the Ferals are marching to attack Forestgold." The villagers glanced at each other, astounded and alarmed, and the crowd generated a disquiet rumble of voices. Darius, who listened intently, wore a supremely disturbed expression. "And it is of dire importance we come to its defense."

"Defense?" a brown and white male Wol'dger in a blue tunic questioned in amazement. "If we are not a part of the fighting, what concern is it of ours? My heart goes out to those townsfolk caught up in the fighting, but this attack benefits us. The Mastgariens will not let this aggression from the Ferals go unanswered. They'll take care of the Ferals without us lifting a finger. Why do we need to get involved?" Much of the crowd nodded in agreement.

"Because there's something you don't know," Hyroc answered. "Yes, this attack will provoke the Mastgariens, and yes, they will assuredly respond by eliminating our foe, but we will be swept up in this as well. They will not solely destroy the Ferals. They will destroy us alongside them." The volume of the crowd increased significantly. "They do not ..." Hyroc started to say.

"Preposterous!" interrupted in astonishment a mostly black muscular male Glacial wearing a cream colored short-sleeved shirt. "Why destroy us? We have nothing to do with this attack. It was all a plot by the Ferals. They are the true culprit."

Hyroc raised his voice to speak over the crowd. "We will be implicated with the Ferals because we are all Wol'dgers."

"Because we are Wol'dgers?" a third Glacial asked, puzzled. "If this were simply due to how our kind looks, why haven't the Mastgariens shown this kind of prejudice until now? We've been here for years without encountering what you're suggesting. Why let us into their kingdom in the first place? It defies all reason."

"Where did you get this information?" a dark gray female Wol'dger questioned. Those around her nodded and briefly voiced their agreement. "Who told you about this plot?"

Hyroc winced, knowing the answer was not going to go over well. "My uncle, Fenrald, and I discovered the plans of the Ferals," he said.

"Your uncle?" someone else said in disbelief. "Why on earth would you listen to him? Don't you know what he's done?"

Fenrald shot Hyroc a sympathetic look that said, "See? I warned you this would happen."

"Yes, I know exactly what he's done," Hyroc said, holding his hands out placatingly. "*But you need to listen to me.*" Crowd members dismissively swiped their hands through the air before turning to leave. "No, you need to listen!"

"No, what he says is the truth," shouted Darius. Hyroc was surprised to see the Mastgar mage speaking. Darius pushed through to the front of the crowd. "Hyroc speaks the truth. Among my people, there is a tremendous dislike for your kin, and it grows stronger with every passing day. This dislike is due to the ones you call Ferals. This anger flares primarily because of their kidnappings of our children. It's the reason I am here: to discover a peaceful resolution to this situation. I now understand the differences between your two sides, but my kingdom still does not. They see Ferals and Glacials as one and the same. As of late, there has been talk amongst the royal court about ridding ourselves of our troublesome Wol'dger neighbors. You would be forced out, even to the point of bloodshed. With every kidnapping, this idea only gains in appeal. If the Ferals attack Forestgold, that will end all talks of peace. They would eliminate you."

The talking of the crowd became frantic and fearful.

"What can we do about this?" someone called out.

"We have to stop the Ferals," Hyroc said sternly. "We have to fight them."

"Fight?" another questioned. "But most of us are farmers! The only things we have close to weapons are our hunting bows. Sure, we can use them to cut down enemies from afar, but if anything gets close, we'll be torn to shreds. We need more than just that; we need swords, axes, spears. *We need weapons.*"

Fenrald snatched a reaping scythe out of the hands of a crowd member. "This is a *weapon*," he said, holding the farming implement over his head. He demonstrated by slashing it through the air before returning it to its owner. Next, he held up a pitchfork. "This is a *weapon*." He made a solid thrusting motion and returned it. He lifted the paw of a Glacial in bear form sitting amongst the crowd. "This is a *weapon*. I've killed men with less. Practically anything can be turned into a *weapon*. We have *weapons enough*. We only need the will to wield them." He returned to Hyroc's side.

"And who's going to lead us, you?" someone questioned. "You? You betrayed your own brother. Why should we trust you?"

"Because I trust him!" Hyroc said. He ignited a blue flame in one hand to emphasize the point. "I am an Anamagi, wielder of the azure flame imparted by the Guardians. When the curse befell our ancestors, those who came before me, Wearla gave them the choice to remain uncursed for their devotion to her and the Guardians. They declined her generous offer. They loved their brethren and did not want to be set apart from their kin. To mark this selfless act, she imbued their bloodline, my bloodline, with the Sentinel Flame. From then on, the Anamagi led and guided our people into prosperity. That is why you were named with the moniker Guidance Wol'dger to honor the Anamagi.

"But Eagle ended all that. He and his followers slaughtered the Anamagi and anyone who followed their ideals. He forced you out of the life you had worked hard to build in Wulfren. He forced all of you into this village in a foreign land. You built new lives here, but Eagle refuses to leave you in peace. He continues to harry and murder you. But fear never got the better of you. You still carried on, continuing to frustrate his plans. Now, Eagle is on the cusp of fulfilling his final scheme where he will *destroy you*, the last remnant of the Guidance Wol'dger. This won't be done at the hands of the Ferals. He will use the blades of Mastgar to do his bidding. They will have no idea those they kill are innocent. And while they come after us, Eagle and his followers will escape safely into the Northlands.

"Whether you want this fight or not, you don't have a choice. It's already on its way. Either we fight the Ferals and come to the town's aid or face the Mastgar army on their vengeful march. And when they come for us, they will come in far larger numbers than us. We will lose that fight, and if we survive that dreadful day, we will have to find another home. Do you want to do that all over again? Do you?" Everyone in the crowd shook their heads. "Then, we must act! Join me. Save the citizens of Forestgold, who know nothing of our conflict. And by doing so, save yourselves. Frustrate Eagle one last time." Several members of the crowd nodded their agreement.

Hyroc indicated Fenrald. "And trust *him*," Hyroc said. "Because I trust him. I know the pain brought by his mistake better than any of you. His mistake killed my parents. His mistake killed his family and the love of his heart, Shandshra. He suffered the same as many of you, and the part he played was unintentional. An accident. Have any of you ever made a mistake, even one that hurt someone else? I know I have." More crowd members began nodding. "Maybe some of you can find it in you to forgive him. Maybe some of you can't. But regardless of your feelings toward him, you need to trust him *now*."

"But we're not fighters," someone said. "Many of us will die if we face the Ferals."

"I know," Hyroc said, somberness touching his tone. "I know I'm asking a lot of you and some of you won't be coming back. *I may not* be coming back. But it is a certainty we will *all die* if we do nothing. This is our only chance. I need you to trust me. Will you follow me?"

Everyone in the crowd nodded emphatically. "I will follow you," someone shouted. A chorus of acknowledgments followed. Then, everyone began chanting, "Hyroc."

Hyroc couldn't help smiling and even caught a brief smile on his uncle's face.

"Okay, I need everyone to listen up," Fenrald shouted, interrupting the chanting. "I need every able-bodied man and even women capable of fighting to collect any blades, axes, shields, or bows they have.

Everyone else needs to grab anything, and *I mean anything*, that can be used as a weapon and bring it back here. You're looking for knives, reaping scythes, pitchforks, rakes, shovels, hammers, or anything that will hurt if you hit someone with it. Be creative. Get some brooms or any long wooden poles. We can tie a knife on their ends to make polearms."

The crowd dispersed in a frantic flurry. They rushed to the shops. Shop owners disseminated useful wares to the nearest person as quickly as possible. They busted down the doors of any with no one attending them, raiding them of anything they could get their hands on. Some crowd members were a little too zealous in their efforts and brought useless tools as makeshift weapons.

"No, how is anyone supposed to use this?" Fenrald said, holding up a wood drill. "Unless they're made of wood or oblige you by standing incredibly still as you drill a hole in their head, this *will not work*. Find something else. And, so help me, I swear if you bring me a cooking pot, I will hit you with it." With a fearful expression, the Glacial rushed off.

When the crowd had finished with the shops, they started on the dwellings. A pile of brooms and fishing rods formed at Fenrald's feet. He was then surprised to see several metallic pans. This item had escaped his consideration. Pans seemed harmless enough, but their weight added severe force to anyone's swing. A hit from one would be effective even against a helmeted foe.

People returned with a combination of swords, axes, and shields. But there were too few of them to make a shield wall. Since they were also fighting North Landers, it was assumed their enemy would employ shield wall tactics; they needed to be prepared to counter with their own shield wall. They required more shields. Fenrald swept his eyes through their surroundings, looking for anything that could serve as a makeshift shield. He had an unusual idea.

"We need more shields," he yelled out. "Grab the doors from every building." Everyone within earshot, including Hyroc, shot a perplexed look at Fenrald.

"The doors?" someone said, puzzled.

Fenrald nodded. "Yes, the doors. I'll show you." He rushed to the nearest shop and used a hatchet to sever the hinges on its door. Then he brought it to the piles of gear, holding it up for everyone to see. "See, do it just like that. And if the doors are too big for you to use, cut them in half. And if there still aren't enough shields after that, grab any planks you can get your hands on. Tie a couple of those together, and it'll work."

Soon afterward, the crowd finished ransacking the village and returned to Fenrald.

"Looks like we've got everything we can use," Fenrald said. "Okay, everyone who can transform, step forward." He gave Hyroc a confused look when his nephew didn't move. "You're not going to fight in your animal form?"

Hyroc shook his head. "No," he said. "I'm going to fight in my natural form. I want to fight as a man, not a beast. Ferals adore the animal savagery of their animal form. I want to show them those tendencies make them weak and they have no power over those on two legs. I am also more agile in my natural form when casting spells with my Flame Claw than in my bear form."

"I see," Fenrald said. "Go ahead and transform," he continued. "The rest of you get yourselves armed. Those in animal form, I want bears over here, wolves here, cats here, birds here."

"Don't forget deer," Hyroc prompted, indicating Iskall, who was nearby in deer form.

"Right, right, the deer, thank you," Fenrald said in agreement before raising his voice to give instructions. "I want deer or anything with hooves over here. Did I miss any animals?"

"Me," a woman's voice said. When Fenrald turned his attention to her, he found she was a huge river otter.

"Uh, you – you can stay right there," Fenrald said. "Any idea what I am supposed to do with a river otter?" he quietly asked Hyroc.

Hyroc discreetly shrugged. "You got me. Are there any rivers around Forestgold? Maybe she can pull people into the water and drown them."

"You, the otter, can stand with the deer." The otter sauntered over to the deer, her body moving in an undulation.

"Hyroc, Fenrald, I have a question for you," Darius said. "Do you have any blue paint?"

Chapter 38

The Storm Breaks

HYROC WALKED DOWN THE TRAIL leading to Forestgold. He marched with the poorest armed soldiers he had ever heard of. Some carried actual shields with swords or axes, but the majority was a different story entirely. Many carried pitchforks, shovels, reaping scythes, or some makeshift polearm. Everyone with a one-handed weapon used a shield made from a door or some planks roped together. These shields wouldn't withstand much punishment, perhaps protecting their user from only one or two blade strikes, but it was better than nothing. He couldn't help wondering how many of those he marched with wouldn't return from the fighting. He forced the thought aside. He needed to focus on his survival. There was a good chance he might not be coming back. This was just as dangerous for him as any of them. It was probably more dangerous for him because he was the last Anamagi. The Ferals hated him. They might single him out and come after him harder than them. If he went into battle distracted, he was going to die.

He checked his equipment to ensure it was ready for battle. He wore a studded leather hauberk and a hardened leather helmet someone had loaned him. His armor was light and didn't restrict his movement. The trade-off for its agility was it would not provide any meaningful protection against a powerful strike or a straight-on thrust from a spear or sword. The armor, however, was not his idea. The owner had insisted he use it because he was the last Anamagi and the owner wanted to give him the maximum chance of survival in the coming battle. The helmet made his head itch and it smelled like an old rug, but it was more comfortable than he expected, having a hole cut out on either side to accommodate a Wol'dger's ears.

Everything was good to go. He was anxious to face his enemy's army. The knowledge he faced a Shade Hunter shadow demon overshadowed his every thought. One had nearly killed him his first winter in Elswood years ago. Not only that, but it also tried to control Kit's mind. He shuddered to think what he would've had to do to his companion if the creature had been able to complete the domination. But, back then, he didn't have the power of the Flame Claw to assist him. Under Eagle's control, this Shade Hunter faced a far more dangerous adversary.

Kit yowled uncertainly beside Hyroc as the smell of smoke permeated the air. Hyroc lifted his eyes above the trees to see an ominous column of black smoke rising skyward. The smoke turned the setting sun and dusk sky dark red. As they approached the town, ash began flitting to the ground.

Fenrald called them to a halt. Forestgold was within sight, but they were out of range of any arrows. The gate was closed, and several town guards manned the walls. With an attack underway by the Ferals, they didn't know if the guards would attack them on sight. There weren't enough of them to breach the wall and then take on the Ferals after sustaining significant losses. This was the town's eastern gate, and the Ferals had attacked the northern gate. If this gate was impassable, they could come around and attack them from the north. Coming at the rear of the Ferals, they might be able to win with minimal casualties, but there was also a risk in doing so. The Ferals might have taken the walls there and had that advantage. If so, their chances of victory were grim.

Darius rode a horse to the front of the column. "Stay back," he warned. "They'll probably see you as enemies." He held up a medallion for Hyroc and Fenrald to see. It was marked with the signet of the Mastgar royal court. "They won't shoot at me if they see this."

"Are you certain?" Fenrald questioned. "You did show up with a bunch of Wol'dgers. They might see you as a traitor."

"Mostly certain," Darius responded. "I'll feel foolish if I'm wrong."

"And dead," Hyroc added.

"Yes, there's also *that*," he agreed grimly. "Well, here I go." He trotted his horse to the gate with the signet held high in one hand. After speaking to the guards manning the wall, the gate opened. He disappeared inside, with the gate closing behind him.

Hyroc crouched so he was at eye level with Kit. "Okay, buddy," Hyroc said, scratching his companion behind one ear. "This is as far as you go." Kit chuffed in displeasure. "I know. I know you want to come with me, but a Shade Hunter is in there. It can dominate you. Remember what happened last time? I have to do this without you. Go wait for us back at the village where it's safe." Hyroc took a deep breath. "I'm going to try my hardest to come back, but – well, if I don't, you have been an incredible friend. Love you, buddy." He wrapped his arms around the cougar's head and shoulders and hugged him. "If I don't come back, make your own path," he whispered into Kit's ear. Hyroc released his companion and gave him one final pat on the head. "All right, go on." Kit chuffed another groan of displeasure before sauntering off and disappearing among the throng of Glacial soldiers.

Hyroc returned his attention to the gate and anxiously watched, hoping to get an answer soon. Every second they wasted cost the life of someone inside the town. After what felt like an eternity of waiting, the mage reemerged. The gate remained open.

"I've convinced the guards that even though you're Wol'dgers, you're not with the ones attacking them," Darius said. "And you are here to help. They agreed to permit you through this gate."

Hyroc held up an arm covered in blue paint, which included a good swath of his body. The rest of the Glacial force mirrored his appearance. Darius had suggested they cover everyone in blue paint so the townsfolk and guards could easily distinguish them from the Ferals.

"Just tell them the ones covered in blue paint are allies," Hyroc suggested. "And the red ones that aren't painted are their enemies."

Darius waggled his head in agreement. "Duly noted," he said.

"Any idea what we're facing in there?" Fenrald asked.

"No, the guards told me it's pure chaos. The ones here have no idea what they're supposed to be doing. They haven't received any orders since the attack started. The Ferals came out of nowhere. They walked right over the guards on the northern wall. They are burning everything and killing everyone they find. There was also something about all the eyes of the animals glowing purple right before they went rabid and started attacking people."

"That would be the Shade Hunter dominating them," Hyroc noted.

"I figured as much."

"Anything I need to know about killing that *thing*?" Fenrald asked. "I've never dealt with a shadow demon."

"Cut its head off. That's how I killed the one that came after me and my friends in Elswood. Or shoot it with lots and lots of arrows."

"So how you kill anything *that's not* a demon."

"Pretty much."

"Got it. Okay, here's the plan. I'm going to split the army. I'll take my force through this gate to stop Eagle's advance through the town. I want you to take your force to the north, where you'll hit the rear of his army. I'm going to take the bears and cats. I need their strength and power to take on Eagle, and the cats will be most effective inside the town, where they can utilize their agility to get on top of buildings and such to ambush Eagle's soldiers. But I will still leave you a few bears, just in case. You'll take the wolves and the deer. They will be most effective outside the wall where they can use their speed out in the open."

"What if they've taken the wall?" Hyroc asked.

"If the gate is closed and they're firing at you from the walls, get out of there," Fenrald warned. "I want you to come back here and join the fight. Now, you should catch them by surprise, and with any luck, outside the wall, you'll encounter minimal resistance. But be ready for anything once you head into the town."

"I got it."

Fenrald laid an affectionate hand on Hyroc's shoulder. "Take care of yourself out there. Keep your head on a swivel and mind your surroundings. And –" His voice shuddered a little when he spoke "and I'll see you at the end of this. Happy hunting."

"I had also better see you at the end of this," Hyroc said. "Happy hunting, uncle."

Fenrald withdrew his hand, turning to leave. He began barking move orders at his soldiers. Hyroc did the same, though maybe a little less abrasively.

"I guess I'm going with you," Freija said, coming up to Hyroc. She wore a dark gray leather jerkin, black pants and brown leather boots. She carried a quiver full of arrows on her back, a bow in her hands, and a dagger on her belt."I'm glad to have you," Hyroc said.

She blew out an exasperated sigh. "Are you scared?"

"Terrified," Hyroc admitted.

She studied him with a look of apprehension. Then, to Hyroc's supreme astonishment, she lurched forward and kissed him. He stared at her, stunned, his face warming.

"That was in case I don't get the chance later," Freija said. "Let's get to it." She walked off to take her position with the other archers.

"Well, mate, you had better make sure you come back from this," Iskall advised.

Hyroc shook his head to recover his focus before heading for the North gate, moving in an arc. The first enemy they encountered was a group of North Landers. They were depositing armloads of plunder from the town into a cart. Hyroc's archers shot them without him having to give the order. Past them was a group of armed Ferals in natural form mixed with North Landers. Several of them were archers who prepared to send out a volley upon spotting Hyroc's forces.

"Shield wall!" Hyroc yelled. A shell of shields fell in around him just as the arrows took flight. The makeshift shields stopped them, but an arrowhead punched through one mere inches from Hyroc's head. "Wolves and deer, come around the sides and take out those archers." A flurry of paws and hooves shot toward the group.

"We need to break and charge that group," Shawnren suggested.

"Shield wall, disperse and charge. Bears to the front."

The formation dissolved as they rushed forward. Hyroc's bears charged through the middle, and the opposing group erupted in cries of terror as the enormous beasts smashed into them. This destroyed all semblance of order within the opposing group as Hyroc clashed with them. Three four-legged creatures wended through the carnage, homing in on Hyroc. As they closed in, he realized they were dogs with purple eyes. The Shade Hunter controlled them! A Glacial wolf tackled one, and Hyroc slashed a second with his sword, but the third got through. Hyroc got up the wooden shield he carried on one arm as the animal ran into him. He lost his balance but kept the shield between him and the dog. The animal pressed against the shield as it snapped its jaws at him. Using his other hand, he skewered the dog with his sword. It yelped, flopping limply against the shield. Hyroc cast its body off as he got to his feet. By now, the enemy group had been routed. The few still alive retreated into the town.

Then, Hyroc became aware of the town's wall. Where the gate should have been, there was a gaping hole. Stone rubble and splintered wood littered the ground as if a gigantic hand had reached in and scooped out that wall section as one might do to a sand castle. Natural form Ferals, accompanied by wolves and bears, poured out of the breach. The wolves sprinted ahead of the group, lunging into the nearest Glacial. The Feral bears barreled headlong into Hyroc's forces but were halted by his bears. A mixture of wolves, pitchforks, and other stabbing weapons came to their aid to bring down their burly adversaries. Hyroc's deer sprang into action to assist those struggling against the Feral wolves. They gored and thrashed with their antlers, stomped, and kicked furiously. Their attacks weren't immediately lethal to the predators, but they managed to hold them off by inflicting pain until those with blades arrived.

Hyroc ran to assist a bear until two heavy chunks of rubble rained down, smashing two Glacials accompanying him. Snapping his attention toward where they had come from, he saw a Feral lifting his arms in a straining motion as if he were lifting something unseen. A chunk of stone levitated off the ground and came sailing at Hyroc. Startled, he threw himself to the ground, barely avoiding the projectile aimed at his head. He faced a rock mage!

That explained the hole in the wall. This mage had used their skill with magically manipulating rock to tear a hole in the fortification. He felt a cracking in the ground beneath him and rolled away. A spike of rock erupted out of the ground where he had been lying. Hyroc scrambled to his feet and sent a fireball flying at the mage. The mage hastily threw their arms up in front of themselves. A large piece of dirt ripped from the ground to block the fireball. The piece shattered with a dusty flare of fire. Hyroc was already running before the flash had cleared. With a sweeping motion of their arm, the mage shattered a piece of stone and sent a fan of shards at Hyroc. Hyroc blocked them with his makeshift shield. The shield's wood creaked and cracked as the shards tore into it, but it held. The added weight of the shards made the shield cumbersome, so Hyroc dropped it as he rushed toward the mage. His opponent's expression showed apparent desperation as he opened a fissure in front of Hyroc. Hyroc saw it coming and preemptively jumped, leaping over the trap. He dispatched the mage with a slash and a stab of his sword.

"THE SKIES STRIKE YOU!" the frigid voice of the Shade Hunter rang inside Hyroc's head.

He saw a mixed flock of birds of prey and ravens bearing down on his forces from the smoke-choked sky. With a shout, Hyroc pointed out the approaching danger. His archers fired, bringing down a sizable portion of the birds. The birds pecked and scratched at his soldiers. Beyond being an unpleasant nuisance and a distraction, the flock wasn't a real threat. The swat from a sword or ax eliminated the danger quickly enough.

"A thicket of horns and thundering hooves trample you," its voice came again. A line of deer bucks burst from the trees, charging at Hyroc's soldiers. Ferals in wolf form and routed enemies from earlier trailed behind the mind-controlled animals.

"Reform the line!" Hyroc shouted. His soldiers fell in around him. "Spears or anything sharp on a pole, to the front, everything else behind them." He grabbed a spear from a dead North Lander, dropping into a crouch and bracing the shaft against the ground at an angle. Soldiers with polearms mirrored him as they prepared to receive the onslaught. The deer slammed into the formation. Hyroc's spear plunged into an animal's chest. The momentum of the deer flipped its rear end forward, throwing it onto its back, and narrowly avoided landing on Hyroc. This scene was replicated for most of his soldiers, with few deer making it through. The ones that got past the first line were immediately brought down by the second.

"Second line, move in front of the spears," Hyroc hastily said. The second line did as instructed. "Now, everyone, charge!" Hyroc and his forces rushed forward to meet the approaching enemies behind the deer.

Ferals and Glacials in wolf form slammed into each other, followed by a cacophonous din of metal and shields. All semblance of order evaporated as the two groups violently fought.

In rapid succession, Hyroc cut down a wolf and a North Lander. He moved to attack a third target in the chaotic flurry of bodies surrounding him.

"You're mine now, Anamagi!" Hyroc heard a familiar enemy's voice announce. The imposing black alpha of The Pack darted determinedly toward Hyroc. Hyroc stabbed his blade at his four-legged adversary, but the agile wolf dodged out of the way. It evaded a series of sweeping sword strokes from Hyroc and snapped at his leg. Hyroc yanked his leg out of the way and gave the wolf a swift kick. The wolf recoiled, giving Hyroc a murderous glare.

"I'm going to make you suffer," the wolf growled.

Before the wolf reacted, it was blitzed by a rack of antlers. The impact threw the wolf off its feet. Hyroc wasted no time driving his blade through his adversary. With a gasp, all signs of life left the alpha. As he pulled his sword from the body, Hyroc noticed the deer was Iskall.

"Nice hit," Hyroc said. His friend acknowledged the compliment with a slight nod.

The two of them rushed off in opposite directions to continue the fight. Hyroc's forces routed their enemy. The survivors retreated through the hole in the town's wall. Hyroc and his soldiers pursued them, entering the settlement. The deer within his forces transformed into their natural form as the tighter confinement of the town's buildings and streets would impede their animal form.

The air smelled heavily of smoke from burning buildings within the settlement. Bodies littered the streets. Initially, the casualties were slain guards, but past these, Hyroc and his soldiers encountered the bodies of men, women, and even children. That shocked Hyroc. He expected to find the bodies of adults, not children. What threat were children to Eagle and his army, Hyroc wondered, feeling sick. Out of the corner of his eye, he caught sight of Freija covering a horrified gasp with her hand. The sounds of battle kept everyone from sinking into contemplation. Hyroc promptly led them to the fighting. The remaining town guards had banded with Fenrald's force and fought alongside the Glacials. Even with the guards bolstering his force, the Ferals outnumbered them and appeared to be forcing a retreat. Hyroc had arrived just in time. Perhaps with his assistance, he could even the odds.

"FOR THE ANAMAGI!" came a collective warcry from Hyroc's soldiers as they assailed the Ferals.

Alarm radiated through the emboldened Ferals, who believed they were on the verge of victory. Their positioning shifted as a large portion rushed to shore up any openings where Hyroc's force attacked. The obstruction of the town's buildings slowed their reaction, preventing them from thoroughly preparing to meet their new adversary. Hyroc's group merged into combat like water added to a bucket. Save for the blue paint, it would have been almost impossible to distinguish the two Wol'dger factions.

Hyroc, Iskall, and Shawnren determinedly fought their way through to Fenrald. His uncle's face was marked with blood and soot but otherwise appeared uninjured.

"I expected you sooner," Fenrald said in a strained tone after he had dispatched a North Lander.

"Sorry, there was a lot more around the North gate than we expected," Hyroc apologized. He jumped past Fenrald to engage a Feral wielding an ax. He and his enemy briefly fenced with their blades before Fenrald joined to finish them off. "Have you spotted Eagle or the Shade Hunter?"

Fenrald shook his head. "No. I thought I caught a glimpse of Eagle at the beginning of the fighting, but I haven't seen him since. And no idea about his pet shadow demon." Fenrald grabbed the shaft of a spear aimed at him, guiding it away from his face. He unbalanced his enemy with a kick to the side of their leg before eliminating them with several sword strokes to their chest.

As the battle raged around him, Hyroc noticed Ferals gathering in a side street away from the fighting. "What's that?" Hyroc asked, indicating the group.

"Don't know," Fenrald said. "But I've got things handled here for the moment. You three, go check it out. It's worth a few more dead Ferals, and I don't like surprises."

Hyroc, Iskall, and Shawnren broke from the fighting. They stealthily crept toward the group. Peeking around wooden boxes, they saw a band of Ferals guarding some Wol'dgers who stood in a circle. The circle members chanted something, but nobody could make it out. Then, there seemed to be a sudden shift in the wind. It started blowing toward the group. Flags waved in their direction as smoke and dust clouds rushed towards them. It was as if something was pulling on everything. Then, a wave of panic crashed on Hyroc! He knew what was happening.

Hyroc cursed. "That's a summoning circle!" he said. "They're opening a gate." Shawnren, Iskall stared at him with uncomprehending expressions. "They're summoning *a shadow demon*. We have to stop them!" Hyroc rushed the nearest guard. Shawnren and Iskall engaged the others. Hyroc caught the first by surprise and swiftly dispatched them. Iskall slipped past the guards as they were preoccupied with his brother and Hyroc. "Kill the summoners!" Hyroc shouted. A swirling black void hovered in the center of the circle. The pull of it grew stronger. The Ferals chanted more fervently. One of the guards realized what was happening and turned to intercept Iskall. Hyroc kicked him in the back, sending him to the ground face-first. While he recovered, Hyroc and Shawnren took out the two other guards, followed by the third. Iskall was already working through the summoners with a blade.

They paid no heed to the deaths of their companions. The void had doubled in size. Hyroc and Shawnren joined the grim work. Then, the last summoner fell. The void disappeared with a sizzling pop. The three of them breathed a collective sigh of relief.

"We did it!" Iskall shouted celebratorily.

"No, we didn't; something came through, look," Hyroc said, pointing at the ground below where the void had been. There stood a two-legged creature about the size of a small child. It had yellow sulfurous skin, spindly legs and arms, five-clawed fingers on its hands, and a skinny tail ending in a point. It had a long, sharp nose, pointy ears, a mouthful of sharp teeth, and two eyes which glowed purple. It appeared momentarily dizzy, as if its entrance into the world had disoriented it.

"What in the Sunless Plains is that?" Shawnren asked in disbelief.

"That's a Mischievion," Hyroc said anxiously.

"They were summoning *this thing*?" Iskall asked. "It doesn't look too dangerous."

"That's *not* what they were summoning," Hyroc said. "It's just what came through. And it's very dangerous! It uh – it really enjoys burning things."

"Well, then, let's get rid of it," Shawnren said, lunging toward the creature. He attempted to punt it across the street with a strong kick, but the creature jumped out of the way sideways and bounced off the wall before landing on the street in front of him. It smiled maniacally, and its eyes glowed with wicked excitement.

"Oh, goody, goody!" the creature announced gleefully. "Wol'dgers. Their hair makes them burn *so brightly*. It smells so nice." It swept its eyes around, growing happier. "So many *flammable houses* made from *flammable trees*. I'll make the sweet perfume of smoke and ash. You three are first." The creature raised its arms above its head, and streaks of glowing orange fire jumped from the nearest flame into its hands. The streaks coalesced into balls of fire that orbited above its head.

"Run!" Hyroc yelled as he rapidly walked back before turning to flee.

The group scattered, taking cover as fireballs chased them.

"How do we kill this thing?" Shawnren yelled across the street to Hyroc as a gala of fire shot past.

"Swords and things will kill it," Hyroc said. "If we can survive to get close enough. I'll distract it while the two of you come around behind it." Hyroc jumped from his cover and sent a blue fireball sailing at the demon while Shawnren and Iskall darted down an adjoining street.

The creature evaded his attack. "No fair, you're an Anamagi," it said. "I'll get rid of your ugly blue fire." In rapid succession, the demon retaliated by throwing fireballs at him.

Hyroc dodged the attack, blocking one flaming orb with a barrier from his Flame Claw. "Are you blind?" Hyroc taunted in his most irritating, pompous tone he could muster. "You can't hit *anything*." He darted down a street in the opposite direction as Iskall and Shawnren.

"I'm not blind!" the creature retorted as it jumped after Hyroc. "But I'll make you blind when your eyes are charcoal."

"The Anamagi is alone," came the cold voice of the Shade Hunter.

Hyroc swept his eyes through his surroundings, but seeing anything as he ran was difficult. *Great, now the Shade Hunter is right here*, Hyroc thought. Two dogs barreled into the street before him, their eyes glowing purple. Hyroc swore as he sidestepped a lunge from one dog and dispatched the second with a sword slash. He wheeled around and killed the first dog. Doing so had delayed him enough for the Mischieviont o catch up to him.

"Run, run, run, you can't get away from me," the creature said with horrific glee in a singsong manner. "Because I'm the one that's here to burn you with fire!" It threw another fireball.

Hyroc used an empty wooden box to block it. He was unharmed, but the impact knocked him off his feet. He rolled out of the way of another attack before scrambling to his feet and dashing down the street. The street opened into a more expansive space with a water well in the center. Here, the air was thicker with smoke, and everything was burning. All the adjoining streets were blocked by burning debris. He was trapped!

The Mischievion arrived and gained a happy, astonished expression when it saw all the fire. "Uh, oh; *you're trapped*," it gloated. It ignited a fire in one hand as it strolled toward Hyroc. "Wol'dgers burn *real good*. Time for an Anamagi torch made out of *you*."

Thinking fast, Hyroc grabbed a bucket of water resting on the well's rim and threw it at the creature. The creature was doused in water, extinguishing the fire in its hand. Sodden, the beast looked disgusted to have water touch it. It affixed a psychotic glare on Hyroc.

"How dare you!" the creature spat. "You're not supposed to throw water on shadow demons. Everyone knows *that*!"

The demon made a sweeping motion with one hand and sent a trail of fire across the ground at Hyroc. Hyroc blocked it with a barrier and used his Flame Claw to pull a glob of water from the well. Hyroc thrust his arms apart, turning the water into a thick mist covering the area.

"I don't want to play hide and seek," the demon growled. "Just let me burn you. You'll make a beautiful candle."

"The mist doesn't hide you from me," the Shade Hunter said. The snapping jaws of a dog materialized out of the mist. Hyroc kicked it in the lower jaw and dispatched it with his sword.

"Tag, *you're dead*!" the Mischievioncalled out from its unseen place before Hyroc heard the whoosh of an approaching fireball. He dove out of the way.

The mist was clearing. The four-legged shape and burning purple eyes of the Shade Hunter appeared. "You should have taken my deal, Anamagi," came the Shade Hunter's hateful voice. "Now, here you die!"

It lunged at Hyroc, and he dodged it with a quick backstep. He jerked his upper body out of the way of a strike from the Shade Hunter's spiked tail. It spat a shard of purple fire at Hyroc, forcing him to block it with a barrier.

"No place to hide now!" the Mischievionshouted as the mist evaporated. While cartwheeling toward Hyroc, it threw a stream of fireballs. Hyroc dodged the initial volleys but had to block one with a barrier. When the fire hit the barrier, the impact force was somehow transferred to him as if a giant hand had slammed into him. It threw him to the ground. The Mischievous hopped on a barrel next to Hyroc, fire in hand. "Aww, your tricks didn't work," it said satisfactorily. "You'll make exquisite ash."

"No, he won't!" came a familiar voice. A wooden board smashed into the back of the Mischievion. The creature squealed in terror as it hit the ground. It landed with a rolling bounce. Dazed, it stood back up. Hyroc threw a blue fireball at it before it could react.

"No fair," the Mischievion screamed before impact. It disappeared with a puff of purple smoke.

"Shadow, that thing *would not* shut up," Iskall said. "That's how we found you."

"What is that damned thing?" Shawnren shouted in shock as he noticed the Shade Hunter.

The Shade Hunter jumped at Hyroc before he could answer. He was still on the ground when it attacked. Hyroc wedged his feet underneath the creature with its snapping jaws close enough for him to feel them moving in the air. He kicked his legs out as hard as he could, throwing the creature off. They regained their footing at the same time. The Shade Hunter shied back as Iskall and Shawnren pelted it with rocks.

"Impatient nates!" the Shade Hunter roared. Its eyes flashed bright purple. Ravens and pigeons materialized through the smoke and started attacking Shawnren and Iskall. They ceased throwing rocks as they tried to shield their heads with their arms. The Shade Hunter rushed Hyroc, overshooting him to strike him more effectively with its tail. When it whipped its tail at him, he severed it with a sword swing. The Shade Hunter let loose a loud wail of pain that sounded like tortured metal being twisted. "YOUR BLOOD WILL COVER THE GROUND!" the creature said furiously. It jolted away from Hyroc to give itself adequate room to lunge at him. Grasping the hilt of his sword with both hands, Hyroc made a hard upward swing, decapitating the monster. The head and body turned to dark purple ash. Hyroc made a sweeping motion with his hand, and a wave of blue fire roasted the birds. Their charred bodies fell to the ground.

"Are you two all right?" Hyroc asked.

"Yeah, it's just a few scratches," Iskall said as he rubbed his head and looked at his hand to see if he was bleeding.

"I now see why you were so concerned with Eagle controlling that thing," Shawnren said. "That four-legged one was nasty."

"Okay, we need to return to the battle," Hyroc advised. The three of them dashed toward the sounds of fighting.

Chapter 39
Full Circle

Hyroc, Iskall, and Shawnren sprinted toward the sounds of clashing metal and the deafening roar of hundreds of voices. They darted around burning buildings, passing bodies strewn everywhere. Ferals, Glacials, humans, and animals all lay together. They came around the corner of a building where a fierce battle raged. The fighting had moved from the town square into the streets leading toward the Western gate.

They had no time to assess the scene as they entered the fray. Hyroc blocked the ax from a North Lander, and then Iskall and Shawnren dispatched his attacker.

"Do either of you see Fenrald?" Hyroc asked anxiously.

The three of them scrutinized the chaotic swarm of bodies surrounding them.

"There," Iskall said, pointing further up the street.

Hyroc found him, but a considerable amount of fighting separated them. The quickest and easiest way to reach him was through a nearby building. It wasn't on fire, but they would have to fight through it because of the raucous coming from inside.

They kicked the building's door open to find it led into the living room of someone's house. An overturned table, broken furniture, and broken serving ware were scattered across the floor. A North Lander and a Feral wolf assaulted a town guard. The guard held them off with a shield, but the situation heavily favored his adversaries. The wolf got around the shield, latched its jaws on the guard's leg, and pulled him off balance.

Hyroc and his companions rushed to assist. The North Lander noticed and came at them with a hard hatchet swing. Shawnren blocked it with his shield, and Iskall went around the side, striking with his weapon. Hyroc moved to deal with the wolf. The Feral reacted too slowly. He killed it with a two-handed downward strike. Iskall and Shawnren had already finished with the North Lander.

"You have my gratitude on the save, friend," the guard said appreciatively as he arduously pushed into a standing position. The guard gasped as he put weight on his leg. He leaned heavily on the wall.

"You can't fight anymore with that leg," Hyroc noted. He glanced anxiously at the fighting outside the door on the house's opposite end. "I don't have the Quintessence to spare on healing you, and they need me out there."

"Go, my brother and I will see him safely upstairs," Iskall said.

Hyroc gave him an appreciative slap on the shoulder. "Thank you. Make sure he barricades himself in."

With that, Hyroc rushed out the door. He eliminated a natural form Feral fighting with its back to him, then fought his way to his uncle.

"What took you so long, *again*?" Fenrald asked crossly.

"We ran into a bit of a shadow demon snag," Hyroc said.

"Another one? It's been dealt with, I hope."

"Yes, it's been dealt with."

"Good, I don't think we could handle any extra problems."

"What's the situation here?"

"Well –" Fenrald paused to block a sword strike from a Feral, then dispatched them with a countering strike. "Well, we're pushing Eagle and his forces back. It looks like the battle has turned in our favor. Eagle knows it and is trying to fall back to the Western gate to escape. We cannot allow that. If he gets away, he'll disappear for a while but continue his mission to destroy us, nonetheless. And this will continue. We have to end this right here, right now. It's the only way we'll be left in peace."

Fenrald scanned his surroundings, realizing the soldiers around him had wiped out all enemies in the immediate vicinity. They stood at one end of a street. They had two choices: take these soldiers and push forward, or fall back to take one of the streets behind them.

"We should push forward," Fenrald said. "Eagle's that way. Soldiers form a line! Shields, short swords, axes, in front. Polearm or anything with a long reach behind them." The soldiers organized themselves as instructed. "Move forward, stay in formation."

The group moved forward steadily, keeping their shields even. A group of Ferals and North Landers surged into the street ahead. "Hold!" Fenrald yelled. A group of archers pushed to the front. "Shield wall." His soldiers fell into a defensive posture with shields in front and above. A volley of arrows whistled into their shields. The archers melded back into the group as the warriors behind tore past. The approaching enemies outnumbered them.

"Strike now!" Fenrald shouted. Suddenly, cat-form Glacials appeared on the rooftops on either side of the street. They pounced on the enemy group from behind, tearing into them with claws and teeth.

"Disperse and charge!" Fenrald said, raising his sword over his head and waving toward the enemy. With a terrifying warcry, Hyroc and Fenrald pressed forward with the soldiers. They clashed with a confused and disoriented enemy. Attacked from both sides, they annihilated their adversaries. "I was waiting for that opportunity," Fenrald admitted.

"Expertly executed, uncle," Hyroc said before paying the big cats a similar compliment. "Cats, back on the roofs. We're advancing. Join our attack when we engage." The big cats nodded, leaping back on the rooftops, disappearing. "As before, move forward." The soldiers reorganized themselves before all moved forward.

They encountered a diminishing force when they approached the street's end. They were only a few buildings from the town's wall. The West gate was nearby. Eagle was close to escaping! Fatigue and weariness on the side of the Glacial forces were starting to slow their progress. Hyroc had lost all sense of time, but it felt like he had been fighting for weeks.

Fenrald rallied the surrounding soldiers into one final push. They clashed with the last vestige of Eagle's Army. A bear form Feral smashed into their line. It mauled one soldier before a Glacial bear of equal size tackled it. They wrestled back and forth; then, the Glacial bear pinned it against the wall of a building. Glacials with pitchforks and polearms came to their aid, stabbing the enemy bear with their weapons.

"That's him!" Fenrald shouted, pointing his sword at Eagle. "*There he is.*" Hyroc looked to see Eagle frantically shouting orders at what remained of his forces as they pushed toward the Western gate. "He cannot get away."

The two of them determinedly fought to reach Eagle. They were so close to fulfilling their hard-fought objective. They had both endured so much pain and waited years for this moment. But it was also on the razor's edge of evading them. Hyroc got separated from Fenrald when he darted through an opening in the Ferals by an attack from some cat-form Glacials.

A tall, broad-shouldered male Feral wielding a long sword blocked his path to Eagle. Hyroc recognized him. He was the one who had beat him during Eagle's interrogation.

"This is as close as you're ever going to get to him," the Feral growled.

"You're wrong about that," Hyroc retorted. He drew a knife with his empty hand. "But I believe we have unfinished business."

"I should have killed you that night, but now's my opportunity to rectify that mistake."

The Feral darted forward, swinging its heavy sword. Hyroc side-stepped a downward strike and blocked a swing with his sword. The two of them struck back and forth with frenetic action. Hyroc slashed the back of the Feral's leg with his knife as he darted past. With a pain-laden yell, the Feral's leg buckled, and he dropped to his knee. He took an ineffective swing, but Hyroc was out of reach behind him. Hyroc slashed him across the back with his sword and drove his knife into their neck before finishing with a hard two-handed strike down the middle of their back. The Feral fell forward lifelessly as a growing puddle of blood formed around them. Hyroc spat on the ground before moving on to Eagle.

"EAGLE!" Hyroc shouted. "This is where it ends."

The one-eyed leader of the Ferals turned, giving Hyroc a wrathful glare. "It took me *years* of meticulous planning to get to this day," Eagle said, sword in hand, as Hyroc approached. "I even sacrificed part of my body to accomplish this." He held up his hand with the missing pinky. "I would finally be rid of the Guidance Wol'dgers. And it was all undone by a clueless Anamagi whelp that, of all things, was raised by human wretches! The irony is almost unbearable."

"Oh, yes, I understand the irony," Hyroc said gleefully. "I, your nemesis, was raised by those so-called *inferior humans*, and you were also defeated with the help of humans."

"And I was beaten by frightened farmers and with PITCHFORKS," Eagle roared indignantly. "That's not an army! That's a mob."

"Either way, now, you're all alone."

"No, I'm most certainly *not* alone. Lynx!"

Lynx's large, powerfully built gray-striped black cat form slinked from the shadow of a building. She was baring her teeth with a fierce growl as she approached Hyroc. Hyroc slipped into a fighting stance in preparation to defend himself. Lynx's cat form was a serious threat. She had the size to take on a bear and the power to kill one. But even as dangerous as she was, he detested the idea of killing her. Sure, she had deceived him with their relationship as the whole thing was just a ploy by her father to ambush him, but he still had feelings for her. After what she did to him, it didn't make sense. Some of the time they shared during her deception had to have been genuine. And when her father had captured him, Hyroc could tell she hated watching what was being done to him. Why else would she have given him some water and tried cleaning his wounds when he was Eagle's prisoner? She even offered to talk her father into sparing him. She cared, she had to. Maybe he could talk her down, avoid fighting, and save her life. But he was prepared to end her if he was wrong and the worse came to worst.

"Lynx," Hyroc said in his gentlest voice. "You don't have to do this." She stopped, her snarl faded, and she tipped her head, regarding him with confusion. "You don't have to do this," he repeated. "We don't need to fight. I don't need to fight you. Just walk away."

"Walk away?" she said, puzzled. "Aren't you mad about everything I did to you?"

"Well, what you did to me didn't feel good, but no, I'm not angry about it anymore." Hyroc pointed at Eagle with his sword. "You weren't the one responsible for your deception. He *was*. You weren't the one who created that trap. He was. He was responsible for every bad thing you did to me."

"Don't listen to him," Eagle warned. "He's just trying to separate us so we're easier to kill. After he's done with me, he will come after you. Now, kill him!"

"I don't want to hurt you, Lynx." Hyroc lowered his sword, moving into a more relaxed and vulnerable position. Lynx looked uncertainly from Hyroc to her father and back. "Lynx, I know our relationship was a fabrication, but not all of it was. Some of your true feelings did come through. I felt them, and I know you felt mine. We shared special moments. I saw a glimmer of how excited you were when I gave you the green crystal cat."

Her eyes lit happily. "You felt the same?"

"Stop it!" Eagle shouted. "Lynx, don't listen to him. He's just trying to get inside your head. He's an Anamagi."

"I would not lie about that, not to you. Please, walk away."

She looked longingly at her father. "But he's my father. He's always taken care of me. I can't just abandon him."

Eagle broke into a more caring tone. "Lynx, darling, I swore I always would protect you." He pointed a clawed finger sharply at Hyroc, his voice regaining its edge. "He is the one I've always warned you about. I have the gift of foresight. I saw him kill you. You must trust me. This is our only chance to stop what I saw from coming to pass. We can only stop him *together*."

"What if he's right?" she questioned. "What if *you're* just lying?"

"LOOK INTO MY EYES, LYNX!" Hyroc shouted. "On the graves of my parents and Marcus and June, I promise you I do not want to fight you. I love you!" The last part he hadn't meant to say. It seemed to escape on its own. Lynx's eyes flew wide with shock, and her mouth fell partly open. "I'm not the liar here." Hyroc pointed an accusatory finger at Eagle. "He is! Practically everything he says is a lie. He is the one who sneaks around in the shadows and messes with people's minds." With a wide wave of his arm, Hyroc indicated everything around them. "And this is all it's wrought! Is all this death and destruction what you wanted? What about the townsfolk? They were innocent victims who had nothing to do with our feud. Why did they deserve to die? And back at your camp, you saw what the shadow demon did to the trees and plants around it. It was sucking the life out of the forest! Is that what you wanted?"

Lynx looked around, her expression growing horrified as if this were the first time she had seen her surroundings.

Hyroc pointed at Eagle. "And it was all *his doing*! I was happily making a life far away in Elswood. I didn't even know either of you existed. But he wouldn't leave me be. He sent monsters to attack me. One of which would have happily wiped out that village to get to me. And those villagers, like these townsfolk, were not even a part of this." Hyroc took a deep breath. What he was about to say next stirred up strong emotions. "And – and what brought me here cost me dearly. It cost me friends and the one person who was the closest thing to a mother I have ever had. No one should ever have to endure what was done to her." Hyroc hastily wiped away a tear. "So I ask you one last time, Lynx. Is this what you wanted?"

She shook her head. "No," Lynx said emphatically. "This isn't what I wanted."

Hyroc nodded. "He's been lying to you your whole life. I don't know what he's made you do, but I know none was your fault."

"No, Lynx, darling, I wouldn't lie to you," Eagle said. "It's not a lie that I love you. It's not a lie when I say I would give my life to protect you."

"Is it true you tried to kill a whole village just to get to *him*?" Lynx asked sharply.

"No, no, I would never do something so heinous."

Lynx's expression turned shocked. "No, you did?"

"All right, yes, I did. I had to do something! But it was a human village," Eagle admitted. "They were only humans."

"You don't have to listen to him anymore," Hyroc said. "Lynx, please, just walk away. Go follow your own path."

Lynx looked from her father to Hyroc and back again. "Goodbye, Father," she said in a sorrowful tone. She turned and sprinted off, disappearing through a cloud of smoke.

"NO, COME BACK!" Eagle shouted in a pain-laden voice. He stared transfixed at the spot from which she had vanished. He fixed a furious, dangerous glare on Hyroc. "She's gone. You took my daughter from me. Even after everything I've done to stop you, you still took my daughter from me. I always knew you would – but I refused to believe it. I understand my mistakes now. I will not make the same ones next time, Anamagi. I *will* come back and finish the job." Eagle looked up as if seeing someone coming behind Hyroc. When Hyroc followed his gaze, he saw Fenrald and several soldiers approaching. "I will avenge her!" Eagle said as he darted toward the West gate.

"He's headed off to join the rest of his forces in the market!" Fenrald said as he came to Hyroc. "I'm ready to finish this. Let's go." He, Hyroc, and the rest of the group rushed off in pursuit of Eagle. They came to Eagle's remaining forces in the market. The Western gate was at their back. The Glacial forces were diminished but still outnumbered them. There was more fighting ahead of them, but victory was assured.

"You are surrounded and outnumbered," Fenrald called out to the Ferals. "Your defeat is assured. Lay down your arms and surrender. Now!"

"We would rather die than bear the yoke of the Anamagi again," Eagle shouted.

"As you wish," Fenrald retorted coldly. He waved his sword forward, and the battle resumed. "Hyroc, with me. He's going to use the chaos of the battle to escape. We have to get to him before he can, or this whole cycle of death will continue."

Hyroc nodded, and the two of them jumped into the fray. They steadily fought through the Ferals to the back of their line at the gate. Several Ferals at the back began to flee through the gate. Eagle joined them when he saw Fenrald and Hyroc coming for him. Hyroc pushed through an opening, but Fenrald got hung up with the enemy soldiers again.

"Go!" Fenrald shouted. "Don't let him escape. I'll be right behind you."

Hyroc did as instructed and rushed after Eagle. He was now through the gate and pursuing his quarry into the forest. Hyroc caught him, catching his breath, bent over with a hand pushed against a fallen tree.

"Eagle!" Hyroc yelled. "It's time to end this."

Eagle pushed himself upright, turning to face Hyroc. "So that fateful hour has finally arrived," he said, drawing his sword. "Isn't it enough for you that you have taken everything from me? Why must you insist on taking my life as well?"

"Well, you killed my parents," Hyroc said. "And as long as you're alive, you'll still just keep doing this, but mostly because you killed my parents."

"Ah, you'll have avenged your parents. Why is vengeance so important to you? Isn't there some moral incentive to avoid vengeance?"

"Maybe, but I don't care. Not with you."

Eagle pointed his sword accusatorially at Hyroc. "Vengeance is a precarious path. Some are never the same once they start down it. Are you truly prepared for the consequences?"

"I'll deal with those consequences when they arrive," Hyroc said. "Right now, all of my attention is focused on you."

"Then, by all means, let's end this, puppet!"

"Gladly!"

Hyroc swiped his sword at Eagle. Eagle blocked it and two accompanying strikes. He backstepped behind the trunk of a tree. When Hyroc came around it, Eagle sent a throwing knife at his head. Hyroc jerked his upper body away from it, and the knife brushed against his cheek. It laid open a thin slice in his face. Hyroc dabbed the injury with his finger to see how much he was bleeding, then came after Eagle again. The clang of steel resounded through the forest as the two exchanged blows. During one exchange, as he blocked a blow from Eagle, Hyroc thrust his hand forward to send a fireball. Eagle slapped Hyroc's hand to the side as the fireball formed and the ball of flames shot over his shoulder. The impact of the fireball on a tree briefly bathed the area in a bright blue glow. Hyroc kicked Eagle against a tree, approaching him with an overhead strike. Eagle jolted out of the way, causing Hyroc's sword to crack into the bark. Eagle punched Hyroc in the stomach as he darted past him. Hyroc doubled over slightly but could still take a swing at Eagle. The tip of the sword nicked Eagle in the shoulder.

"You understand why I did it, don't you?" Eagle said, backpedaling.

"Because you're a crazed warmonger?" Hyroc retorted. He took another swing at Eagle, who blocked it.

"No, I did it because I saw our potential, and the Anamagi stood in the way of a better future. It was nothing personal."

Hyroc struck as he answered. "IT ALL FELT PLENTY PERSONAL TO ME!" Hyroc followed his blow with a quick series of powerful strikes. He got through Eagle's guard and slashed him across the chest. It was merely a glancing blow, but it opened up a gash that issued blood, creating a growing dark spot in Eagle's tunic. Eagle darted out of Hyroc's reach, checking the wound with his hand. When it came away marked with blood, he stared at his hand in astonishment as if he was suddenly aware he could be harmed in this fight.

"No!" Eagle said. "This isn't what I saw. I don't die here." He blocked a strike from Hyroc before sprinting away. He came to a stop when a figure blocked his path.

"Yes, *you will*," Fenrald growled.

"You're – you're alive? What? No, you're not supposed to be alive, still." He thrust an accusatory finger at Hyroc. "You did this. What did you do?"

"I did nothing," Hyroc said. "You did everything!"

Hyroc and Fenrald rushed him. With both attacking simultaneously, Eagle could do nothing but defend against the constant barrage of blows. Eagle backpedaled frantically as he fended off their blades, trying to prevent either of them from getting behind him. When an opening presented itself, Eagle darted out of reach.

"I saw both of you lying dead in the streets of that town. It was burning, and all its citizens were dead. Then, I saw myself, my daughter, and all the Ferals escape safely into the Northlands. The rage of Mastgar descended upon your village. They slew all there and burned it to the ground. I saw the charred bodies of the villagers heaped into a pile. I saw the end of the Guidance Wol'dger and the Anamagi. I saw it! It remained the same for all these years. Why has it suddenly changed?"

"You saw wrong!" Fenrald said as he and Hyroc charged in for another attack. Similarly, they pushed Eagle into an uncontrollable retreat as they assailed him with their swords.

"No!" Eagle shouted. "I saw it. I know I did. I did something wrong. But I can fix it. I will fix it!" He darted through an opening in the attack, scooped up a handful of dirt as he moved, and threw it in Hyroc's face.

Hyroc's eyes stung as dirt blinded him. While he was momentarily unable to see, he couldn't defend himself. Eagle came for him, and Fenrald shoved Hyroc out of the way. Fenrald exchanged blows with Eagle to take his attention off Hyroc while he recovered. Eyes watering, Hyroc used his Flame Claw to pull the dirt from his eyes. The dirt pulled away, and his vision cleared. Wiping away the residual tears, he returned his attention to Eagle. Just as he turned, he saw Eagle get through Fenrald's guard and stab him in the abdomen. Fenrald's whole body seized up, and his sword fell to the ground with a metallic clang.

"NO!" Hyroc screamed as he rushed to his uncle's side. Eagle jogged away. Hyroc slid to the ground, using his arms to embrace his uncle. Fenrald was bleeding badly, but he was still breathing and conscious. Hyroc ripped a strip of cloth from his tunic beneath his armor and shoved it onto the wound to help stanch the flow of blood. He got a start when Fenrald seized him by the collar. "Don't waste your time with me!" Fenrald growled. "Go."

"No, I am not going to leave you," Hyroc argued.

"You must. If he gets away, more lives will certainly be lost. Leave me! *Finish this.*"

Reluctantly, Hyroc stood. Dread filled him as he ripped his eyes away from his injured uncle. He knew this was probably the last time either would speak. He bolted after Eagle. Eagle hadn't made much progress, as his fatigue was starting to take its toll.

"Eagle!" Hyroc shouted as an uncontrollable rage bubbled up inside of him. "This is where this ends."

"No, this is not the end," Eagle said breathlessly. "Not for me. It's yours."

Eagle rushed at Hyroc, shedding all signs of previous fatigue. The ferocity with which he attacked forced Hyroc only to defend. When Hyroc got an opening, he retaliated. But as he struck Eagle's blade, he flung his other hand forward and squeezed Eagle's injury. Eagle groaned in pain as he desperately tried to shake free of Hyroc. He backhanded Hyroc in the face, which caused him to flinch and let go. Eagle backpedaled.

"I would've thought an Anamagi was above such savagery," Eagle said grimacing.

"You taught me nothing is off-limits with you," Hyroc said, stepping forward. They exchanged another round of strikes. "You've taught me quite a *lot* over the years."

"Really? Do you now see the merits of me trying to wipe out the Guidance Wol'dger, and you wish to pledge your loyalty to my cause?"

"No, you taught me the value of friendship and compassion."

"Friends?" Eagle spat. "You're referring to those flat-faced humans you followed around like a lost puppy. It's disgraceful for one of *us* to even associate with those weak humans, let alone to call them friends. You're a traitor to all Wol'dger."

"Call me what you wish. I don't care, but I would die for them."

"I'll happily oblige your request." Eagle and Hyroc exchanged a series of fierce strikes. They separated after Hyroc landed a series of punches on Eagle and kicked him away.

"I must admit you have a formidable hook," Eagle said.

"You also taught me *that*," Hyroc said coldly. "If you hadn't separated me from my parents, I may not have learned how to fight. There's a lot I should thank you for."

"Thank me?" Eagle puzzled.

"Yes. Thank you for sending that Shade Hunter after me in Elswood. Without it, I may never have started on this path. And if not for its essence corrupting those spiders, I would never have learned bravery. I also must thank you for sending that witch and their blood werewolf hostage. Einar was his name; he may never have been set free if I hadn't done it. But I must thank you, especially for the witch. Defeating him and saving all the lives of those villagers turned my friends and me into outcasts. And our search for a new home inevitably led us out of Arnaira and into Mastgar. Then, I came here. You see why I have to thank you. You helped me find my people and the last of my family. I may never have arrived here if you had just left me well enough alone. Everything you did only led me back to you. So thank you."

Eagle's eyes widened with the startling realization Hyroc was right. Hyroc's arrival was all his fault. He merely led him closer every time he tried to get rid of Hyroc. And if he had left Hyroc alone, Hyroc would never have intervened, and his plan to destroy the Guidance Wol'dger would have succeeded. He, alone, was at fault for the failure of his plan.

"It's very ironic, don't you think?" Hyroc said. "You were your own worst enemy."

"Well, I won't make the same mistake twice," Eagle said. He and Hyroc exchanged a round of sword strikes. "Why won't you die!" Eagle attacked Hyroc again, but Hyroc easily fended off his blade.

"But I've always been closer to you than anyone else." Eagle stared at him, confused. "Everything I am is because of you."

"Enough of this!" Eagle shouted. He rushed at Hyroc, and the two of them exchanged blows. Hyroc got through Eagle's guard and slashed him across the abdomen. It was a grievous wound.

"You made me who I am," Hyroc said before Eagle fell.

Eagle was bleeding badly, but he was still alive.

"I am defeated," Eagle said in a pained voice. "Now, claim your vengeance. End my suffering."

Hyroc grabbed the hilt of his sword with both hands; the blade faced down as Hyroc prepared a killing strike. "You ruined so many lives," Hyroc said. "Lives of people I knew, people who made me a part of their family. I lost so many of them. You took so many away from me. You took my mother, Shrana. My father, Jasok. Svald, Helen, Walter, Harold. I almost lost my friends alongside them. You took my home in Elswood away from me. Everything I've ever held dear, you've taken from me."

"Then fulfill your vengeance upon me for all your grievances," Eagle said.

Hyroc shook his head. "No," he said. Hyroc tossed his sword aside. Eagle regarded him, baffled. "I've taken so many lives because of you. I'm tired of taking lives. I *will not* take any more because of you."

"Then, you're as weak as I have always thought. You can't do what is required of you. I should never have expected anything less from an Anamagi."

"Perhaps it is a weakness I can't make myself do it. I won't, *but he will.*"

Hyroc stepped out of the way as Fenrald charged forward and drove his blade into Eagle. "For my brother, his wife, my love, Shandshra, and my family," Fenrald growled. Eagle went still. It was over.

Hyroc patted Fenrald comfortingly on the shoulder. "We did it," he said relieved. Fenrald happily grabbed Hyroc's head and pulled him closer. Suddenly, his hand slipped from his sword, and he fell to the ground. His wounds had depleted the last of his strength.

"No, no, don't leave me," Hyroc pleaded. "Just hang on until I can get help."

"I'm sorry, my time is all but spent," Fenrald apologized.

"No, don't talk like that."

"This isn't so bad. I go to meet my family and my ancestors without regret. It will be a glorious and joyful celebration. We saved our people. One couldn't wish for a better death than to die protecting those you love. I will tell them your great deeds if they do not already know. They will be proud of you."

Tears streamed down Hyroc's face as he felt the life slipping out of his uncle. All he ever did was lose people he cared about. He had watched the life slip out of Marcus as sickness took him, powerless to do anything. As was he the night he lost June. He didn't want to do it, but twisted by shadow demon essence, she was too dangerous, and he had to dispatch her. There was nothing he could do to fix her. Now, he would lose Fenrald, the last of his family, and he could do nothing.

"I lost my parents," Hyroc said. "BUT I WILL NOT LOSE YOU!"

Hyroc shoved his hands on top of Fenrald's wound, feeling hot blood on his fingers. Fenrald weakly gasped in pain. Hyroc funneled as much magical energy through his hands and into the wound as he could muster without losing consciousness. He focused on the skin, muscle, and the sinew. Then, his focus moved the energy to the organs, extending his intent to repair any damage that had occurred to them. He next guided it onto the bone. He could feel the energy knitting everything back together. Anything vital was fixed along with the bone. Hyroc extended his attention to creating blood to ensure the blood loss that had already occurred would not be fatal. He reversed his focus as he backed out, stitching the wound back together from the bottom up. He severed the flow of energy, nearly falling face-first to the ground from the sudden hit to his strength as he depleted his Quintessence reserve.

Fenrald gasped loudly as life surged back into him. Fenrald wore a bewildered expression. After a long moment, he turned his attention to Hyroc. "You – you – you saved me," Fenrald said. He got to his feet and held a hand to help Hyroc stand.

"Yes, uncle, I saved you," Hyroc said mirthfully.

"Thank you. How am I ever supposed to repay that?"

"I don't want you to repay me. I just want you to be my uncle."

"I can do that. Yes, I can do that." He embraced Hyroc in a brief hug.

"The whispers lied to me," Eagle said in a ghostly, thin voice. "They said I would defeat the Anamagi. He said I was making a better world. He said I couldn't fail."

"Who lied to you?" Hyroc asked. "Who told you this."

"Drakashon." Eagle drew his last breath.

So passed Eagle, the leader of the Feral Wol'dgers, the bane of the Anamagi.

Chapter 40
Lamentations

THE RED SUN SHONE DOWN on Forestgold through a smoky haze. The fires from the battle had raged through the night, but, for the most part, they had burned themselves out. The damage was mainly confined to the buildings near the northern gate. The charred ruins and smoldering shells of structures were one reminder of the carnage. The rest of the town was still largely intact. Glacials and townsfolk alike worked to clear the streets of debris and corpses. The bodies of the Ferals were heaped onto carts and unceremoniously dumped into a trench outside the town. The remains of the slain citizens and Glacials were treated with the utmost respect. They were placed on carts before being wheeled off for dignified burial wherever the family wished.

Practically all the attacking Ferals had been killed, with few escaping into the surrounding forest. They would move away into the Northlands if they had any sense. But despite the advantage the Glacial forces held in numbers over the Ferals, repelling a far better-armed enemy had exacted a heavy toll. They had expended much Glacial blood to achieve this victory. Every family from their village felt the sting of loss. But none could say their lives had been lost in vain. Without their sacrifice, the Glacials and their village would have been lost.

Hyroc and Fenrald stood off the side of the road, watching the somber procession of carts trundle past. They offered the passersby what little condolences and encouragement they could. They honored each of the fallen by laying a stalk of violet lupine across their bodies. It seemed a meager tribute to their valiant sacrifice, but it was all they could offer. Despite the necessity of defeating Eagle's forces and the glory the fallen had achieved, Hyroc couldn't help feeling sorrowful so many had to die.

"You know what I've been having trouble figuring out?" Fenrald said in a hushed, reverent tone after laying a lupine stalk on one of the fallen. "Why did Eagle's visions of the future regarding the battle end up being so far off? His seer abilities always seemed to warn him when I came for him because I could never catch him by surprise. He seemed to know what I was going to do before I even knew I was going to do it. And yet, when he came here to execute his meticulous plan, after years of patient planning, he died when we were supposed to die. I don't understand what happened."

Hyroc laid down another lupine stalk. He rubbed his furry chin for a long moment before answering. "I think it's because he was seeing possibilities or possible futures. During your animal form training, when you first got your transformation ability, do you remember the red Spirit Stone that took you to the red cave?"

"Where you had to fight that twisted image of yourself? Fenrald asked. Hyroc nodded. "Yeah, I remember it well. That was the scariest part of my training."

"Well, I think it was something similar with Eagle. That twisted image was actually a version of yourself. If you had followed a different, obviously much darker path, there was a possibility you might have turned into that."

"Ah, I see. I faced a Feral possibility of myself."

"Precisely. But you didn't turn into that because you made the wrong choices or right choices, depending on how you want to think about it. You made different choices, which took you on a different path. That different path led to a different outcome or future. You started in the same place but ended up somewhere else."

Fenrald stared at him, confused, not comprehending what he meant. "Okay, my Guardian mentor explained it to me like this. Time is like a stream. It flows only in one direction: forward. But when you drop a stone in it, the flow changes. The bigger the stone, the bigger the change. Our decisions are like those stones. They change the flow of time a little, but we still end up in pretty much the same place. Now, if you block the stream, symbolizing a huge decision, the stream will go somewhere else or get stuck and flood. And you can think of the flooding as an obstacle in your life you need to overcome. Eventually, the stream will break through the blockage and continue on its original path."

"I think I understand," Fenrald said.

"Now, think of that stream metaphor regarding Eagle seeing the future. He saw upstream into the future. His and your decisions were small stones, which means no matter what either of you did, it wouldn't cause much of a change. That's why he could predict what you would do: you couldn't change the stream enough for it to be a problem. Therefore, he always saw you coming. I was in a different stream, and no matter what I did, it had no bearing on either of you. That is until I arrived in Mastgar. When I arrived, I dropped a huge stone into the stream of you two. That caused a considerable change in your streams, which altered the flow so much that what Eagle originally saw was no longer correct."

"If I understand what you're saying correctly, if Eagle had meditated to check the validity of his visions, he would have seen something else?"

"I believe so. But there's one more thing. Whenever Eagle saw me in a vision or however that worked, he sent something to kill me. And when he did that, he dropped a bunch of big stones in his stream. Or my stream depending on how you look at it. And those stones piled up enough to block his stream, which altered it and caused the flow to change. That change, then, made it flow into my stream."

"So his actions to keep you away only brought you closer."

Hyroc nodded. "Yes."

Fenrald grunted a laugh. "I see. That's quite an ironic twist of fate." He was quiet a moment, but his expression turned thoughtful.

"But there's one last thing I don't understand. Eagle was convinced you would kill his daughter, which caused this whole mess. But you didn't kill her. You let her live."

"I know, I've also been giving that some thought," Hyroc agreed. "Maybe I was on course to kill her before Eagle acted and changed things. I don't understand either."

An awkward silence descended as both pondered the conundrum.

"Wait," Fenrald eventually said. "Actually, in a way, I think you did kill her." Hyroc shot him a quizzical look. "The person she was, enslaved by her father's will and devoted to his cause, did die. You killed that version of her by destroying the original person she was and creating a new, better version."

"That's an interesting way of putting it, but you're right. I changed the person she was."

"I guess, in a way, Eagle was correct. It just wasn't in the way he expected."

"I think we can agree things would have been much better without the need for all this bloodshed."

"I agree."

Hyroc heard the joyful yowl of Kit. The cougar wended through the queue of figures and carts and bounded excitedly toward him. In his eagerness, he bumped into Hyroc's leg, nearly knocking him over.

"I'm happy to see you too, buddy," Hyroc said, catching himself with an outstretched hand on a tree trunk. He crouched and held out his hand to rub between Kit's ears. The big cat rubbed affectionately against Hyroc's hand while purring loudly.

"FERAL!" they heard someone yell atop the town's wall. Another call sounded from ground level. Town guards marched to intercept their adversary. Fenrald and Hyroc drew their swords, with Kit following as they moved to join the group. In the trees, Hyroc saw a four-legged shape with the red animal mark come into view. He recognized that Feral. It was Lynx.

"Hold!" Hyroc yelled. The guards came to a halt, regarding him with astonished expressions. "This one's friendly."

"Friendly?" Fenrald questioned, taken aback. "That's Eagle's daughter."

"I'm well aware of who that is, uncle." Fenrald grabbed his arm when he took a step forward.

"Wait, this might be some trap. This might be one final attempt from her to avenge her father by killing you, the last Anamagi,"

"It's not a trap."

"Need I remind you she struck up a relationship solely to lure you into a trap."

"You don't need to remind me. I remember it well. This is *not* a trap. Trust me." Fenrald loosened his grip.

"Okay, but I'll be right here should you need anything. You only have to call."

"Kit, stay," Hyroc said to his feline companion. Hyroc walked over to Lynx. "Lynx, it's good to see you," he said with slight trepidation. "What brings you back here?"

Lynx scanned her surroundings cautiously before transforming into her natural form. "I wanted to thank you for talking me into leaving." She gazed toward the pile of bodies outside the town. "Otherwise, I would be with the others right now."

"I don't want you to thank me. I know it was already a hard enough decision for you to make. I'm sorry about your father. He left me no other choice. You understand that, don't you? If he had given me another choice, I would not have done what was done."

"Yes, I understand. I said my peace, so I should get going and stop making those guards nervous."

"Wait," Hyroc said, lunging forward to grab her arm. "I don't want you to go."

She turned to give him a baffled look. "You don't? Why? I'm the daughter of the man who killed your parents and made your life so miserable. Why would you want me to stay?"

"Because I love you. I meant it when I first said it last night, and I mean it now."

"Even after everything my father did to you?"

"I don't blame you for any of it. He lied to you and made you an unwilling participant. I know this, but I don't blame you. It wasn't your fault." Hyroc moved his head forward to kiss her. Lynx pushed a hand against his chest and held him back. Hyroc regarded her with confusion.

"No, I can't," Lynx said, her tone revealing she was greatly conflicted. "Every time I look at you, I'll be reminded of the pain and suffering my father caused you. And in your village, whenever someone looks at me, they'll be reminded of *him*. And my glowing red animal mark will be a stark reminder of my shame for everyone to see. We can't be together. I'm sorry. My father had determined my course all my life, and now I must find my own path. A path far away from anything he had influenced. Goodbye, Hyroc. Thank you for this gift." She rubbed the green crystal cat. "Words cannot convey my gratitude for saving my life." She kissed him on the cheek before walking off.

Feeling downtrodden, Hyroc watched her until she disappeared into the trees. He turned and headed back to the open road beyond the forest.

"Everything all right?" Fenrald asked. He lifted a hand to put on Hyroc's shoulder, but Hyroc moved past too swiftly.

At the forest's edge, Hyroc sat at the base of a tree and slumped against its trunk. He covered his face with one hand and let out an exasperated breath. Then he felt someone grab his arm and gently rub his shoulder. He turned his head to see Freija. She grabbed his hand, giving him a comforting look. Hyroc smiled somberly, but he was happy. This was home.

The End

Epilogue

HYROC STRODE UP TO THE gate of Vettenfelth, the capital of Mastgar. Its walls were tall and made from large gray blocks of stone. Turrets and towers topped with dark green roofs adorned the fortification at even intervals. Its walls seemed to stretch on endlessly. Hyroc was amazed by the size of the city. It dwarfed Forna and Forestgold and was bigger than both combined. It may have even been more prominent than The Tree of Memories. Enormous tracts of green farmland surrounded the city, with only a modest gap of bare soil separating them from the wall. The city was nestled into a bowl-shaped valley surrounded by low mountains and steep hills.

A constant crowd of bodies, carts, and carriages flowed through a sizeable wood-roofed tunnel. The tunnel ended at a short drawbridge that spanned a furrowed stream leading through an open gate and into the city. Towering spires filled the capital, and enormous rectangular structures, bigger than any buildings Hyroc had ever seen, were spread throughout. Hyroc had no idea it was possible to concentrate so many people in one place. He received the usual stares from bystanders he passed, those who had never laid eyes on a Wol'dger, but their looks gravitated more to wonder than fear.

Hyroc stepped to the side of the street, reviewing a map of the city that instructed him to reach his destination. He was glad of the forethought of it as the city was more challenging to navigate than an unfamiliar forest. Confident of his destination, he rolled the map before continuing. The murmur of voices clashing in the air increased as Hyroc approached the market district. When he reached the market proper, the sound of so many voices vying for dominance reminded him of the roar of a waterfall. *How could anybody concentrate amid so much noise,* he wondered. He gazed through the windows of the various shops, trying to find his destination. It was here somewhere. The sign over one shop caught his attention. "The Grumpy Wol'dger," he read aloud, baffled. He shook his head in humored disbelief. This had to be it. He eagerly rushed over to it! He had long awaited this moment.

"ELSA, DONOVAN," Hyroc called.

The brother and sister duo poked their heads out of the shop, affixing him with joyful expressions. "Hyroc!" they both yelled in greeting. They no longer wore clothing made from unsightly animal skins patched together. Their garb was fine, but despite its richness, it was not flashy or extravagant, and it still retained the hearty, rugged quality suited to the woods. Hyroc even thought he saw a golden necklace around Elsa's neck. His friends seemed to have settled quite well into their new surroundings.

Hyroc hugged Elsa before he and Donovan shook hands and patted each other on the shoulders.

"It's so good to see you again," Elsa said. "We've missed you since leaving you with your uncle and the Glacials. How is he?"

"Fenrald's good," Hyroc said.

"I bet the two of you have had to do a lot of catching up," Donovan said.

"Yes, *a lot,*" Hyroc agreed. He indicated the shop's sign. "I don't need to guess whose idea that was," he sighed.

Donovan beamed mischievously.

"Come on inside," Elsa said.

"Yes, I'd like to see what the two of you have here."

The shop was nearly twice as large as his uncle's cabin. Furs of every kind dominated the interior of the shop. Various animal mounts adorned the walls, including a scythe horn and a bear skin rug. The contents of this room were worth more than he had ever possessed. Though it was not of greater worth than his Flame Claw. He was content with that but wasn't opposed to having a little more if an honest opportunity presented itself.

Elsa ushered him over to a chair at a table at the back of the shop before setting a kettle to boil in a hearth. Hyroc aimed the palm of a clawed hand at the container, using his Flame Claw to accelerate the heating of the water. White steam quickly began to issue out of it. His friends regarded him with astonished comprehension. They had been doing without the convenience of his Flame Claw for so long they had almost forgotten about it. Hyroc smiled.

"Right," Elsa acknowledged as she donned leather gloves to retrieve the hot kettle. Donovan divvied out the cups and helped Elsa pour the tea.

"How did the two of you get all of this?" Hyroc said, indicating the room with the sweep of his hand.

"It was kind of a weird coincidence," Donovan said. "The night we arrived in the city, we bought a room in a tavern. While we were having our supper, a visiting Mastgar Baron overheard our conversation. We must have said your name, and he recognized it. And you're not going to believe this. You remember that girl Sandra we rescued from that slaver caravan." Hyroc nodded. "That Baron was her uncle."

"You're kidding me," Hyroc said surprised. He sipped his tea as it had now cooled enough to drink. The hot tea had a pleasant, earthy taste.

"I'm as serious as a shadow demon attack," Donovan assured him. "He was so grateful for our assistance in rescuing her he invited us on a hunt with him."

"What did Curtis think of all this?"

"He wasn't with us when we went hunting with the Baron," Elsa interjected. She pointed to the shop roof to indicate something obscured from view by the roof. "We had already dropped him off at the mage school on that tall hill overlooking the city."

Hyroc nodded his understanding.

"During that hunt," Donovan continued, "that baron was so impressed by our hunting prowess he hired us to lead his future hunts. Then, we got to trapping and hunting for pelts between them. Slowly, word got around about us. Then, before we knew it, we were getting all kinds of contracts with the Mastgar royal, which were very lucrative. Then one thing led to another, and then here we are."

"I'm glad for the two of you to have done so incredibly well for yourselves," Hyroc said happily.

"Thank you," his friends said in turn.

"And what about you?" Elsa asked. "I heard you and the villagers got into it something fierce with the Feral. We've heard all kinds of stories about a town getting demolished and a battle. What on earth happened after we left?"

Hyroc looked distant for a long moment as he stared thoughtfully into the cloudy white substance in his cup. "Eagle is what happened," he said. "He had plans beneath his plans. All these long years, he had been working toward a goal nobody saw coming. We narrowly stopped him before his master scheme came to fruition. He almost won. It was only through the expenditure of an immense amount of Glacial and Mastgar blood that we defeated him. But he and the Ferals are no more."

"Good," Elsa said.

"Good riddance," Donovan agreed. "He deserved nothing less from what he did to our families. I'm sorry we missed it."

Hyroc nodded. "Yes, justice was served," he said. Hyroc retrieved a bottle from his knapsack and flipped the cork out with his thumb's claw. "I propose a toast." Everyone tossed the dregs in their cups into the hearth before Hyroc refilled them with a clear brownish liquid from the bottle. They raised their cups. "To all those we lost along the way. To our mothers, fathers, uncles, aunts, grandfathers, and grandmothers, friends –" Hyroc paused in saddened contemplation "and unfortunate adversaries with no choice." They clanged their cups together before drinking.

Hyroc walked up the tall hill overlooking the Mastgar capital. He was amazed when the school came into view. It looked like a castle with its many spires reaching high into the sky. It was an imposing structure, yet its fortified appearance had a friendly air. He passed through the gate, coming into an immaculate garden that stretched in all directions with strange trees behind bright green hedges. There were no gardeners; enchanted tools floated about tending to various chores. Hyroc passed a pair of clippers trimming a hedge as he approached the school's main entrance.

"Hyroc!" a familiar voice called. Hyroc smiled when he saw Curtis running out the door to greet him. The boy was garbed in fine dark blue clothing inlaid with some shiny metal, forming the school's various insignia and sigils. "I'm so glad to see you." Hyroc nodded his appreciation before pointing curiously at the pair of enchanted sheers. "I know," Curtis said happily. "Isn't it amazing no one needs to do the chores around here?"

"Yes, that sounds fantastic. I'll have to learn how to do that sometime."

"You really should; I bet it would make your life much easier. The mages here teach classes on that if you want to learn."

"I will keep it in mind. How are you getting along here?"

"Well, I'm the only lightning mage here, so the teachers and students always ask me to do things with my lightning. I guess it's been a long time since they've had one of me, and they are very excited to work with it. They have also been helping me to focus and better control my ability. Watch this." Curtis lifted his hand and sent a lightning bolt skyward. It moved in a figure-eight. When the front of the bolt curved down toward Hyroc, he realized it had the head of a snake. It even started moving in a serpentine pattern. Curtis didn't maintain the spell long before dismissing it and excitedly turning toward Hyroc.

"What did you think?" Curtis asked expectantly.

"That was amazing."

"LOOK OUT!" another student in the garden yelled. Hyroc turned to see a fireball flying straight at him. Hyroc used his Flame Claw to protect his hand and scooped the fireball out of the air. It turned from orange to blue. "Wow, he's got blue fire," a nearby student said.

"How do I make mine turn blue?" another asked jealously.

"Hey, no roasting the Wol'dger," Hyroc said half-humoredly. He closed his fist to extinguish the fire he held.

"Sorry," the attacking student said.

"Since the three of us left you at the Glacial village," Curtis asked. "Has anything happened?"

Hyroc smiled. "*You have no idea.*"

Hyroc stepped into Darius Ashfin's office. The mage sat on a soft padded chair.

"Hello again, my Wol'dger friend," he said as Hyroc sat. "Tea?" He made a swirling hand motion, and a tray that held cups and biscuits and a hot steaming kettle floated in front of them. Hyroc gave his cup a dismissive wave but indicated he would accept a tea biscuit. Seemingly of its own accord, the kettle poured a cup of tea for Darius before the filled cup, and the biscuit floated over to a small table next to Hyroc. Then, with a waving motion from the mage, the tray floated away.

"How go things at the village?" Darius asked before taking a sip of his tea.

"Good, everything's good," Hyroc said. "They're prospering as allies of the Crown. And the rebuilding of Forestgold is progressing faster than anticipated."

"Good."

"I wanted to ask you about something while I'm here. Right before Eagle died, he mentioned something about whispers. Do you know anything about what he was saying?"

The mage rubbed his chin as he thought. "Yes, I believe so. There is something called the Wraith Whispers. They are in a channel similar to a shadow demon's speech, and you cannot perceive it unless you are tuned into the channel as you are. But to hear the whispers, you must delve deep into a peculiar dark magic. A specific ritual is required, but you'll be able to hear the whispers for a short time at the end. Nobody knows where these whispers originate, but many warnings exist against listening to them. Many a mage or warlock have met a grizzly end by listening to them. Some have received great rewards, but rarely. Simply put, listening to them is usually a good way to die."

Hyroc nodded. "It seems Eagle fell into the former category," he said darkly.

"Indeed."

"With his final breath, Eagle said the name 'Drakashon.' Do you know what that is?"

The mage was suddenly more intrigued. "No, I am unfamiliar with that name. I could dig into the school's archives and get back to you if my research yields anything."

"I would greatly appreciate that."

"But I can leave you with this. There are things in this world that are unfathomably ancient, far older than humanity's history. Some of these things are almost elemental in nature, persisting similarly to fundamental forces in the world. We barely understand them. They are like the air we breathe. *They simply are.*"

"Interesting," Hyroc said.

"Indeed. But be aware the answers you seek will all likely lead to nothing."

"Or just be so incredibly dull they won't even deserve mention."

The mage laughed, raising his cup in a salute of agreement.

If you enjoyed this book, the complete Sentinel Flame Series, Hyroc, Tree of Memories, Outcasts, is available at https://www.adamfreestone.com/ or Amazon.com

https://a.co/d/8XfiNHo

https://a.co/d/9iH4LxE

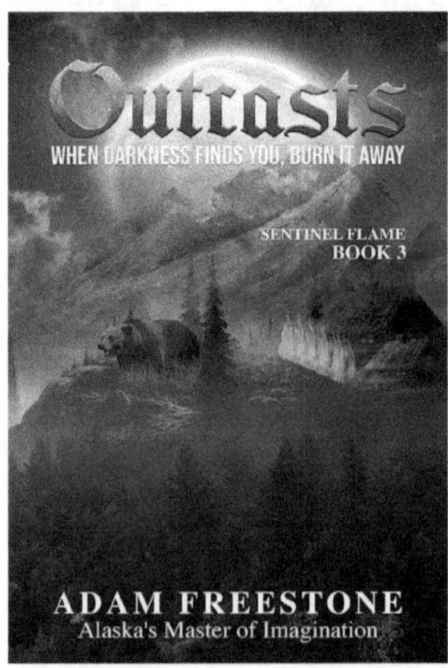

https://a.co/d/fRqbyWZ

www.ingramcontent.com/pod-product-compliance
Lightning Source LLC
Chambersburg PA
CBHW071144020726
47502CB00002B/265

* 9 7 8 1 5 9 4 3 3 7 6 6 6 *